THE VALLEY BETWEEN US

By
Cristi Slate

Copyright © 2024 Haven Press

All rights reserved.

No part of this book may be reproduced, or stored in a retrieval system, or transmitted in any form or by any means, electronic, mechanical, photocopying, recording, or otherwise, without express written permission of the publisher.

ISBN: 979-8-9905986-1-4

Cover design by: Rebecacovers

Printed in the United States of America

This book is dedicated to the brave Caucasus women who shared their personal stories of bride kidnapping with me and gave me the inspiration to write this book. For their safety, all people and place names have been changed.

And to Andrew, my favorite forever.

CHAPTER 1

Tbilisi, Georgia

October, 1991

The forest green Lada idles by the curb, its bumper firmly attached with what appears to be an entire roll of duct tape. The three men inside wait silently, watching in their side mirror as the oblivious young woman with long auburn hair approaches.

"That's her," the driver grunts to his companions. "The one I've been telling you about." He lowers his sunglasses and slowly presses on the gas.

***

Tbilisi is beautiful in all seasons, but Dina loves it best in the fall. By the first of October, the grapevines hang lush and full with clusters that are such a deep dark purple, they are almost black. There is something about the crumbly red stones of the ancient buildings that tie together so beautifully with the yellow leaves of the white-barked aspen trees that line the river. The water is the murky brown of milk tea, and notoriously polluted, but on a crisp day with blue skies and sunshine, Dina finds it lovely.

Dina hurries, berating herself for yet again being late to English class. She pulls her threadbare coat tighter as a cold breeze blows off the river to her right. She pushes thoughts of her tardiness out of her mind, realizing happily that in three days it will be St. Andrew's Day and class will be canceled. As always, her family will gather together in the kitchen to make a giant batch of *khinkali*— little savory meat-filled dumplings that take forever to make but are worth the effort. This year, with money being so tight, they'll probably only be able to make a few meat *khinkali*— the rest, they will fill with mashed potatoes and garlic.

Dina's stomach rumbles at the thought of *khinkali*. Suddenly, the sound of a car slowing beside her draws her attention and she looks over her shoulder. A dark green soviet Lada creeps along beside her. The windows are tinted, so she can't see the driver, but she can hear the thumping bass of the music inside the car. At first, Dina ignores the car and continues her walk to class, but after a few minutes, when she realizes the car is still beside her, her heart begins to beat faster. She picks up her speed, but the car holds pace with her. She runs her hands nervously down the sides of her white-washed jeans.

Dina looks around, but no one is nearby. Nothing but her and the car, bumper rattling, moving in perfect sync beside her. Feeling slightly foolish, she breaks into a run, her purse slapping noisily against her side as she spreads her toes in an attempt to hold her low heels onto her feet as she runs. The car speeds up to keep pace with her. Dina sucks in a breath, ignoring the stitch in her side— she realizes with relief that she is almost to campus. Suddenly, the wide front door of the nearest building opens and a rush of students floods out. Dina thrusts herself in amongst them, bending over with her hands on her knees as her breath comes in ragged gasps.

When her breathing has slowed and her heartbeat normalized, she stands up and looks back towards the road just in time to see the Lada speed away with a screech of tires.

***

By the time class is over, the green Lada seems like nothing but a bad dream. Slightly embarrassed and sure she overreacted, Dina doesn't mention the incident to any of her classmates. Still, she knows it's better to be safe than sorry— after all, Tbilisi has been a den of crime and corruption ever since Georgia seceded from the Soviet Union in April and left a power vacuum that the mafia has been more than happy to fill. Dina, like everyone else, has heard stories of people kidnapped or murdered over pitiful sums of money. Only a few months before, Anna's uncle had been murdered right in front of his small bread kiosk for not paying the mafia the twenty rubles they had demanded from him. Dina shudders, glancing around to make sure she doesn't see the green car. There is no sign of it. But just in case, she decides to ask Nika to walk her home. He's been her best friend ever since they'd met during the first week of freshman year, when they'd been the only freshmen to place into an upper-level English translation class with a notoriously hard professor. Many evenings spent studying English together late into the night in the library had cemented their friendship and earned them good grades in the class.

"Hey Nika!" Dina shouts across the leafy quad, waving her arms enthusiastically at the gangly boy with dark curls hunching awkwardly against a tree across the lawn.

***

Nika has been scanning the quad for her ever since class got out. His pulse quickens when he finally spots her, waving and calling out for him. He hurries over, almost stumbling over his long legs and big feet.

"Hey!" he says, trying to play it cool and hide how out of breath he is from the short jog.

"Would you mind walking me home?" Dina asks, her green eyes looking up at him through long lashes. "I know it's in the total opposite direction of your house, so you definitely don't have to if it's inconvenient!"

"No problem! I'm happy to," Nika hurries to assure her.

"Are you sure?" Dina raises an eyebrow.

"I'm positive," Nika smiles, running a slender hand across his scraggly attempt at a mustache.

"Great!" Dina pulls her backpack higher on her shoulders and takes off with purposeful strides in the direction of the metro. Nika hurries to catch up. He has been smitten with her since freshman year, but so far, she just seems to view him as a friend. *And why wouldn't she? She's way out of your league. She's gorgeous and funny and so self-confident. And you're awkward and nerdy and shy. But she did just ask you to walk her home. Maybe there's hope...* With it being their senior year, Nika has been starting to feel a bit desperate that he is running out of time before he and Dina graduate and go their separate ways. Of course, he's never actually been brave enough to ask her out... so for now, he soaks up the time they get to spend together and hopes that, somehow, her feelings will change.

Nika glances sideways at Dina, bouncing along beside him, animating the story she is telling with her usual big hand motions and vivacious smile. Nika realizes guiltily that he's been so distracted by thinking about her— about *them*— that he hasn't actually been listening to what she is saying.

"—and then, Giorgi came running up the street, yelling that Dato was bringing home a dead cat he'd found behind the neighbor's garage and wanted to dissect it! Can you imagine??! I mean, we all know Dato is a science genius and is planning to go to medical school someday, but he's only in seventh grade! Ugh, can you imagine how many germs a dead cat must have?? Who knows how long it had even been dead." Dina shudders and Nika laughs— stories about the antics Dina's younger siblings get into are a constant source of humor and conversation.

"What did your mom do?"

Dina rolls her eyes. "Gah, you know she usually lets her golden boy Dato get away with anything. Apparently, though, she draws the line at cutting up rotting cats! She made him and Giorgi bury it out in an abandoned lot. Mariam went with them and cried as they buried the cat. And it was just some random stray!" Dina laughs and shakes her head at her youngest sister's well-known obsession with animals, her long auburn waves moving in a way that makes Nika long to run his fingers through them.

Eventually they get to the tall gate at the top of Dina's street. The gate, as usual, has been left open and Nika can see into the tiny concrete courtyard, surrounded on every side by ramshackle homes crammed tightly together. All the neighbors share the bit of communal courtyard space, which currently contains a tricycle, lots of laundry drying on lines, and a rickety little round table with two crates next to it to serve as chairs. Baba Tamara sits on one of the crates, wearing a floral robe and smoking some grass rolled in butcher paper— the cheapest substitute for a cigarette these days. She grunts and lifts a hand in greeting to the young people before going back to reading the newspaper.

"Come inside? It's probably only soup for dinner, like usual, but we can always add more water and salt to the pot!" Dina offers, gesturing up the narrow wooden staircase at the back of the courtyard that leads up to her family's two-room apartment.

"I wish I could," Nika says regretfully, running a hand across his scraggly black mustache, "but I have piano lessons at six o'clock. I've got to get to the metro soon if I'm going to make it back to Vake in time."

Dina nods in understanding— Nika is an incredibly talented pianist and teaches lessons to children at a local music school in the evenings to help pay his way through college.

"See you tomorrow then!" She gives him a quick hug and then bounds up the stairs to her family's apartment, where Nika can hear excited squeals from her younger siblings at their oldest sister's arrival. Before Nika turns to go, a door slams upstairs and Giorgi and Mariam run out onto their balcony and wave excitedly down at him, trying unsuccessfully to convince him to stay for dinner.

As Nika walks home he wishes, not for the first time, to live in a family like Dina's. True, her family is extremely poor, *though the same could be said about most people in Tbilisi these days*, but they are boisterous and close and truly seem to love each other. Things haven't always been ideal for them— Dina's father had drunk himself to death a few years earlier, but her grandfather had stepped in so that Dina's mom didn't have to raise five kids on her own.

Nika's own family is quite different— smaller, quieter. He is an only child of parents who are married to their careers. His father, the principal violinist for the Tbilisi City Orchestra, lives and breathes music. He is constantly either practicing or performing, and is rarely home. The main time he spent with Nika during childhood was spent sitting at the piano, drilling Nika for hours on arpeggios and hand drills. Though Nika would've preferred to spend his time reading, he didn't complain about the time at the piano because it was the one place he had his father's attention.

Nika's mother is a surgeon and also works long hours. As an adult, Nika respects the lifesaving work that she does. As a child, he had resented constantly playing second fiddle to her patients. He'd loved the few times he had gotten legitimately sick as a child and so had her momentary full attention.

Quiet and shy by nature, Nika had grown up sticking close to home and preferring the company of books and his piano to that of people. That all changed when he met Dina, his first real friend. She was all the things that he was not— vivacious and loud, comfortable with people, popular. And she cared so much for her family— she'd been working side jobs since she was only eleven to help provide for her four younger siblings. Her four younger siblings who Nika too had grown to love. Dina had pulled him into her noisy family, where Nika had felt immediately accepted. Regardless of what happened with them in the future, Nika would be forever grateful to her for opening up his world and painting it with color.

CHAPTER 2

San Francisco, California

May, 2018

"Seriously, Call, you're going where?" Lucy asks, eyebrows raised over her dry martini. The San Francisco bar is slammed with a late-night crowd, but Callie and Lucy are tucked into a corner by the window. The strands of lights outside the bar glitter on the dark water of the Bay.

"Georgia— the country of," Callie replies firmly, twisting a strand of her shoulder-length chestnut hair with frustration. She has already told Lucy at least six times. It's not that hard to remember, for crying out loud.

"I mean, who even knew there was a country of Georgia??!" Then Lucy gasps in horror, "Everyone is going to think that you're moving down south!"

Callie laughs, "Obvs I would never do that!"

"Well, at least you have some standards!" Lucy giggles with relief. "What about Lucas?"

At that moment, a waiter squeezes his way over to their table and sets down a dish of creamy spinach artichoke dip, surrounded by a circlet of sliced French bread, each piece toasted to golden perfection. Callie orders a second glass of wine, and moans dramatically, "Who needs Lucas when you can have spinach artichoke dip and wine?"

Lucy looks suggestively, "Girl, spinach artichoke dip cannot meet all your needs."

"Well, it's going to have to do for now because Lucas and I are done," Callie sighs. She looks away from Lucy and stares up at the ceiling, willing herself not to cry over some dumb boy.

Lucy reaches across the table and grasps Callie's hand. Everyone in the office thinks Lucy is a ditsy blond who only cares about fashion and partying, but Callie knows that, deep down, Lucy loves her.

A bachelorette party squeals raucously from the bar and Lucy looks at Callie with concern, "Girl, are you sure you're ok in here? It's really loud and crowded. We can go somewhere else if you need."

"It's fine," Callie insists, holding up a slice of golden bread topped with steaming spinach dip, "It's worth dealing with the noise for the best dip in San Francisco. Plus, Dr. Paekl says it's good for me to stretch myself, to occasionally force myself to be in uncomfortably overstimulating places."

"If you're sure," Lucy says, "You know this place is my jam. So back to you and Lucas— what really happened between you two? You guys seemed so solid for so long. I mean, you were the dream team. There was a running pool in the office on a wedding date for you guys!"

"Ugh, did not need to know that!" Callie half laughs, half groans. "Well, no one is going to win that pool now. Lucas is a great guy, you know that. And for a long time, things seemed really good. For a while, they were better than good." Callie gives Lucy a sad smile and slowly finishes her wine. She breaks a slice of French bread in half, hands half to Lucy, and dips the other half in the still warm spinach dip.

"I guess, though, we just want different things in life. Lucas loves sports and loves reporting on sports. He lives for the next story. Plus, his travel schedule is so insane that I barely ever saw him. And even when he is home, he happily works eighty-plus hours a week if he's onto something. The reason he stays so trim is that he forgets to eat half the time because he is so engrossed in work!"

"Yeah, I never do that," Lucy grins over a mouthful of dip and smacks her round butt ruefully.

"Me neither!" agrees Callie. "I mean, I love reporting. I think what we do is interesting and important. I just think there are other things in life too. There just got to be too many times when I played second fiddle to some work assignment of Lucas'. Plus someday," Callie blushes, glances furtively around her, and lowers her voice,

"Someday, I think I'd like a family. And that doesn't seem to be on Lucas' radar or in his plans."

"Girl, you said that like it's some capital offense. You know it's not a crime to want a family, right?" Lucy raises her perfectly plucked eyebrows.

"I know," Callie sighs. "But admit it— at our age and stage in San Francisco, no one is married, and NO ONE has kids. Seriously— when was the last time you even saw a kid??"

Lucy frowns and answers slowly, "I honestly can't remember. Look at you, being all counter-cultural! It's your Southern roots coming out! We knew they had to be in there somewhere! You can take the girl out of North Carolina, but you can't take North Carolina out of the girl!" Lucy jokes affectionately.

"Tell me though, are you going to this 'Georgia' place just to get away from Lucas? Cause you know you could do something way less extreme— like move across the Bay or something. And then at least you could keep your job and— most importantly— still see me!"

"It's not just Lucas," Callie promises. "I've been wanting to change things up for a while, try something different. This summer seems like a perfect time. There's nothing holding me here— Suzanne has agreed to give me a three-month leave of absence from *The San Francisco Chronicle*, and the volunteer work I'm gonna be doing in Georgia seems fascinating. I'm hoping to be able to do some good for a change. And honestly, I'm pretty burnt out from covering the local politics beat. At this point, I'm pretty convinced that all politicians are sleazebags. I'm ready to rub shoulders with some everyday people, and to be off the beaten path."

"I get that. But man, *The Chronicle* is gonna suck without you," Lucy insists. "How long will you be gone? And what exactly will you be doing?"

"I'm only gonna be gone three months, and I'm sure you'll be having so much fun that your summer will fly by," Callie grins knowingly at Lucy, who shrugs one bare shoulder in agreement. Lucy's summers are always an epic string of romantic flings, typically followed by heartbreak for either her or the guy involved, and weekend travel to exotic places. Though Callie loves Lucy, she would never want to live the kind of drama-filled life Lucy seems to enjoy.

Callie glances out the window, soaking in the view of her beloved Bay and the mountains across the water. She is going to miss this place when she leaves.

"I will fly into Tbilisi, the capital of Georgia. From there, I will go out to this little Ramazi village—"

"Whoa, wait." Lucy's eyes go wide, "Ramazi?! As in Ramazistan — that place in Russia that has been all over the news for that recent terrorist attack? Ummm, I do NOT give you permission to go there!"

"Relax," Callie grins, "I'm not going to actual Ramazistan. There is apparently a small Ramazi diaspora in the Georgian mountains, and I will be going there. It's perfectly safe. A local lady runs a guesthouse. From the information she sent me, it looks beautiful. She's trying to modernize it and start to draw Western tourists into the area. Which, after your reaction, I can see why she's having a hard time doing that!"

"So, what…" Lucy frowns, "you're gonna be redecorating her guesthouse rooms or something? I mean, we all agree that you have an enviable grasp of interior design, but…."

"I'll advise on that some," Callie nods, "but mostly I will be helping with social media. They don't have an Instagram account or Facebook, and their website is pretty pitiful. The owner, Leila, is hoping to be able to get some different grants as well to try to improve things in the region. Apparently, it's a pretty poor area and she's hoping that bringing in tourist money will help the local economy. After spending the past four years writing about sleazy California politicians and local elections, I'm hoping that this will be a chance to actually do some good in the world," Callie admits softly.

Lucy laughs, "Look at you, going all Mother Teresa on me! But are you sure it's wise for you to go somewhere so off the beaten path and away from western comforts? With your sensory issues and all? I mean, San Francisco is hard on you— how will you handle somewhere rougher?" Lucy asks, eyes full of concern.

Callie hesitates, gently biting her lower lip, "I've thought about it long and hard. Thanks to Dr. Paekl, I feel like I've made a bunch of progress this year. I've learned my triggers and have some new coping techniques…"

Lucy nods supportively, well aware of all the self-work Callie has put in.

"Honestly," Callie admits, "I'm just really tired of living in fear, of living hampered by my hypersensitivity. I feel like I've cultivated this very careful bubble-life, where I try my best to stay away from situations and places that will put me into sensory overdrive. Places like this bar," Callie gestures around her at the noisy, crowded room and shivers involuntarily. "It's exhausting, trying to control everything. Plus, I don't want to look back and regret missing out on amazing experiences because I was too afraid."

"So you figured if you're gonna take the floaties off, you might as well just plunge head first into the deep end?" Lucy laughs, finishing off her martini with a lusty swig.

"Pretty much," Callie agrees, raising her glass, "Here's to hoping I don't drown!"

"No way, babe— you're a brave woman and I'm super proud of you." Lucy leans over and squeezes Callie's hand reassuringly, "Your summer is gonna be amazing."

CHAPTER 3
Tbilisi, Georgia

October, 1991

For days, life goes on as usual for Dina. She sees no sign of the green Lada. Her family celebrates St. Andrew's Day on Thursday by stuffing themselves with dumplings and then heading to Freedom Square to watch late-night fireworks explode in the sky over the top of Mtatsminda, the low mountain ridge that stretches across the western edge of Tbilisi. Eight-year-old Mariam falls asleep on Dina's shoulder in the metro on the way home (it's almost midnight, after all), and Dina and Sofi laugh their way out of the metro and over the three streets to their apartment, dragging a half-asleep Mariam, who stumbles like a drunkard between them and mumbles grouchy complaints the entire way.

By Friday, Dina has mostly forgotten about the Lada. It's foggy and starting to drizzle, and her main priority as she walks to campus is trying to keep her old umbrella covering up the curls that she spent so long ironing into her long auburn hair that morning. Dina mutters and kicks at a pebble as a gust of wind sweeps the umbrella inside out and she hears another spoke snap. She had been saving money to buy a new skirt, and she's furious to realize that she is going to have to spend her money on an umbrella instead. She frowns at the river, bends and picks up a rock, and throws it with all her might into the muddy water. She hears a faint, satisfying plop as the rock disappears from sight, and she feels slightly better about the world.

She's bending over to pick up another rock when she hears the noise of a car slowing down beside her. She turns and barely has time to register the dark green Lada before its back doors open and two men with thick beards and dark clothes rush towards her.

At first, neither of them touch her. They stand, threateningly close on either side of her, and one says, "Get in the car!" in a stern voice. He's speaking Georgian, but with a thick accent that Dina can't place. Dina backs away from them, looking around in panic to see if there is anyone close by to hear her if she screams for help. The gray, foggy streets are deserted. Later, Dina will remember noticing a mangy street dog rummaging through trash next to a building across the street — the only sign of life nearby, and no help to her at all. Dina takes a deep breath and realizes she will have to save herself. She nods and pretends to obey and heads towards the car. She glances out of the corner of her eye to see the two men relax their stance a bit, thinking she is complying.

Just as she is about to reach the Lada, she sees that the man to her left has stopped a few feet away from the car, leaving a small opening. With a sudden burst of speed, she darts through the opening and takes off sprinting up the street. She can hear the loud rush of her frantic breaths and the beat of her feet pounding the pavement. She curses herself for yet again wearing impractical heels that are terrible to run in.

From behind her, she hears the men shout in a language she doesn't recognize. She takes a quick glance behind her and sees them running towards her. Her heart rate escalates and blood pounds in her ears as she quickly kicks off first one shoe and then the other, almost tripping as the second shoe gets caught on her foot. Finally she gets it off, and sprints the fastest she has ever run in her life, ignoring the pebbles on the ground that cut into her feet. She realizes that if she turns left at the next block, only a few meters ahead of her, and goes one block north, she will hit Rustaveli, Tbilisi's main street. Surely there she could find someone to help her. At the last moment, she swerves to the left, taking the side street that leads towards Rustaveli. She hears the men behind her, gaining ground.

Suddenly, she hears the noise of a car coming up behind her. She can hear the thumping of music inside it and the rattle of the duck-taped bumper. *It has to be the green Lada. I'm not going to make it*, she panics, tears of fear and anger running down her face.

The Lada pulls up beside her and the tinted window lowers. Dina glances over and sees a bearded heavyset man wearing sunglasses.

She continues to run, despite knowing that it is useless to try to outrun a car.

"Good game, girl!" the driver shouts from his window cheerfully. "We always like a woman with spirit! We'll be seeing you again!"

To her shock, Dina hears the car slow to a halt and glances back to see the driver waiting in the middle of the alley for his two compatriots on foot to catch up with him and hop in the back seat. They slam their doors and speed off past her, the driver giving her a jaunty wave out his window.

Dina limps to the top of the alley, where it corners up against Rustaveli. As soon as she makes it, she immediately collapses against the wall of the alley, shaking so hard that she can feel her teeth rattle inside her head. Her breath comes in ragged gulps, and sobs of terror and relief tear from her throat as she tries to calm herself down. She coughs and gives her face an awkward scrub with her sleeve when she realizes that snot is running from her nose into her mouth.

"Miss, are you alright?" Dina looks up to see concerned eyes looking down at her from the face of a hunched-over old woman, who, even standing, isn't much taller than seated Dina.

Dina nods distractedly, hoping the old lady will leave her alone. But the woman comes closer and bends down towards Dina's feet.

"I don't think you're ok," the woman says softly, pointing at Dina's feet. Both feet are covered with grime, and the left one is pouring blood from a deep gash that Dina hadn't even felt. *I must've stepped on glass*, she thinks with surprise.

"Can I help you find your shoes? Or help you get home?" The old woman looks at Dina kindly, offering a hand.

Eventually, Dina nods numbly and attempts to stand. She is shaking so hard that it is difficult. The old woman, herself not super sturdy, offers Dina an arm. "I'm Larissa, dear. What's your name?"

"Dina. I think my shoes are that way," Dina points back towards the river, and slowly the two of them make their way out of the alley. They find Dina's shoes just where she left them, looking abandoned, lying a few feet apart. Dina picks them up and moves to put them on, and then realizes nonplussed, that she will ruin them if she puts her dirty, bloody feet in them. And they are her only good shoes.

"I'm going to ruin my shoes if I put them on!" she sobs, feeling as if it is the end of the world.

"Hush dear, sit down." Larissa gestures to the low stone wall that lines the river, and Dina sinks onto it obediently. Larissa moves beside her and places a large purse on the wall with a loud thunk.

Larissa digs around in the purse, and eventually pulls out a handkerchief and holds it towards Dina. It's white and delicate and beautifully embroidered with flowers around the edges.

"Use this, dear."

Dina shakes her head, "I can't use that! I will ruin it!"

"Nonsense! You think I've lived to my age and not learned how to get dirt and blood stains out of laundry? Turn sideways, and put your feet up on the wall." Larissa commands.

Dina complies, lifting her legs onto the wall. Larissa takes Dina's right foot in her hand, caked with grime, and very gently wipes off as much mud and dirt as she can. Tears trickle down Dina's face and she isn't sure if she's crying from shame or gratitude. *Probably both,* she realizes. Larissa finishes the right foot and slowly slips Dina's shoe into place. Then she lifts Dina's left foot, which is a bloody mess. Larissa frowns with concern, "This might need stitches. Or if not stitches, definitely cleaned thoroughly, sterilized, and bandaged. Do you have someone who can help you with that?" Dina nods, and Larissa seems satisfied. She tends to the left foot even more tenderly and carefully than she cleaned the right foot and eventually ties her handkerchief around the foot like a tourniquet to try to stop the flow of blood.

"Where do you live, honey? Is your home safe?"

Dina nods.

"Let me help you home then." Seeing Dina's hesitation, Larissa adds, "I won't take no for an answer! Besides, I'm retired— there's nowhere else I need to be now anyway." She smiles and offers Dina her arm. Dina slips off the wall and gradually puts more weight on the injured foot, which has now started to throb. Slowly the pair make their way to Rustaveli metro station and then ride the red line to the eastern edge of the city, where Dina lives. Larissa insists on walking

Dina all the way to her gate, though Dina tries to tell her she doesn't need help. At the gate, Larissa gives Dina a quick pat on the elbow then turns and begins a slow hobble back down the street in the direction of the metro.

***

"Why aren't you in class? What's going on?" Dina's mom Natela asks, glancing at Dina with concern as she stumbles through the front door of their apartment and crawls straight into the bed that she shares with Sofi in the small back bedroom. She follows Dina into the dimly lit room and sits beside her on the bed. Dina turns to face the wall and curls up tight, eyes closed. Natela rubs the small of her daughter's back through the threadbare blanket Dina is wrapped in. Having raised five kids, Natela is fairly used to kid "crises". She patiently massages Dina's back, thinking wryly that her fireball of a daughter is going to have to learn to control her emotions someday before it gets her in trouble.

"Did you and Anna have another argument? Being best friends can be hard, but you girls always make up," Natela offers, as Dina shakes her head.

"Bad grade on a test?"

Dina shakes her head again and curls up tighter under the blanket. "Well," Natela offers with a placating pat on Dina's back, "I'm sure whatever it was will seem better in the morning." She starts to stand when Dina flings herself over in the bed, eyes blazing with fury.

"It won't ever be better! You have no idea what you're talking about! Three men tried to kidnap me today and I barely got away!"

Natela's hand flies to her mouth and she stumbles against the door frame, "Oh my God! Here in Tbilisi?? What happened? Where were you? Who was it? Are you hurt?" The questions pelt from her lips as Natela rushes to her daughter and squeezes her hands tightly.

"I'm ok, Mom," Dina sighs loudly. "It happened right downtown, almost at Rustaveli. I think these guys have followed me before— I saw their car a few months ago too."

"Why didn't you tell me?" Natela places her hands on both sides of her daughter's cheeks as Dina pulls away, curling back in on herself.

"I'm so sorry honey, this is not your fault. I'm just so shocked, and so thankful you're safe," Natela wraps Dina in a hug, and Dina buries herself in her mom's familiar embrace. They sit there for a few silent minutes, and Natela can smell the sweat in Dina's hair.

"Dina," Natela says softly, pulling away and looking into her daughter's eyes, "We need to go to the police and you need to tell them and me everything."

Dina moans, "No, Mom, please! You know they won't do anything anyway! The police here are worthless and so corrupt— half of them are criminals themselves anyway, or in the pocket of the mob. And I have no clue who it was who tried to abduct me, so how would the police even be able to find them? Just let me stay home. Please." Dina pleads so heartbrokenly, and the points she made were so accurate, that Natela eventually gives a reluctant nod.

"Ok, but I'm calling your grandfather and Nika and Sofi and you need to tell the four of us exactly what happened, and we will come up with a plan to try to keep you safe."

"Not Nika," Dina whispers, burying her face in her hands.

Natela looks around the room, this room where Dina had spent her whole childhood. Dina's beloved stuffed bear Bappo sits on the dresser, missing one eye and losing stuffing through a crevice under his arm. Drawings of horses cover the walls from when Dina had been in her horse obsession phase. The blanket on the bed is pink and frilly— Dina had wanted it more than anything for her ninth birthday. Now it is faded and frayed around the edges. Natela sighs, hating that her little girl isn't little anymore, and is having to face adult problems.

She places a warm hand on Dina's arm, "I'm sorry, but we have to include Nika. He is with you more than anyone, including at university when the rest of us are not around. Plus, he's a man and more threatening than your sister." Dina sighs, realizing her mom is right—her sixteen-year-old sister Sofi is wispy and thin and often lives in a world of her own imagination. She would be no protection at all.

"Fine," Dina whispers, "but let me sleep 'til they get here."

Natela leaves the room, pulling the curtains closed and quietly shutting the door behind her.

***

That evening, Natela sends Dato, Giorgi, and Mariam to play at the neighbors', while she, Grandfather, Sofi, and Nika gather in the kitchen. As usual in the evenings, the electricity is out, so Sofi lights a bunch of candles. Since the electricity being out means that the heat is also out, the room is frigid. Everyone sits around the table in their winter coats. Grandfather has his raggedy blue beanie hat pulled down tight over his ears— Sofi had knit it for him years before, when she was just learning to knit in awkward, uneven beginner stitches. With how frequently their heat is out, he rarely takes the hat off these days. Natela serves bowls of steaming cabbage soup and *lobiani*—a thin pastry filled with beans. Dina is conspicuously absent.

When everyone is gathered and eating, Natela pokes her head in Dina's pitch-black room, "Honey, everyone's here. Can you come out?"

A few minutes later, Dina exits her room, limping slowly to the kitchen table. Sofi's eyes widen at her older sister's appearance— Dina, who loves fashion and normally spends ages in the morning perfecting her hair and makeup, to the chagrin of all of her family members who have to share a bathroom with her, is a mess. Her eyes are puffy and she has black mascara trails running down her cheeks. Her auburn hair looks dank and tangled— is that a leaf Sofi sees in it? Dina silently hunches into the lone empty stool at the table, not looking at anyone. Everyone glances at each other with worry in their eyes.

Natela clears her throat, "I asked you all here tonight because some men tried to kidnap Dina when she was walking to university today." Nika turns pale. Grandfather's spoon falls to the table with a noisy clatter. Dina sits like a statue, seeming not to hear. Her only movement is spinning a slender silver ring on her finger in constant circles.

"We have to go to the police!" cries Sofi.

"I wish that would help," says grandfather, voice thick with regret and anger, "but it won't. The police won't do anything. They would probably just tell us it was an attempted bride kidnapping and to go home."

"But bride kidnapping doesn't happen these days, not in Tbilisi!" Sofi insists.

"It's rare now, but not unheard of. We have to protect Dina ourselves!" Grandfather's eyes are fierce, and it is clear he will do what he can to protect his granddaughter.

As Grandfather's words sink in, everyone realizes that he is right. Bride kidnapping is an ancient tradition in Georgia— historically, if a man didn't have money for a wedding or dowry, he could kidnap a woman and marry her immediately. For centuries, it had been viewed as an acceptable way to get a wife. The Soviet Union had technically outlawed it, but it was still widely practiced in the Caucasus mountains which ran along Russia's southern and Georgia's northern border. The whole family knew that Grandfather's own parents had been married after his father kidnapped his mother.

"Dina," Natela says gently, "We need you to tell us exactly what happened so that we can come up with a plan for keeping you safe, to protect your future. We want your life to be better than that of the women who have gone before you."

Everyone waits, staring at Dina, who remains hunched over, looking at the floor. Eventually, falteringly at first, she begins to tell her story. Her voice is emotionless and she leaves out no detail and never looks up. By the time she gets to the end, Nika looks like he wants to vomit. Grandfather's gnarled fists are clenched on top of the table.

When Dina finishes, Sofi jumps up and throws her skinny arms around her sister, eyes full of tears, "Oh, Dina, that must have been awful! I'm so sorry! You were so brave!"

Finally, Dina looks up at Sofi, and her own eyes fill with tears as she hugs her sister. "Thank you," she whispers.

Natela clears her throat, "Let's get to the practical part of figuring out how we prevent this from happening again. Dina has a bright future here in Tbilisi— we don't want to let these men ruin it for her."

Dina describes the car and the men as best she can. They all agree that the men must be from one of the predominantly Muslim people groups that live up in the mountains since they'd had beards and thick accents and had been speaking a language Dina didn't understand. Plus, bride kidnapping is much more common and accepted among the mountain peoples.

Dina promises her family and Nika that she will stick to home for the foreseeable future, aside from when she needs to go to class or her part-time job at the corner store near their house. In return, her family and Nika promise to accompany her whenever she has to leave the house. Since Nika lives across the river near their university, they agree that Grandfather will walk her to the metro every day, she will ride it through the city and under the river, and Nika will be waiting for her on the other side.

Normally, the idea of having to basically be babysat would've been extremely distasteful to Dina, who relishes her independence. But on this night, she just gives a tired nod of agreement to her family's plan before hobbling back to bed without saying goodnight to anyone.

CHAPTER 4

San Francisco, California

May, 2018

Callie stands on her tiptoes on her wicker desk chair and stretches her fingers as high as they will go up her wall, attempting to take down her favorite painting. It's a sunset over the Blue Ridge mountains, where her family would camp every October when she was a kid, back before her mom got sick. The leaves in the painting are a glorious riot of reds and yellows, oranges and golds, and every time Callie looks at it, a well of nostalgia stirs within her, and she remembers how much she really does love and miss her family and her home state. *Which is probably the reason Dad bought me the painting*, she thinks with an affectionate eye roll.

When she finally gets the painting down, she places it carefully against the side of one of the big cardboard boxes on the floor. Looking around the room, she moans— *how can I still have so far to go?!* Callie had always prided herself on living a pretty neat, minimalist lifestyle, but she realizes with chagrin as she boxes up her belongings that perhaps she wasn't as minimalist as she had thought. Clothes are strewn across the bed, shoes cover the floor, and a mostly empty suitcase sits beside a handful of cardboard boxes.

The room is small, with white walls, high ceilings, and large windows. On this abnormally fog-free day, you can catch the tiniest corner of the Golden Gate Bridge through the window. Callie gathers the plants from around the room and lines them all up on the window sill. Hopefully her summer subletter won't mind watering them. She glances up at the life-saving blackout shades rolled up at the top of her window and a twinge of doubt stirs in her stomach. Her eyes shift to the white noise machine plugged in beside her bed. *How am I ever going to sleep without all the things I need?* Callie worries, fingering her iPhone with its sleep app that is a poor substitute for her state-of-the-art white noise machine. She leaves the machine where it sits, waiting to box it up for storage until the following day so that she can sleep one last night to its soothing whir.

Callie turns to her dresser, opening up the top drawer and scooping out a hairbrush and hair clips and tossing them into her suitcase. As she pulls random things from the back of the drawer, her hand pauses when she feels something smooth and rectangular. With knots in her stomach, knowing exactly what it is, she pulls it out.

We look so happy, Callie thinks, running her finger across the framed photo of Lucas and herself that had sat prominently on her dresser until a few weeks before, when everything had gone wrong between them.

In the photo, Callie is wrapped in a thick flannel blanket on the porch swing of a cabin they'd rented for a ski weekend with friends, before they'd even officially started dating. Back when everything first began. Callie had been smitten with Lucas for over a year, but too shy and insecure to do anything about it. He was the big man around the office— the life of the party, the hot guy that pretty much everyone had a crush on. Callie had felt ridiculously cliché even liking him at all. But he was so winsome that she couldn't help it.

And then that ski weekend, she'd twisted her ankle on the first day of the trip and he had been the one to offer to accompany her back to the cabin. They'd sat on the porch swing just the two of them all day, wrapped in blankets and drinking cup after cup of hot chocolate as snow fell in white glory on the woods around them. And Lucas had picked every single marshmallow out of his cup and added them to hers because he knew that she loved them. An afternoon that had started with easy chatting slowly gave way to deep conversation, sprinkled in with a healthy dose of flirting on both sides. Callie's stomach had been in knots as she tried to convince herself that he was just being nice, that he couldn't possibly actually be interested in *her.*

And then he'd pulled out his phone to take a selfie of them, and just as Callie had grinned at the camera, he'd leaned in and kissed her cheek. In the picture, she is laughing with surprise and joy, not even caring that his kiss jolted her cup and spilled droplets of hot chocolate on the blanket in her lap. And Lucas' face— she's always loved his face in the picture— he looks as mischievous as a little kid, like he knows he is doing something naughty but that he also knows he is going to get away with it.

And that was how it all started, on that creaky mountain swing, the two of them laughing with frozen fingers and cheeks red from the cold. *If only it could have stayed that fun and simple. But you broke up with him for a reason, Call. He wasn't willing to commit. It's over.* Slowly, Callie pulls her trashcan towards her and tucks the picture in, frame and all. *You've spent far too many days grieving over this. It's time to move on. You're about to leave, get a fresh start in a whole new country. Put Lucas behind you,* Callie takes a deep, centering breath and turns back to her dresser, focusing her mind on the task at hand— trying to figure out what to take with her to Georgia and what to leave in storage.

Leila, the Ramazi guesthouse owner, had emailed that she needs to dress modestly in the village— preferably long skirts or dresses and high-necked shirts. Definitely no pants or shorts. Callie pulls out a black turtleneck— modest enough, but probably too warm. She's read that Georgia gets super hot in the summer. Being from North Carolina, Callie knows a thing or two about hot summers. Where she's from, you can at least spend a hot summer in your bathing suit at the pool. *Doesn't sound like that will be an option in the country of Georgia,* she thinks with chagrin.

Callie finds one brightly patterned floral maxi dress in the back of her closet, but the top is spaghetti straps. She groans in frustration. *Is nothing I own appropriate?* She eventually gathers a couple of t-shirts, two button-down dress shirts, and a light jacket. She realizes she is going to have to buy some floor-length skirts and try to find a modest floor-length dress. *Do they even make those anymore?* Callie berates herself for her uncharacteristic procrastinating and leaving packing till the final day— her flight is tomorrow morning! Her roommates will be home from work in a couple of hours for their farewell dinner, and Callie still hasn't finished clearing out her room. No time for a trip to the store. Thank goodness for Amazon's new two-hour delivery option that they're testing out in San Francisco! Callie opens her Mac and types in "modest floor-length skirt" and "modest floor-length dress". A few minutes and a hundred dollars later, she has a couple of items checked out and on their way to her. Relieved, she turns back to her room and begins to sort through toiletries.

Two hours later, as Callie debates which shoes to pack *(sandals? hiking boots? tennis shoes?)*, she hears a knock at the door.

"Coming!" she shouts with relief, rushing to open the door and receive her Amazon delivery.

But when she opens the door, it's not a delivery guy.

"Lucas? What are you doing here?" Callie stammers, cheeks reddening and stomach dropping. Callie had said an awkward goodbye to Lucas at work the day before and definitely did not expect to see him again before she left. And yet here he is, all six-foot-two of solid man.

Lucas leans against the doorframe and rakes a hand across his blond crewcut. He has clearly come from work— he is in dress pants and the blue button-down that Callie bought him for Christmas the previous year. It brings out the bright blue of his eyes and Callie loves it on him. A more calculating man would've worn it on purpose, but Callie knows him well enough to know that he likely had just blindly reached, half asleep, into the closet that morning and pulled out whatever shirt his fingers first touched. Clothes are not Lucas' top priority, and yet he somehow manages to look amazing in whatever he wears. Callie had sometimes been jealous at the ease with which he pulled off looking fabulous.

Come on Call, pull yourself together. Stop admiring his eyes and figure out what he's actually doing here, Callie rebukes herself.

Lucas takes a slow step towards her and says, "Can I come in? Can we talk?"

Callie hesitates for a minute, then backs away from the door and lets him through. She follows him to the living room, where he lowers himself into the tan couch that is so fluffy that Callie and her roommates have dubbed it "the cloud". Lucas sinks into the couch with a contented sigh and pats the spot beside him. But instead of taking the seat right beside him, Callie sits at the far edge of the couch and tucks her bare feet up under her. She's in sweatpants and a tank top, with no makeup and her hair in a messy bun. She had been planning to get dressed up soon for the roommates' dinner, but of course Lucas showed up when she looked like a scrub. *Why do I even care?* Callie reprimands herself. *It's not like he hasn't seen me looking like a scrub plenty of times before. And I'm not trying to impress him— we broke up, for crying out loud. Get a grip.*

"Callie…" Lucas hesitates, seeming unsure of what to say next. Which is very unusual for Lucas, who usually knows exactly what he wants to say.

Lucas reaches his hand towards Callie and, hesitantly, she takes it. He looks into her eyes with heartbreaking sincerity, "Callie, the past few weeks since we broke up have been awful. I have missed you more than I can express. I know I haven't been the best boyfriend, and there are lots of areas I need to grow in. You were right when you said I spend too much time at work, and that I need to create better life boundaries. I've just always cared so much about work. Good journalism can change the world! And sports are awesome!" Lucas grins, laughing at himself. But then he pauses and his blue eyes turn serious, "But since you left…" Lucas hesitates, and Callie looks down at their intertwined fingers. His fingers are warm and soft and so familiar. They feel like home.

"Since you left, nothing else has felt like it matters. Work has felt flat. Pete and I went out to Tony's and I swear my favorite pizza tasted like cardboard. I miss you, Callie. We never should have broken up— we belong together. Can we please fix things?" Lucas slides across the couch, till he is right next to Callie. He runs a hand down her cheek and then cups the side of her face. For a beat, Callie feels a twinge of offense that he would just assume that she would come running back the second he beckoned. She had broken up with *him*, for crying out loud! But then she closes her eyes for a moment and leans into his hand. She has truly missed him.

"Callie," Lucas whispers, putting one finger under her chin and lifting it to eye-level with him. "There's something I need to tell you that I should've told you a very long time ago." He pauses and Callie's breath catches.

"I love you, Callie. I've loved you for a long time— I was just too busy with work and too stupid to say it. But then once I lost you… well, it was a wake-up call."

Callie's pulse races. Throughout the 18 months that they dated, she had waited for him to say those words. They always had lots of fun together, but Lucas rarely got serious, and never said the "L" word or seemed interested in thinking about the future together.

"I love you too," Callie whispers, and before she can think, Lucas' hands are in her hair, pulling her tenderly towards him. His lips close over hers and she moans with pleasure as his hands move down her back, caressing slowly. *Why did I ever break up with him?* Callie wonders, caught up in the joy of being well kissed.

As Lucas' kisses grow deeper and more insistent, Callie reluctantly pulls away.

"We have to stop. I have to finish packing and get changed for our final roommate dinner," she murmurs, running a finger across his lips and down the faint white scar on his chin that was leftover from a nasty table run-in when he was a toddler.

Lucas moans and playfully tries to pull her back into his arms.

"Seriously babe, I really have to finish packing," Callie stands up.

Lucas looks nonplussed, "Wait, what? You're still leaving?"

Callie twists her fingers together and sighs, "I have to go," she replies. "My plane leaves tomorrow morning. Leila is expecting me; I can't let her down. She needs my help this summer. Plus I've already taken a leave of absence from work and sublet my room."

"But what about us?" Lucas frowns. "How are we supposed to be together if you leave? I don't understand why you just can't help Leila remotely. And you know Suzanne would take you back at work in a heartbeat. And if you need someplace to live, I'm pretty sure I could find you a spot in my bed." Lucas gives a mischievous wink and Callie swats him. "Lucas, you know full well that I'm not planning to move in with any guy unless I'm married to him."

"I know, I know," Lucas laughs. "Southern Baptist roots run deep!"

"Whatever," Callie rolls her eyes. "Summer lodging aside, I can't cancel my trip. I committed to it, so I have to go."

Lucas frowns and scoots backward on the couch, "But I just told you I love you. I want to make our relationship work. I thought this meant we were back together. Did you not just experience that kiss?"

Lucas grins, "We obviously should be together. Sparks like that don't just happen every day!"

Callie gives a half-smile. In many ways, he's right. She knows she still loves him. And making out with him is definitely high up on the list of her favorite things to do in the entire world. She's been waiting for years for him to say "I love you", and now he finally has. Maybe this is just the first step towards the life and family she has dreamed of with him. *If I leave now, will it ruin things? Will I be giving up my chance to make our relationship work?* Callie twists a strand of dark hair around her finger, her stomach in knots as she waffles over what to do.

Lucas sits sprawled across the couch, one eyebrow raised as he waits for her answer with a smug grin on his face.

"I'll tell you what," she finally announces, trying to give no sign of how fast her pulse is racing. "You and I can give things another go." Lucas pumps a fist triumphantly. "But!" Callie quickly adds, feeling like she is gambling her future, "We're going to have to do it long distance because I committed to this summer project and I'm sticking to my word."

Lucas grimaces but holds out his hand, and Callie quickly takes it, relieved. "Deal, partner," he grins and gives her hand a firm shake. "But expect to be very thoroughly kissed when you return home if you make me live like a monk for the next three months!"

Callie laughs and throws her arms around his neck. "Maybe you should start now— stock up some for while I'm gone!"

"Now you're talking!" Lucas crows, and happily pulls Callie onto his lap, leaning in to fulfill her suggestion.

Just then, there is a knock at the door. Lucas curses under his breath, and Callie reluctantly leaves the warmth of his lap to answer the door. This time, it actually is her Amazon order. Which reminds Callie that she has a lot of packing still to do, plus she needs to get ready for her final roommate dinner.

"I'm sorry babe, but you really are going to have to leave. I've got to pack and get ready."

"No!" Lucas moans. "At least let me see you before your flight. When do you leave?"

"My flight isn't 'til noon, but I want to leave for the airport by nine o'clock at the latest since you never know what traffic will be like."

"Perfect! I will be here at eight for a final breakfast— or perhaps something more exciting than breakfast," Lucas winks.

"Deal," Callie smiles, a deep dimple appearing in her left cheek. "Now get out of here before my roommates return and start grilling us." Callie swats at Lucas and he reluctantly stands.

"I missed you, Callie. I'm really glad we're back together," he whispers into her hair as he gives her a quick hug.

Callie closes the door behind him and slides to the floor. *What on earth just happened?* She twists a strand of hair around her finger, emotions aswirl.

CHAPTER 5
Tbilisi, Georgia

Winter, 1991

The winter is long and abnormally cold and snowy. Dina thought she might've seen the green Lada once, from far away, but she couldn't be sure— Ladas are a very common car in the former Soviet Union.

Dina, who has always been a straight-A student, struggles to keep herself motivated. Her grades begin to slip and she realizes that she doesn't even care. Her hands shake at random times and she stuffs them in her pockets, hoping no one will notice. All she wants to do is sleep. But half the time when she sleeps, she has nightmares that replay that awful autumn day. In some of her nightmares, she escapes, to wake up drenched in sweat and shaking with relief. But in others, the men actually succeed in kidnapping her. And when she wakes, she can't keep herself from playing out the "what ifs" in her head and re-hearing the driver's laughing threat that he would be seeing her again. It feels so incredibly unfair— with one act, they have stolen her life. Now, everywhere she goes, she looks over her shoulder. She never leaves the house alone, and she stays home in the evenings instead of hanging out with her friends. Her friends have been hurt and confused because, aside from Nika, she doesn't tell anyone what happened. *You were strong and brave, and you got away,* she keeps reminding herself like a mantra. But no amount of self-talk can rid her of the nagging feeling that somehow it was her fault, that she had done something to draw the men's attention.

One gray afternoon not long after the attempted kidnapping, Nika had tried to talk to her about what had happened, but Dina stonewalled him and said, "I already told you everything; don't make me have to relive it." And so neither of them mentioned the incident again, and they pretended it was normal for Nika to walk her to and from the metro every day, and to and from all her classes. He is happy for any time he gets with her, even if she is a shadow of her former self. And she is grateful for his quiet constancy.

***

By the beginning of March, it has been almost five months since the attempted kidnapping, and nothing else has occurred. Everyone begins to breathe again and let themselves believe that surely it is over — probably whoever was looking for a wife had realized Dina would be too much trouble anyway and decided to go for easier prey, though Dina always feels a twinge of guilt whenever she feels hope from that thought.

With her birthday only two weeks away, Dina's family tries to convince her to have a party and invite her girlfriends from high school and college.

"It's not every day you turn twenty-one, Dina," Natela smiles firmly at Dina, "It's time to put last fall behind you and move on. Get back to living your life. Reconnect with your friends. Call Anna! Celebrate! I can make you an apple cake and Grandfather can grill kabobs. We could have a picnic at Vake Park if you want."

Dina looks up from the sink, where she has been peeling her way through a giant pile of potatoes and carrots for that night's soup.

"That sounds nice, actually. Thanks, Mom. I will call the girls and invite them for next Saturday. Is that good?"

Natela comes around the table and squeezes Dina's shoulders, "That's great, honey. I'm sure they will be happy to reconnect with you." Natela grabs a basket of wet laundry and heads to the balcony to hang it on the line.

"Oh, Mom?" Dina calls after her, pausing her peeling. "I actually won't be home for dinner tonight. Nika has a birthday present for me but he says he has to give it to me at his house."

"Ok honey, that's fine. But why is he giving it to you so early?"

"Remember, he applied for that piano competition for a chance at an internship with the Tbilisi Philharmonic? His audition is next week, so he said he's going to hole up like a bear all week next week and practice. Tonight works well anyway because he doesn't teach on Monday nights and I don't have to work."

"Alright honey, you have a good time. Just make sure he walks you to the metro afterward, and make sure Grandfather knows what time to meet you."

***

That night, Dina is in a cheerful mood, almost like her old self, as they walk through the majestic tree-lined streets of old Tbilisi, heading deep into the city, where Nika lives. The trees are still bare after such a cold winter, but the day has been unseasonably warm and sunny. Plus, Dina had called two of her friends that morning and they had happily agreed to a birthday picnic. Anna had been thrilled to hear from her, so Dina is feeling upbeat.

"So, what is this big birthday surprise you have planned for me?" she asks, throwing an arm through Nika's. Every cell in his body ignites at her touch, but she hums along beside him, oblivious.

"Oh, it's really not that big a deal."

"Well, it must be something big if you couldn't bring it to my house! How am I supposed to get it home, huh?" Dina gives his arm a light conspiratorial punch.

"Oh, it's nothing like that," Nika hurries. "It's not even a thing, really." He smiles over at her, "Hold your horses and you'll see. You're as impatient as a kid."

"I can't help it if I like gifts," Dina grins back at him.

As they walk in comfortable silence, the sun begins to set through the trees and the sky turns a soft pink with dark purple at the edges. The street lamps come on, throwing circles of warm yellow light onto the broad sidewalks. Nika resists the urge to reach for Dina's hand.

***

"Okay, are you ready for your gift?"

When they had arrived at Nika's, they'd had a snack of open-faced sandwiches with salami, cheese, and pickles, followed by tea and chocolate, like always. Nika's parents are both working, so they have the apartment to themselves.

"Of course!" Dina claps her hands and stands from her chair in the small kitchen. Nika's apartment is right off the main boulevard in Vake, located on the fourth floor of a stately, historic building. Like most of Old Tbilisi, the building itself is a bit crumbly on the outside, but Nika's grandparents had renovated the interior of their apartment when Nika's father was a young boy, so it is in pretty good shape. Though not large, it has tall ceilings and nice wallpaper and elegant, if old-fashioned, furniture. Dina has been to the apartment often to study since it's practically impossible to get studying done at her home with all the chaos of her siblings running around.

Dina follows Nika through the corridor and into her favorite room— the sitting room, which has floor-to-ceiling windows framed by deep red velvet curtains with gold sashes. Dozens of potted plants fill the room— Nika's grandmother had had a green thumb, and Nika's mother had kept up the care of the plants since Nika's grandmother passed away two years before.

There is only room for one small couch in the room, where Dina now sits. Most of the floor space is taken up by a stunning Steinway grand piano. According to Nika's father, it's one of only three in the entire country of Georgia. Dina has been haranguing Nika for years to find out how his father had finagled getting it, but his father keeps the story tight as a vault. Dina's sure that the story involves the black market, but she will never find out the truth. The piano is the prized family possession, and Nika loves it almost as much as his father does.

Nika sits down at the piano, looking suddenly shy and nervous. Dina is surprised, since sitting in front of a piano is one of the few places where Nika normally seems confident and at ease.

"I… I wrote you something." Nika says softly, glancing up at Dina. He runs a hand through his unruly black curls and his left leg bounces nervously up and down.

"Like… a song?" Dina asks in surprise. As far as she knows, Nika's father is the composer in the family, not Nika.

Nika nods, "I haven't composed much before, but I wanted to do something special for you for your birthday, and this seemed like a good idea. But maybe I should play it some other time…" Nika begins to close the piano lid.

"Haha, no you don't!" Dina exclaims. "This is probably the one time in my entire life that anyone will ever write me a song, and I am not leaving 'til you play it! Got it?"

Nika blows out a breath of air and nods, "Okay. But I won't get my feelings hurt if you don't like it. But I hope that you do like it. Because to me, this song is you."

"What?" Dina frowns, confused.

"I... I tried to sum you up with a song, tried to capture the essence of who you are, of how I see you, with music." Nika presses both hands down on the piano bench, frustrated with not being able to find the words he wants. He glances at Dina, who is staring at him as if seeing him for the first time.

"Play it," she whispers.

From the first note, the song is joyful and full of life. It reminds Dina of the sound of a bubbling brook, and she smiles at Nika and he smiles back at her. But a few minutes later, as the song enters its second movement, Nika inserts a thundering, crashing dissonant chord with his left hand, and suddenly the song switches to a minor key. For a few measures, it sounds threatening— fast, scary. Dina sits still, in shock. It is as if she is hearing the soundtrack to her emotions during the attempted kidnapping. Her heart beats fast and her palms begin to sweat. Dina is not so sure she wants to hear the rest of the song. But then the music shifts to a slower section. It is quieter, and at first sounds somber and sad. But gradually, slowly at first, Nika adds in occasional major chords, which sound to Dina like whispers of hope. Nika looks back up at her, never breaking eye contact as he finishes the piece. The major chords increase in number until finally, at the end, the song loops back into the joyful thread of the opening movement. The final section isn't quite as bubbly as the opening movement, but to Dina, it sounds rich with joy and hope.

Dina is stunned. The music itself had been incredible, but more than that, she realizes something—

"You see me," she whispers, holding Nika's eyes, tears in her own. Nika nods, chest full of emotion. He is no longer scared or nervous or unsure. *Now is the moment,* he thinks, *I can finally tell her how I feel about her.*

"Dina, I—"

Just then, they are interrupted by the shrill ring of the phone on the hallway wall. "Argh," grunts Nika, feeling an uncommon rush of frustration and anger. "I should probably get that. Don't go anywhere!"

Dina nods, still in shock and astonishment. *Was he about to tell me that he likes me? He was, I'm sure of it. I could see it in his eyes and feel it in his fingers as he played. How long has he felt this way about me? How did I never see it before? How did I never notice him before, never feel anything other than friendship for him before? Or maybe I did, and I just didn't acknowledge it? He is rather tall and awkward and gangly. And his pitiful attempt at a mustache has got to go. But maybe I could like him,* she realizes with surprise. She twists the slender silver ring on her right hand, pleasant butterflies stirring in her stomach as she anticipates his return.

But when Nika walks back into the room, his face is serious. "Dina, that was Sofi. You need to get back home right away— they think your grandfather has had a stroke. Your mom is on the way to the hospital with your grandfather, so you need to get home to be with your siblings."

Dina gasps and puts her hand to her mouth, "Oh no! Oh, poor Grandfather! Nika, can you walk me to the metro? I've got to get home now!"

"Of course," Nika replies, grabbing his jacket and handing Dina hers.

Dina frets out loud about her grandfather throughout the walk to the metro. When they get to the top of the stairs, Nika asks with concern, "Are you sure you will be okay getting home by yourself?"

"I'll be fine," Dina rushes. "It's only a couple of blocks." She starts quickly down the stairs before pausing and running back up to Nika. She grasps both of his hands in hers and stares into his eyes, "Nika, your song was beautiful. I can't believe you wrote it for me. I don't think there will ever be another gift in my life that means as much as that song." She tightens her grip on his hands. "I'm sorry we got interrupted. But once my grandfather is better, we will pick up where we left off, ok?" She smiles and stands on tiptoe to surprise him with a quick peck to his cheek before dashing down the stairs. He watches her till she gets to the bottom, where she turns and shouts up, "Oh, Nika— you should play that song at your competition next week!"

***

The doctors confirm that Grandfather has had a stroke, and they keep him for observation for a couple of days. Every day, Natela brings her father breakfast, lunch, and dinner, since the hospital does not provide any meals. The first night, she also brings sheets, a pillowcase, a towel, and toilet paper, since Georgian hospitals don't provide any of those items either.

After three days, Grandfather begs Natela to bring him home— he can't get any sleep and is fed up with the noise in his large ward. He is sharing a room with eleven other patients, who all have visitors of their own coming at all hours to bring them food. When Natela realizes that the doctors and nurses are critically understaffed and swamped, she decides to bring Grandfather home where at least someone can watch over him around the clock.

And so, just like that, all of their lives change. The family arranges their schedule in shifts so that someone can be with Grandfather at all times. Even Mariam takes shifts, which she takes very seriously and proudly. Giorgi, on the other hand, often has to be yelled at for disappearing out into the street to play soccer with his friends when he is supposed to be watching Grandfather.

For a few days, Dina stays home from university to help. She calls her professors and explains the situation and they all graciously agree to let her make up her work. Nika promises to take extra-detailed notes to share with her.

When Dina returns to university the following week, she walks herself from her house to the metro. She's a bit nervous at first, but nothing happens so she calms down. Despite his busy practice schedule, Nika still meets her at Rustaveli station and walks her the last few blocks to class. Dina is so preoccupied with worry for her grandfather that Nika decides to hold off on bringing up the topic of their relationship and his feelings for her.

"Hey Dina, I won't be able to walk you to and from class tomorrow," Nika says with regret on Wednesday. "My audition is at

2:00 p.m., but then I have to be at the philharmonic throughout the afternoon."

Dina waves him off, "Seriously, it's not a big deal. I don't even know why you're walking me to the metro these days anyway—everything is clearly fine. Grandfather hasn't been able to walk me to the station on our side of the river since his stroke, and nothing has happened. So don't worry about it."

"I feel really bad. I wish I could." Nika frowns.

Dina lays a hand on his arm and looks up into his deep brown eyes, "Seriously Nika, it's no big deal. Everything will be fine."

CHAPTER 6
Tbilisi, Georgia

~~~~

May, 2018

Callie fastens her seatbelt, closes her tray table, and exhales in relief. The past 24 hours have been an exhausting, emotional whirlwind: packing up her room, getting back together with Lucas (*yay!!*), the goodbye dinner with her roommates, late-night drinks with Lucy, and then morning breakfast and, yes, make-out session with Lucas before catching a cab to the airport. Traffic had been terrible, and she had stressed for a while that she might miss her flight. But once she had finally made it to the airport, the line at security was lighter than normal. And Callie had only had one checked bag and one carry-on, so it hadn't taken her long to get through the airport. She had been pretty dang proud of herself for packing so light. *It didn't hurt,* she had thought, *that so few of my clothes were appropriate to bring!*

Callie has the window seat she pre-selected, and next to her are a man and a woman with a little baby. At first, she had been dreading an international flight next to an infant, but the kid actually sleeps most of the time. Unlike the baby, the father does *not* sleep. He sits in the middle seat, his broad hips squished uncomfortably close to Callie's. He watches movies the entire flight, the fluorescent glare from his screen, which he has turned up to maximum brightness, shining obnoxiously in Callie's eyes. She tries to ignore it, turning her head towards the window. But no matter what she does, she can still feel the glow through her eyelids. *Calm down, this won't last forever. Deep breaths,* she tells herself, channeling Dr. Paekl. Finally, unable to sleep, she gives up and decides to distract herself by catching up on a couple of movies she hasn't seen. But unlike her seatmate, Callie makes sure to turn the screen brightness to its lowest level so that she won't bother those around her. *Common courtesy,* Callie thinks, darting a critical frown at the oblivious man next to her. She leans against the window, waiting for the plane to land for her new adventure.

***

Despite massive amounts of pre-trip googling, Tbilisi manages to surprise Callie. Downtown looks straight up European, with a brightly lit main drag lined on both sides with majestic buildings decorated with classic European scrollwork and statues and floral motifs.   Her boutique hotel is super cute and modern, with a giant comfortable bed and the softest sheets Callie has slept on in ages. And the coffee shop next door to her hotel is hip enough to fit in on any corner in San Francisco. And the caramel macchiato, Callie's favorite guilt trip, is only two dollars! *You can't find a caramel macchiato for $2 in San Francisco! I'm liking this place already,* she thinks.

After giving herself twenty-four hours to catch up on sleep at her hotel and start getting over jet lag, Callie decides to explore the city. She had mapped out a detailed plan of the top ten things to see in Tbilisi, but in a spur of uncharacteristic adventurousness, Callie leaves the paper on her bedside table and resolves to venture out without a plan. A thrill of excitement stirs in her stomach.

She turns left out the door of her hotel, away from the main street, and back into a warren of tiny streets. The hotel receptionist had told her proudly that Tbilisi had been founded in the fifth century, and from the buildings around her, she can tell. The streets she walks are cobblestone, and tight enough that she wonders how on earth even a single car would fit through. On both sides, ancient two-story stone buildings, all connected to each other, line the streets— it looks like mostly shops on the first floor and homes on the top floor. Many of the upper-floor homes have brightly painted balconies with intricately carved railings and a plethora of plants. Callie pulls out her iPhone and starts snapping pictures. *How does Tbilisi not make a regular appearance on travel blogs and newspaper recommendation lists of places to travel to?* Callie makes a mental note to write to Suzanne and suggest they send one of their travel writers to do a piece on Tbilisi. *Thinking like a journalist, even when I'm on a leave of absence,* Callie grins to herself.

After getting lost a few times, Callie eventually meanders her way back to her hotel, proud of herself for stepping out of her comfort zone. Though reluctant to leave Tbilisi since she has barely explored it at all, she's ready to get started on her real reason for being in Georgia. She slips out of the pants that she'd been wearing on her walk through Tbilisi and changes into a long black skirt and a light blue t-shirt. *Guess this is what I'm gonna be wearing for the next three months,* she thinks ruefully. She gathers her things back into her suitcase, says an internal goodbye to her soft sheets and chic room with its blue walls and white couch, and heads downstairs to the hotel lobby to wait for her driver. Leila had promised to send a driver at noon, and Callie is excited and nervous to finally be making her way to the village. She is guessing that it will be a far cry from the surprising level of modern comfort that she has enjoyed in Tbilisi.

While she waits, Callie admires the hotel lobby. Yellow couches sit at pleasing angles throughout the room. A couple of giant bright green monsteras in ornate pots give the room a vibrancy. A crystal chandelier adds opulence to the vibe.

"Excuse me, Miss Leffler?"

Callie turns as a voice close to her says her name in clear but accented English. Before her stands a young man, probably about her age. He has dark hair, cut with swoopy Justin Bieber bangs, a neatly trimmed beard, and caramel skin. He is dressed in a black button-down shirt, black pants, and black shoes. *This must be my driver,* Callie breathes with relief. She had been a little worried that Leila wouldn't send someone, or that there would be a mix-up of sorts. To save money, she hadn't opted to upgrade her Verizon phone plan to include international calls and texts, so she is pretty much stuck in the Dark Ages with an iPhone that is good for nothing but taking photos.

In addition to being relieved that her driver has found her, Callie is comforted to find that he speaks English. She has been very impressed with the level of English spoken by many people in Tbilisi, but Leila had warned her that few people in the mountains speak English.

Callie smiles and sticks out her hand to shake her driver's hand. His eyes widen for a moment and he hesitates, eventually leaving her hanging when he tucks his hands awkwardly in his pockets. Callie's cheeks redden and she quickly pulls her hand back. The driver attempts to smooth things over with a polite nod and a bow from the waist.

"I'm Callie. Nice to meet you! You must be my driver!" Callie tries to speak loudly and clearly, unsure of how much English the guy actually understands.

"I'm Abdullah, nice to meet you," he gives another formal little bow. "Ready to head to Sureti?"

"Sureti?" Callie asks, racking her brain. The village she's going to is called Khev.

"Sureti is the name of the valley we live in," Abdullah explains. "It is about a three-hour drive from here." His English is formal, almost British, and his accent is fairly thick. But Callie is relieved to realize that he speaks at a high level. She hopes that he lives somewhere close to Leila's guesthouse so that she will have at least one other person in addition to Leila with whom she can communicate.

"Is this everything you have?" Abdullah points to Callie's large black rolling suitcase and her bright orange backpack. "That's it," she nods, feeling a twinge of pride at her light packing.

Abdullah picks up her large suitcase with one hand and her backpack with the other and walks out the door.

"You don't have to do that! I can carry my own—" Callie begins, but it's too late. She quickly follows him outside and watches as he puts her things in the big trunk of a rusty sedan that looks like it might be older than Abdullah. Callie tries not to show her nervousness that the car might die on them on the journey, and starts to open the door to the front passenger seat. Abdullah hurries over and makes a stop motion with his hand.

"So sorry," he says, looking a bit flustered and embarrassed, "but you will need to sit in the back. It's not appropriate in Sureti for an unmarried man and woman to sit in the front of a car together."

Callie turns pink and says, "Oh, of course, I'm so sorry! I didn't even think," and rushes to climb into the backseat. *I'm such an idiot, making cultural mistakes from the very first minute! How many hundreds more am I going to make??* Callie is certain that she is going to be unintentionally breaking cultural norms all summer. *How on earth will I, an agnostic millennial from San Francisco, fit into a tiny, conservative Muslim village?* Callie despairs, beginning to question the wisdom of her trip.

Abdullah asks Callie a few polite questions: how her flight was, where she was from, what she did for a living, and then they lapse into uncomfortable silence. Well, it isn't actually silence, since the sedan seems to be missing part of its muffler and drives with a mix of roars and ominous clanks. The back seat is a wide bench of cracked vinyl with stuffing coming through in various places. Callie wiggles around awkwardly, trying to find a place to sit where the vinyl cracks won't rub against her legs. She is appalled, though not exactly surprised, to find there are no seatbelts. There is going to be a lot she will have to adjust to.

After a few minutes of driving, they leave stately Old Town Tbilisi and enter the non-touristy part of the city. They pass whole streets of crumbling buildings, some with additions attached to them that look like they were built with whatever scrap wood and sheets of tin that the locals could find. Homeless dogs and cats abound, roaming the crowded streets. Eventually, they drive through a gray industrial area, where factories neighbor car part stores with stacks of tires leaning in precarious towers in front of them. After what must've been an hour, they finally make their way out of Tbilisi's congested, windy streets and get to the freedom of an open highway.

The sedan clanks its way along, going a good ten miles per hour slower than any of the cars around them. *Well, at least we are going slow enough that I probably wouldn't get very hurt, even if we have a wreck without a seatbelt,* Callie thinks as she stares out the window and soaks in the sights of the countryside around her. The land is slightly hilly, with a little scrub brush, but very few trees. The grass is the vibrant green of late spring and early summer.

Gradually, the low hills give way to higher hills, and abruptly they begin to climb up a steep winding mountain road. *These views look like they could be from the lake district in England,* Callie thinks, entranced. Soon, she loses the ability to focus on the beauty around her as the car rattles and groans around each hairpin turn, and Callie realizes that she is clutching the door handle with white knuckles. She forces herself to let go and take in a couple of slow, calming breaths. Abdullah is driving slowly and carefully, but the curves are still making her head swim. *If only I could sit in the front seat and have a better view of the road, maybe then I wouldn't feel so carsick,* Callie thinks. *Maybe asking Abdullah about himself will get my mind off of the dangerous road and my swimming head, though he doesn't seem overly eager to converse.*

"Ummmm, excuse me, Abdullah? Are you from Sureti?" Callie hopes that she is pronouncing the name of the valley correctly.

"Yes."

Abdullah's one-word answer doesn't give Callie much to work with.

"What do you do for a job? Do you work for Leila at the guesthouse?"

"Yes."

"Have you worked there long?" Callie asks, feeling aggravated at the one-word answers. *This guy is impossible to converse with!*

"Basically my whole life," Abdullah replies, and it seems he has a hint of a smile in his voice. "Leila is my mother."

"Oh!" Callie exclaims, "I had no idea! Well, I'm very glad to meet Leila's son! Do you live at the guesthouse?"

"I live on the property, but not in the actual guesthouse. Our family lives in a separate building."

"Oh yes," Callie jogs her memory, trying to recall the pictures Leila had sent her. "I think I remember seeing a couple of other buildings on the property in the photos that Leila sent me."

They lapse back into uncomfortable silence as Callie goes back to staring out the window and taking deep, calming breaths. They reach what seems to be the peak of the mountain pass, and then begin a descent through a lush forest with trees that canopy the road. If not for the rattling of the sedan, it would be totally silent. Occasionally another car passes them, or a newer car speeds around from behind them, but for the most part, they're alone.

Callie rolls her sweatshirt into a loose ball, places it against the window, and leans on it. *If this guy won't talk to me, I might as well try to get some sleep.* She closes her eyes, doubting she will be able to sleep through the racket of the car and the stomach-churning hairpin twists of the road. But the next thing she knows an hour has passed and she wakes groggily as the car comes to a rumbly stop. *I must still be jet lagging and catching up from not sleeping on the plane,* Callie realizes. Before her is a tall green gate that Callie recognizes from Leila's photos. She berates herself for sleeping through the town. *Though I suppose I will have plenty of other opportunities to see it,* she thinks. *Since I'm certainly not going to want to face that mountain pass again anytime soon!*

As Callie gets out of the car, a woman comes out of the gate. Though Callie has never seen a picture of her, Callie is sure this must be Leila. She is of medium height and slender build, with long wavy hair covered at the top by a thin headscarf. Her floor-length gray dress is topped by a neat cream-colored apron. She walks with a straight back and exudes calm and control.

"Welcome Callie," Leila bows her head formally, and Callie smiles, though she doesn't go in for a handshake— she learned not to do that with Abdullah. "We are very grateful to have you here," Leila continues.

Callie follows Leila through the gate and is immediately in awe of the grounds of the guesthouse. The few pictures she had seen did not convey the beauty and riotous colors of the incredible flowers and landscaping all around. Clearly, Leila is an expert gardener. To the left of the entrance is a large two-story white building with front columns and a stately porch. Callie knows that this is the main guesthouse. Beside the main guesthouse is a smaller building, which Leila explains holds her office and the family living quarters. To the right a grassy yard expands, overhung with grapevines. Leila leads Callie behind the guesthouse, where there is a large vegetable garden, more flowers, and an apple orchard. In the apple orchard stands a picturesque wooden gazebo with benches inside. Behind the apple orchard are chicken coops and a few smaller buildings. *Perhaps a barn? Or tool shop?* Callie wonders.

Leila finishes giving Callie the tour of the property, and then leads her to a room at the far end of the main hall on the second floor of the guesthouse— the room where Callie will be living for the next three months. The room is large with white walls, big windows, and tall ceilings. Callie grins to realize that the bones of the room are not too different from her room back in San Francisco. Though the idyllic mountain view out the back guesthouse window is nothing like the urban view from Callie's apartment! The decorations in the bedroom at Leila's are scarce— two sets of bunk beds and two simple wooden dressers are all the furniture the room contains. The floor is carpeted with a red patterned rug that reminds Callie of traditional Turkish rugs she has seen, and a couple of framed photographs of mountains hang on the wall.

Leila explains that this room is the women's sleeping quarters— guests book a bed per night in the room, like in a hostel. Two doors down are the men's sleeping quarters, in which guests also reserve beds per night. In addition, they have a couple's room with a queen-sized bed reserved for married couples, as well as a family room with both a queen-sized bed and a bunk bed for people traveling with their children. Callie is grateful to see that, at least for tonight, there seems to be no one sharing her room. She's hoping to get a good night's sleep to try to catch up from her lingering jet lag. She glances around the room and speaks hesitatingly, "Ummm, excuse me Leila, but is there a bathroom with this room?"

Leila motions for Callie to follow her out of the main building and down the path towards the orchard. Callie frowns, confused.

"Unfortunately," Leila explains, "indoor bathrooms are not common in Sureti. Many homes in the town still use outhouses. It's considered more sanitary to keep the bathroom away from the home, plus many homes do not have indoor plumbing."

Leila leads Callie toward a small building near the chicken coop. From the outside, it looks like a wooden outhouse straight from an episode of "Little House on the Prairie". Callie glances inside— instead of having a seat or a bench, there is just a circular hole cut into the wooden flooring. Next to the hole is a pitcher of water. Callie searches the small space, relieved to spot a roll of toilet paper hanging on a nail on the wall. Surprisingly, the outhouse doesn't stink, which is likely thanks to multiple slits cut in the walls to provide ventilation. A fly hovers lazily above the opening in the ground and Callie begins to seriously regret her decision to come. *Three months of squatty potty outhouse?? I'm not sure I will be able to handle that. I may be speed dialing Dr. Paekl at this rate,* Callie wrings her hands nervously.

Well, at least I know the number one thing to recommend that Leila change if she wants to attract Western clientele, Callie thinks, steeling herself as she resolutely closes the outhouse door behind herself.

***

The food at dinner that night is so incredible that Callie is once again glad she decided to spend the summer in Georgia. The first course is soup— a vegan lentil stew flavored with fresh mint leaves, which gives it a unique, fresh taste. The stew is served with the most incredible stuffed cheesy bread Callie has ever tasted— Leila explains that it is called *khachapuri* and is pretty much the national pride of Georgia. *Lucas would love this,* Callie thinks, missing him. Lucas is obsessed with pizza, and the previous fall he had decided to try all sixteen top-rated pizza places in San Francisco— starting with their favorite, Delfina's. By the time Christmas had come, Callie was sick at even the thought of pizza. Not Lucas though— he rated every restaurant and continued his quest through the spring, although Callie had mostly declined to join him at that point. *Khachapuri* reminded Callie of a salty, doughy pizza, just without the sauce.

Just when Callie thinks dinner is over, Leila brings out the main dish— golden fried chicken smothered in a creamy garlic sauce. It's served alongside a tomato and cucumber salad mixed with a light dressing of ground walnuts. Callie has never tasted anything like it, but she immediately loves it. There are also potatoes, sliced thin and grilled with onions and mushrooms.

Callie moans with satisfaction when she is so full that she can barely move. *I'm going to have to watch my waistline while I'm here!* she realizes. *I'm not going to be able to stuff myself with khachapuri cheesy bread every night if I want to fit into my clothes when I get home!* Callie's San Francisco diet was super simple and predictable— coffee and oatmeal for breakfast, a salad for lunch at work, and either takeout or something quick and easy for a late dinner at home before bed. She has to admit, it is super nice to have someone cook for her. Her roommate Megan would sometimes cook for their monthly roommate dinners, but other than that, Callie has been fending for herself for the past few years. And cooking is not her strong suit. *Maybe I could learn a recipe or two here and impress Lucas when I get home!*

Though the food is amazing, dinner itself is slightly awkward. There are no guests currently staying at the guesthouse, so Callie sits alone at the large table in the downstairs dining room. Leila goes back and forth to the kitchen, serving Callie like the most attentive of waitresses.

A few minutes after dinner starts, when Callie is still working on her first course of soup and cheesy bread, she gestures to the seat across from her and says, "Leila, please sit and eat with me! You don't need to serve me!"

"Oh no," Leila replies. "In our culture, we do not eat with guests. It is our honor to serve the guests who are a gift from Allah to our home." Leila bows politely and returns to the kitchen.

Though she tries multiple times to get Leila to sit and eat with her over the following few weeks, Callie is not successful. Most evenings, there are other guests to engage with at dinner. But on the rare evening when Callie is alone, she brings a book to read or her laptop to the table with her so that it isn't quite so awkward and lonely to sit at the huge wooden table by herself.

***

"So, what do you want me to work on first?" Callie sits at the dining room table, a cup of steaming tea warming her hands and a nubby white blanket pulled around her shoulders to protect against the crisp evening mountain air— despite it being June, the nights still get surprisingly chilly.

Leila sits in front of Callie, a pen hovering above her open notebook. Abdullah is next to Leila. Though Callie has seen him around the property multiple times in the forty-eight hours she's been at Leila's, he has said barely a handful of words to her. Every time she saw him, he seemed hard at work on the land. She couldn't help but notice his lean frame and tight muscles. *I guess I would be in tip-top shape too if I was constantly baling hay and chopping wood,* Callie thinks wryly.

The previous evening they'd had overnight guests— three guys backpacking from the Netherlands. But the guys had left at sunrise to get an early start on a long day of hiking, so Leila and Abdullah and Callie once again have the guesthouse to themselves. They'd agreed to have a meeting to talk through their plan for Callie's time. This meeting is the first time Callie has seen Leila sit down, as well as the first time Leila has willingly shared a table with her.

"I think the immediate priority is updating the website, as well as creating Instagram and Facebook accounts," Leila explains, her back straight and stiff in her chair. "If you post to those throughout your time here, then by the time you leave, we should have a decent base in place for us to continue when you are gone." Callie nods in agreement and sips her warm tea as Leila continues, "Abdullah has agreed to keep up the accounts when you leave, so it would be best if you worked with him on setting everything up, and it would be great if you could teach him how to create posts in a way that is appealing to a western audience." Callie glances at Abdullah, right at the same time as he glances at her. He gives a slight, formal nod.

This guy is gonna be a blast to work with, Callie thinks with an internal eye roll. His English had been fine in the car, but would he really be capable of creating social media content that was up to Western standards? Plus he seems really stiff, almost anti-social. *Couldn't barely get two words out of him! Is he that way around everyone, or just me? Maybe he doesn't like Americans?* Callie is afraid that she has her work cut out for her in partnering with him.

Leila looks down at her notebook, where she has a page full of notes in squiggly Georgian script. "Once you've set up the social media accounts, I would love for you to help advise us on how to modernize the property so that it is appealing to Western guests."

Callie smiles, trying not to sound judgmental, "I can tell you the first thing you need to do— get real bathrooms!" Callie had made an uneasy peace with the outhouse, but she did not enjoy using it. She especially dreaded having to put on boots and a jacket to go tramping through the dark when nature called in the middle of the night. She was sure American guests would not be up for using the outhouse.

"I've been telling her that for years!" Abdullah laughs, his brown eyes crinkling. *He has nice eyes when he smiles,* Callie thinks, surprised to see him warming up.

Leila grimaces at him good-naturedly, "There are lots of things you've been telling me for years! I've been busy focusing on essentials, like getting heat and running water. Plus, most of our guests so far have been Russian or European backpackers who don't seem to mind the outhouse."

"But you're wanting to change that, right? Expand your clientele?" Callie asks.

"Yes, absolutely," says Leila, making a note in her notebook and turning to Abdullah, "I give you permission to start looking into building bathrooms."

Abdullah gives a quick fist pump and his eyes light up with more excitement than Callie has seen from him so far, "I know just where we should put them! I think we should build two, each with a full shower, right next to the main house!"

"Wait," Callie frowns, "you wouldn't add them to the current rooms?"

"We had a whole construction team here when we put running water into the kitchen," Leila explains. "We asked them about adding bathrooms to the main house, but they said that we'd have to gut the whole thing and move multiple walls, install pipes inside of them, and so on. It would be a ton of work and very expensive. It's a lot more feasible to build nice bathrooms that are close to the main house, but in a separate building."

"Ugh," Callie groans, "So that would still mean boots and coat and walking outside at night to use the bathroom!"

Leila shrugs, "Unfortunately, yes. But it is the best we can do. Anyway, most people who come this far off the beaten path are fairly adventurous and not expecting 5-star, modern accommodations." Leila reaches for a strand of hair that had escaped from under her headscarf and tucks it back in. She wraps her thick sweater tighter around her thin shoulders. Abdullah lounges in short sleeves, seemingly impervious to the cold.

"There are two other things on my list," Leila glances down at her paper and then up at Callie. "Not top priorities for now, but things I want to get to while you're here. The first is having you help advise us on decorating the rooms. I try to stay up on modern trends, but out here, I feel hopelessly behind. It would be good if you could make a trip to Tbilisi one day and help us choose updated decor— pillows, blankets, rugs, lamps, etcetera."

"I would love to!" Callie replies enthusiastically, "That sounds like my idea of a good day! Interior design is one of my favorite side hobbies. Can't promise professionalism, but I definitely enjoy it! And honestly, from what I can see, you have a really good eye. Your style is clean lines and minimalism, which is definitely in right now."

Leila blushes and smiles genuinely, clearly pleased by the compliment.

"Enough talk about decorations! Be right back," Abdullah hops up from his seat and goes into the kitchen, returning with a plate of scone-like pastries and a bowl full of tiny, bright red strawberries. Callie's mouth begins to water.

"Picked them from the garden this morning," Abdullah says, offering the bowl to a grateful Callie. *You would think I wouldn't have room for anything after the giant dinner Leila fed me only two hours ago, but apparently, there is always room for strawberries. And anyway, they're healthy! And taste amazing and smell so good!*

Callie enjoys the berries as Leila shares the final item she wants help with— applying for grants to international foundations to try to get money to improve the valley.

"Obviously this point is super important," Callie hesitates, choosing her words, "but I have no background in grant writing or dealing with foundations. Plus, I don't know the needs of this valley. So I will try to help you with this one, but I can't promise anything."

"I understand," Leila nods, "but at least we can try. Sureti Valley is full of good people who have had hard lives and need help but are too proud to ask for it. So maybe I can ask for them."

"That's great that you want to help your community," Callie says. "How did you guys get the idea to start this guesthouse?" she asks, curious.

"That's neither here nor there," Leila stands abruptly and her face looks like someone has pulled a curtain shut across it. She thanks them curtly for the meeting and announces that she is heading to bed. Abdullah stays seated, looking unflustered by his mother's odd behavior, his mouth full of scone. Leila coughs, gives him a meaningful glance, and Abdullah hurries to his feet and wishes Callie goodnight before following Leila around the corner of the guesthouse to their home across the patio.

That was weird, Callie thinks. *Leila obviously did not want to answer that question about how they started the guesthouse, and she didn't seem to want Abdullah to stay and sit with me. I wonder why?* she shrugs, deciding not to let it bother her. At least they'd made progress tonight, with Abdullah actually starting to talk to her. *We better learn to talk soon if we are supposed to do so much collaborating!*

Just then, Callie's cell phone rings. Her screen says "unavailable", so she figures it's Lucas calling from San Francisco on his lunch break. She is excited to talk to him— they haven't talked since a brief call on her first night in Tbilisi.

"Hello?" Callie leaves the well-lit dining table on the patio and walks out to a little bench in the dark semi-privacy of the grape arbor.

"Callie?" Lucas' voice sounds tinny and far away.

"It's me; can you hear me?" Callie asks.

"Callie? You're breaking up. I can't really hear you."

And that is how the entire five-minute long conversation goes. Callie heads back inside to get closer to the Wi-Fi router, hoping that will solve the problem. It doesn't. By the end, Callie is so frustrated that she wishes she could throw her phone. She's kicking herself for not biting the bullet and paying for an international phone plan. She had wanted to tell Lucas everything— about how cool and hip Tbilisi was, about the long awkward car ride to Sureti, about the guesthouse. About hospitable, organized, but slightly aloof Leila. About Abdullah, who she can't get a read on. She would definitely leave out the information that she finds him attractive.

Eventually, Callie gives up, "Sorry babe, I can't hear you at all. If you can hear me, know that I love you and will try to call you tomorrow. Maybe we will have better reception then."

Scratch adding bathrooms as top priority, Callie thinks with frustration, *The first thing Leila needs to do here is get decent Wi-Fi!*

CHAPTER 7
Tbilisi, Georgia

March, 1992

Dina hurries along the river, hoisting her heavy backpack on her shoulders, frustrated at herself for being late. *I should've started curling my hair earlier! Gah! Why am I always late?? I've gotten used to being on time for once these past few months with Grandfather pushing me out the door on time every morning to meet Nika at the metro, but now that I'm back on my own, I'm back to my old habits of constantly being late everywhere! Oh! Nika! His audition is in a few hours!* Dina crosses herself and says a quick prayer to St. Gregory, the patron saint of musicians.

The spring day is light and breezy and Dina wishes she'd left her coat at home and just worn a sweater instead. She is about to cross the street to the university when car tires screech beside her. She doesn't even have time to react before two men (the same two as before, she will later realize) hop from the car, grab her arms from both sides and push her headfirst into the back seat. She starts to scream and scratches them as she attempts wildly to climb out the door, but it's too late. They duck into the car, slamming the doors behind them. The windows are up and Georgian techno music blares from the speakers. Dina quickly realizes no one outside would be able to hear her scream, but that doesn't stop her from continuing to call for help.

After a few moments of useless thrashing and screaming on Dina's part, the driver pulls up at a stoplight and turns around in the front seat.

He speaks loudly to make himself heard over the thumping of the music, "And here we are. I told you we'd meet again. You be a good girl— we promise we won't hurt you. But you've got to stop screaming— you're giving me a headache. And it won't do you any good anyway," he gestures to the darkly tinted windows.

Dina glares at him, but reluctantly acknowledges that he is right about the screaming. She stills, realizing she should conserve her energy for a time when she might have a chance to escape.

As they wind through the streets of Tbilisi's warren-like old town, Dina's heart thumps loudly in her chest and all of her senses are on hyper-alert. She smells the body odor of the men on either side of her and the heavy cologne wafting back from the man in the front seat. *Boom bop bop* the dance music pulses as Dina's mind races. The car is old and rickety; she can feel the cracks in the seats through her skirt and pantyhose. Her breath comes quick, panicked. *How can I escape? Could I jump out?* She looks at the heavyset guys on either side of her— there is no way she's getting past them. The one on her left was likely a wrestler in his youth— short and stocky, ripped muscles, with a giant cauliflower ear. The one on her right has a bit of a pudgy gut but still looks quite strong. When he glances at her, she notices that he is missing at least three teeth. She turns to the car's tinted windows and realizes with a sinking feeling that no other drivers will be able to see her. *I will have to wait 'til we stop to try to escape*, she concludes, wishing she could come up with a better plan.

Unfortunately, the men don't seem to have a plan to stop. Dina's hands tense when she realizes they're on the outskirts of the city, and then leaving the city behind. *They're probably from one of the mountain villages, just like I originally thought. If they take me to their village, there will be slim chance of me escaping.* Her stomach turns and she's worried she will be sick.

"What's your name?" the guy in the front seat calls back, his voice friendly and casual. Dina raises her eyebrows and crosses her arms, looking out the window and refusing to answer.

"Hey, talk to him. Saidun's a great guy— give him a chance!" Cauliflower Ear grins at her, gesturing to his buddy in the front seat. "He's been smitten with you for ages, ever since he saw you outside the university last year when he was in Tbilisi for a supply run for his farm! Look at all the trouble he went to to come all this way back here to get you!"

"And plus, Saidun comes from one of the wealthiest families in Khev," Toothless chips in. "You're a lucky girl!"

Dina bites her lip, their words confirming her suspicion that this is a bride kidnapping. *At least he plans to marry me, not murder me,* she grasps at straws of hope. *He will probably take me to his family home. I will have to try to 1) escape before we even get there, 2) convince his family not to let him marry me, or if that doesn't work, 3) run away.* Dina pulls her arms tight against herself, trying not to touch up against either of the guys in the backseat with her. To their credit, they both sit as far away from her as possible. She watches as the low, scruffy plains around Tbilisi gradually rise into hills. If her best guess is correct, they will soon be heading for the Zudi Pass— a desolate mountain highway where there will be no chance of getting help. *I have to try to escape before we get to the Pass!*

Dina scans the horizon in panic— they are in the countryside, with no signs of civilization around. Suddenly, over the far hill, Dina spots a decrepit gas station with one lone pump.

"I need a bathroom! Please stop!" Dina announces hurriedly, pointing at the distant gas station.

All three men immediately look distinctly uncomfortable, glancing at each other with uncertainty. Cauliflower Ear shakes his head slightly at the driver, Saidun.

Saidun replies, "Come on, guys— this lady is our guest; let's show her the courtesy and hospitality we are famous for! And plus, where's she going to go anyway?" He laughs, spreading an arm expansively at the open plains around them.

Dina grasps the edge of her seat as Saidun floors the car into the gas station and screeches to a halt in front of the pump.

This is my chance, Dina thinks, desperately scanning for a gas station attendant and planning to scream for help as soon as she sees one.

And then she notices the ripped plastic bag over the handle of the pump and the broken, boarded-up window of the tiny, dingy kiosk that is as dark as night inside. Her heart falls.

"Come on," Toothless beckons as he stands outside the car door, waiting for her. *Ok, on to Plan B,* Dina steels herself as she scoots out of the car. *If there is no one here to save me, I'm going to have to save myself.*

"There's an outhouse back there," Cauliflower Ear points out across a field filled with knee-high weeds.

Dina steps carefully around a pile of old tires and broken-up boards. Plastic bottles and other trash litter the ground. She glances back to see Saidun gesture towards her and then towards Toothless, who reluctantly begins to follow Dina across the field. When she looks Toothless in the eyes, he blushes and quickly looks away from her. *This is good,* Dina thinks. *He is uncomfortable— maybe he won't come close.* Her heart begins to beat faster when about halfway across the field, her wish comes true— her "guard" stops awkwardly in the middle of the field, clearly deciding he has gone as far as is appropriate. Dina continues on alone, estimating that there are about thirty yards between her and the outhouse— enough to give her a good head start. With a jolt of relief and gratitude, she realizes that the door to the outhouse is on the back side of the small wooden structure, the side that can not be seen from the car.

As nonchalantly as she can, Dina picks her way through weeds and trash around the side of the outhouse. When she gets to the back side she glances in the partially open door and almost gags— the "toilet" is a hole in the ground that has been used by so many passersby that the sewage has spilled above the ledge in a rank stew of urine, feces, and old newspaper, which passes for toilet paper in Georgia. Steeling herself, Dina ignores the bathroom and instead focuses her attention on the surrounding land. Hidden from sight behind the outhouse, Dina figures she probably has a good five minutes before the men might think to come to check on her.

She desperately scans the area around her. The grass is waist-high, which could provide some cover if she is willing to crawl through it. *At this point, I'm willing to try anything.* Unfortunately, the field is large and barren with no trees in sight. There is, however, a copse of bushes and brambles about twenty yards to the back left of the outhouse. Determined, Dina sinks to all fours in the weeds and begins to army-crawl her way through the grass in the direction of the bushes. Damp dirt quickly soaks her hands and knees and thorns tear at her pantyhose. Dina ignores it all, panting as quietly as she can as she speed-crawls through the grass, hoping she is going in the right direction. She doesn't dare poke her head up to verify.

"Hey!" she recognizes Saidun's voice, calling to Toothless. He shouts out something in a language that Dina can't understand. *Probably telling him to check what's taking me so long,* Dina's stomach turns and she doubles her pace. With relief, she spots the bushes not far ahead of her. As quietly as possible, she creeps behind the bushes, brambles biting into her hands as she crawls. Behind her, she hears a loud shout and knows the men have discovered her escape. Heart pounding, she lowers herself as close as she can to the ground. *Crash, crash*— the noise of the three men searching the field thunders towards her.

Please don't see me, please don't see me, she prays, cursing her bright purple blouse. Her fists tighten as she hears the unmistakable thud of boots plowing through the underbrush toward her.

"Aya!"

Her stomach drops at the exultant shout that she knows means she has been spotted. She scrambles to her feet but it is too late— Saidun is already almost upon her. She expects him to grab her, but when he gets a couple of feet away, he stops short, seemingly unwilling to touch her. Unlike the laughter that had filled his eyes that first time when she had run in Tbilisi, this time there is no humor in his face.

"Enough," he says, his thick chest panting from the exertion of running and searching for her. "This is ridiculous. Where did you think you would go? We won't hurt you. I am going to give you a good life. You should be rejoicing, not trying to run! Now come back to the car and behave," he waves his hand towards the car.

Dina stands slowly, brushing a myriad of dirt, leaves, and sticks from her clothes and skin. For a few minutes, she refuses to move, arms crossed tightly across her chest, breathing heavily and glaring at Saidun. He purses his lips and raises his eyebrows. Finally, realizing she has no other recourse, Dina follows him back to the car.

Not long after leaving the abandoned gas station, the road twists upwards into a snowy mountain pass. The higher they climb up the steep windy roads, the deeper the snow drifts around them. Dina holds her breath as Saidun takes the hairpin curves at a stomach-dropping speed. At one point, they skid around a curve, their tire less than a foot from the edge of a sheer drop-off. The men laugh when Dina lets out an involuntary shriek.

"Hey, don't worry!" Toothless reassures her, "Saidun is a great driver! He's driven over this pass in every kind of weather."

"And, I just bought new snow tires— I'm the only Ramazi in all of Khev who has them. These babies can handle anything— they've got grip like a mountain goat," Saidun grins at her proudly over his shoulder, her escape attempt seemingly forgotten in his pride over his new tires. *Ramazi. They're Ramazis,* Dina thinks, heart sinking as she remembers all the terrible rumors she has heard about Ramazis over the years.

For the rest of the afternoon, the men talk animatedly amongst themselves in the car in a language Dina doesn't understand but assumes is Ramazi. At one point, Cauliflower Ear offers her an apple, which Dina turns down— the dangerously curvy snowy road combined with dread over her situation has her stomach in way too many knots to eat. Finally, near dusk, they drive through a small village. Dina stares hungrily out the windows, trying to memorize every turn in case she needs the information in the near future. The pot-hole-filled gravel roads are lined with high walls on every side— Dina assumes that behind each wall is a family compound. Eventually, they pull up to a tall blue gate. Saidun blares his horn a couple of times before hopping out of the front seat and banging on the gate. His two buddies stay in the back seat, hemming Dina in.

Before long, the gate is opened by a stocky older woman in a long dress and a headscarf. Her body shape is so similar to Saidun's that Dina assumes that it must be his mother. The men in the car watch raptly as their buddy talks animatedly to the woman, pointing to the car. Dina is relieved to see the woman completely lose it, gesturing wildly and yelling furiously. *His mother is going to say no! She's against this! She's going to make him take me home!* Dina sags with relief against the worn back seat of the Lada. She watches the interaction carefully. Through the gray light of dusk, Saidun gets progressively more animated. Soon he too is throwing his arms up in the air and yelling. Dina hears a squeak and looks across the street to see a neighboring gate open and an elderly man stick his head out, clearly watching the drama with interest. Though the front window in the car is cracked, Dina can't understand a word the driver and his mother are yelling at each other. Throughout the whole episode, Cauliflower Ear and Toothless sit motionless and mute.

Dina waits, hoping the woman will come to the car. *Maybe she will talk with me, maybe even have someone drive me back to Tbilisi!*

Dina's heart sinks when the woman slams the gate resoundingly in Saidun's face. He storms back to the car, face red and livid and arms crossed tightly against his chest.

"Твок лвыв зщыду!" he rants to his buddies once he swings into the front seat and slams the car door so hard that the whole car rattles.

"Ир родла ло двак кроп," the guy on Dina's left replies, patting Saidun's shoulder placatingly.

Saidun throws the car into gear and screeches down the street, flinging dust and stones from the gravel road behind his spinning tires. He drives through a couple of small streets until he gets to a field, where he pulls the car over under some trees. Dina's heart starts to thump again and she anxiously twists the slender silver ring on her right hand, a birthday gift from her mother in better times. It's now fully dark and she is in the back of a car with a furious man whose life plans were just foiled. She tenses, preparing herself to run if the need or opportunity presents itself. *If a door opens, I will run for it and try to make it to one of the houses,* she decides.

But no door opens. Instead, the three men talk animatedly for a long time, of course never bothering to translate anything for Dina. It seems like they're getting nowhere. *Maybe I could talk them into taking me home,* Dina thinks.

"Excuse me," she butts in, and all the guys immediately are silent, staring at her in surprise, as if they've almost forgotten she is even there. Or maybe they're just surprised that she will risk speaking up?

"Was that your mom?" she asks the driver hesitantly.

He pauses and then nods reluctantly.

"I'm guessing she doesn't want you to marry me?" Dina asks, hoping her guess is correct.

"I'm a grown man! She can't control my life!" the driver spits out in Georgian. "If my father had been home, things would've been done properly! He never would have lost his head like my mother!"

"If your father had been home, he would've made you turn around and drive back to Tbilisi," Cauliflower Ear ribs him. "This is why we did this now, when he's gone— remember?"

"Well I'm an adult and I will marry who I want to marry!" Saidun huffs, his thick chest thrust out.

"Please, I know you don't want to make your parents mad," Dina pleads. "I'm sure they want what's best for you! Find a girl here, someone from your same language and culture! I would be a terrible Ramazi wife! You don't want me! Just take me back to Tbilisi, please. I'm begging you," Dina cries. "I just want to go home. My family will be so worried about me," Dina pleads, trying to catch the eyes of all three men, hoping to gain at least one of their sympathy.

"It's too late to go back tonight," Saidun sighs. "We'll go to my uncle's for the night and figure stuff out there. He's much less judgmental and more understanding than my mother," he rolls his eyes and puts the car into gear, bumping over grass and roots as he heads back towards the road.

***

They drive for maybe fifteen minutes, out of one tiny village and into another. Behind the compound walls that line the streets, Dina barely registers the majestic forms of towering, snow-covered mountains. They stop at the gate outside another walled-in compound, and again Saidun gets out alone. This time, he knocks politely on the gate. Almost immediately, the gate is thrown open by an older man with a sleek gray beard. He and the driver talk for a long time outside the gate, and eventually, the driver turns back to the car and gestures to Dina and to his buddies to come inside. Dina's heart races, *This is my chance. I have to convince his relatives to let me go.*

Dina is led through a courtyard surrounded on every side by low, squat buildings. The uncle leads them into one of the buildings, into a dark smokey living room with low ceilings and pea-green brocade couches. He gestures for Dina and the men to sit down, and all four men almost immediately begin talking animatedly, with loud voices and lots of hand gestures. A headache begins to grow behind Dina's eyes and she realizes she hasn't had anything to eat or drink since breakfast that morning. *Breakfast at home in Tbilisi*, she thinks, tears welling in her eyes.

"Excuse me," she butts in in Georgian, speaking extra loudly to try to make herself heard.

"I need to go home," she addresses her plea to the uncle, who looks as shocked at hearing her speak as if she'd grown a second head. "Please, my family will be desperately worried. They've probably already called the police."

The men look at each other and shrug carelessly. Dina realizes that route of reasoning won't work.

"Aren't you Muslim?" she asks, grasping at straws. "You don't want him to marry me— I'm an Orthodox Christian."

Uncle shrugs, "You will be whatever religion your husband is. Be quiet while the men come up with a plan. Don't worry your pretty little head— you are lucky Saidun chose you. Ramazi women are the happiest women on earth. They did a study in 1983 that said so. We men take care of our women and provide for their every need," he says proudly, stroking his luxurious gray beard. At that moment, a young woman enters the living room with a silent bow. With her eyes never lifted from the floor, she carries a tray of tea and desserts to the low table in the middle of the room and begins to pour tea for each of the men. She looks to be about fifteen and her face is a riot of painful-looking acne. The men ignore both Dina and the girl serving tea and go back to their discussion in Ramazi. Suddenly, Dina finds herself overwhelmingly exhausted. The intensity of the day hits Dina like a load of bricks and she sinks against the firm couch, wishing for nothing more than to be safe at home in her own bed, trying like usual to wrestle some blankets from her sister Sofi, who perpetually hogs them.

Dina is startled to feel a gentle tap on her wrist. It's the young girl, timidly offering her a cup of tea and a plate of cookies. Stomach rumbling, Dina gladly accepts both, knowing she will need whatever fortification she can get for what is to come.

The men talk for hours and to Dina's infinite frustration, she can understand nothing. *If only I could understand what they're saying,* Dina thinks, *I could know how to best argue for my freedom.* But it's no use— their conversation drags on and on into the wee hours of the morning. At some point late in the evening, the young girl brings in a meal of boiled lamb on top of small noodles, with a buttery garlic sauce to dip the noodles in. To Dina's surprise, despite the stiffness of the couch and her trepidation of what the night may bring, she begins to doze off after the heavy meal. Eventually, she is woken up by the clearing of a throat near her face. She opens her eyes to see Saidun looking down at her indulgently.

"Sorry we bored you to sleep," he smiles. "Let's get you to a real bed!"

All of Dina's senses go into immediate high alert. *What is going to happen now? Where will he take me? What is he going to do to me?* She looks around in desperation at the other three men, but none of them are paying her any attention— one is yawning, one is scratching his chest, and Uncle is standing impatiently by the door out to the courtyard. Dina looks around for the young girl who served them food, or any women for that matter, but sees none.

Saidun and his two buddies hug goodbye, and Dina watches them leave through the outer gate. The courtyard is dimly lit by one naked flickering bulb. Dina pulls her coat tight about her, thankful that she has it— it's spring in Tbilisi, but up in the mountains, the March air is biting. Snow still lies in piles around the courtyard. Dina shivers, her long legs clad in nothing but her thin skirt and cheap nylons.

Uncle gestures and Saidun and Dina follow him, Dina's breath shallow and quick and her fists clenched. They enter the largest building at the edge of the courtyard and step into an entryway crowded with shoes. Wordlessly, Uncle, Saidun, and Dina all remove their shoes. As per Soviet custom, Uncle and Saidun both put on slippers to wear inside the house. Uncle hands Dina a pair of blue velvet women's slippers with delicate silver stitches. They're too small and they pinch her feet, but Dina puts them on anyway and follows the men down a narrow hallway with a couple of closed doors on either side. With no ceremony, Uncle opens a door and indicates for Dina to go inside. She stands in the doorway, unsure what to do— knowing she can't stay in the hallway indefinitely, but also so scared of what will happen if she goes into the room with Saidun.

Saidun gestures impatiently to the room, "This is for you. Get a good night's sleep. We will figure everything out tomorrow, okay?" He tries to make the last sentence sound kind, and then gives a giant, noisy yawn and rubs a hand down one side of his face. "I'm heading to bed. Goodnight," he gives a half bow and heads down the hallway. Uncle gestures impatiently to the room again and at last, Dina heads inside.

The room is small and sparse, with a little loveseat that has been folded out into a bed. The walls are covered with gaudy gold wallpaper that is peeling in places. Dina sinks onto the bed with exhausted relief. *Did I really just get off so easily? Is Saidun actually going to leave me be for the night?* She rushes to check the door and finds to her deep disappointment that it doesn't have a lock. As she stands there, she realizes that she really really needs to pee. And she has no idea where a bathroom is. *Am I even allowed outside of this room?* Dina wonders. *Maybe I could try to escape! And if anyone catches me, I could just say I'm trying to find a bathroom!* Her heartbeat quickens as she tries to think through what an escape scenario would look like. *My attempt this afternoon was an utter failure. Would tonight be any different? Where would I go? Even if I were able to get out of the compound gate, the likelihood of any of the neighbors just bringing me straight back here is quite high. Could I escape into the forest?* Dina remembers the cold air, the piles of snow, and the mountain pass with a sinking feeling— there's no way she would survive outside overnight in this weather, and certainly no way she could make it back home on foot. *I'm going to have to try tomorrow to convince them to take me back. Or try to escape during the day and find someone to help me. Maybe I could somehow call or get a letter to my mom and she could come and get me?*

Multiple scenarios run through Dina's head as she paces back and forth, trying to keep her mind off of her complaining bladder. Finally, she can hold it no longer and opens her door, peering into the long hallway, which is dark and deserted. She slips out into the hallway, walking up and down it. All the doors are closed, and she's hesitant to try them, thinking it likely that people are sleeping behind most of them. She paces the hallway, squirming with increasing discomfort, unsure of what to do. Finally, in desperation, she decides that her best option is to sneak outside and pee somewhere in the yard. As quietly as she can, she slips on her shoes and sneaks out the door to the courtyard, which is thankfully still lit with the dim, flickering bulb hanging from a wire. She heads around the back corner of the house, her left shoe sinking in a snow drift that she didn't see. It's pitch black behind the house so Dina doesn't dare go too far.

Finally, she squats in the darkness, awkwardly trying to snake her hose down her legs under her skirt. She shivers as a rush of icy air hits her legs. *How did this happen?* she thinks, tears streaming down her cheeks as she squats in the black night, trying to hold her underwear and pantyhose out far enough so that her stream of pee doesn't hit them, and wet snow seeps through her thin shoes.

CHAPTER 8

Sureti Valley, Georgia

June, 2018

Callie's first few weeks at the guesthouse pass slowly, so different from her perfectly organized, extremely busy life in San Francisco. In San Francisco, Callie was up by 6:00 a.m. every day, either heading for the gym in bad weather or out for a run on a clear day. She was home by 7:00 for a quick shower and breakfast of a banana and six ounces of oatmeal with twelve raisins before arriving at work by 8:00. Actually, most days Callie arrived at work at 7:55— she is fastidiously punctual and hates being late. She also has little patience for others being late. *It isn't that hard to be on time, for crying out loud.* Lucy was perpetually late, which frustrated Callie to no end. Sticking to a predictable schedule and routine helps Callie feel a sense of control, and gives her the stability she needs to be able to cope when curveballs come her way, though she tries to minimize curveballs as much as possible.

The Chronicle offices hummed with activity all day— half of the staff was in a constant rush to finish whatever story they were working on in time for the 2:00 a.m. print deadline, while the other half had the unfortunate problem of working online, which meant not even having a set stop time— the internet never sleeps, and so rarely does the staff. Lucas worked at the online desk, which partially explained his inability to ever distance himself from work. Despite serious cutbacks in print subscribers over the past decade, *The Chronicle* had bought into the need for online advertising early and so had been able to maintain a large portion of its staff.

It had taken Callie a while to adjust to the pace of life at Leila's. Leila and Abdullah were up early every morning, gathering eggs from the chickens, preparing breakfast, and doing general chores around the property. Callie, however, had the luxury of being able to sleep in for the first time in years, that is when other female guests weren't sharing her room and waking her up with their morning noise. Most days she did wake up at 4:00 a.m. when the call to prayer sounded over the village loudspeakers, and then again at 5:00 a.m. when the roosters started crowing, but usually she was able to roll back over and go to sleep. For the first few days, she felt guilty about sleeping while the family was working, and she tried to get up early and help Leila around the property, but Leila seemed horrified and offended at the idea and shooed Callie quickly back to her room.

One morning Callie attempts going for a run, which turns out to be a fiasco. When the rooster crows at 5:00 a.m., she's unable to get back to sleep. After tossing and turning for a while, she decides to get up. Aware that she can't run in a floor-length skirt, she puts on a pair of leggings, a long T-shirt and tennis shoes and slips out the green front gate. The weather is cool and slightly foggy, with a damp mist. Callie breathes the fresh air deeply, relishing the chance to stretch her limbs. She starts with a slow jog, gradually warming up after a couple of weeks of not running. *Man, I've missed this.*

"Ду фывлдо зуш ячбй!" Callie hears someone shouting and turns to see an elderly woman yelling and frantically waving her arms. Callie looks around, wondering if the lady is yelling at someone else. But there is no one around. So Callie stops running and heads over to the woman, who must be at least eighty, judging by the number of wrinkles that wreath her face. When Callie gets close, the old woman grasps her arm and starts tugging her back to Leila's.

"Oh no," Callie explains slowly and loudly in English. "I'm going for a run. I don't need to go back there. I'm going this way, to the river," Callie points across the lush green field in front of her.

But the old woman clearly doesn't understand. She shakes her head and continues to pull Callie toward Leila's. Frustrated and confused, Callie gives in, following the woman back to the guesthouse. It is a long, slow trek. When they finally get back to the guesthouse, the woman calls for Leila at the gate, says something in Ramazi, and then pats Callie's arm with a kind smile and starts hobbling off back towards her house.

"What was that all about?" Callie asks. "I was just trying to go for a run and she stopped me and dragged me back here!"

"I'm sorry about that— I should have warned you," Leila looks uncomfortable and apologetic. "Unfortunately, you cannot go running here."

Callie blushes, both embarrassed and annoyed, "Because I'm in pants?" she asks.

"Well, mostly, yes," Leila replies. "But even if you somehow figured out how to run in a floor-length dress," Leila gives a small half-smile, "it still wouldn't be culturally appropriate." Leila hesitates, staring out at the grapevines and picking at a corner of her apron. Eventually, she takes a deep breath and continues, "I've had a lot of troubles over the past few years, trying to start this guesthouse. Women don't normally run businesses here. In addition, many people in the town are against encouraging foreigners to come to Sureti Valley — they think foreigners will bring Western ideas and loose morals. I do not agree with them, but I have to walk the fine line of trying to make Westerners feel welcome, and, in return, bringing much-needed tourism money into the valley, while also trying to show my neighbors that we can welcome Westerners while still maintaining our values." It is the longest speech Leila has given since Callie arrived, and Callie nods with understanding, grateful that Leila is finally opening up to her. She hadn't realized what a tight spot Leila is in. She worries that by her own behavior, she might have accidentally compromised Leila and the guesthouse in some way.

"I'm so sorry, I had no idea— I'll just do workout videos in my room from now on."

"Excellent, thank you," Leila nods curtly.

"Would it be okay for me to take a walk around the town and explore?" Callie asks hesitantly.

"That would be perfectly fine. I will have Rosana take you out later this morning."

"Oh, seriously, no need! I can just go out on my own!" Callie replies.

"Rosana will be happy to take you. I know you Americans are very independent, but at least let her show you around the first time so that I know we won't lose you. After that, it should be fine for you to go walking by yourself."

"Is it… it's safe, right?" Callie asks awkwardly.

Leila laughs drily, "Probably much safer than where you came from in the US! Everyone knows everyone here and looks out for each other, and they look out for guests as well. You will be quite safe. The biggest thing you have to fear is being invited in for tea or a meal at every other home you pass," Leila smiles as Callie raises her eyebrows in confusion.

"People here are quite welcoming to guests," Leila explains. "And you're the first American who is living in our village for a lengthy chunk of time, so people are understandably quite interested in meeting you. I've already had multiple families tell me they want to invite you over for a meal."

"Really?" Callie asks, shocked.

"Absolutely. Once you've had a few more days to get settled in, I will have Abdullah accompany you to some meals. He will translate for you. And it will give you a good chance to get a feel for how people here live and what the needs are in the community. If we end up applying for any grants, it will be essential that you have seen what daily life for people here is like."

***

"Alright marketing guru, you teach and I will follow!" Abdullah announces as he waits for the clunky old Dell office computer to slowly pull up the home screen. From the office window, they can hear the mostly happy shouts of what sounds like an entire circus but is really just the four children of an American family currently staying in the guesthouse. The couple and their twin four-year-old boys have been staying in the family room, and the nine- and eleven-year-old girls have been bunking with Callie. After not having been around kids very much in San Francisco, Callie has been enjoying hanging out with the girls. She even taught them how to make homemade paper dolls one afternoon, which they had loved. It had brought back fond memories for Callie of afternoons spent making paper dolls with her sister June when she was a kid. Though she won't lie— she's looking forward to a return to peace and quiet once they leave.

The sun shines through the office window and Callie twists a strand of hair, waiting impatiently for Abdullah's computer to finish booting up— her sleek MacBook Air has been ready to go since the moment she opened it. She decides to use their waiting time to cover a couple of topics. "First of all, I am not a marketing guru! I've spent the past few years working for a newspaper, so I am aware of some marketing strategies and principles, but I'm not a professional by any means. But I will do my best."

"No problem, I didn't mean to put pressure on you. Anything you know is more than we know!" Abdullah encourages, his left leg bouncing as he sits in front of his noisily whirring computer.

"Okay, the first thing we need to do is set up Instagram, Facebook, Airbnb, and Trip Advisor accounts for this place. My understanding is the only site you are on is booking.com?"

Abdullah nods, "That's where all our clients have come from so far. Well, that and word of mouth."

As they talk, Callie grows increasingly impressed with Abdullah's English. "How did you learn such good English? You have an accent, but your vocabulary is amazing."

Abdullah shrugs, "My mom studied English and she spoke it and Georgian to us from the time we were little. My grandparents spoke to us in Ramazi mostly, and we went to elementary school in Russian and high school in Georgian. So basically from the time we were kids, we spoke all four languages. Plus, all the best TV and movies are in English. When I was a kid we would get pirated DVDs for very cheap in Tbilisi and bring them here and watch. Name a famous American movie, and I bet I've seen it!" he grins, seeming to be much more at ease here on his home turf than he had been alone with Callie in the car.

Together, they work their way through setting up profiles on each of Callie's recommended sites. However, she's baffled by the lack of quality photos— *my grandma could've taken better photos, which goes to show how awful these are!* Callie thinks.

"Are these all the photos you have?" Callie asks, trying to keep her voice neutral.

Abdullah shrugs, "Photography isn't our specialty. They've been fine so far." He glances at Callie and laughs at the expression on her face. "Ok, I can tell from your face that they aren't fine!"

"Let me show you what we're ideally looking for," Callie pulls up some top Airbnb hosts, as well as some Instagram travel influencers. "Photo quality is key. Good photos are what is going to draw people here. Honestly, I'm not sure how you've gotten people here so far, with the photos you have." Callie admits.

"I know how!" Abdullah leans back in his chair, both feet off the ground. "We're the only place to stay within fifty miles in any direction! So if people want to come to this area, we're their only option." His amber eyes crinkle in a smile and he shrugs.

"Zero competition!," Callie laughs. "That's one way to succeed in business! But that's not the main thing you have going for you— your main draw I think is the number of five-star reviews you guys have. Though you haven't had a ton of guests, almost all of them have given glowing reviews about your hospitality, food, and the beauty of the property. Honestly, reading the reviews is what convinced me to contact your mom about coming here."

"Really?" Abdullah raises his eyebrows.

"Absolutely. I was interested in taking a couple of months off of work and doing some sort of internship abroad, so I looked on gogive.com. It's kind of like a clearinghouse website where people post internship opportunities abroad that they're hoping to fill, and people like me can use filters to search for what we're looking for. I specifically was searching for an internship where I could use my writing, social media skills, and love of design and fashion. Your mom's post came up as one of the top options for an internship for someone with my specific skill set. But once I looked into you guys deeper, it was the reviews on booking.com that made me actually want to come here. It seemed like you guys had a lot of untapped potential. Plus your mom was really on the ball with communication."

Abdullah listens attentively, his face straight. Finally, at the end, he grins, "You know it was me who put that post on gogive.com? You were writing with me part of the time."

Callie's eyebrows rise in surprise and she swats at him, "Hey! And you let me go on telling you about it as if you were hearing this for the first time?!"

"It would have been rude to interrupt you," he shrugs with a glimmer in his eye. "Did I do a good job sounding like my mom on the computer?"

Callie laughs, "I am very impressed at your ability to mimic a middle-aged woman!"

"Ha, I have lots of experience. We share one email account for the guesthouse. It's in my mother's name of course, but she and I work together to handle client communication. Often people will spend half their time writing with me and half their time writing with her, but I have so perfected writing like her that no one ever knows the difference." Abdullah leans back in his chair, looking at ease chatting with Callie and not in any hurry to get down to business. Callie, on the other hand, is tightly wound with the internal American drive for productivity.

"Well, your mom clearly trusts you, which is good! And I'm sure she's glad for your help. Now— back to the topic at hand— reviews," she says. "Like I said, reviews are everything. Well, reviews and photos. You guys have great reviews going for you— now we just need to get you good photos. And then get those broadly disseminated."

"And you can do that?" Abdullah puts his front chair legs back on the ground and raises his eyebrows.

"I can try. Unfortunately, I didn't bring my good camera, so I won't be able to get professional quality photos. But even with my iPhone, I can for sure get better photos than the current ones. And I've got some ideas for marketing. My best friend at work, Lucy, has an ex-boyfriend, Max. Well, she has lots of ex-boyfriends, but one is a pretty famous travel Instagrammer. Last I checked, he had over two-hundred thousand subscribers. She burned her bridges with him when they broke up, but thankfully I didn't. I'm gonna contact him and see if he would be willing to do a post on this place. The best thing of course would be if he could actually come visit, but even a post from him would go really far to get us actually on the map. I've also talked to some of the travel writers at *The Chronicle*, where I work in San Francisco, and they're willing to do a piece on the guesthouse as well."

Abdullah crosses his arms, and raises his eyebrows, "I'm impressed! That's a lot of good ideas! We better get working on those bathrooms ASAP if we're going to have loads of Western guests," he laughs.

"The sooner we get bathrooms, the happier I will be!" Callie grins.

Just then, a timer beeps on Abdullah's watch and he hops up, "Mind if we call it quits for now?" He hurries towards the door.

"Sure," Callie says, caught off guard by his abrupt departure. Something of her confusion must show in her face because he pauses and holds up his watch.

"Time for prayers," he explains. "Muslims do them five times a day, at set times."

"Oh," she nods, "of course. I suppose I'll see you later," she finishes lamely. Abdullah gives her a jaunty half-bow and disappears down the hallway.

***

One morning, Callie comes downstairs with a new idea to suggest. She isn't quite sure how it will go over— so far, Leila hasn't let Callie into the kitchen a single time, despite Callie suggesting many times that they allow her to just make herself a simple meal instead of them always feeling like they need to make her elaborate feasts for every meal. Leila always says it isn't a big deal for them to cook for Callie as well since they often have guests they are cooking for anyway.

Callie has been pleasantly surprised to note that Leila has a steady stream of guests coming through the guesthouse. Rarely are all four rooms booked, but often at least one of the rooms is booked. Abdullah explains that summer is their best season— in January and February, they can spend weeks snowed in, without a single guest.

Callie slides her hand down the smooth stair railing. It is a light smooth oak, stained a rich, deep honey-yellow. The posts of the railing are intricately carved with grapevines curving around them. Callie has been admiring them ever since she arrived. The gazebo around back is made from the same wood and also has intricate carvings.

Callie takes the final steps two at a time, turning quickly around the corner towards the kitchen.

"Leila!" she says with surprise, "I'm so sorry— I didn't see you coming and almost ran into you!"

"No problem," Leila nods formally and continues walking, carrying a big basket of wet clean sheets towards the clotheslines in the back.

Callie joins Leila and walks alongside her. "I've been meaning to ask," she says, "the woodworking here is amazing. Did you hire a local carpenter to do it?"

Leila gives a rare smile, "Sort of— Abdullah did most of it. His grandfather was a woodworker and taught him the tricks of the trade. A lot of the furniture in the bedrooms was carved by his grandfather. Abdullah tinkers around in his grandfather's old workshop, but these days the guesthouse keeps him so busy that he rarely has time to carve." Leila looks sincerely regretful.

"Wow," Callie replies. "He's really talented. He could sell woodworking like his for loads in the US. And that's so cool that his grandfather taught him. I feel like I know almost nothing about your family— I'd love to hear more about this grandfather and the rest of your family!"

Leila's eyes harden and she says, "You are here to be a business partner. Please let us maintain professional courtesy and keep the past in the past. I will not ask you about your family, and you kindly refrain from prying into mine."

"I'm so sorry," Callie stammers. "I really didn't mean anything by it, honestly." *Wow, I'm never going to touch that topic again!* Callie cringes. *Clearly stepping on some kind of landmines! I wonder what they are?* Despite herself, curiosity stirs in Callie. But she knows now is not the time to press.

"Back to Abdullah's carving," Callie says, returning the conversation to a safe topic, "does he sell it here?"

"Unfortunately there's not much of a market for it here," Leila looks relieved to be back on neutral conversational ground. "Most people have more critical needs than fancy furniture. Anyway, what was that idea you wanted to run by me?"

"Oooh, I had a great idea!" Callie clasps her hands in excited anticipation, "What if you offer Ramazi cooking lessons to the guests who come?"

"Well, most of our Western guests are not the biggest fans of Ramazi food— it's very carb-heavy, lots of noodles and fried dough, as well as lots of gamey meats like lamb. We tried serving it for a while at first and often got complaints."

"Well, how about Georgian food? The Georgian food you make is incredible! And Americans love learning to cook international dishes."

"That's a good idea," Leila muses.

"You'd have to let someone into your kitchen!" Callie jokes with a glint in her eye, "Maybe you should give me a trial cooking lesson to iron out the kinks."

Leila eyes Callie with false sternness, "Alright young lady, we do a trial cooking lesson. But don't expect access to my kitchen after that! You are still our guest."

"Deal," Callie nods, sticking out her hand for a handshake. After her conversational faux pas of a few moments before, she is pleasantly surprised when Leila takes her hand and shakes it.

***

"*Baba!*" Callie and Leila are interrupted by a squeal ricocheting off the high walls surrounding the gate. They turn just in time for a curly-haired missile to collide full-speed into Leila's skirts. Leila laughs lightly, surprising Callie. She bends down and carefully untangles an adorable little boy from her skirt, speaking to him first in Ramazi and then turning to introduce him to Callie in English.

"Callie, meet my grandson Daud! He is two and a half, and has just as much energy and spunk as his mother did at his age!" Callie grins at the little boy, who looks up at her curiously. He has Leila's coloring— from the auburn curls to the bright green eyes.

"So you are blaming me for his energy? I hardly think that's fair!" A short young woman in a hijab approaches slowly, wheezing. "I seem to remember Abdullah being the one bouncing off the walls!"

"Abdullah had energy, but he was never as noisy and chatty as you!" Leila smiles affectionately and turns towards Callie. "Callie, meet my eldest daughter Fariza."

"Nice to meet you!" Callie exclaims. "I've heard so much about you!"

"Did they tell you I was about to pop?" Fariza moans dramatically, putting her hands on her very round stomach. At barely over five feet tall, her pregnant belly is even more pronounced. Callie gives her a quick once-over— she certainly looks nothing like her beautiful, stately mother. Fariza's eyes are too close together, her build is stocky, and her thick black hair frizzles out from under her hijab in an untidy braid. But her green eyes are merry and her grin infectious and Callie immediately likes her and feels more at ease around her than she does around aloof Leila.

"Guess how many months pregnant I am?" Fariza demands, both hands on her hips.

"Oh," Callie reddens, feeling distinctly out of her area of expertise and not wanting to offend, "I really have no idea." *She looks like she could give birth any minute though!* she thinks.

"Seven months! Barely seven months! I still have ten more weeks to go! How on earth will it be possible to grow any larger?! I am like a whale already!" Fariza laughs self-mockingly.

"But our favorite whale!" Abdullah jokes, coming around the corner carrying a giant box of apples from the cellar.

"Hey! You are not allowed to say that! Only I can complain about my size!" Fariza swats at him as he ducks easily.

"Abduwa! Abduwa!!" Daud jumps up and down, thrilled to see his uncle.

Abdullah quickly sets the box of apples down and swings a laughing Daud up onto his shoulders, then gallops around the courtyard as the little boy cackles with glee.

"He's all yours!" Fariza shouts at Abdullah. "I'm going to help Mom in the kitchen. Don't let him near the gate or the woodworking shop or the farm equipment!" she warns.

"I've got him!" Abdullah rolls his eyes good-naturedly up towards his nephew. "Can you believe she thinks I cannot take care of a two-year-old?"

Daud responds by giving Abdullah's hair a painful yank and shouting, "Run, horsey!"

Callie stands under the tangled grape vines alone, watching Abdullah gallop off towards the back orchard with his nephew, and Leila and Fariza walk arm in arm towards the kitchen. She shifts from foot to foot, feeling lonely and very far from home and family.

***

Later that afternoon, once everything is blessedly quiet thanks to Fariza putting Daud down for his afternoon nap in Leila's bedroom, Callie decides to do an Instagram post on the incredible woodwork around the guesthouse. She takes some photos of a beautiful desk in one of the guest rooms, with gracefully arching legs that remind her of Queen Anne furniture from England. She squats close to the leg of the desk, trying unsuccessfully to get just the right angle. Eventually, hoping no one sees her, she lies across the floor and angles her iPhone so that it catches a ray of sunlight streaming in through the sheer curtains on the open window. *Not too shabby*, Callie thinks, admiring the resulting photo.

She is photographing the balcony railings when Abdullah walks by.

"What are you doing?" he pauses, looking confused.

"Oh!" Callie hops up, "I was just photographing this woodwork for Instagram! Your mom told me you did it— you're really talented!"

Abdullah looks momentarily taken aback by her enthusiasm, but then he thanks her formally and heads away, towards the back pasture.

"Hey, Abdullah, I was thinking— maybe you could show me your workshop?" Callie runs down the staircase to catch up with him, "It would be great to have pictures of it for the post I'm gonna do about the woodworking. Oooh, and maybe I could get some shots of you doing actual carving? That would be fabulous!"

"Oh, I'm not sure," Abdullah looks embarrassed, "The wood shop is a mess right now— I don't get out there that often…"

"Oh, okay, don't worry about it," Callie interjects quickly, sensing his hesitation and not wanting to step on his toes. "I can just do a post about the stuff that's already done."

Abdullah glances at the small building behind the orchard that contains the wood shop and runs a hand down his beard. *I don't normally like facial hair, but his beard looks really good on him,* Callie admits to herself. Abdullah straightens, clearly having made a decision. "I'll tell you what— let me clean up the wood shop a little bit this afternoon, and tomorrow I can show you around and you can take whatever photos you need for the post. Deal?"

"Deal!" Callie grins, "People are gonna love it!"

***

The woodshop building is super old, for sure older than Callie, and maybe older than Leila. *This place looks like it's gonna collapse,* Callie thinks, slightly concerned. There are three almost identical old buildings on the property— one housing the woodshop, one housing the chickens, and one that Callie will only find out the grim truth about much later.

The windows of the woodshop are so grimy that she can't see in them, and the entire building, which measures probably no more than one hundred square feet, is tilting slightly to the left. The clapboard wood that had been used to build it has long since weathered to a dirty gray and Callie notices green lichen splotched liberally across the boards.

"Knock, knock!" Callie calls out, opening the rusty metal door with a screech of hinges. When she enters, Callie isn't sure exactly what "cleaning" Abdullah had done the day before, because the entire floor is still covered with literally thousands of wood chips and wood shavings. In the middle of the room, a big metal machine stands in hulking silence. Once Callie's eyes have adjusted to the dim lighting filtering in through the grimy windows, she notices that dozens of tools are hung neatly on nails scattered across the walls. *This must be the cleaning Abdullah was talking about.* Callie pulls out her iPhone and takes some shots of the workshop. She glances at her phone— Abdullah had told her he would meet her out here at 3:00 p.m., but it is already 3:15. Lightly aggravated, Callie begins to tap her foot impatiently.

Just then, Abdullah comes rushing through the door, "You're here! Sorry I'm late— I got held up with a delivery of produce I was picking up."

"No worries," Callie smiles quickly, tamping down her frustration. "I'm looking forward to seeing what you do! I've never actually been in a woodshop before." Callie moves closer to the big machine in the middle of the room and runs a finger along the smooth metal cylinder in its center.

"It's not very exciting," Abdullah shrugs, "but I find it rewarding. I was close to my grandfather and it reminds me of him; we spent many hours together in this shed. He was an expert craftsman— trained in the ways of our ancestors. Few woodcutters today still use the ancient methods, which is very sad because it means that they are dying out. For example, my grandfather never used nails— he would always make handmade pegs to attach things. Young people today don't want to spend the time and effort to do things the old way," Abdullah explains, running a hand through his dark hair. "I try to do things as much like my grandfather taught me as possible, but even I take shortcuts to save time. I use nails— I admit it!" Abdullah looks legitimately regretful. "If I had more time, I would be able to do more of the old methods. But as it is, I barely manage to do woodwork even with cutting corners."

"Ok," Callie suggests, pulling out her phone again, "How about you make something and I will just take pictures of the process?"

Abdullah starts to laugh, and he laughs so hard that Callie almost gets offended, "What??! What did I say??"

"Callie, do you know how long it took me to make each railing for the balcony?" Abdullah asks, still catching his breath.

Callie shrugs, biting her lower lip, "I don't know— a couple of hours? Multiple hours?"

"Weeks, Callie! Each one! Or years, depending on how you count! First I had to find a tree that would be right for what I wanted to make. For railings, I normally use dogwood. To be the right thickness, the tree has to be at least fifteen years old. Then my buddies and I chop down the tree and let the wood sit and dry out, normally for at least two years. Sometimes more— my grandfather's rule was one year of drying for every inch of thickness in the wood. You can speed it up a bit by covering the wood in dried shavings, but I normally still wait a couple of years before working with a piece of wood."

"A couple of years?!" Callie raises her eyebrows. She can't imagine waiting multiple years to work on something. Ramazis must have more patience than Americans.

"Then, once the wood has dried out, I have to cut it to the right size. Then I place it on the lathe," Abdullah gestures to the large metal machine in the middle of the room. "I use the lathe to turn the wood to the shape that I want." He demonstrates the various parts of the metal lathe in the center of the room and Callie follows him around, duly impressed with the amount of time, skill, and effort needed for woodworking.

"Here's what I was thinking," Abdullah suggests, pointing to a large pile of shavings in a dark back corner that Callie hadn't noticed amid all the other shavings. "I have a number of projects in that pile that are in process, but not finished yet. I call it my Corner where Dreams go to Die," Abdullah gives Callie an embarrassed grin.

"Your Corner where Dreams go to Die?" Callie laughs out loud. "I'm pretty sure I have like ten of those!"

"And what is in Callie's Corner where Dreams go to Die?" Abdullah raises his eyebrows as he leans back against the lathe.

Callie twists a strand of chestnut hair and bites her lower lip, thinking. "I wanted to be a writer for a while, but of fiction, not news," she admits. "When I was really little, I wanted to be a ballerina until I took ballet and was terrible at it! I would come home so distraught after each class that my mom let me quit after only three lessons! In college, I took some painting classes, which I really loved. And I love interior design, but I've never done anything with it professionally. So basically I have a huge Dead Dreams Corner," Callie rolls her eyes.

"Maybe you can take something out of your Dead Dreams Corner this summer, dust it off," Abdullah suggests.

"Maybe," Callie hems noncommittally. "For now, let's work on getting something out of your Corner Where Dreams go to Die," she grins.

"Deal," Abdullah winks, heading over to the corner. "What if I work on one of these a bit, and you can photograph the process? And then we will hit two rabbits with one rock!"

"That's great," Callie agrees. "But— hit two rabbits with one rock?"

"Ummm, it's an expression of ours. It means to do two things at once, or solve two problems at once."

"Oh! We have a similar saying— to kill two birds with one stone! I've never understood why you would even want to kill one bird, but I suppose it came from back in the day when people had to hunt for their food."

"Well, if that is the case, then I can say that the Georgian saying is wiser because rabbits are much tastier than birds!" The corners of Abdullah's eyes crinkle in a smile as he digs under the sawdust to get to his pile of abandoned projects, finally selecting a long piece of wood that Callie recognizes as a partially finished railing, similar to the ones that line the balcony.

Callie shudders, "I could never eat a bunny!"

"You've never had rabbit??" Abdullah looks pityingly at her. "It's delicious! I will ask my mom to make one for dinner one night soon."

"Ugh, please don't," Callie winces at the prospect.

"You're missing out then," Abdullah shakes his head and moves over to the lathe.

When he switches the lathe on, it comes to life with a roar that makes Callie jump. *Glad Abdullah had his back turned and didn't see that*, she thinks, cheeks reddening. Callie checks the lighting in the room (*not great*) and edges her way to find the best angle. For a few minutes, she just watches Abdullah. He is bent over the lathe, clearly concentrating on the spinning piece of wood. His dark hair falls over his eye as he presses what looks like a dull metal knife up against the side of the rotating piece of wood on the lathe, using firm, solid motions to gradually carve the wood. Callie watches, mesmerized, as the piece of wood rounds under his knife to the shape of a railing. He presses the metal instrument at various places and various angles, adding dimension to the railing. Under his strong hand, curves form like magic as the lathe whirls. Callie's breathing quickens as she watches the muscles in his lean forearm strain as he presses the knife hard against the wood.

Abdullah coughs lightly and then yells over the noise of the lathe, "Is there something I need to do differently for your photos?"

Callie blushes, very glad that the room is too dark for Abdullah to notice. "Oh no, this is great!" Callie shouts back. "Keep going! I was just figuring out angles and lighting."

Abdullah nods and goes back to the lathe. He's so engrossed and focused that it's as if he doesn't notice Callie at all. She looks through the lens of her phone, trying not to notice Abdullah's lean muscles, frustrated at the iPhone 7's poor quality in low-lighting situations and wishing she had her real camera from back home that had somehow not made the "essentials" list for packing. *Why did I not think to bring my camera?*

"Hey Abdullah, my iPhone camera isn't great in low-lighting situations. Is there any way we could get more natural light in here? Maybe open the door and the windows?"

Abdullah stops the lathe, and Callie is as shocked by the sudden silence that descends upon the room as she had been by the noise when the lathe first started. He opens the door, which complains loudly, and then heads to the window. "Honestly I'm not sure if this thing even opens. It's probably been years since someone opened it." Abdullah fiddles with the latch on the window, which at first seems entirely stuck in place.

"Don't worry about it, I think the lighting from the door is enough," Callie offers quickly, not wanting to inconvenience him.

"Nope, I will figure this out!" Abdullah grabs a mallet off the wall and hammers the latch until it finally gives in and turns. Then Abdullah is able to wrench open the window— not fully, but enough to let in a stream of sunlight that completely changes the lighting in the room.

"Perfect! Thank you!" Callie claps.

Abdullah nods and heads back to the lathe. This time, Callie braces herself for the noise and is proud when she doesn't jump. She pulls out her phone right away and begins to take pictures. At first, she heads outside the studio and gets a shot of Abdullah through the open doorway, back bent over the lathe. Then she moves inside and gets a couple of shots in profile as he concentrates on the wood. Finally, she moves extra close to the lathe, taking zoomed-in pictures of just the wood, and the lathe, and Abdullah's hands. *Woah, he has nice hands— wide and strong and calloused— very manly.* She tries various angles, and in one picture she manages to capture a shaving flying off of the piece of wood.

"Ok, I think I have what I need!" Callie shouts, and Abdullah shuts off the lathe.

"Now I just need a picture of the craftsman!"

"Ummm," Abdullah looked embarrassed, "Really? Didn't you already get enough?"

"I basically got your backside!" Callie laughs.

"Oh, that won't do," Abdullah looks distinctly uncomfortable and Callie berates herself for yet again putting her foot in her mouth in this conservative culture.

"Maybe you can tell me what other photos you need?" Abdullah asks smoothly.

"Well, you know on Instagram people want a face to go with the story." *And you have a nice face,* Callie adds to herself.

"Okay, fine," Abdullah crosses his arms across his chest. "But first let me see the other photos you took." Callie hands over her phone and Abdullah scrolls through, starting with the photos she just got of his hands, and going all the way back to the ones of his grandfather's chair.

"These are really good," he says earnestly, looking up at her. "They look like something from a magazine. You have a good eye."

"Ha! Or I've just spent way too much time scrolling through influencers on Instagram!" Callie laughs off his compliment but is secretly pleased.

"Don't sell yourself short," Abdullah looks at her intently, his amber eyes warm. "These are really good. Corner Where Dreams Go to Die material," he smiles.

"Maybe," Callie smiles back. "I did dabble in photography in high school. My high school even had an ancient darkroom that I used one semester after borrowing an old film camera from my dad. I really loved it, but basically haven't touched it since then."

"Seems like a good time to dust off an old dream," Abdullah hands the phone back to Callie, and then stands awkwardly against the lathe. "I trust you with the camera... but don't exactly trust myself as your model. I've never had my photo taken before, not in a serious portrait... so I'm not sure what to do."

"No problem," Callie reassures him, feeling comfortable as she settles into work mode— she's been watching *Chronicle* photographers talk down nervous clients for years. "Most guys are uncomfortable posing for pics. It's my job to help you find a pose that feels natural. Try picking up the piece of wood you were just working on and hold it in your hands as you lean back against the lathe. Good. Now move a little to your left and try crossing one leg over the other. Nice. Now freeze and look at the camera."

Abdullah stays statue-still, holding the partly finished railing in his hands. At first, Callie gets a couple of full-body shots, and she's happy with the results. The room around is dark except for a stream of light coming in through the open window, which glints off of Abdullah's hair. Callie is surprised to notice hints of auburn, like Leila's, as the sun hits his hair. He's wearing worn jeans, dark shoes, and a black button-down collared shirt, with the sleeves rolled up to his elbows. His face is so serious that Callie almost laughs.

"Come on! Your audience is American! You gotta smile for a picture for them!"

"Uggh— I feel so awkward! I officially do not like this. How did I ever let you talk me into doing this?" Abdullah complains with a frown.

"I'll tell you what— close your eyes and think of something funny, and then as soon as you open them, I will snap a pic. Ok?"

"Worth a shot," Abdullah looks unconvinced. But he closes his eyes, and a minute later a smile is playing across his lips. Callie creeps closer, positioning the phone for a close-up face photo. In a moment, Abdullah opens his eyes and looks surprised for a moment to find her so close to him. Callie snaps a pic but is aggravated to see that his face looks surprised in the photo, like he was caught off guard.

"Ok, so what was so funny?" she asks, phone still posed.

Abdullah laughs, "I was remembering when I let Daud help me gather the eggs last week and he pelted the chickens with two of them before I could stop him."

He looks towards Callie as he explains, laughing, and she snaps the photo. *Gotcha!* she thinks victoriously.

"Hey, you tricked me!"

"But it worked, didn't it?" Callie grins. "It seems like your nephew is a trip! Hey, you showed me how you turn the wood, but you didn't show me how you carve it."

"That's because that is the super long part! Stick around for the winter, and you will find me whittling away on cold snowy evenings when it's impossible to get anything else done. I suppose I can show you a little bit now if you want."

Abdullah talks her through the various knives and tools he uses, how to find the best wood for a certain piece, and his thought process for deciding what to carve. Even though Abdullah likely had learned very little about Michelangelo in his Ramazi village school, the way he talks about the carvings finding him reminds Callie of a quote she'd heard years ago that Michelangelo had supposedly said, something about his job as a sculptor simply being to let free the sculpture that already resided under the marble. *It seems like artists are alike at heart across centuries and cultures.*

They move outside and sit on two stumps after Abdullah says he needs better lighting to see to carve. Abdullah leaves the railing he'd been working on inside and instead brings a small block of wood outside. When Callie watches him carve, she is even more impressed— under his nimble fingers, a horse no larger than Callie's thumb begins to appear from within the wood. The details he is able to bring to life with a tiny knife are incredible— she's never seen anything like it. She watches him for a long time, fascinated, only occasionally remembering to take a few photos.

Her Instagram post that night gets a hundred and twenty-seven likes and eight comments— not a lot in the grand scheme of things, but the most since they'd launched their new account the previous week.

"High five!" Callie calls out that evening, showing Abdullah her phone as she passes him in the orchard on her way back inside from her dreaded pre-bedtime outhouse visit. He hesitates for a moment, glances to make sure that no one is around, and brings his hand up to meet hers.

CHAPTER 9
Sureti Valley, Georgia

March, 1992

The first night at Uncle's house is unbearably long. There is one small wooden chair in her room, which Dina pushes up against the door. Not because it would be able to keep Saidun out, but because she's hopeful that the sound of it scraping against the floor would wake her if someone tried to come in. She tosses and turns in bed for hours, tensing at every sound she hears, terrified that he is coming to have his way with her. Finally, exhaustion overtakes her and she falls into a fitful sleep. She is surprised and relieved to wake up to sunshine streaming through her window in the morning, having passed the night blessedly undisturbed.

***

Dina brushes her hair the best she can with her fingers, but yesterday's careful waves are now a tangled mess. She has no clothes to change into, so she reluctantly exits her room in her clothes from the day before, despite the underarms of her purple blouse being stained with sweat and body odor from the stress of the previous day.

Just as she's leaving her room, a matronly woman in a floor-length dress and headscarf comes bustling down the hall towards her, her arms full of cloth.

"Tsk tsk tsk," she says in surprisingly unaccented Georgian, "You can't go out like that! Here, these are for you— I'm sorry we didn't think about them last night. It was just such a shock, with you coming so unexpectedly and all." She hands Dina a rolled-up bundle, which Dina opens to find contains a simple dark brown floor-length woolen dress, thick tights, two pairs of underwear, a headscarf, a thin white nightgown, and a towel.

"Follow me. I will show you where to bathe." The woman bustles off down the hallway, and Dina follows her to an outhouse and attached outdoor bathhouse with a giant barrel of water in one corner.

"I'm Albina, Saidun's aunt, by the way. My husband's sister is Saidun's mother."

Dina nods, not quite following the track of family relations.

"Wait!" Dina stops the woman at the bathroom door with a desperate grasp on her arm. "There's been a mistake! I have to go back home— my family will be worried sick about me! I can't stay here. I can't marry Saidun! I'm in university— I was about to graduate from my final year. Please, you have to help me— I've been kidnapped against my will!" Dina begs, hoping that this woman may have pity on her and be willing to help her.

But the woman just smiles kindly and pats her arm, "Calm down, dear. I know it seems overwhelming now, but it will be all for the best. My husband kidnapped me over twenty years ago. At first, it was hard, but then things settled down and now I have a home and wonderful children. I know your case is different than the usual bride kidnapping here, since you aren't Ramazi. Believe me, it has been quite the scandal! But the neighbors will adjust to the idea and so will you. You will be fine— stop worrying! Now clean up and then come to the kitchen for breakfast."

Dina is utterly taken aback— this is not at all the reaction she was expecting or hoping for. Before she can attempt another tactic, the woman bustles away, leaving Dina alone at the outhouse door.

***

Once Dina is dressed, she stares in the small bathroom mirror and does not even recognize herself. The frumpy brown dress is nothing like the bright, modern styles she usually wears. Her long auburn waves, her secret pride, are hidden under a headscarf that she tied so poorly that it keeps slipping down over her forehead like a child on a slide. She forwent bathing when she felt how icy the water in the barrel was, so her hair feels greasy. *What I wouldn't do for a hot bath!* Her face looks pale and bare without her usual lipstick and mascara. Her green eyes alone are recognizable. *You made it through yesterday,* she tells herself, staring into her eyes in the mirror and straightening her shoulders. *You can make it through today. Today is going to be the day that you figure out how to go home,* she tries to convince herself.

At the door, Dina waffles. Most of all, she would prefer to go back to her room, close herself in, and try to come up with a strategy to either talk her way out of her situation or run away. But her stomach growls so forcefully that she decides to go find that promised breakfast before she does anything else.

When she passes the living room, she is shocked to see it packed with men— probably at least twenty men in all. She recognizes Saidun, his uncle, and the two men from the car. They're gathered around a table laden with food, and clearly in the midst of a heated debate. *This must be half the men in this village,* she thinks with amazement. *And I'd bet good money that they're here trying to figure out my future,* she frowns with trepidation, half-tempted to go in and speak for herself. But she quickly realizes that there isn't a single woman present in the room and that anything she says would be likely to backfire. So she quietly slips past, in search of the kitchen that she'd been instructed to find.

She locates the kitchen easily thanks to the din of female voices coming from a building across the courtyard. The scene when she enters is like walking into an anthill after a child has stirred it with a stick– utter chaos. Seven or eight women, rushing to and fro, stirring pots, washing dishes, prepping plates to be ready to be carried to all the men across the way who doubtless are waiting for the rest of their breakfast.

When Dina enters, it's as if someone pressed pause on a movie — everyone freezes and stares at her. Dina looks at the faces— a couple curious, a couple hostile, and a couple looking too tired to care about anything. Albina, the woman from the hallway, smiles at Dina and points to a small table in one corner of the kitchen, "Sit down, sit down! Let us get the rest of this food out to the men and then we will get you some breakfast— you must be starving!"

Dina sinks into a chair, watching as the women return to their labor and start speaking to each other in their unintelligible Ramazi. She feels a twist of guilt for sitting while the rest of the women are working so hard. But Dina knows that, not knowing her way around this kitchen, she would likely just get underfoot if she tried to help.

Plus, honestly, she has zero desire to put any effort into preparing food for the men who are trying to ruin her life.

The women run giant bowls of steaming oatmeal and plates of bread and cheese out of the kitchen and across the courtyard to the men. Once they have all the men served, the skittish, pimple-faced girl from the night before brings Dina a bowl of oatmeal. It's milkier than Dina is used to and highly sugared. But she eats it gratefully, glad to have something so filling in her stomach.

When she finishes eating, Dina offers to help the girl who brought her breakfast with the giant pile of dishes that has accumulated. But the girl looks horrified, "Sit down! You are our guest! Of course you cannot wash dishes!"

"Sit down! Sit down!" A chorus of women echo from across the room.

Dina watches as the women work together. She feels a gut-twisting stir of homesickness as their coordination with each other reminds her of her mother and sisters— that wordless co-laboring that women have shared in kitchens through time eternal. How many meals has Dina prepared with her mother and sisters, the work made easier by the sharing and the community?

"Ok, dear," Albina approaches Dina again, "I'm done here so you can come with me and my daughter Dogmara and I will get you all measured," Albina waves absently across the room and the teenage girl hurries over.

Dina looks up, confused.

"For your wedding dress," Albina explains as if it's obvious.

Dina pushes herself back in her chair, shaking her head vehemently, "I already told you, I'm not getting married! I have to go back to Tbilisi!"

"Yes, yes, whatever you say, dear. Let's just get you measured just in case," Albina holds out a hand, and Dina looks around to see the women in the kitchen watching with rapt, frozen curiosity. Reluctantly, she stands and follows Albina silently from the room. *I will figure out a way to get out of this. And soon,* she promises herself.

***

"Dogmara?" Dina approaches the awkward teenager cautiously, not wanting to scare her off. Dogmara seems kowtowed and skittish at best, but Dina figures that she is her only potential chance for help. Dina has been watching all afternoon for a chance to catch Dogmara alone. She finally lands her moment when she sees Dogmara head to the barn and hurries to follow her.

Dogmara looks up from the barn floor, her cheeks reddening as she freezes in the midst of mucking out the cow's stall, "Yes?" she asks haltingly.

"I don't want to bother you," Dina motions to the hoe in Dogmara's hands. "You can keep working."

Flustered, Dogmara gives the hoe a stab so weak that it doesn't move any of the dirty hay.

"So, have you lived here your whole life?" Dina asks, trying to build rapport.

Eyebrows raised and eyes darting around furiously, Dogmara nods. Dina sighs— *this is not going well. I need to just get to the point.*

"So you know I'm from Tbilisi?" Dina asks, and Dogmara nods mutely.

"My family is still there— my mom, my grandfather, my four younger brothers and sisters. They have no idea where I am. They're probably worried sick about me."

Dogmara shifts her shoulders and lowers her eyes to the barn floor.

"It's not your fault!" Dina hurries to reassure her. "I just don't want them to worry. So I thought... I thought maybe you could help me?"

Dogmara's startled eyes fly to Dina's face and she begins to quickly shake her head.

"Please," Dina begs, reaching an arm out and grasping Dogmara's sleeve. "Can you imagine what it would be like for your mom if you disappeared one day and she had no idea if you were alive or dead? I can tell that your mom loves you. That would break her heart. She would be so desperate to know what had happened to you."

Dina watches Dogmara's body language closely and is relieved to see her blow out a slow breath of air and her eyes cloud with empathy.

"It would be so hard for my mom," Dogmara whispers. "I am sorry for your mom. But I cannot do anything to go against my family. So I do not think I can help you."

"I don't need much! Just a small favor!" Dina jumps in quickly, reassuringly. Sensing the time is right, she slips a folded piece of paper out from under the waistband of her skirt. "I wrote this letter to my mom. Just to tell her that I am safe, so she won't worry. Could you mail it for me?" She holds the letter out towards Dogmara, eyes pleading.

"I don't know," Dogmara frowns, biting her lip. "Probably you should ask Saidun or my parents if it is okay and have them mail it?"

"But would they mail it?" Dina asks, knowing she and Dogmara both know the answer.

"Please? For my mom? I knew that only you, of everyone in the family, would understand a daughter's concern for her mother," Dina presses.

Slowly, looking like she already regrets her decision, Dogmara takes the letter and tucks it into her apron pocket.

"Thank you!" Dina breathes, squeezing a startled Dogmara's hand in a burst of relief and gratitude.

As she leaves the barn, Dina prays that Dogmara won't read the letter before she mails it. Because if she does, she will see Dina's plea for rescue.

CHAPTER 10
Sureti Valley, Georgia

June, 2018

Abdullah grabs a bag of fresh lamb meat, a loaf of bread, and some tomatoes and cucumbers from the garden. He bows goodbye to his mother and heads through the gate and down towards the river. The sun is out and the day has been hotter than usual for the mountains. A trickle of sweat runs down Abdullah's back by the time he gets to their spot by the river.

Musa, unsurprisingly, has arrived first. Short and stocky, and with a bright red beard, Musa is always looking for any excuse to get away from his controlling parents, his unhappy wife, and his three little kids. Abdullah knows that Musa's home life is miserable, but Musa is crude and brash and often rubs Abdullah the wrong way. But they've been buddies since elementary school, when Musa had stood up to a bully who'd been picking on then-scrawny Abdullah. Abdullah owes him one, and so tends to let Musa's rough side slide. Plus, Musa is often the one who brings laughter to their group, which can certainly tend towards solemnity.

Abdullah tosses the bag of lamb to Musa, who catches it expertly before setting it on a stump. Wordlessly, the two men split up and comb the forest for useable sticks and logs for firewood. By the time they return to the stump, Abdullah's cousins Ibra and Ali have arrived. As usual, Sayid is late. But since it means he is probably home helping Fariza, Abdullah doesn't mind. His brother-in-law is not your usual Ramazi man.

The four men greet each other with the traditional two-handed handshake— first grasping the other man's hand, and then their forearm as they bow towards each other. Out of respect, the younger man leans deeper into his bow than the older man. Sayid is the oldest of the group, but only by a few months. And he has yet to arrive anyway.

The friends work together to build a fire, their movements showing that this is something they have done countless times before. They talk and joke easily as they work. By the time the fire has died down and the coals are red and hot, the sun is starting to set behind the mountains. Abdullah threads the lamb he brought onto Musa's skewers, alternating meat slices with pieces of onion, peppers, and eggplant that Ali brought. He then carefully angles the skewers over the top of the hot coals, resting them on stones that Ali has propped on either side of the fire.

"Well, look who it is, the black sheep of Khev!" Musa jokes as Sayid finally arrives, sheepishly offering a thermos of tea and a tin of cookies. "What were you doing— home in your apron, baking *khichini*?"

Everyone laughs and Sayid grins, "Sorry I love my wife! It's not my fault that Allah gave me the most beautiful woman in the valley!"

"You're supposed to sleep with beautiful women, not cook with them!" Musa ribs.

"Who says you can't do both?" Sayid winks and everyone laughs and rolls their eyes. They all know Sayid doesn't actually cook, but he does help around the house and is way more involved with his kids than any other father they know.

"It's like we always say," Ali repeats a line that the guys have been saying for years, "Something went wrong in the Ramazi man factory when Sayid was created! You know you are our favorite mutant Ramazi!"

Everyone ribs Sayid, but secretly they all respect him. He is gentle, a word pretty much never associated with men in Sureti, but he is firm and honorable. He's a devout Muslim and a teacher at the local *madrasa*. Abdullah quietly thanks Allah, for probably the hundredth time, for giving his sister such a great husband.

"Speaking of sleeping with beautiful women...," everyone groans as Musa returns to his preferred topic of conversation. The guys all know Musa visits prostitutes on his monthly work trips to

Tbilisi, but they pretend not to know so as not to dishonor him. "Abdullah, brother, we have all seen that hot piece living at your place!"

Abdullah sits up straight and glances at Sayid. "Callie is at my mother's guesthouse for work. She is a professional, there to help with the business. That is all," he says firmly.

"Woah!" Ali laughs, eyebrows raised, "Look who has his hair ruffled more than a startled alley cat! I think you hit a nerve, Musa! Come on Abdullah, what's going on?"

"Nothing is going on, I promise." Abdullah insists.

"That's not what the rumor mills are saying," Ibra tosses in. "I hear you two are seen together quite a lot."

Abdullah blows out a breath in frustration, "We're working together— that's it. She is consulting on the guesthouse for my mother, nothing more."

Ibra nudges Abdullah suggestively and says, "Maybe you could get her to consult on *your* guesthouse!" He winks and all the guys but Sayid laugh. Abdullah frowns— he knows if he tries to defend Callie, they will only latch onto the topic harder, like dogs with a bone. He stays silent, hoping they'll move on to some other topic of conversation.

"Seriously, my brother," Musa looks at Abdullah earnestly. "We all know Western women are whores who have no morals. This is your chance! Obviously, you can't do anything in Sureti or you'd have massive trouble, but you could come up with some excuse for a work trip to Tbilisi and screw her there. She probably knows all sorts of dirty tricks that our women would never think of!" Musa looks distinctly envious of the suggestion.

"Enough!" Abdullah shoots up to standing and shouts louder than he intended. "Musa, your words are filthy and disgusting and you should be ashamed of yourself. Our prophet Muhammad, peace be upon him, honored women, and we must do the same, whether they are Muslim or not. And Callie is not a whore." Abdullah crosses his arms firmly across his chest and thumps down onto his stump.

His friends exchange curious glances, sensing that something is going on— Abdullah rarely loses his cool.

"Abdullah is right," Sayid interjects mildly. "We must copy our prophet's example and respect the honor of the women around us, whether they are Muslim or not." Everyone nods in reluctant agreement as Sayid continues, "Callie is a guest of our family, and I expect her, as a guest, to be treated with respect."

"Ok, no more giving you grief about the American woman," Ibra agrees, "But seriously brother, you have to be more careful. Your family has had enough issues with the scandal of your mother running a business as an unmarried woman. She doesn't need any more headaches."

"I know," Abdullah acknowledges. "Callie has a boyfriend back in America. She and I are just friends, nothing more."

At that, the whole circle begins to laugh so hard that soon Musa is wiping tears from his eyes. "Dude, 'just friends'?! What have you been doing, watching American sitcoms? You know men and women cannot be friends!" Everyone laughs in agreement, and Abdullah sits in silence. After a moment, he lowers himself to the edge of the coals and, one by one, begins to remove the kebabs from the fire pit.

CHAPTER 11
Sureti Valley, Georgia

March, 1992

Through the high window at the back of her room, Dina can hear a cacophony of guests milling in the courtyard— it sounds like the whole village has come for the wedding.

Turning to Dogmara, Dina shakes her head again, arms folded tightly over her chest and eyes blazing, "I'm not putting it on! You can't make me!"

"Please," Dogmara pleads desperately, glancing towards the door fearfully. "You *have* to put it on! You don't have a choice!" She holds the long white dress out towards Dina.

Dina straightens stubbornly and turns her back to Dogmara, who gives a low moan. Dina hears the door open behind them, and Albina's voice. "She still hasn't put it on?" Albina asks, coming over to Dina and laying a gentle but firm hand on her shoulder. "Come on dear, let's get this over with. There's no running from fate. And look at this dress— it's beautiful! You will be stunning in it!" Dina glances at the dress, which is a slender floor-length white dress with long sleeves and a high neck. It has beautiful, intricate gold beading up and down the chest. Dina knows that it is the height of Ramazi fashion, but it is nothing like the kind of wedding dress she would have chosen for herself. *And Saidun is nothing like the kind of man I would have chosen for myself. And this is nothing like the life I would have chosen for myself,* Dina thinks with hot anger.

"Take your dress and give it to someone else!" she hisses, glaring at the women. "I refuse to do this!"

The two women glance at each other, and Albina takes the dress carefully from Dogmara's arms and lays it out across the bed. When they quietly exit the room, closing the door behind them, Dina sinks into the rickety wooden chair in relief. *Did I convince them? Did holding my ground work? It has to work,* she thinks in despair, knowing that sheer stubbornness is her only card left to play. *Dogmara probably never even mailed my letter,* she glares at the door.

She looks up at the sound of a firm knock on the door, and instinctively scoots back farther in her chair when Uncle enters the room. He is dressed from head to toe in what must be his finest suit and his long silver beard is gleaming. But all Dina can focus on are his eyes, which are blazing with fury.

"Enough!" he hisses as quietly as possible, glancing towards the high window, clearly trying to be careful that the gathered relatives and neighbors do not overhear their conversation. "You have behaved like a child for long enough. It is time to accept the hand that Allah has dealt you. Do you think our family wanted this marriage? Huh? You are a shame to all of us! My poor sister may never get over the shame of having her beloved only son marry a *kafir*, an infidel. I have spent the past two days working day and night to try to get everyone in agreement so that my nephew can marry the woman he wants to marry. And how am I thanked for all of my hard work?! By this!" he flings his hands towards her, his eyes hard.

Dina stands up, almost knocking over the chair, "I never asked you to spend the past two days arranging everything! You shouldn't have— it was all for nothing because I will never marry him!" she hisses back. "Take me home!"

Uncle laughs harshly and gestures out the window, "It's far too late for that. This wedding is happening, whether you want it to or not."

"I will not get marri—!" Dina starts to shout towards the window desperately but is cut off when a rough hand covers her mouth.

"Do not ever do that again," Uncle's eyes glimmer dangerously, and Dina shrinks away from him.

"Sit," he points her to the chair, and she reluctantly sinks into it.

"My idiot nephew is going to have his hands full," he rolls his eyes and sighs with exasperation. "Listen to me carefully. This wedding is happening, regardless of what you want. I have already spent my hard-earned money to pay for everything, which is far more than you deserve. My entire family has treated you as an honored guest this week, and this is how you are spitting our hospitality back in our faces?" Dina glowers at the floor, her breathing shallow and quick. Uncle bends down close to her face, "You had plenty of chances to accept your fate with dignity, to be grateful for the chance to start a marriage and family with a successful man from a good family. I doubt you had such chances in Tbilisi," he snorts with derision.

"But since you are incapable of controlling yourself, it seems I will have to resort to giving you some harsher incentives. Your family lives at 46 Tenidze Street, right? How long have they lived in that apartment, with such cheap rent? What would happen to them if suddenly their rent tripled?" Dina's eyes, wide and wild, fly to Uncle's face. "How about Natela, your mother? What would happen if she suddenly were to lose her job at the laundromat? How would the family get along then? Your poor invalid grandfather would never be able to support them, would he?"

"You would threaten my family?" Dina accuses in a hot whisper, and Uncle holds up his hands placatingly.

"Your family is perfectly fine. And *you* have the opportunity to make sure they stay that way. My arm of influence is long," he says it flippantly, but Dina is sure that he means it. *I'm going to have to go through with this,* she realizes, stomach sinking and tears forming in her eyes. *I can't put my family at risk.*

"Seems like we have an understanding. Apparently, you're a smart girl after all," Uncle stands, nods formally at Dina, and leaves the room quickly.

I will go through with this today, Dina decides, *but somehow, someday, I will escape.*

A few minutes later, Albina and Dogmara return. Both look relieved when Dina mutely lets them take off the brown woolen dress she's wearing and help her into the long white wedding dress. It takes them a while to button up the dozens of tiny white seed pearl buttons on the back of the dress. When they're done, Albina places a white cylindrical hat on top of Dina's head, with a long gauzy veil behind it that almost reaches the floor.

"Here, dear," Albina holds a cloth out towards Dina. "Wipe those tears off your face and let's get some makeup on you so that you don't look so pale and puffy-eyed."

Dina acquiesces to their ministrations silently, dreading the day and the night ahead. She steels her nerves, reminding herself that she will do whatever it takes to protect her family.

***

The wedding ceremony lasts all day. When Dina is finally dressed in her wedding gown and covered in so much makeup that she barely recognizes herself, Uncle and Albina lead her out to the courtyard, where she is met with raucous cheers. Someone thrusts a large, empty water jug into her hands and the crowd starts cheering in Ramazi. Dina's eyes dart around— she has no idea what people are saying or what she is supposed to do with the pitcher in her hands. She sees no sign of Saidun.

"Коуш лува арац!" someone shouts, and Dina is pulled along with all the young people in the crowd, out the gate of the compound and towards the river that runs behind the property. Dina glances around at the young people around her, who all seem to be enjoying themselves, excited about whatever is going to happen next. *How am I having a wedding where I don't even know what is happening?* Dina despairs.

When they get to the river, the girls in the crowd nudge Dina towards the water. She stares at them, uncertain of what she is supposed to do.

"Dip the jug in! Make sure to get as much as you can— the more water you get, the better wife and daughter-in-law you will be!" one of the girls whispers to her in Georgian. Awkwardly, Dina bends towards the water, trying not to get her pristine white skirt wet or dirty. She scoops up as much as she can as the crowd of young people cheer unintelligibly, and then lead her back to Uncle's house. When she enters the courtyard, the group around her suddenly goes silent. She looks towards the house and sees Uncle and Albina. Beside them is a couple about their same age. She recognizes Saidun's mother from the night of the kidnapping, when Dina had seen her yelling at Saidun from their gate. The woman glares daggers at Dina. Beside her stands a lean man with an expressionless face. Dina assumes this must be Saidun's father.

"Go give them the jug," one of the girls behind Dina whispers. Dina crosses the courtyard hesitantly, holding the jug out toward Saidun's parents.

Saidun's mother takes it, glancing inside with a snort of derision. "Лов щыгйс лоырва рйтс," she huffs, holding it out for her husband and Uncle to see. Clearly, Dina has not managed to bring nearly enough water. A mixture of shame and fury rumble in Dina's stomach — *how dare they judge me on some dumb superstition that I didn't even know about?*

The rest of the day passes in a similar blur of confusing new traditions and activities, culminating in a giant feast. Dina is relieved to find that for most of the rest of the day, she doesn't have to play an active role— apparently the bride's job at Ramazi weddings is to stand in the corner like a beautiful frozen princess, looking demurely at the floor as a symbol of womanly submission. In her current state of mind, Dina finds standing silently in a corner and not having to interact with anyone to be a relief. She does however continue to notice the frosty glares that Saidun's mother keeps throwing her way. *These do not bode well for whatever time I am stuck here,* Dina thinks worriedly. *Hopefully, I won't have to see her very often.*

The past few days keep running through her head— should she have done something differently? Was there some window when she could have gotten away that she didn't take advantage of? She racks her brain and is grateful to at least be able to tell herself that she had done what she could. Maybe Saidun will surprise her. So far, he hasn't seemed so terrible in their interactions. *Aside from the fact that he kidnapped me, of course,* Dina sighs.

What will his family be like? Will we live here, with his scary uncle, unempathetic aunt, and timid cousin? The not knowing is gnawing at her stomach. Dina feels like it would be much easier to face what was coming if she at least *knew* what was coming.

And what about the letter I sent to Mom? Did it ever get mailed? Did she get it? Will she come? What will happen if she comes?? They will never let me go home with her. Would they harm her? Oh, I never should have sent that letter! A knot of fear for her family forms in Dina's stomach.

***

The wedding lasts late into the night. For most of it, the women are in one room of the banquet hall and the men are in another. By the time it reaches midnight, Dina can tell from the raucous noise coming from the men's side that most of them are drunk. Dina shivers. Her childhood memories of her father's drunken rages resurface. *Would Saidun be a mean drunk too?* With the gender separation of the ceremony and reception, she has barely seen him all day.

By the time the party winds down, Dina's calves ache from standing all day in heels. Her eyes are dry and gritty and all she wants to do is curl up and sleep and escape from this crazy alternate reality she has stumbled into.

"Come on, dear, let's get you to your new home," Dina feels a hand pat her elbow, and looks down to see Albina standing beside her.

"Wait, I'm not staying here?" Dina asks, confused.

"Thankfully, Saidun's parents have finally agreed for you both to go there now that you are married. Don't look so glum! They have one of the best houses in their village— you will be well taken care of there!"

"But! But!" Dina stutters, unable to figure out what to say next. After the glares she has been getting from Saidun's mother, she has a sinking feeling that living with Saidun isn't going to be the only unpleasant part of her new life.

"Here, dear, I've gathered your things for you," Albina hands Dina a small plastic bag, which Dina can see contains the clothes and shoes she was kidnapped in, as well as the brown woolen dress, headscarf, and nightgown that Albina had given her. "You won't be needing your old clothes anymore," Albina smiles, "But I thought I'd send them with you just the same— a little piece of home for you to hold onto."

"Thank you," Dina whispers, clutching the bag to her chest.

Aside from the noisy grinding of the car across potholes, the ride is silent as Uncle drives Dina and Saidun to Saidun's family home. The men sit up front, and Dina is alone in the backseat, her heart thumping madly in anticipation of the night ahead of her. In the darkness, she can't make out the mountains.

When Uncle drops them off at the blue gate, the courtyard is well lit but deserted. Dina follows Saidun past a grape arbor and up the steps of a large white home. It is two stories tall and has big white columns on the front. Even in her frenzied state, Dina is impressed with the size and beauty of the place— it's easily quadruple the size of her family's cramped Tbilisi apartment.

The room Saidun leads Dina into is fairly spacious, though the dark carpets hanging on the walls give it a claustrophobic feel. There is a double bed and a dresser. It is meticulously clean, but still smells musty and distinctly masculine. Dina quakes inside when she realizes that this must be his bedroom.

"The Taj Mahal, my lady!" Saidun turns towards her with a grin, sweeping his hand sloppily around the room as he sways slightly. Dina stands against the wall, heart hammering. "What is mine is now yours!" He says magnanimously, clearly trying to make her comfortable. "Here, this drawer is for you!" He opens one of the dresser drawers, and points towards the plastic bag that Dina is clutching against her chest. Reluctantly, she hands it to him and he drops it in the drawer and gives it a hearty push shut.

"Now what do you say you and I get to know each other better, huh?" Saidun plops on the bed and pats the bedspread beside him. Dina remains frozen against the wall. *He seems to be a good-natured drunk, so that's good,* she thinks, mind racing.

"I'm actually really tired. It was a very long day. Could we... could we get to know each other some other time and just... just go to sleep tonight?" Dina asks desperately.

Saidun sticks out his lower lip in an exaggerated pout, "Now what kind of wedding night would that be? Come on, you don't have to be scared. I won't hurt you."

Dina shakes her head mutely and Saidun sighs noisily and begins to remove his boots. He gives a large yawn, "Okay, you win. We can take things slowly— I'm tired anyway. And pretty drunk," he grins, stripping off his shirt. Dina averts her eyes, blushing at the sight of his barrel chest carpeted with thick dark curls. He flops back on the bed and is snoring by the time his head hits the pillow.

Dina collapses to the floor, shaking with relief. After a few moments, she stands up, planning to change out of the uncomfortably heavy wedding dress and into the white nightgown that Dogmara had lent her. But when she goes to take her dress off, she realizes that she can't unbutton it— the dozens of tiny seed buttons that line the back are something only someone else could remove. She stands frozen with indecision for a few moments, but finally her exhaustion and aching feet win out and she gingerly lays down on top of the blanket on the edge of the bed as far away from Saidun as she can possibly get. The wedding dress is stiff and hot and uncomfortable, but eventually she falls into a restless sleep.

***

Dina startles awake later that night from the feel of a hand running down her side. Immediately wide awake, she lays as still as possible. *Maybe if I pretend I'm asleep, he will leave me alone and go back to sleep,* she thinks in desperation. The hand moves from her side to the back of her dress, where she can feel the tiny buttons being slowly undone. The process takes quite a while and is accompanied by a number of muttered curses.

Pretend to be asleep, pretend to be asleep, Dina repeats like a mantra in her mind.

"Hello, wife," she feels Saidun's hot breath on her neck as he whispers in her ear. His breath smells like sour wine and Dina's stomach clinches. "What do you say you and I get to know each other better?" Saidun rolls her over towards him and Dina knows she can no longer feign sleep.

"Touch me and I will scream," she threatens in a desperate whisper, scooting to the edge of the bed.

Saidun just laughs, "I like your spunk! Most of the women here are too docile and boring— no challenge at all. But I knew from the first time I saw you in Tbilisi— walking with your head held high and your hips swaying suggestively in those tight jeans— that you would be a good time. Come on now, I won't hurt you! And besides, you know screaming would be pointless. You wouldn't want to scandalize my little sisters. Or, god forbid, make my mother mad," Saidun pulls a face that conveys the depth of trouble they would be in if they made his mother mad.

Dina lays on the edge of the bed, tense as a spring. *There is nothing I can do,* she realizes with a sinking feeling. Until this very moment, she had been hoping against hope to find some way to escape. But now here, in the middle of the night in this pitch-black bedroom, she knows that there is no escape.

CHAPTER 12
Sureti Valley

June, 2018

The sun is shining brightly as Callie makes her way through the village, headed for the tiny corner store a couple streets away from the guesthouse. When Rosana had realized that they were short on sour cream for dinner, Callie had quickly offered to run to the store to get some. The village is a fascinating place and she soaks up any chance she can get to explore it.

Callie shields her eyes from the sun as she dodges around giant potholes in the dirt road. She can't see any houses because they're all hidden behind tall walls and gates. Callie wonders curiously what life is like inside those walls. Leila had told her that a family in the village is planning to have her over for dinner on Saturday night, which Callie is both excited and nervous about. It will be her first time in a traditional Ramazi home and she's very aware of how lacking she is in knowledge of their traditions. But hopefully that will be a chance to learn. Abdullah will go with her, and he said they're going to one of the wealthier, less conservative families.

"Hello!" the wrinkled old vegetable seller shouts at her when he spies Callie come around the corner. Callie hurries over to his stand, which is really just a metal stool on the side of the road surrounded by a bunch of cardboard boxes full of produce. Five or six street dogs laze in the shade behind Abbas' chair. Callie met Abbas the week before when Rosana took her shopping and he had been extremely friendly, despite not speaking a word of English other than 'hello'.

"Woah," Callie shies back nervously as the street dogs hop to their feet at her arrival and begin excitedly sniffing her. Her heart begins to race— she's uncomfortable around stray dogs. When one starts to lick her hand, Abbas jumps to his feet and starts swatting the dogs and shooing them away in Ramazi. Callie gives him a grateful smile.

Abbas gestures for Callie to follow him into the rickety one room general store next to his produce stand. Inside, Callie barely glimpses a teenage girl in a headscarf hidden amongst giant stacks of paper towels, pasta, soda, toiletries, tools, and other sundries. As the one store in town it is required to carry a wide variety of items.

Abbas speaks excitedly to the young woman, who blushes before speaking to Callie in hesitant English, "I am Amina. I am studying English in school," she says, turning an even deeper shade of red. "I apologize for my bad English. But my great uncle Abbas wishes to welcome you to our family's store."

"Nice to meet you," Callie smiles. "I don't think you were here when I came before."

"I only work after school," Amina explains. "Maybe you met my mother or my aunt."

Abbas gestures excitedly and spews out a stream of Ramazi.

Amina blushes again, "My uncle says come to our home. To be guest."

"Oh!" Callie smiles, warmed by the old man's friendliness to someone he barely knows. "Thank you— that would be lovely! Maybe Leila can schedule a time with your family?"

Amina relays the message to Abbas, who frowns.

"He says... come now," Amina struggles to communicate in her limited English.

Now? But I'm supposed to be buying sour cream and helping with all the guests arriving this afternoon. Does he really mean this minute? Will I offend him if I say no or postpone? Callie twists a strand of her dark hair, wishing Abdullah was with her to help navigate the murky cultural waters.

Abbas gestures insistently towards the door, and Callie finally gives an awkward laugh and decides she better follow him. Life overseas is supposed to be an adventure, right?

"Oh! Amina!" Callie calls out as she heads out the door. "I was supposed to get sour cream for the guesthouse. Would you be able to take some to them? And maybe tell Abdullah that I've gone with your uncle?"

Amina nods and Callie hopes that she understood.

***

Abbas leads Callie across the street, in the opposite direction of the guesthouse. A couple of the street dogs start to follow him, but he good naturedly shoes them away. As Callie walks beside him, she wonders what she's gotten herself into and hopes that it will turn out alright.

They walk for ten or fifteen minutes through the village till they finally reach a small road, if it can be called that, on the edge of town. It's more mud than anything else, and Callie gingerly picks her way amongst the puddles. She looks around in fascination— unlike the properties in Leila's more affluent part of town, these homes clearly can't afford high walls and gates. Instead, most are surrounded by chain metal fences. Which means she can actually see into the yards and see the houses, most of which are ancient hovels in various states of disrepair. Chickens and cows and dogs abound, as do tools, sheds, and farm equipment. Behind the homes, the mountains rise in majestic splendor. These houses have been built right at the very base of the mountains. Abbas waves to a few neighbors as they pass, each of whom eyes Callie with wide-eyed curiosity. A few give her friendly waves.

At the end of the street, Abbas stops and points excitedly to a small stucco home that is surrounded by flowers so beautiful that they almost rival Leila's. Two small children spot Callie and Abbas from across the yard and run over excitedly. The girl, probably around eight or nine years old, is wearing a full hijab in a beautiful bright turquoise fabric. The boy, who looks a few years younger, gives Callie a huge grin— which is made even cuter by the fact that he's missing his two front teeth.

"Eliina!" Abbas points to the girl. "Halil!" He points to the boy and gives him a playful nuggie on the head. Abbas says something to the children and then heads to the house, leaving Callie standing awkwardly in the yard. *He's probably alerting his family to the fact that he invited a foreign guest over!* Callie thinks, hoping her intrusion doesn't cause too many problems for Abbas' family. She feels a guilty twinge as she imagines the women having to scurry to pull together a meal in the kitchen.

Unexpectedly, the little girl reaches over and grabs Callie's hand, pulling her across the yard.

"Hello! I'm Callie," Callie smiles at the children, wishing she could communicate.

"Cats!" the girl says, pulling Callie. They cross a bare yard littered with lumber and tools, most looking like they had rusted in place decades ago. They come to what was once a wooden chest of drawers, but is now missing all the actual drawers. The girl leans down and points inside and Callie bends beside her. Nestled on a blanket inside the chest is an orange cat nursing multiple tiny kittens.

"Cats!" Eliina repeats happily, reaching in and scooping up a fluffy kitten and holding it out to Callie. Gingerly, she accepts it. It's so new that its eyes are still closed. Delighted, Callie gently strokes the soft fur.

"It's beautiful," Callie smiles at Eliina, who nods.

"Do you speak any English?" Callie asks. *Amira from the store seems to have learned English in school— maybe Eliina has too?*

"Little bit," Eliina shrugs.

"Good job!" Callie encourages. "Did you learn it in school?" she asks, enunciating slowly and clearly.

"School? Yes!" Eliina nods excitedly.

"Do you know anything else in English? Maybe songs?" Callie racks her brain, trying to think of something easy that the girl might know.

"Songs! Yes!" Eliina glances furtively around and then begins to sing "Twinkle Twinkle Little Star." Her accent is thickly Ramazi, but her voice is clear and lovely.

"Wonderful!" Callie claps. Eliina grins and transitions into "London Bridge." She's about halfway through the song when she stops suddenly, her eyes going wide and fearful. Callie turns to see a wiry middle-aged man with a long beard and large nose stomping towards them across the yard. The frown on his face makes his displeasure quite clear. Callie watches in horror as he grabs Eliina's arm and hisses at her under his breath. Eliina shrinks under his hold and runs back behind the house as soon as he lets her go. *I can't believe he manhandled her like that,* Callie thinks, appalled. *She wasn't even doing anything! I hope I didn't get her in trouble somehow.*

The man watches Eliina with a frown and then turns to Callie. The anger that he'd shown towards the young girl is completely wiped from his face and he bows politely to Callie and then escorts her through the lovely flower garden and into the small home.

The home, which looked so decrepit from the outside, has clearly been carefully and lovingly remodeled on the inside. The walls are covered with gold wall paper in a swirling design. Delicate lace curtains that look hand-crocheted hang from the windows. Heavy burgundy brocade sofas fill the small room. To Callie, who loves light and airy design, the low ceilings and excess furniture feel oppressive. *But it's probably the fashion here, it's just not what I'm used to,* Callie reminds herself.

The wiry man gestures to one of the couches and Callie quickly sits down, unsure of what to do. The man stands in awkward silence, not looking at her. After a few moments, two women rush in from the neighboring room carrying a folding table. They glance at Callie surreptitiously, but don't say anything. Callie wonders if they're quiet because of the language barrier or because of the watchful eye of the man in the corner.

As Callie sits, the women set up the folding table in front of her, and quickly cover it with a tablecloth and dishes and silverware. Callie feels so uncomfortable sitting as they mutely serve her, but her experience with Leila has taught her that it's highly unlikely they would accept any help.

I can't believe he's just standing there, watching them work and carry heavy things and doesn't do anything to help. Callie catches herself judging the man in the corner before stopping to remind herself that this is a different culture with different gender roles and that she needs to be understanding and accepting when things aren't what she's used to. But it's hard to do.

"Eat!" Abbas ducks through the low doorway, a grin wreathing his wrinkled face. The women and the man in the corner all stand straight in respectful attention when Abbas enters. He smiles at them and gestures to the table. The man in the corner waits to sit until Abbas has sat first. The women continue to mutely serve; neither of them sit. Callie realizes with a knot in her stomach that the meal will just be her, Abbas, and the man from the corner.

***

"Oh, you're here!" Relief washes over Callie as Abdullah ducks through the doorway. The past hour had been so uncomfortable— the women bringing unending plates of strange dishes, mostly suspicious looking meat and various fried and boiled kinds of dough. Abbas smiling at Callie and repeating, "Eat! Eat!" over and over again— it's clearly one of the only words he knows in English. Odd food textures are really hard for Callie to handle, and at one point she was afraid she might vomit when they placed a long piece of something on her plate that she later found out was lamb entrails. Callie was strongly regretting her agreement to come.

"Experiencing your first Ramazi hospitality?" Abdullah grins as he bows respectfully to each of the men in the room.

"I'm about to burst," Callie exclaims. "And they keep pressing more food on me!"

"You're an honored guest! And what else can they do since they can't talk to you?" Abdullah takes a seat at the table, and graciously accepts the multiple plates of food that women in the family rush to surround him with.

With Abdullah there, the whole mood in the room noticeably shifts. The man from the corner, Rashid, relaxes into his seat and he and Abbas begin to tell Callie some of the folklore from the region, with Abdullah translating. Abbas especially is clearly delighted to have an audience for whom all his stories are new and interesting.

The next hour passes surprisingly quickly. Abdullah is an excellent translator–his amber eyes sparkle and he's quick to laugh along with Abbas, who's stories are so outrageous that soon Callie is laughing as well.

When Callie eventually asks the men to tell her about their family, she expects them to talk about their wives and children. But instead, they start with stories of their great-great-grandfathers, who fought against the Russians in a previous century.

"Just roll with it," Abdullah winks at her out of the corner of his eye when he notices her surprise. "We Ramazi venerate our ancestors and honor them by keeping their memory alive." The women quietly bring in tea, delicious cakes, chocolate, and sliced fruit as Callie and the men talk long into the afternoon. Callie is relieved to have food that is more familiar.

"I wish they could sit with us. Could we invite them?" Callie whispers to Abdullah, glancing at the women.

Abdullah subtly shakes his head, "Sorry, it would make them feel really uncomfortable. It's not their custom."

"But it doesn't feel right for me to sit here while they serve me," Callie whispers back.

"It might not feel right to you, but it's what they're used to," Abdullah assures her.

"It feels so offensive though," Callie says under her breath, glad that no one in the family can understand their quiet conversation.

"Things here are different. If they aren't offended, then there is no need for you to be offended for them," Abdullah chides gently, the kindness in his amber eyes softening his words. Callie's feelings tangle — she loves the way he's looking at her, but she's unsure if she agrees with his words.

Just then there is commotion at the door and Halil comes running in with Eliina close behind him. The women quickly rush over to hurry the children into the other room, but Rashid waves them away and pulls Halil onto his lap. Halil grins and grabs a handful of chocolate from the center of the table as Abbas laughs and Rashid musses the boy's hair.

"This is my son Halil," Rashid tells Callie through Abdullah. "He's six years old and already a brilliant wrestler!" Halil grins at Callie and lifts one shirt sleeve to show her his muscles. The women smile— they clearly love this precocious little boy.

"And this is my daughter Eliina. She was the youngest girl in her class to start wearing the hijab. And she did it because she wanted to, not because we made her." There is pride in his voice as he smiles at his daughter, who returns his smile shyly.

"It's very nice to meet all of you," Callie says, starting to be genuinely glad she came. "Perhaps now that we're done with our meal the ladies could show me the beautiful garden outside?" Callie asks Abdullah.

Abdullah nods encouragingly that Callie has figured out a culturally appropriate way to spend time with the women, and she finds herself unexpectedly basking in his approval. He translates the question for the women, whose faces light up with smiles as they lead Callie out into the rosy glow of sunset peeking out from behind the mountains.

***

Dear Callie,

I can't believe you've been gone two weeks already. I have definitely missed you. It has officially sucked that your wifi is so bad that we can't even get Skype or FaceTime to work— tell Leila that the first thing she needs to work on is getting high-speed internet for her Western guests! And that she should work on it while you're there ;-)

Everything around the office is the same as always. Lucy says hi. She has a new boyfriend (no surprise). She met him at some celeb party she was covering. I don't see it lasting, but she seems smitten. Let me guess— she's either texted you all about it or totally ghosted you because she's so caught up in the new romance?

Two nights ago I got assigned (aka I begged to cover) the Padres/Dodgers NLCS game. Whoever wins 4 out of 7 goes to the World Series. This was the third game in the series and WE WON! I know you could care less about sports :-P, but it was awesome as a lifelong Padres fan to be there for their victory. I couldn't help but be a bit triumphant and smug in my piece that I wrote about the game :) I've attached it, but you don't have to read it if you don't want to :)

Did I mention I miss you? I keep thinking about our kiss the night before you left. Wow was that hot. Can you come home again ASAP so we can get back to that?

Since Skype and FaceTime aren't working, maybe we could go old-school and email? I want to hear all about your adventures and your life there. Educate me, babe— I know basically nothing about Georgia! (Though, unlike you, I actually did know it was a country :-P)

Love always,

Lucas

Callie grins as she reads Lucas' email— she can practically hear his voice through the computer. Being out of touch *has* been super frustrating. Maybe his idea of sticking to writing each other emails will allow them to still connect while being less frustrating than attempting calls where they can't even hear each other.

Callie grabs her laptop and heads out to one of the new swings she'd encouraged Leila to get for the back orchard. It's a two seater and super comfortable. In the week since they'd purchased it, Callie has seen guests sitting in it a lot.

Dear Lucas,

It was great to hear from you! I miss you too. I like your idea of going old-school and emailing. Let's try it :) I'm glad you got to go to the Padres game, and that they won (you're right— I normally wouldn't care at all about that, but I'm glad for your sake!). And tell Lucy hi for me— she has definitely been ghosting me. I assumed she was distracted with some new guy lol.

Things here are good. I'm starting to feel settled in. The guesthouse is really charming and the surrounding land is beautiful. The family who runs the guesthouse has been welcoming and I think I've been able to help grow their business. I've updated their website already and started an Instagram account and a Facebook account. We've already seen an uptick in bookings. Plus, I've made some suggestions about things to improve/change around the place. I did suggest better wifi, but unfortunately, that is low on the list of priorities, down below things like "build actual bathrooms." Did I tell you they only have an outhouse here?? You would be super proud of me for using it! Though I am still not a fan, I've adjusted and sucked it up. It's not as stinky as I was afraid it would be. Though I am definitely looking forward to getting back to modern plumbing.

I'm not sure if Leila (the guesthouse owner) likes me. She's pretty hard to read, and seems kind of aloof. The few times I've tried to ask her any personal questions, she changed the subject. In general, Ramazi society seems pretty private (though they're very warmly welcoming to guests; they just don't tell you all their secrets :). I've already been invited for meals in two homes since I've been here. The poverty at the first place was pretty sobering (I'm kind of cocooned away from it at the guesthouse). It was a tiny building with no running water and multiple generations sharing a couple of rooms.

I've had a hard time adjusting to the culture here— it's so different from what I'm used to. Abdullah (Leila's son) keeps reminding me that different doesn't necessarily mean wrong. Though I'm particularly wrestling with the treatment of women here, and the treatment of kids. I saw a dad manhandle his daughter because she was singing (I didn't know at the time why he was mad at her—

Abdullah had to explain it to me later). Apparently conservative Muslims think it's a sin to sing. And I was the one who asked her to sing in the first place :(

As for women, I knew coming in to expect women to have social restrictions and not to be treated as equals. But it's one thing to know it in your head and another thing to see it. Every home I go into, the women basically don't say anything. They serve the meal silently and then leave the room. Never once have they been allowed to sit with me. I always end up sitting with the men (a privilege given to me as an honored guest). Normally they ask me about America (I have been getting lots of questions about what I think about Trump!) and then they proceed to tell me their family history back 6 generations. No joke. It is incredible here how much family history people know and how much they value their family history. And I realized that that is something that we Americans have lost. I can't even tell you the names of my great-grandparents, much less 6 generations back! There are definitely good things about the culture here too, which I'm starting to appreciate. Both times I've gone to meals at peoples' homes, the entire family has walked me the mile plus back to Leila's guesthouse afterwards, just out of respect and politeness for me as a guest. We definitely don't show that kind of hospitality to our guests in the US!

Ok sorry, this has gotten super long and I know you're super busy. Everything here is just so different and complicated and I'm trying to process what I think about things. It's nice to be able to share with someone. I miss you too :) And yes, the kissing before I left was memorable :)

Write me back! Love,

Callie

Callie closes her laptop, feeling happy to have reconnected with Lucas and also slightly guilty for her inexplicable attraction to Abdullah. *Get it together*, she commands herself, not for the first time. *You love Lucas. He loves you. You're back together. Remember that kiss you just wrote about? Plus, Lucas is American— he understands you in a way that someone from another culture never could. Abdullah is just a friend, that's it. Not even a friend, really— more a co-worker. Yeah, a co-worker. Who just happens to be good looking. It's not the first time in your life you had a good looking co-worker, and you always dealt with it before. So do it again this time.*

***

Callie is startled awake by a loud drilling sound. She groggily glances at her iPhone and realizes guiltily that she'd fallen asleep while typing up a draft business plan for Leila. *Oops, definitely did not mean to sleep for the past hour! I need to get back to work ASAP. Everyone here works 24/7— gosh, I'm such a lazy person in comparison to them. I don't think they ever stop! Speaking of stopping— what is that awful noise??* Callie throws a cardigan over her tank top and slips on sandals under her floor length skirt. The drilling continues unabated and Callie grits her teeth, feeling like she is going to lose her mind if she has to continue to listen to the awful racket. She heads outside, determined to try to find the source of it and see if she can find out when it is going to stop. Dr. Paekl had helped her realize that knowing the end time for bothersome sensory stimuli could help her bear it.

She blinks in the bright June sunlight as she heads down the porch stairs and is surprised to see a group of eight guys gathered in the yard. They are jabbering loudly in Ramazi and have already dug two giant holes in the ground *For septic tanks maybe?* Callie guesses. Callie can see one of the men jackhammering the concrete of the walkway. *That explains the noise that woke me up!* Callie thinks. *They're building the bathroom! Wow, that was fast! Hope they finish ASAP! Both for the sake of my ears AND so that I can stop having to use the outhouse!* Callie darts a glare back towards the outhouse.

Callie watches them unnoticed for a few minutes, but then one of the guys spots her. He immediately nudges his buddy, who nudges the guy beside him. In a minute, all eight guys have stopped their work and are standing stock still, staring at Callie in respectful silence.

"Hi," Callie waves, feeling distinctly uncomfortable and unsure of how to handle all the attention. "Thanks for helping with the bathroom!"

Abdullah translates her words to the men, who all nod, still standing mutely frozen. Clearly they are not used to interacting with foreign women.

"Well, carry on!" Callie gives a half-hearted wave and hurries back upstairs to her room. *What a disaster! You just acted like you were 12!* Callie moans as she flops on her bed. *Massively awkward!*

Callie hides in her room for the rest of the afternoon, fighting a thumping headache that she's sure is a result of the jackhammering. At seven o'clock, feeling grumpily hangry, she reluctantly heads down for dinner as usual, hoping the guys will be gone. The noise of the drilling is gone, so she takes that as a good sign.

The volume of voices at the table alerts her before she even gets there that her wish has not been granted. When she enters the dining area, there's a flash of movement and a loud scraping of chairs as all the men hurry to stand up in her presence. Callie blushes, "Really, you can sit down!"

Abdullah translates, but the men remain standing.

"We can't sit until you sit," Abdullah explains quietly, pulling out a chair beside him for Callie, who quickly sits down. All the men follow suit.

Ugh this is going to be so awkward! Callie thinks, running a hand through her shoulder-length brown hair and tightening her cardigan about her. *Yet again, I'm the only woman at a table full of Ramazi men!*

The dinner is awkward at first, but eventually conversation gets moving. Callie asks the men questions about themselves and their work and they, in return, ask her about America. At first the questions are bland and polite— What's the weather like? What American food do you like? etc. But fairly quickly they move into topics that Callie, as an American, finds sensitive— politics and religion. The men all have strong opinions and are unafraid to share them. There clearly is no concern for political correctness or worry about stepping on someone's toes. Abdullah translates, and occasionally whispers an apology before he translates a question or comment. Some of the things the men ask about are based on fact, but others are so out of left field that Callie doesn't know whether to be amused or appalled.

"Is it true that American kids are raised on nothing but hamburgers and french fries and Coke?" one man asks, truly curious to verify this rumor that he has heard.

"Is it true that all Americans are atheists? We heard that no one goes to American churches anymore so they are turning them all into shopping malls," another asks.

"We heard that the streets of America are super dangerous— people carry guns everywhere and can shoot you anytime. Are all black people gangsters?" asks a stocky man with a bushy red beard. Callie flinches from the racist assumptions. She quickly tries to set the men straight, but from their faces, is unsure if what she said has penetrated. Clearly worldview here is quite different.

After an hour and a half around the table, Callie is exhausted and wishing for some socially acceptable way to be able to excuse herself. The men, however, seem to be in no hurry at all. They decide to go for a second round of tea and Callie moans inwardly, knowing how long these table hangouts often last. Leila brings out a fresh teapot and desserts and all the men rise respectfully and give her small bows. Leila smiles at them affectionately— she has known these men since they were babies, toddling around her yard with Abdullah.

When Leila returns to the kitchen, a tall lanky guy with glasses sits up straight across from Callie, "Oh! Has Abdullah told you about the stone of Islamil?"

Callie shakes her head and the guy across from her launches into a twenty-minute monologue about some famous rock in Sureti that was apparently the site of some famous battle a couple hundred years ago with someone who Callie has, of course, never heard of. The rest of the men all nod along with the story, looking engrossed. Even Abdullah's animated translating can't keep Callie's mind from wandering. *Why on earth would I care about some random battle hundreds of years ago?? Why do they still care about it?* But clearly they do. After the twenty-minute long battle story from Glasses, Red Beard takes over with his own long monologue about some feat one of his relatives did hundreds of years ago.

Callie tries to look interested and pay attention, but she can feel her headache growing and she wishes the dinner would end. Abdullah darts a quick glance at Callie and she gives him a pleading look as discreetly as she can. He accurately interprets her signal and laughs, "Well gentlemen, I think this was enough Caucasus history for our guest for one evening! We should probably let her head to bed! And you fools all need to leave too so that you can get a good night's sleep and be back here early in the morning to pour the foundation!"

The men all nod good-naturedly and begin to stand. Callie tosses Abdullah a grateful grin and bids goodnight to the guys before heading upstairs. As she changes into her pajamas, she can't help but compare the evening she just spent with a night back home with her guy friends in SF— which would probably have included going out for pizza, maybe drinks at a bar, and then piling onto someone's sofa late at night and cracking up over dumb YouTube videos together. Or just watching a movie on Netflix if they were feeling lazy. Some days, Sureti feels like a different planet.

***

The neighborhood guys continue to show up every day for the next couple of days and work on the bathroom. Every time Callie passes them, they all politely stand to attention. She gets used to having them around at meals, and also grows accustomed to their long, excited monologues about ancient Ramazi history. They make quick progress on the bathrooms, which Callie is doubly thankful for— first of all, because she can't wait to no longer have to use the outhouse. And secondly, because the construction noise is driving her crazy, as if the jackhammer is literally inside her head. She takes multiple walks down to the river to escape the noise and offers to walk into town with Rosana every time she goes grocery shopping. For the most part, Abdullah is unavailable to work with her because he is busy with the construction. Though she tries to keep herself busy by helping with guests and updating their social media accounts, Callie realizes with a slightly guilty twinge that she really misses his company. *I just miss him because he's one of the few people here I can speak English with,* she tries to tell herself.

One afternoon, Callie is sitting at the picnic table furthest back in the orchard (trying to get as far away from the construction noise as she can), when Abdullah surprises her by joining her.

"What are you doing here?" she asks, eyebrows raised.

"Those jokers don't need me," he grins. "They've got everything under control."

"How's it coming?" Callie asks, hoping he will tell her that they're almost finished.

He shrugs, "We'll probably have the main structure done by the end of the day today. Tomorrow we're going to do the plumbing, and the next day, lay tile. So probably we'll be done with the major parts in three days. And then after that it will just be detail work. Which is why I was coming out here actually," Abdullah pulls up his phone and scrolls through his WhatsApp messages.

"What do you think of these tile options?" Just as he hands her photos of tile to scroll through, loud pounding of a hammer reverberates from the direction of the bathroom.

Oh my gosh, that is so loud. Pounding. I don't know how much longer I can take this. Focus, Callie. He told you it will only be a few more days. Deep breaths. Look at his phone— which tile would look best? Callie grimaces, trying to concentrate on the photos in front of her. But the noise of the hammering throbs in her brain and finally she reluctantly hands the phone back.

"I'm so sorry, I can't concentrate through all the noise," she admits reluctantly, cheeks getting hot.

"Noise?" Abdullah asks, genuinely confused.

"The hammering," Callie says as if it was obvious.

"Oh, I didn't even notice it. It's bothering you all the way out here?" Abdullah looks surprised and Callie blows out a long breath of air, then nods.

"I'm just... really sensitive to sounds. Well, to all sensory things — smells, tastes, how things feel, etc. I've been that way since I was a kid." Callie shrugs, glancing at him to see his reaction. His eyes are raised with curiosity.

"I have sensory processing issues, or heightened sensitivity," Callie explains. "It's more common than you'd think, actually. My therapist has been helping me work through it and try to develop strategies to cope with it."

"Therapist? You mean, like, psychologist?" Abdullah asks tentatively, clearly confused.

Callie nods, "Yeah, I've been going since last year when some of my sensory issues started affecting my ability to do my job well. It's been really helpful."

"But... you're not crazy," Abdullah says sincerely.

"Umm, obviously I know that," Callie replies, starting to heat up. "Why would you say that?"

"Here, only crazy people go to psychologists. Normal people don't need psychologists." Abdullah shrugs as if what he is saying is the most obvious thing of all.

"Well, maybe they should!" Callie spurts out. "I'm sure there are loads of issues that people around here have that psychologists could really help with!" Her shoulders tense and she finds herself clenching her fists in her lap.

Abdullah runs a hand through his dark swoopy bangs and looks doubtful, "I don't know... maybe. But mostly, we just deal with things ourselves. Or talk through them with our friends."

"Or stuff them inside and never deal with them," Callie blurts, thinking of aloof Leila but not about to say her name.

Abdullah laughs, "Actually, that is probably the most common of all! Problems solved!" He wipes his hands against each other cheerfully as if dusting them off.

"Yes well, you know that doesn't *actually* work, right?" Callie asks, frowning. "I mean, it isn't healthy to just sweep all your problems under the rug and never deal with them."

"Maybe not. But it is what people normally do here." Abdullah lifts both hands in a *What can you do?* gesture.

"Honestly, lots of people in America do that too," Callie admits. "It's what I did for years, until it got to the point when I couldn't run from my issues anymore."

Abdullah nods, his eyes empathetic. "Back to what you were saying. This... what did you call it? Sensory issues that you have? What is it like?" He looks sincerely interested and not combative, so Callie takes a calming breath and tries to figure out how to explain it in a way that maybe he will understand.

"Well, whenever people are around sensory stimuli, like sounds or smells or tastes, etc, their brains react to those stimuli. For your typical person, the more intense a stimulus is, the more intensely their brain will react. So take for example that hammering. It's far away and not super loud, so your brain receives it as a light stimulus and will respond lightly, registering it but allowing you to move on and even tune it out. Or if a day is a little bit warm or a sweater a bit itchy, your brain will register it, but not overreact. Which allows you to tune out the stimuli and carry on with your day."

"That sounds about right," Abdullah nods, his leg bouncing and shaking the table as he listens.

Keep going, Callie tells herself. *Just ignore his leg.* As the whole picnic table bounces, she resists the urge to lash out at him and tell him to sit still. She takes a deep breath and continues, "But that's *not* how my brain works. My brain responds really intensely to *most* stimuli. So imagine how many synapses would be firing in your brain, and how annoyed and distracted you would be, if someone was blowing a horn super loud in your ear right now."

"I might punch them," Abdullah grins.

"Right??!" Callie agrees. "*That* is what it feels like inside my brain *all* the time. Like that "light" hammering from across the orchard has the synapses in my brain firing as intensely as if a horn was blowing in my ear. It makes it almost impossible for me to concentrate on anything else."

"Wow, that sounds really frustrating and difficult," Abdullah leans towards her, his amber eyes warm.

"It can suck," Callie blows out a breath of air. "I drove my parents crazy with it when I was a kid! I would never wear socks with seams, or play outside if it was hot at all, or eat anything if I didn't like its smell or texture. And I didn't like to go to crowded places because the sounds just pushed me over the edge. I definitely had multiple meltdowns!"

"Yeah, that would never fly here," Abdullah laughs. "Kids just have to do whatever their elders want, whether the kids want to or not." It is clear from the way he says it that he thinks the Ramazi approach to childrearing is the correct one. Callie, with an American view on things, cringes internally. Though, truthfully, she realizes, Abdullah and Fariza seem pretty emotionally healthy and they were raised in a very rigid, hierarchical society.

"There are good sides to being hypersensitive," Callie adds, feeling slightly defensive.

"Like what?" Abdullah frowns, seeming unable to come up with any.

"Well, while negative stimuli drive me crazy, I think I appreciate positive stimuli more than your average person. For example, it might cross your mind that your mom's *khachapuri* smells and tastes great, but for someone with hypersensitivity, good smells and tastes send all our neurons into a fireworks party. I'm convinced that many food critics and chefs have hypersensitivity. And lots of artists as well— because beauty speaks to them in a louder and more intense way than it does to regular people."

"So— for you— the bad senses are worse and the good are better?" Abdullah asks, confirming that he's understood.

"Pretty much," Callie nods. "I'm often not sure if it's worth it, experiencing everything more intensely. And getting stuck in an attention rut and being unable to concentrate on anything else, like with the hammering. But I do feel like I appreciate many things deeply as a result. So, in that regard, it's good I guess."

"Thanks for trusting me enough to share," Abdullah's voice is low, his eyes holding Callie's for long enough that her heart starts to beat faster. "Like I said, people here don't normally open up about their issues, so it's refreshing. And let me know if there is ever anything I can do to help make things more pleasant, or less frustrating, for you." Abdullah says sincerely. "Except for the construction noise. I'm afraid if you want a bathroom, you're going to have to suffer through that," he shrugs apologetically.

"It will be worth it, I'm sure," Callie smiles. "And honestly it really helps knowing that I will only have to deal with it for a couple more days."

"On that note, I'm gonna head back to work and see if I can get the guys to speed things up for you," Abdullah stands and pats the table twice before loping across the orchard. Callie watches him go, aware at once of how different their cultures are, but also warm inside at how willing he had been to try to understand her.

CHAPTER 13
Khev, Georgia

March, 1992

The afternoon after the wedding, Dina sits at the table, her head lowered. The women of the family sit around her, eating lunch and speaking in Ramazi. Dina is so exhausted from the sleepless night that she doesn't even care that she can't understand what they're saying. She tries to eat her soup, but the headscarf tied around her head keeps coming undone and dragging on the table. She notices one of the sisters, the smaller dark-haired one, looking at her with pity from across the table. Dina quickly breaks eye contact; she can't handle any emotional connections at this point. She needs to figure out how to get out of here. After last night, she can't stay. Like he promised, Saidun tried to be gentle. But the whole thing was so awful, so repulsive, so degrading... Dina chokes on the spoonful of soup in her mouth. She forces herself to take a deep calming breath and try again.

The soup is thick and hearty, tomato-based with lots of vegetables. It is seasoned in a way that Dina isn't used to, but it is warm and filling and she realizes she is very hungry. Just as she spoons a large bite towards her mouth, her headscarf comes completely undone and one end of it falls into her bowl of soup.

"You've got to be kidding me!" Dina mutters, flinging the entire thing off in frustration.

"Дʌа зщо курокре ерит тва ʌоку ваоʌудʌамг!" the mother shouts, gesticulating wildly towards the headscarf. Too exhausted and frazzled to care about the consequences of her behavior, Dina glares back and eats her soup with set shoulders and deliberate bites.

"Длу вал флоц фылмтйзышя!" more shouting from the mother, followed by anxious comments from the sisters. Dina ignores them all and continues to eat.

Finally, the mother switches to Georgian, "Stop eating! Cover your head! Do you have no shame?"

Dina grits her teeth and slowly raises the headscarf, which now smells of soup, to her head.

"Here," the smaller sister says timidly in heavily accented Georgian, "I will show you how to tie it so that it will not come undone." She stands up from her chair and moves behind Dina, taking the scarf gently in her hands and wrapping it expertly around Dina's head. Dina is surprised by how firm and settled the scarf feels once it's tied in place.

"Thank you," Dina offers the sister a sliver of a smile, which the sister returns warmly.

"My name is Hava," she offers quietly. "And that is Marta." she gestures across the table to her taller sister, who simply gives a head nod.

"Сывт фывдло шуйз ов й ыш ицвчйц влол," the mother says, and Hava quickly returns to her seat and finishes her meal in silence. The only sound is the radio on the sidebar, a man's voice droning away in a monotone monologue in Ramazi. Dina didn't even realize there was a radio station in the Ramazi language. A few weeks later, Hava explains to her that it is broadcast from across the mountains in Russia — that Georgia doesn't allow Ramazis to do their own broadcasts.

For all the times Dina is in the dining room over the next few weeks, she never hears music on the Ramazi radio station— just that same monotonous man's voice. She can't understand anything he says, so she has no clue what he's even talking about. Politics? Religion? The men listen intently when they eat, and it often spurs them into active conversations and debate. Though she can't understand the words, Dina can tell by the body language that all the neighbors and workers around the table respect Saidun's father Anzor, and listen to what he has to say during the discussions.

Five times a day, the regular radio programming is paused as the call to prayer comes across the radio waves in Arabic. Simultaneously,

Dina can hear the call to prayer coming over the loudspeaker from the neighborhood mosque. At first, it jolts her every time, especially when it wakes her at 4:00 a.m. Saidun just grunts in his sleep and rolls over. From what Dina can tell, he is not actually very devout. But during the day, when he's with his father and the other men from the community, the men all dutifully head to the dining room from wherever they are on the property when they hear the sound of the call to prayer, unfurl their prayer rugs, and kneel, face to the floor, heads pointed east towards Mecca. When Dina gets up the nerve to ask Hava why the men pray and the women don't, Hava just shrugs, "Women don't have time to set aside and pray like the men do— our hands are always full with chores and cleaning and cooking and babies. But I think Allah understands," she smiles. "We let the men take care of religion and we take care of everything else. And someday, when we are old and our hands are less full, we will have time to devote to Allah ourselves."

CHAPTER 14
Sureti Valley, Georgia

June, 2018

"So, what do you do?" a girl from Indiana with long black hair pulled in a high ponytail asks Callie politely, as she passes her a plate of steaming mashed potatoes.

"I'm a journalist," Callie explains, "but I'm taking the summer off from my day job and am here helping with social media and marketing for the guest house."

"Oh my gosh!! Are you the one who does their Instagram??! I *love* your page! Those woodworking pics you posted were, like, so awesome!! My friend Sam is, like, really into woodworking, and he somehow found that post. Maybe, like, hashtags? Anyway, I don't know. But he knew I was coming to Georgia and so after he found it, he, like, sent it to me and told me I should totally come here! So I looked up your account and your pictures were, like, so enticing! And I know this is, like, way off the beaten path, but I just *had* to come here!" the girl bubbles so enthusiastically that Callie can't help but laugh.

"Yup, that's me. Well, us, really. Abdullah, whose family owns and runs this place, is doing it with me."

"Well, you guys are, like, totally awesome!" the girl gushes. Callie smiles inwardly, amused at how incredibly different dinner is this evening with a table full of new American guests, versus the night before when she got a Caucasus history lesson from the men that stretched back six generations and took multiple hours to tell. Family history and storytelling are *not* American strengths or values—Americans tend to be much more focused on the here and now and on their own lives. Callie cringes when she realizes that she's going to be sharing a room with this chatty American girl for the next three days.

Rosana is bringing out tea and dessert when Callie hears a knock at the gate. She excuses herself from the table and walks through the deepening twilight towards the gate— they have been expecting an American couple to arrive all afternoon— perhaps this is them?

The sky is still tinged with pink along the edges of the mountains, but higher up, it's already a deep purple. The heat of the afternoon sun is gone and Callie pulls her cardigan around herself as a cool breeze wafts across the garden, carrying with it the heady scent of lilac blossoms.

"Welcome to Leila's Guesthouse," Callie smiles, opening the gate to find the couple they had been expecting. They're older, *maybe in their mid-60s*, Callie guesses. The man is tall and thin with a large, crooked nose and a head full of thick, white hair.

"Nice to meet you! I'm Rob," he grins, shooting out a big gnarled hand and giving Callie a vigorous handshake. "Barely found this place in the dark! You'd think we'd never been here before! Woohee, what a journey! Sorry we are late! Got a flat tire on the way here, can you believe that? Our driver had a spare thankfully; changed it himself on the side of the road. Wow, what a drive that was— beautiful pass!"

"Oh hush, leave this poor girl alone. She looks like a deer in the headlights with all your yakking." A short, plump woman with her gray hair in a messy bun comes up beside Rob and thrusts a suitcase towards him. "Here, take this!"

"Yes, ma'am!" Rob salutes cheerfully, and heads towards the trunk of the car, where he helps the driver unload so many suitcases that it looks like they're planning to move in for good.

The woman notices Callie's inadvertent eyebrow raise at the number of suitcases and laughs ruefully, "I know, I know! Ridiculous! Can you believe we have been world travelers for years and this is still how he packs? Can't go anywhere without a million books," she smiles indulgently at her husband. "But after forty years of marriage, I've just come to accept that I'm not gonna change him, so I might as well love him as he is, ridiculous quirks and all! I'm Pat, by the way. Here, do you mind carrying this, hun?" she hands a backpack to Callie, who grabs the handle of a rolly suitcase in addition to the backpack and leads the way into the guesthouse courtyard.

"Rob! Pat!" Abdullah enters the courtyard from the direction of the bathroom construction, covered neck to toe with grime that hints at the amount of hard work he's been doing all day.

"Abdullah!" Rob and Pat smile at him like he's their long-lost son, and Rob goes in for a handshake.

"Woah!" Abdullah laughs, holding up his grimy palms in demonstration, "Let me clean up and then I would love a handshake!"

"Deal!" Rob grins, "What are you guys working on that has you so dirty?"

"Building a bathroom!"

"Actually, two bathrooms," Callie chimes in, standing next to Abdullah in the twilight dusk.

"Two bathrooms!" Pat exclaims, clapping her hands. "Honey, we picked the perfect time to come for a visit!"

"Well, you probably should've waited a couple of weeks," Abdullah laughs, his amber eyes crinkling. "They're not done yet."

"We don't need bathrooms!" Rob exclaims. "Bathrooms are for wimps! We're more than happy to rough it out!"

"You, maybe," Pat rolls her eyes good-naturedly. "I, on the other hand, appreciate a good bathroom!"

"Callie does too," Abdullah glances warmly at her. "She's the one who was able to convince my mom to finally agree to build the bathrooms." Callie blushes at the praise in Abdullah's voice, as if she's accomplished something monumental.

"Well, my dear, it seems I owe you one!" Pat gives Callie a nod of appreciation.

"I think you all will enjoy getting to know one another," Abdullah smiles at the group. "You are all great people. And hungry people, probably! Dinner is ready if you want to head to the dining room. Rob and Pat, my mother can't wait to see you guys! Just leave your suitcases here— I will clean up and then I will take them up to your room."

"You don't have to do that," Rob begins when Pat stops him with a light hand on his lower back. "Let him, honey," she says gently. "With the way your lower back has been flaring up recently, you don't need to lift any more than you have to." Rob nods reluctantly, and then smiles at Abdullah, "Gotta do what the doctor orders!" he says, glancing pointedly at his wife.

"Hah! If you always did what I ordered, you wouldn't have hurt your back to begin with! It's when you ignore me that things go wrong!" Pat smiles conspiratorially at Callie and loops an arm through hers, "Now let's go find that dinner Abdullah was talking about! It has been *way* too long since I had *khachapuri*, and Leila's are to die for!"

Callie allows herself to be led back to the table, thinking, *I think I'm gonna like these quirky new guests. And I sure hope I'm as cute with my husband when I'm their age someday!*

***

The first few days Pat and Rob are at the guesthouse, Callie doesn't see much of them or Abdullah. They've been gone visiting families in the village most of the day every day. Callie tries not to admit to herself how much she misses spending time with Abdullah. *It's probably just that there aren't really many other people my age to hang out with around here,* she justifies to herself.

She had been surprised to learn over dinner the first night that the couple had booked their room for almost a month— most guests stay for only a couple of days. Rob is a Ph.D. linguist, and he's doing a study on the preservation of minority languages. So they're in the Sureti Valley for research for his job, hence all the visits and interviews with locals, which Abdullah is translating for. Pat recently retired from a career as a middle school teacher, and so has the flexibility to travel with her husband. Callie's impression of them improves each time she engages with them.

One morning, as she heads out towards the dreaded outhouse, she sees them sitting in the rocking swing, across the back orchard. Pat's head is leaning on Rob's shoulder and his arm is draped around her. They look so comfortable together that a twinge of longing stirs in Callie's stomach. Trying not to intrude, Callie averts her eyes. But when she leaves the outhouse, she can't help but peek at them again. She notices with surprise that both their eyes are closed and a large book is open across Rob's lap. *They're Christians,* she realizes, like a lightbulb clicking on in her mind. It makes sense— the kindness, the joy, the loving marriage. The old-fashioned values. She had been around families in her church growing up that seemed to give off the same kind of vibe. Honestly, it reminds her of how her parents used to be. *Except Dad will never experience this, the sweetness of growing old together.* Callie's heart aches for her dad and she determines to email him when she gets back to her room.

She takes one final glance at them across the yard, her stomach turning uncomfortably. *I hope they won't judge me, if they find out I used to be a Christian but don't consider myself one anymore. I need to be on my guard around them.*

***

"Tea?" Pat offers Callie a box of black tea packets. "No thanks," Callie shakes her head. "If I drink any caffeine after about 3:00 p.m., it's almost impossible for me to fall asleep at night."

Pat nods empathetically in the falling dusk as Abdullah scrapes his chair back from the patio table tucked under the overhanging grapevines.

"Be right back," he smiles. In a couple of minutes, he returns with a plastic grocery store bag filled to the brim with what looks to Callie like dried grass.

"What am I supposed to do with this?" She wrinkles up her nose at him.

"He's trying to ask you to take over feeding the cow," Rob jokes.

"Hey, this precious stuff is not for the cow!" Abdullah looks mock-offended. "This is the best herbal tea you can find. My mom and sister gather it from the mountainside every summer. It has nettle, thyme, echinacea, and rose hips and is good for reducing blood pressure, strengthening the heart and respiratory system, calming nerves, improving the immune system, and bringing a calming night's sleep."

"I trust you," Callie laughs, "but it definitely looks and feels like a bag full of grass."

"If you do not appreciate our special medicinal tea, and do not want to sleep like a baby tonight, then I can just take this back," Abdullah tugs the bag in her lap with a grin.

"No way are you taking this back now!" Callie pulls it back. "If it will do even half of the things you promised, I'm keeping it!"

Abdullah nods smugly. He reaches into the bag and pulls out a generous pinch of the mixture, which he then sprinkles into the bottom of a pot and fills it with boiling water. Callie bends close to the teapot— in the deepening gray shadows of twilight, she can barely make out the pinks and reds and yellows of flower petals swimming alongside bits of grass.

"Let it steep for a while and then it will settle," Pat suggests. "And it is great with honey."

Callie takes both of Pat's suggestions and is pleasantly surprised to find the tea delicious.

"Alright, you won me over," she smiles at Pat and Abdullah.

"You're lucky there are no other guests tonight, otherwise I wouldn't have brought this out. Gotta keep the good stuff hidden," Abdullah jokes, his eyes twinkling as he runs a hand back through his dark bangs.

Callie looks around the vineyard. In the darkness, she can barely make out the shapes of the unripe grapes hanging only a few feet above her head. But their sweet, heady scent reminds her that they are there. In the slivers of space between the vines, the sky is almost pitch black and stars are beginning to appear. In the silence, she can hear the buzz of insects flocking to the light hanging over the courtyard. The table tucked away under the grape vines feels warm and secure. It's nice to have a night with no other guests, being able to just hang out in the darkness with Abdullah and Rob and Pat. Callie sighs with pleasure and stretches out slowly in her wooden chair.

"I really love it here," she admits quietly. "It's so peaceful."

"We love it too," Rob nods, reaching across the table and wrapping his large knobby hand around Pat's smaller pudgy one. He gives it a squeeze and the two of them smile at each other.

"You guys... you seem like you have a really good marriage," Callie comments, adding another spoon of mountain honey to her tea. *Keep them talking about themselves and then hopefully conversation won't get around to you,* Callie strategizes.

"We do now," Rob gives Pat's hand another squeeze.

"We didn't always," Pat smiles.

"Unfortunately, I wasn't always as winsome and charming as I currently am," Rob laughs and Pat rolls her eyes.

"What changed?" Callie asks, curious. She has seen a lot of marriages start strong and then fall apart, but rarely has she seen one start poorly and then improve. She glances over at Abdullah. He's leaning back in his chair, a steaming cup of tea cradled in his hands. His golden eyes are intense and curious as he too listens in.

"We were college sweethearts," Pat begins.

"She fell for me hard and fast," Rob winks.

"Stop interrupting," Pat swats him. "We got married the weekend after college graduation and spent our honeymoon camping in a mosquito-infested campground in Tennessee," Pat laughs.

"Real memorable, let me tell ya'." Rob grins.

"We were too poor for anything else," Pat explains. "We were pretty happy at first. But we got pregnant with our first son not long after our honeymoon, and I had to quit my job when he was born. So money got even tighter. Rob was stressed trying to provide, and I was exhausted and frazzled being a new mom. Our patience with each other ran thin pretty quickly. And then Rob's brother moved in, and things went to hell in a handbasket."

Rob nods, "My family was pretty dysfunctional, and I basically had to raise my younger brother Steve. But he was a great kid and we were super close. When he wasn't driving me crazy," Rob grins and Callie and Abdullah both nod. Annoying siblings is something that they can both empathize with.

"Steve was my world. Of the two of us, everyone always thought he would be the one to go somewhere, to make it out. He had somehow inherited all the brains, good looks, *and* athletic ability of the family!"

"He didn't get *all* the good looks," Pat gives Rob a gentle rub on his cheek and he shrugs cheerily.

"Anyway, Steve was the quarterback for our high school football team. He had a scholarship to college lined up and everything. Then senior year he got injured a few minutes into the second-to-last game of the year— massive fracture to his left leg. He had multiple surgeries and it effectively ended his football career."

"What's worse, and what we didn't know at the time," Pat continues, "is that he got addicted to the pain meds that he started taking after the surgery. He held it together well for a long time, even went to a couple years of college, but eventually he had to drop out. His whole life began revolving around drugs. He tried to stop multiple times and couldn't. We even helped get him into rehab once, but it didn't take."

"Anyway, it's a long rough story," Rob waves his hands. "The gist of it is, it got to the point where I pretty much lived in constant fear that he would overdose."

"Which he did," Pat adds, "One night we got a call from Grady Hospital in Atlanta–the doctors said it was miraculous that Steve had even survived. They told us they could either release him to family custody or put him in government rehab."

"I couldn't send him to a government facility, so I drove to Atlanta and picked him up," Rob explains and Abdullah nods— clearly, he would do the same thing in a similar situation.

"Our marriage was already really strained. I was pregnant with our daughter, and our boys were exhausting toddlers. Three kids in under four years– I don't recommend it! Rob was working two jobs to try to make ends meet. We were fighting all the time. And then add to all of that a drug addict."

"It was a dark time," Rob nods, running a thick wrinkled hand across his chin. "Long story short, Steve lived with us for two long months."

"It felt like about two years," Pat laughs and Rob again reaches for her hand.

"We saw first-hand the horrors of addiction. Steve and Rob had always been thick as thieves, but Steve didn't hesitate to lie to our faces and manipulate us. We realized pretty quickly that he was still using, though he denied it. Soon stuff started going missing around the house— money from our wallets, Rob's watch, etcetera. Everything came to a head one night when Rob was gone working the second shift at his night job and some of Steve's addict buddies came and robbed our house. I was pregnant with Stephanie, asleep in our room with our sons Matt and Alex asleep in the room next door. I woke up to the sound of someone roaming around the living room. In my groggy state, I assumed it was Rob home from work. I didn't even get out of bed."

"When I got home, the house was trashed." Even though it has been decades since the burglary happened, Rob's eyes are still sad. "I was terrified that something had happened to Pat and the kids. I've never been more scared in my life than running through that house and searching their rooms. I was so relieved to find them safe and asleep in their beds."

"Rob woke me up and I was terrified too. I couldn't believe that I'd slept through all the noise. Steve and his pals had taken anything they could— our TV, all electronics, books, money, etcetera– anything they thought they might be able to sell. They even took the boys' tricycles," Pat adds sadly.

"That must have been terrible. I cannot believe that a brother would do that to his brother," Abdullah says quietly.

"Addiction is an awful thing," Rob explains. "It makes people do things that they would normally never do."

"So what did you guys do?" Callie asks, sipping the last of her now-cold tea.

"We called the police," Rob admits. "I felt so guilty, having to call the police on my baby brother."

"But it's what ultimately ended up turning him around," Pat adds. "He did a year in the county jail."

"Forced him into sobriety for the first time in years," Rob explains. "I visited him every week. At first, he refused to see me. Understandably, he blamed me for turning him in."

"But you kept going," Pat squeezes Rob's hand and he squeezes back.

"Steve got real involved in a Bible study in jail— the chaplain was a former inmate himself, had a crazier story than Steve's. Steve really liked the guy. One day when I went for my attempted weekly visit, expecting Steve to refuse to see me like usual, I was surprised when he showed up. And even more surprised when he asked for my forgiveness for all the wrong things he had done when he was using. And he told me that he didn't blame me for turning him in."

"At first we were suspicious and didn't trust what was going on. We weren't religious ourselves— we thought Steve had just caught on to some temporary fad or something," Pat explains. "But we were wrong. We had *lived* with him, so we knew first hand how completely trapped he had been by his addiction. We watched the next few years after Steve started following Jesus, how his life radically changed. He got out of jail and the changes stuck."

"We'd been really worried that once he got out, he would be pulled back into addiction," Rob explains. "But he wasn't. He turned his life around, got involved with a good church, married a great lady, and they're still married twenty-plus years later. He's got two kids of his own, and he and his wife have gotten involved with a ministry to foster kids."

"Compared to him, we had always been the stable and functional ones. Our problems didn't seem so bad next to his. But once he turned his life around, we started to examine our own lives. And acknowledge that there was a lot in our own lives that wasn't so pretty," Pat explains. "Basically, we started looking into Christianity out of selfish, jealous motives! We thought that maybe if it could fix his problems, it could fix ours too," Pat laughs.

"And it didn't fix all our problems," Rob grins at Pat. "It wasn't some bandaid or magic bullet."

"Definitely not," Pat laughs, swallowing the rest of her tea. "But the more we began to examine Jesus, the more appealing he became. We got curious to know who he was, and why he was the way he was. Eventually, we both decided that we wanted to take the leap and try following his teachings."

"It seemed like not much of a risk, since we were such an exhausted mess at that time," Rob explains.

Pat nods in agreement, "It's been a long road, and not without its bumps. But slowly, as we've walked with him, God has transformed our lives and our marriage. We're really thankful." She leans over to Rob, and he places a gentle kiss on her head.

Callie glances at Abdullah, who is leaning forward in rapt attention, clearly fascinated by their story. Callie twists a strand of her dark hair around her finger, feeling torn inside. On the one hand, she really likes Pat and Rob. They are so genuine and real. But something about them being here, listening to them share about their faith, makes her feel like her past is following her across the ocean. *It's like I'm a hermit crab who has gotten rid of my old shell and moved into a bigger, brighter new one. But my tight old shell keeps following me around the sea,* Callie thinks, blowing out an annoyed breath of air. *Though Pat and Rob don't seem to feel like the shell of religion is restrictive...* Callie admits to herself.

***

Callie is helping Leila set the table for lunch when Abdullah rushes in, breathless.

"It's done!" he shouts, his amber eyes gleaming. "Well, not entirely done... not decorated or anything, but functional!"

Callie thrusts the pile of plates she had been holding onto the table, relieved when none of them break. "Show me now!"

The short walk to the new bathrooms becomes a procession, as they're quickly joined by Pat, Rob, Leila, and a couple of other curious guests.

Abdullah stops in front of the closed bathroom doors and turns to face the small crowd. A couple of his local buddies stand to the side of the bathroom, proud looks on their faces as everyone oohs and ahhs over their handiwork. The two bathrooms are in a small neat building, a few feet away from the main guesthouse. They are side by side, and each one gleams with clean white tile and boasts a Western-style toilet, a shower, and a sink. If you walked into a similar bathroom in America, you wouldn't think anything of it— it would just seem like an average bathroom. But here in Sureti Valley, it is state-of-the-art, cutting-edge. As far as Callie has seen, no one in town has anything like it.

Abdullah bounces up and down on his toes, his lean body full of pent-up energy. "Ladies and gentlemen, without further ado, I hereby reveal to you these two beautiful bathrooms, with running water and everything, which we dedicate with honor to Miss Callie Leffler!"

Callie blushes. "We'll get you a plaque, hang it right on the wall!" Pat jibes, elbowing Callie in the ribs. Callie covers her face with both hands and laughs, "Perfect! Just what I've always dreamed of!"

A few hours later, Callie is sitting at the picnic table in the orchard updating their booking.com listing with some new bathroom photos when a shadow passes across her screen. She looks up, squinting in the bright June sunlight, to find Abdullah leaning over her shoulder.

"Hey, this is looking good! People will be thrilled to know we have an actual bathroom," he jokes. Abdullah leans closer over Callie's shoulder and she sucks in a breath, taking in his clean scent of wood shavings and sunshine. She blushes, hoping he doesn't notice. He seems unaware of his arm glancing hers as he reaches for the trackpad on her laptop to scroll through the other pictures Callie has added to their listing. "Your pictures are much better than the ones we had up there," he admits freely.

Callie nods, trying to seem engrossed with her task— trying not to show the heat and sparks that are flooding her shoulder and arm from the places where his skin has brushed hers. "See how the wide-angle zoom really opens up the rooms in the pictures? That's a trick real estate agents use when taking pictures for houses they're trying to sell," she chokes out. "Oh— and look at this! Remember that couple we had last week from Sweden? They left a glowing five-star review! Here, read it," Callie clicks through to another page and tips the computer screen up toward Abdullah.

He reads silently for a moment, showing no sign of being affected by or even aware of their closeness. *I need to stop imagining things,* Callie chides herself. He gives a contented nod and turns the computer back towards her, "This is looking great. We can't thank you enough for your help for our family." Abdullah's words sound polite and formal, but when Callie glances up, the way he is looking down at her is anything but formal. Her stomach flips.

"My pleasure," Callie replies, looking away. There's a pregnant pause, and then Abdullah slides onto the bench across from her.

"I actually came out here to ask for your help. We've finished the grunt work on the bathrooms— the part we know how to do!" he gives a light, self-deprecating laugh. "Now we need expert decorator help, which is most definitely the part we do *not* know how to do!"

"Honestly, I think they look really good how they are. I love the white tile— it's very modern and minimalist. I don't think you need much decoration. And your mom is better at decorating than you guys give her credit for— she has a good eye. But what specifically are you wanting my help with?"

"Well, we need to choose faucet handles, light fixtures, shower curtains, and floor mats. I started to look and, I will admit, got overwhelmed by the amount of options. I showed my mom a sample of the light fixtures I thought we should get and she groaned and sent me to ask you," Abdullah grins.

"Well, I love design!" Callie exclaims. "Is there a store here where we can go look at options?" she asks, frowning doubtfully.

Abdullah laughs, "You've seen the entire town! We don't even have a coffee shop or a gas station— there's certainly not a home goods or building supplies store! We'll have to go into Maidana. It's about an hour's drive. Are you good if we go in tomorrow?"

"Hmmm, I don't know. My schedule is looking pretty full tomorrow. I'm really not sure if I can make the time. I mean, I have to update Instagram, help set out the dishes for lunch... I'm just not sure if I can spare the time," Callie teases.

"You joke like you're not doing a lot, but I see how much you work," Abdullah stares at Callie intently from across the table, his eyes sparkling golden in the afternoon light. "Why are you here? Why did you come? Why do you want to help us? You're not making any money here," Abdullah's voice is earnest, and Callie can tell that he's been wanting to bring this up for a while.

"Well...," Callie pauses, twisting the ends of her hair as she pulls her thoughts together, "Honestly, I think I selfishly wanted a change of scenery and change of pace. My life in San Francisco was really busy — I worked super long hours and then had a jam-packed social schedule whenever I wasn't working. And I was getting pretty burnt out at my job. This seemed like a way to unplug and reset my life, maybe reevaluate some things, while also hopefully doing some good and being useful along the way."

"And have you been able to reset? To reevaluate?"

Callie shrugs and bites her lip. She picks up a small stick lying on the table and gently pulls it along the lines of one of the groves in the wood of the picnic table. "I've definitely been able to unplug, thanks to the terrible internet here," she jokes. "And, probably as a result of not being so distracted by my phone, I've had time to reevaluate. I'm not sure I want to go back to my job when this summer is over. Oh wow, I can't believe I said that. I haven't admitted that to anyone. I'm not even sure I knew it until it just came out of my mouth." Callie raises her eyebrows in surprise.

"Why don't you want to go back?" Abdullah asks, sitting forward, his eyes intently holding hers. "I thought you liked journalism?"

"I do," Callie rushes to assure him. "It's just that I've been covering local politics and elections and so many of the candidates are so sleazy," Callie gives an inadvertent shiver.

"Sleazy?" Abdullah frowns. "I don't think I know this word?"

"Sorry! Your English is so good that sometimes I forget you aren't a native speaker!"

Abdullah glows at the compliment, "Thank you! My mom taught us well, from the time we were babies. There was a lot of pressure to be good in English with our mom as the most sought-after tutor in town! Though I did my best to slack off when I could," he grins. "Honestly it was watching all the American TV shows with friends in college that really got my English to the next level! You could say I learned much of my English from Ross, Rachel, Joey, Chandler, Phoebe, and Monica."

Callie laughs, "I would never in a million years have pegged you as a *Friends* fan! You seem far too respectable for that!"

"Ha! Maybe I am not as respectable as you think," he gives her a cheeky wink and drawls, "How *you* doin'?" with his best Joey Tribbiani impression.

Callie cracks up, putting a hand on the side of her face as she raises her eyebrows, "I certainly did not see that one coming!" she gasps through her laughter. Abdullah grins, casually propping his chin on his hand as he leans forward, clearly pleased with himself. Callie's stomach flips— she is enjoying this relaxed, flirtatious side of Abdullah far too much.

"Wait, how did we even start down this rabbit trail?" Callie asks, steering the conversation back to safer ground.

"Sleazy. I was wondering what the word means."

"Ha! Joey Tribbiani is a great example of it, actually!" Callie laughs, explaining. "It usually refers to someone who tries to be showy and attractive, but underneath actually has bad morals or questionable judgment. Joey is a pretty harmless version of it. We use it a lot in the US to describe politicians."

"Ah," Abdullah commiserates. "We know something about corrupt politicians— Georgia's former president is currently in jail for corruption!"

Callie nods, "Yeah, politicians are the worst. I mean, there are obviously some who are good people who truly want to help people. But there are a lot who just seem to be chasing money and power. And I'm tired of covering that beat. I just want to find a job that feels meaningful, but that I also enjoy doing. Is that too much to ask?" she laughs self-mockingly.

"Probably not in America. In America, you can be picky with jobs," Abdullah shrugs one shoulder lightly. To Callie, his words sting. He keeps talking, not even realizing his words had hurt, "Here, most people are just trying to survive. The only requirement for a job is if it pays enough money so that you can feed your family."

"I shouldn't have said that, what I said," Callie says, not wanting him to judge her. "I didn't realize how entitled, how American, it sounds to expect a job to be fulfilling."

Quickly, Abdullah thrusts out both hands in a stop motion, "No, no, no! That's not what I meant! I think it's wonderful that there are places in the world where people have the luxury of choosing the kind of job they want. It's just unfortunate that that same privilege doesn't extend to the rest of the world."

"You're not making me feel any better," Callie laughs weakly.

"Seriously, don't feel guilty. This has nothing to do with you— it's been this way for multiple generations in our country. We're still just getting back on our feet after everything collapsed after the Soviet Union fell apart. My mom doesn't talk about her past much, but my Aunt Marta told us a couple of stories about how hard it was back then."

"Do you know why your mom doesn't talk much about her past?" Callie asks. She's been curious all summer and feels like she finally has an opening to ask.

But Callie is disappointed when Abdullah merely shrugs, "Life was hard back then. Lots of people don't want to talk about the '90s."

When she realizes he isn't going to add anything, Callie changes the topic of conversation to faucet handle options and Abdullah willingly moves on.

***

"Miss Callie Leffler, I have come downstairs to invite you to a dance," Rob's blue eyes sparkle with mischief as he approaches Callie at the dining room table. The late afternoon sun is lowering towards the horizon and Callie is about to wrap up her work for the day before offering to help set the table for dinner.

"A dance, huh? You and me? What type of dance? I should warn you, I'm a pretty terrible dancer!" Callie forces a laugh, closing her laptop and gathering her books in a pile. Inside, her stomach turns — she finds dancing in public awkward and embarrassing. Plus, it's normally a sensory overload— Callie has a quick flashback to a college frat party. Strobe lights. Pounding, thumping music. Sweaty bodies gyrating around her. The exit nowhere in sight. A random drunk girl spilling her beer down the front of Callie's tank top at the exact same time when a guy she didn't even know had pressed up against her backside, thrusting in time with the music. Callie's vision had started going dark and her breath had come in ragged gasps and she had pushed her way frantically through mobs of oblivious, wasted partiers, trying to find the exit. Only later did she realize she'd been having a panic attack. Ever since, she has tried to avoid dancing situations whenever possible.

"Well, you might like to know that I am an expert dancer." Rob raises his head proudly and grins, unaware of Callie's inner turmoil.

"He thinks he's an expert because he and Pricilla Wingsbee won some dance competition in the fifth grade," Pat says drily, entering the room.

"Hey! You didn't have to spoil my ask!" Rob feigns offense. "And I will have you know, that was a very challenging competition! We beat out eight other couples from our school *and* our rival school!"

"Of course you did. How could I forget?" Pat grins at him indulgently before giving Callie a wink.

"And anyway, tell the poor girl you aren't asking her to actually dance," Pat prods him before turning to pour herself a cup of tea from the sidebar.

"Not dancing together?! I'm heartbroken!" Callie throws a hand to her chest in mock distress, while internally breathing a sigh of relief.

"Maybe some other time!" Rob grins. "But actually, I'm inviting you to come—"

"—with *both* of us–," Pat inserts.

"Of course with both of us! I'd never go anywhere without my Pooh bear!" Rob throws a lanky arm around Pat's round shoulders and pulls her close. She swats at him playfully.

"What he's been *trying* to do this whole time is invite you to a local dance performance. It's going to be on Saturday night, two villages over. Word on the street is that their dancers are pretty good," Pat explains.

"Ramazi dance is my favorite!" Rob enthuses, thrusting his arms out wide and then pulling them in quickly as he jumps up into the air.

"Please do not take that as a sample of what Ramazi dance is really like," Abdullah ducks into the dining room carrying an armful of bread from the local bakery.

"Hey now! You're the one who taught me everything I know!" Rob pushes out a mock-offended bottom lip.

"Well, clearly you had a poor teacher," Abdullah laughs as he leaves the room to head into the kitchen.

"He's really good, actually," Rob nods his head towards Abdullah's disappearing back. "Though he doesn't often have time to perform with all his duties around here."

"Will he be performing in this upcoming dance?" Callie asks, curiosity piqued. With the lithe way Abdullah walks around the farm, she can only imagine what his dancing would be like.

"You can help me try to talk him into it!" Rob answers. "But even if he doesn't dance, the performers are supposed to be excellent. You should come— get a feel for the culture, as well as get some good pics for social media."

"Sounds good," Callie agrees, internally determined to talk Abdullah into performing.

***

The concert hall two towns over is hot and dark and crowded. It seems to Callie that every single citizen of Sureti Valley, plus some Georgian tourists as well, must have shown up for the show. Clearly this dance is a big deal.

Callie adjusts her headscarf self-consciously, feeling at once awkward wearing one and grateful for the semi-anonymity it grants her in a crowd full of covered women and dark-haired men. Pat had recommended she wear a headscarf to the event, and Callie is glad she listened.

"Why is it so hot in here?" Callie whispers behind her hand to Pat, who chuckles good-naturedly beside her.

"I came prepared," Pat grins, pulling a small folding fan out of her giant purse and offering it to Callie. "I've been to enough of these events to know how warm they get!"

"You're a life-saver!" Callie takes the fan with deep gratitude. The air it provides is minimal, but better than nothing.

As Callie sits fanning herself, the lights come on on the stage and the audience begins to stomp and clap and cat-call. Callie raises her eyebrows in surprise to Pat— she definitely did not expect it to get this rowdy!

A drum beat starts and a line of men march out onto the stage, dressed in identical traditional Ramazi costumes of long black coats covered with buttons and gold braiding, knee-high boots, and short round hats. Long knives are strapped across their chests.

The men move in perfect synchronization. Their movements are big and intense, full of jumps, thrusting arms, and spins. It almost looks like a choreographed fight. Though the actual movements and music are nothing like Irish river dance, there's something about the energy of it that feels similar to Callie. The music pounds in a way that feels almost militaristic. As it increases in volume, the men's dance movements increase in speed and intensity. Callie searches the dancers but doesn't see Abdullah.

The song ends and the audience goes wild. The next song begins, softer than the previous one. A line of slender young women in floor-length white dresses glide in from stage left. They wave their arms in perfectly synchronized graceful arches as they swirl and twirl around the room. Their movements look effortless. The men form a circle and the women dance around them, and then the women circle in the middle, and the men dance around them. And then the men and women all form a giant half-circle and the crowd begins to stomp in anticipation.

And then Callie sees him— Abdullah marches in from stage right. Unlike the other male dancers, his costume is a deep hunter green. The male dancers all take a knee, clapping in rhythm in his direction.

Abdullah takes a giant leap, and it seems like he is flying across the stage. The audience shouts and whoops. His feet move in a dizzyingly fast step pattern and Callie's heart beat quickens. *Wow, he's good.* He drops to his knees and dances on them and the audience goes crazy.

Just as he gets back to his feet, someone shouts and all eyes go stage left, where a stunningly beautiful woman enters in a white dress that is covered with delicate gold lace. Her long dark hair is in a single braid down her back and covered with a gossamer lace veil. She glides over towards Abdullah and spins around him, her large dark eyes always focused demurely on the floor. He adjusts his movements to hers, and they circle each other. Her movements are graceful and ethereal and lovely and his are intense and strong. Callie's gut twists as she wonders if there is anything going on between the two of them. She is so lovely— how could he not be attracted to her?

"She's supposed to be a swan, and he is supposed to be a warrior eagle," Pat whispers in Callie's ear. "See how they don't touch— they're supposed to dance around each other, but they're never allowed to touch or make eye contact."

"It's really beautiful," Callie whispers back, unable to keep her eyes off of Abdullah and the dark-haired beauty gliding around him. She belatedly pulls out her phone and starts to film.

**

"So, what's going on between you and Abdullah?" Pat asks mischievously, startling Callie as she comes up to her from behind. Callie blushes furiously, quickly averting her eyes from where she'd been watching Abdullah chop wood across the back pasture— his graceful movements and strength are a beauty to see. Not as intense as his dance moves, but still hot.

"What? Nothing!" Callie tries to feign nonchalance as she picks up a wet sheet from the basket in front of her and hangs it on the line.

"Oh really," Pat grins, "Because I've been reading on that bench in the orchard and watching you two— in the past ten minutes, you've hung a total of one sheet and one pillowcase. And Abdullah, on the other hand, has chopped far more wood than he chopped before you came outside."

"Oh," Callie blushes again. "Really, it's nothing. We're just friends," she insists.

"From my experience, Ramazi men don't have female friends," Pat picks up a towel and pins it to the clothesline. "I've seen the way you two look at each other— with enough sparks to start a fire. It's clear there's more than just friendship on both sides."

Callie's cheeks get hot— *are my feelings really that obvious? And is Pat right— does Abdullah have feelings for me? How can he? He's a local star— people utterly mobbed him after the dance the other night. And I'm a nobody who sticks out like a sore thumb here.* Callie sighs, holding a wet pillow case in her arms and glancing across the field towards Abdullah. "So I like him. He's attractive—"

"Very handsome," Pat nods appreciatively.

"—and kind. And hard working. And many other things…" Callie pauses.

"But?" Pat nudges.

"But…" Callie sighs, "I already have a boyfriend, Lucas. And Lucas is great. We probably have lots more in common than Abdullah and I do. It's just that Lucas feels really far away right now, and communication has been spotty since I've been in Georgia. And I've really enjoyed the time I've gotten to spend with Abdullah. This is a whole different world from the US, and he has opened it up to me."

"Long distance can be hard," Pat replies empathetically. "But you're right about Abdullah— his world is very different from yours. In fact, US culture and Ramazi culture are about as diametrically opposed as you can get. Trying to make a marriage work between the two cultures would be extremely challenging, to say the least." Pat lays a gentle hand on Callie's arm before pulling another piece of wet laundry from the basket.

"Woah, back up!" Callie puts up her hands. "No one is talking about marriage here! It's just a harmless summer crush, that's it. Seriously. It's not a big deal." Even as she says the words, Callie knows she isn't being entirely truthful.

"For you, maybe not," Pat concedes. "But I think Abdullah may feel differently. Men here don't get the chance to experience female friendship very often— the genders tend to stay pretty separated. And you are fun and beautiful and independent— things Abdullah has probably not rubbed shoulders with in a close way before. Just be careful, okay? You two are wonderful, and I've come to care for both of you. I just don't want either of you to get hurt," Pat gives Callie a quick squishy hug and smiles at her in a motherly way.

Callie nods at Pat, her voice lodged in her throat. When Pat walks away, Callie sinks into a nearby bench, processing. At first, she feels a wave of embarrassment and defensiveness. *It's not fair for her to judge me,* Callie thinks hotly. *I haven't done anything wrong.* But as Callie sits in the orchard, looking out towards the mountains, her anger dissipates and she gradually realizes that she is grateful that Pat cares enough to get involved, to talk with her about her heart. *I missed out on this,* Callie realizes. *This is the kind of conversation my mom and I could have had if she was still alive.* Callie quickly scrubs away a tear on her cheek as she, not for the first time, wonders how on earth she is supposed to navigate adulthood and relationships without her mom's guidance. It feels incredibly unfair.

CHAPTER 15
Khev, Georgia

March, 1992

Dina's first week passes in a mind-numbing blur of backbreaking work all day and nights in bed with Saidun that Dina tries her best to block from her memory. She has never been more physically and emotionally exhausted in her life— she feels like her body is on the verge of a breakdown and her soul is shriveling inside her. Saidun's mother, Khadijat, clearly detests her. She glares at Dina whenever she sees her, and is constantly commanding her to do chores in Ramazi. She then switches to Georgian, berating Dina for not understanding or obeying the first time. One evening, Dina tries to talk to Saidun about asking Khadijat to be kinder to her, but he quickly shakes his head vehemently, "That's between you and my mother! I would never get involved in women's issues!"

"But it's not just women's issues! I'm your *wife*! Don't you care how I'm treated??" Dina throws her arms in the air.

Saidun frowns, defensive, "My mother is a good person! I forbid you to say anything negative about her! You're just a woman— hush and be quiet. You need to learn your place. You aren't supposed to have an opinion on things anyway."

"Not supposed to have an opinion??!" Dina's voice raises and her cheeks get hot. "I'm a human being! I went to university! I was one of the students who attended protests for Georgian freedom the past few years in Tbilisi, picketing to break away from the Soviet Union. Remember when Soviet tanks ran over twenty people and killed them three years ago during the protests? I was *there* that day! I stood up for freedom! I have had a voice and will continue to have a voice! You said you wanted a wife with spunk— well, now you have one!" Dina is nearly shouting and she doesn't even care that Saidun's face is getting increasingly stormy.

"Well, I was clearly wrong!" Saidun walks toward her threateningly, puffing out his chest. Dina stands her ground for a moment and then backs up against the wall. "It's not good for women to think too much. A woman's place is in the home, cleaning and cooking and taking care of children. *Certainly* not getting involved with politics," Saidun laughs with disbelief, shaking his head. "Those days are over for you, and the sooner you forget they existed, the better off you will be. I am the head of this marriage, and you do what I say. No questions asked. And my mother is in charge of the women, so you also do what she says, no questions asked. I am sick and tired of her complaining to me about how useless you are."

"Useless?!" Dina screeches, fists clenched. "I have worked harder this past week than I have ever worked in my life!"

"Then you have had a soft life," Saidun snorts with derision. "You think you worked hard this week? Just wait 'til summer— you'll be so tired then, you will be able to sleep standing up! Ramazi life is hard, but it has made us strong," Saidun pounds his puffed-out chest. "Did you know that in 1848, two hundred Ramazi soldiers fought in the Zudi Pass against almost six thousand Russian soldiers, and we not only held the pass, but we sent them back to Russia with their tails between their legs!" Saidun boasts as proudly as if this ancient feat was something he himself had taken part in. Dina sinks to the chair in their room, her eyes glazing over as Saidun starts in on one of his nightly Ramazi history lessons. As Saidun rants, Dina allows her mind to wander back to those protests— she remembers how Nika went with her despite his peaceful nature and personal aversion to large crowds, how he had stood beside her, quiet and steady, as she and the other students shouted and waved their placards, and how he had rushed her away to safety the second things got dangerous, and then offered a shoulder to cry on when she fell apart later when the news came that twenty-one people had been killed, including one of their classmates. He had told her afterwards that he so admired her strength, her willingness to stand up and fight for what she believed in. *How different my life would have been with him instead of with Saidun,* Dina despairs. *How did I not see how wonderful he was when he was right in front of me?*

"Are you listening to me?" Saidun glares at Dina accusingly, and she hurriedly returns her attention to her husband.

***

Dina is startled in her dishwashing by the sound of a man clearing his throat behind her. Alone in the kitchen, she instinctively spins around in fear. *How long will I be so jittery?* she chides herself. She takes a calming breath when she sees that it is only Saidun's father Anzor standing awkwardly in the doorway, seemingly unable to step across the threshold into the women's world that is the kitchen. She has had almost no interaction with him so far, but at least he has not been downright hostile towards her like Saidun's mother.

Dina stands still, unsure of what to do or how to act. Every interaction feels like a field of landmines strewn with dangers that she can't see, unknown cultural cues and expectations and rules lying just below the surface. She fidgets with the ring on her finger as she watches him, waiting for him to make the first move. He's of medium height like Saidun, but lean and slender. Saidun clearly got his barrel chest and thick-set figure from Khadijat's side of the family.

Anzor runs a hand down his white beard, which contrasts with the still-dark hair on the top of his head. Dina is unsure how old he is — early 50s, maybe? He moves spryly, like a much younger man, but his skin is dark and leathery and wrinkled from years of working in the sun. Glancing around behind him, Anzor moves into the kitchen towards Dina. She stands frozen, unsure of what to do. Seeming to sense her fear, he extends a placating hand in her direction.

"Excuse me," he says politely, in Georgian, but with a surprisingly Russian accent. "Something came in the mail, and I believe it is for you." He pulls a small, plain envelope from the pocket of his wool jacket. Dina gives an inadvertent gasp when she recognizes her mother's handwriting on the outside of the envelope. She hungrily grabs the letter and clutches it to her chest.

"Thank you!" she whispers.

He nods, looking uncomfortable. There is a long pause and then he clears his throat, "Umm… it is probably best if you did not show my wife or son this letter. I don't know how your mother got our address, but there could be problems if my family finds out she is writing… my wife is still trying to figure out how best to deal with this difficult situation that our son has put us in."

The situation he has put YOU in, Dina thinks bitterly. *What about the situation he has put ME in? Your idiot son has ruined everything for everyone!*

But instead of speaking her mind, Dina nods politely and thanks Anzor again. As he exits the kitchen, Marta enters, raising her eyes in curiosity at her father's departing form. Dina quickly turns back to the dishes, tucking the letter into the pocket of her skirt. All afternoon it burns there, like a warm, fiery coal of hope, alive in her pocket. She can't wait to escape the kitchen and find a moment to read her mother's words, which she hopes will contain a plan for how to save her from this horrid mess and, somehow, a plan to do it in a way that doesn't put Dina's family at risk.

In the late afternoon, Dina catches a window of opportunity to read her letter. She pretends to be heading to the outhouse behind the main house, but just before she gets to the outhouse, she ducks to the left and hides behind a large tree. Though there is slushy snow at the base of the tree which seeps icily into her boots, she doesn't care— she knows that from this angle, no one can see her from the main house. Hurriedly, she tears open the envelope and pulls out a one-page letter in her mother's careful cursive penmanship.

My dearest Dina,

Praise the Lord that you are alive! I cannot tell you how relieved we all were to receive your letter. When you did not come home from college last Thursday, we feared the worst— that you had been kidnapped and maybe even killed. We went to the police, but they couldn't help us. Your grandfather even insisted on hobbling out of his sickbed to visit two morgues to see if they had had any bodies come in that matched your description. Thankfully, none did. And so we waited and prayed. And now God has answered our prayers! I am so grateful that you are at least safe and sound.

I'm sorry my daughter for your hardship. I know this was not how you were planning your life to go, and not how we were hoping your life would go either. We all tried so hard for many months to prevent this from happening, but now it has and we must deal with it. Often life throws us sharp turns, and we must steel ourselves to meet them as best we can. Broken dreams are hard to stomach, especially for someone who is a strong feeler like you are. I know something of what hardship is like— I did not expect your father to die and leave me with five children to raise, but he did and so I had to gather my strength and rise to meet the challenge.

Bride kidnapping is an honored tradition in Georgia, especially in the mountains. As you know, your great-grandfather kidnapped your great-grandmother and they ended up having a happy marriage. I know you are young and modern, and maybe things will change in the future, but for now, I am afraid that you are stuck where you are. We have been discussing it for days, trying to figure out if there is any way we could get you out of this situation. But I'm afraid if we were to try to come and get you, it would likely make your situation even worse. Your new husband probably would not let you go, and even if he did, your honor would be so ruined that no man would marry you in the future (I am sure that by the time you receive this letter, you will already be married). And so I think you must try to make the best of it. Be a helpful, loving wife. Serve your husband as best you can. Try to learn their culture and language. Hopefully, with time you will grow to love him. Grandfather and I will pray that you will be blessed with children. Children can make even the unhappiest of marriages seem worth it. As you remember, your father (God rest his soul) was not a perfect man and was often hard to live with, especially when he drank too much. But thanks to him, I have the five of you, who are the biggest blessings I could ever have asked for.

Dina, you have always been strong. Remember when you were only ten but you beat up that 12-year-old bully Irakli for picking on Sofi? You were strong physically, but also had strength of character and will. I believe that will serve you well in this new role. Try to adjust to this new life, but never forget, inside, who you are and where you came from.

I love you with all of my heart. Grandfather sends his greetings and says you are in his prayers every day. Sofi, Dato, Giorgi, and Mariam miss you every day and are relieved that you are safe. Nika is heartbroken. I ask you, for both your sakes, to please not try to contact him. I'm afraid he would do something foolish that could get you both hurt or killed.

Love always,

Mother

P.S. I don't know what Ramazi rules and traditions are, but if they will allow you to come home to visit sometime, we would all very much like that. Please continue to write to us.

Dina clutches the letter in her hand and slowly slides down the trunk of the tree she had been hiding behind for privacy. Muddy spring snow soaks her skirts and she doesn't even care. Tears come, hot and fast and unwanted. "No!" Dina whisper-shouts in frustration and anguish under her breath. How could her mother do this to her? Her life is so miserable. She had been counting on her mother and grandfather to come swooping in to rescue her the second they found out where she was. But instead of rescuing her, they were going to leave her in misery, with the worthless words to "be strong". How could they do this to her??

A wave of hopelessness washes over Dina and she gives in to the feeling and weeps into her skirt. Her life, as she knows it, is over. There will be no rescue.

"Dina!" Khadijat's stern voice shouts across the courtyard. Everything in Dina wants to ignore it, but she knows she would pay dearly for it later. It's not worth it. So Dina stands, dries her tears, tucks the letter into the bodice of her long dress, and heads back to the courtyard.

"Where have you been, you worthless girl!" Khadijat shouts at Dina, throwing her arms in the air in frustration. "No Ramazi girl would be lazy like you, always shirking chores, always forcing me to have to come find you!"

Dina looks at the ground mutely, knowing that saying anything or defending herself is pointless. Khadijat gives a huff and heads back to the kitchen, Dina following obediently behind.

***

For days it drizzles unending cold rain. Dina puts on thick stockings and wears multiple layers, including her winter coat, everywhere she goes, but she is still cold (except for in the kitchen, where the fire blazes to a heat that leaves sweat running down her face and back). The rest of the family seems impervious to both the heat and the cold. Hava tells her that they're just used to it.

White fog rolls in over the mountains and covers them completely. Dina realizes with surprise that she misses being able to see them— glancing up at them throughout her day has become a bit of solace and stability in an otherwise unpredictable and unhappy existence.

Saidun is more irritable and gruff than usual— he is frustrated that the bad weather is delaying the hunting trip that he has been planning into the mountains with his friends. Dina can't decide whether to be relieved that he is leaving or horrified that she's being left home with his mother. She decides that it is perfectly acceptable for her to be both.

One morning, Dina wakes up to find Saidun's side of the bed empty— as usual, he has gotten up before her. In Tbilisi, she loved to sleep in lazily on the weekends when she didn't have class. In Khev, she doesn't have that luxury— the rest of the family is up before dawn every day, and Khadijat reprimands her anytime she dares to sleep past seven o'clock. Judging by the sun outside the window, she's verging on being late, and earning herself another lecture. Dina reluctantly gets out of bed, bracing herself for the rush of cold air.

She is quickly dressing in the dim light of the room when she is surprised by a light rap on her door. When she opens it, she's almost blinded by a flood of sunlight streaming into the room.

"Spring has come!" Hava smiles excitedly outside her door, "And we got Mother's permission for you to spend the day helping us in the garden! Grab a quick breakfast and meet us out back."

When Dina gets to the back garden, Hava and Marta are already kneeling in the freshly tilled soil. The soil is deep brown, almost black, and looks damp. Dina grins when she sees the sisters— both have been warm and welcoming to her in the small pockets of time when they've been able to interact without the hovering presence of their stern mother.

"The men tilled it yesterday so that they can go hunting today and tomorrow while we plant!" Hava explains, waving Dina over.

"Two days of men-less peace!" Marta thrusts a fist in the air and grins.

"Hooray!" Hava agrees.

"Ha, that's what you say, but we all know you're going to be pining away for Isa while the guys are gone!" Marta snorts, "We've all seen the way you look at him! 'Oh Isa,'" Marta speaks in a syrupy imitation of Hava, placing her hands demurely under her chin and fluttering her eyelashes, "'Oh Isa, you're so strong and manly and I'm just a delicate girl— could you please carry this bucket of water for me?'"

Hava blushes beet red, picks up a clod of dirt, and throws it straight at Marta's face. "Hey!" Marta exclaims, startled— she was not expecting her gentle diminutive sister to retaliate.

"Hush before someone overhears you," Hava insists, "And come on, we need to get working." She turns to Dina and rolls her eyes, "Ignore Marta. We invited you out here because spring planting is one of our favorite days."

"Mostly because we get to do it alone, without adult oversight," Marta grins. "Took us almost 19 years, but Mother finally trusts us to push a seed under a bit of dirt," Marta rolls her eyes and nudges Dina's shoulder. Dina smiles back.

"Have you ever planted a garden?" Hava asks.

"Actually, no," Dina admits. "I grew up right in downtown Tbilisi. I was surrounded by pretty much nothing but solid concrete. I had a few potted plants in my room, but I don't think that counts."

"Don't worry, we will teach you!" Marta tucks her long black hair further under her headscarf and pulls out a basket filled with dozens of containers of seeds. Then she hands Dina a piece of paper, "This is our map, where we've drawn out the plan for the garden." Dina is slightly overwhelmed by the variety of things they will be planting— carrots, tomatoes, peppers, beets, cabbage, squash, pumpkins, onions, eggplant, zucchini, strawberries, dill, basil… the list goes on. She notices a surprising omission, "What about potatoes?"

"Oh, this garden doesn't have nearly enough room for potatoes! The whole town has a giant communal potato plot that we use commercial equipment to farm. The men are in charge of the potatoes. We do everything else."

"Leave it to the men to take care of one thing while the women take care of thirty-five things," Marta rolls her eyes, expertly sorting through seed packets as they talk.

"Marta," Hava reprimands. "They're on their way to hunt now. You know that's also important work."

156

"Work!?" Marta snorts, handing Hava a packet of small, dark seeds, "Have you seen how they carry on and cavort about their hunting trips?? I guarantee you there is more drinking than working going on on those trips! Imagine what it would be like if we could take trips with our friends," Marta sighs wistfully.

"I went to the beach in Batumi last summer with three of my closest girlfriends," Dina shares.

"Really?!" Hava and Marta's eyes are wide. "With no men?? And no adults?"

"Yup, just us girls," Dina grins. "It was a blast. We rode the train there, stayed at a hotel on the beach, laid out and sunbathed during the day. I got burnt to a crisp my second day, which I do not recommend! And then in the evenings we would get popcorn and ice cream from street vendors and explore the town after dark. One night we even saw the moon rise over the ocean!"

"That sounds magical!" Marta sighs. "We will never get to do anything like that."

"I'm sorry," Dina feels tears well in her eyes, grieving both for Marta and Hava and the restricted lives they live as well as for herself, because she realizes with sinking despair that she will never be able to do anything like that ever again.

"It's fine," Marta shrugs, "We make our own fun! Just wait 'til canning day— that's a blast!" She rolls her eyes sarcastically and even Hava laughs, "Ugh, canning day is the worst! Sterilizing so many jars in hot water, stirring giant vats of stewed peppers all day. Basically a whole day of sweating!"

"Sounds terrible! I helped my mom can a couple of times in the city, but mostly she was so busy at work that we just got canned goods from our relatives who live outside of Tbilisi," Dina admits.

"Lucky you!" Marta makes no attempt to hide the jealousy in her voice. "Okay, enough chit-chat! For some of the things on our map, you can plant the seeds directly into the dirt— like cucumbers, carrots, radishes, pumpkins, squash, etcetera. Others, like tomatoes, are a lot more likely to succeed if you first plant them in tiny containers indoors where they can be warm, and then transplant them outside once it's a bit warmer. So this morning we will work on the things that can go directly into the dirt, and then this afternoon we will plant seedlings in pots inside."

"This year," Hava interjected excitedly, "Mother has agreed to let us have a small corner of the garden for planting flowers."

"She of course thinks they're a waste of space and time and energy. Why would you want to have something whose only purpose is beauty??" Marta raises her thick eyebrows wryly, nudging Dina.

"I'm planning to plant sunflowers, mums, gladiolas, and foxcomb. The gladiolas will bloom in the spring, the sunflowers in the summer, and the mums and foxcomb in the fall. Have you noticed the garden four houses up?" Hava asks, expertly digging three-inch deep holes three inches apart, and dropping a cucumber seed into each before gently covering them up. Dina attempts to copy, but her attempts are slow and sloppy. *I hope that doesn't affect how they grow. All I need is for Khadijat to be able to blame me when there aren't enough veggies this summer.*

"I haven't noticed any neighborhood flowers," Dina says, "I haven't been out much, and I've honestly been kind of focused on my own problems."

Hava places a slender hand on Dina's arm and nods sympathetically, "We know it's been hard for you here."

"I just don't understand why your mother hates me so much," Dina says quietly. "I mean, I know that I wasn't her first choice as a wife for Saidun. But it's not like it's my fault," Dina rolls her eyes. "So why does she blame me?"

The sisters glance at each other, and Hava replies, "It's not that she hates you. It's all just very, very complicated. Before you and Saidun married, Mother had tentatively arranged for Saidun to marry the daughter of one of the wealthiest, most influential families in the village."

"It would've been a real winner of a match-up, very beneficial for both families," Marta nods. "But Saidun wanted nothing of it— said the bride was too fat and that her nose was too big," Marta snorts, digging holes so expertly that she doesn't even have to look at what she's doing. "Men!"

"When Saidun first brought you home," Hava continues, "Mother was furious. She almost invoked *kharam*," she says with eyebrows raised in legitimate horror.

"*Kharam*?" Dina frowns, confused.

"Tsssssck!" Marta slashes her finger across her throat.

"Marta, you're no help," Hava chides. "But basically, she's right. Mother threatened to cut him off. If she had invoked *kharam*, it would have meant he was dead to our family. We never would have been able to speak to or about him again."

"People really do that?" Dina raises her eyebrows, unable to imagine a parent cutting ties with their child.

"It's rare, but it happens," Hava sighs.

"Lucky for Saidun, he's the only son," Marta snorts. "So Mother couldn't cut him off! If she had, then she and Father would have had no heir! No son to take care of them in their old age, no one to pass the family name down to, no one to give them grandchildren."

"Uncle eventually convinced her that the deed had already been done and that the quickest way to still the rumor mill was to get you guys married right away. And so she and Father acquiesced. But they've been paying for it ever since."

"Obviously, since I'm such a terrible daughter-in-law," Dina spits out defensively.

"Relax, sister!" Marta laughs and lays a calming hand on Dina's arm. "She didn't mean that at all. She meant that our parents have been paying for it with the neighbors— half the village sided with the other family, the one who feels their daughter got unfairly shunted. And so now half of Mother's friends won't talk to her. Some have been really mean."

Dina nods slowly, beginning to understand all the layers of complexity in the situation. It had been so easy to live inside her internal pity party that she'd had barely a thought for how the marriage might be affecting the extended family.

"What about you two," she asks the sisters, concerned. "Has it affected you guys?"

"Well, we've gotten a wonderful new sister-in-law," Hava smiles warmly.

"And anyway, we don't need those snakes who stopped talking to us," Marta waves a hand in the air. "Our closest friends have stuck by us."

"I'm glad," Dina says, relieved.

"There are good people here," Hava insists, eyes intent. "I know you have had a rough first season, but you'll get used to it, really you will. We will introduce you to some of our friends— I'm sure you'll like them. And you've got to get to know our great-aunts, our grandfather's six sisters. They all play the harmonica and the accordion and are hilarious when they're together! And there are some wonderful things about living in Khev. I mean, just look around at all this beauty! Eden couldn't have been more beautiful than this," Hava sighs, panning out her arm to encompass the orchard right behind them—the tiny, pink-white buds just beginning to open on the cherry trees, the blue sky above them, the green mountains all around them.

Dina nods slowly, "It's beautiful—you're right. And I will try to appreciate it more."

Hava's dark eyes blaze as if trying to send some secret message, "It helps. It can be a saving grace."

"Humph, I should've known you three would've done next to nothing by now," Khadijat's voice over their shoulders startles all three girls. "Dina, you're useless here. Your rows look like they were dug by a blind troll. Get to the kitchen and do the breakfast dishes instead. Hava and Marta can finish this— hopefully quicker without you holding them back and distracting them."

The sisters pass regretful glances before mutely getting back to work.

Dina reluctantly stands and heads towards the kitchen.

"What do you think you're doing?" Khadijat shouts after her, "You will destroy the kitchen covered in mud like you are! Do you have no common sense? Change your clothes and clean off and *then* do the dishes. Idiot girl, do I have to tell you everything??"

Dina stiffens her back and walks towards her room to change, not saying anything.

***

One evening, Dina is in the dining room all alone. The women of the family are in the kitchen cleaning up from dinner, and Khadijat has sent Dina to dust the shelves and the good china that the family rarely uses. Dina savors the solitude, for once grateful for Khadijat's obsessive cleanliness. *If only I could have actual silence, without the unintelligible droning from the radio,* Dina thinks. As she dusts around the base of the radio, her fingers suddenly dart towards the dial. Glancing furtively around to make sure that no one is coming, she gives the dial a quick spin to 91.5, her favorite Georgian radio station.

Through crackly static, Dina is shocked to hear the familiar voice of her favorite evening DJ, "—and coming up, we have our top 7 at 7:00! #1 on our charts tonight, making waves all around the world, we have *I Will Always Love You* by Whitney Houston!"

Dina quickly lowers the volume on the radio as Whitney Houston's powerful voice croons through the speakers. As the second verse begins, Dina sinks to the floor, huddled up against the side of the shelf. She closes her eyes and sings under her breath as tears leak down her cheeks.

"......*Bittersweet memories*
That is all I'm taking with me
So goodbye, please don't cry
We both know I'm not what you, you need
And I, I
Will always love you, ooh, I
Will always love you, you
I hope life treats you kind
And I hope you have all you've dreamed of
And I'm wishing you joy and happiness
But above all this, I wish you love

After the Whitney song, an upbeat, poppy tune plays next. Something American, which must be brand new because Dina doesn't recognize it. She quickly scrabbles behind her and turns the radio entirely off. In the silence, her shoulders shake with sobs. How is it possible that she is close enough to home for her favorite radio station to reach her, but also so far that she might as well be in a different world? And a world that she hates vehemently.

The last stanza of Houston's song twists in her gut— Houston hoping for life to treat her listener kindly, that they'd have all they dreamed of, including joy and happiness and love. *I will never have any of those things now,* Dina thinks bitterly. *My whole life is ruined,* she tucks her knees up and cries into her skirt, not even caring about the streams of snot pouring from her nose as she weeps. After a while, she gathers herself, eternally grateful that no family member entered the dining room while she was crying. She picks the dusting rag up and starts on the china, moving her hands in careful precision around the delicate pieces. Before she leaves the room, she turns the radio back on to the Ramazi station. She promises herself that she won't turn it on to the Georgian station again— it is too painful.

***

Saidun returns from the hunt in the best mood Dina has seen him in. The men managed to shoot three deer, which will provide their families with much-needed meat. Saidun rarely talks with Dina— normally she is working with the women and he is working with the men. And since men and women do not eat together, she rarely interacts with him outside of their room, which she is deeply grateful for.

But this evening, glowing from the hunt, Saidun throws himself down in the chair in their bedroom as Dina is mutely unpacking his bag.

"The hunt was amazing! The second evening, towards sundown, we even saw a bear! Maga didn't believe me at first when I told him I saw it, but once I got everyone to quiet down, I pointed it out to them through the thicket and they all saw it. It was huge! Biggest bear I've ever seen in the mountains!" Saidun jumps up animatedly and throws his thick arms high in the air to show the size of the bear.

His dark eyes are alight as he continues his tale, "You have to be careful, of course, when you see a bear. Never know what it could do. They're super dangerous, after all. You've seen Salid Magamed down the street, with the limp?" Dina nods— she'd seen the old man out and about with his cane. "Got it from a bear attack!" Saidun announces. "I wasn't afraid though," Saidun puffs out his barrel-like, muscular chest. "I just pulled my rifle up, set my eye to the scope and drew a good bead on the bear. I would've killed it too, had the idiot Maga not sneezed and startled the bear! It turned and fled through the forest, but not before I landed a bullet in its side. We tracked it by the blood trail, but it got dark before we found it and we had to stop," Saidun says with regret. "Can you picture how great a giant bearskin rug would've looked in the dining room?"

Dina wrinkles her nose— she is not a fan of decorating with animal skins. Plus, she feels distinctly sorry for the wounded bear.

Saidun notices her face, and sighs, "I'm not happy about how it ended, either. I wish I had killed it instead of leaving it in pain. It's not good to leave an animal in pain." Dina is surprised to see real regret and compassion in his dark eyes. *How can he feel compassion for a bear's pain, but thinks nothing of the pain he causes me?* she wonders in amazement.

"Make sure you get every bit of dirt out of those pants," Saidun instructs, pointing to the mud-encrusted clump in Dina's arms. "If you can't handle it, give it to my mom. She's a professional at laundry," Saidun leans back against his propped up pillow and stretches his socked feet across the bed.

***

Dina clears the mens' dishes from the lunch table, gathering empty soup bowls and plates greasy with remnants of lamb, polenta, and stewed vegetables. As usual, multiple neighbors and relatives have joined Saidun and Anzor for lunch. Almost every meal, Dina and the women are cooking for at least ten men. *Do they never eat at their own homes?* Dina wonders, annoyed. The women, however, never complain. They seem to see it as an honor that so many guests come to their home. As Dina clears the dishes, she keeps her gaze down at the ground, walking as silently and unobtrusively as possible. For their part, the men either pretend not to notice her, or truly do not notice her. She tunes out their conversation— it's in Ramazi like usual, so she doesn't understand it anyway.

Her ears automatically perk up when Saidun unexpectedly switches to Georgian. "Women are like horses," he explains expansively, clearly continuing the conversation the men had been having before Dina entered the room. All the men nod in agreement, as if this is a theory they are well familiar with.

"Some women come to you docile and obedient— easy to train." Saidun continues.

"And easy to ride!" one of the neighbors pipes up, earning him loud laughter from some of the men around the table and a disapproving frown from Anzor, which quickly stifles the merriment.

"And other women," Saidun continues, "come to you wild and obstinate, like a feral horse." Dina freezes in the back of the room, flushing as she feels the eyes of a couple of the men flicker her way.

"But fortunately," Saidun laughs, "I am an expert horseman! I have yet to meet a horse I could not train!" The men nod in agreement — Saidun is well known in Khev for being one of the best horsemen in town. Many a neighbor has called on him to break a horse for them.

"The key to breaking a horse (or a woman!) is to be strong and firm. They have to know without a doubt that you, and only you, are in charge! You have to break every last bit of their will, until all desire to stand up to you is gone from them. Then, once they're broken, you can build them back up to be tame and obedient."

Dina feels a combination of fury and fear stir in her chest— *how dare he compare me to a horse?? Is this what he's been trying to do this whole time — break my will?* She shivers and darts a glance at him and realizes that he is looking pointedly at her and the whole room is frozen in awkward silence. Dina looks around at the men— half of them have the decency to look uncomfortable. The other half look like they agree with Saidun.

Dina straightens her back, "Some horses can never be broken," she says with reckless fury, before rushing out of the room.

"That's what she thinks!" Saidun shouts, and the sound of laughter follows Dina as she slams the door behind her.

***

Dina runs into the kitchen, her arms full of dishes and her heart beating fast. She knows she will pay for her insolence. All day, she finds excuse after excuse to not leave the relative safety of the kitchen with the other women. Before dinner, she asks Hava in a whisper if Hava can serve the food to the men while Dina stays in the kitchen and works on dishes. Hava raises her eyebrows in questioning concern, but Dina just mutely shakes her head. After a moment, Hava nods and gently takes the pot of soup from Dina's arms, "Of course, anything you need." She serves the dinner to the men and clears the dishes and asks no questions.

Normally Dina is anxious to finish cleaning the kitchen after dinner while Saidun hangs out with the other men so that she can escape to her room for what is often the few minutes of solitude and downtime that Dina gets in the long, grueling work days. But tonight, she takes her time and lingers over the cleaning. She even gets a rag and attacks the baseboards (which, with Khadijat's standards of cleanliness, are actually quite clean already). Finally, when it is so late that Dina hopes against hope that Saidun might already be asleep, she uses the outhouse and then creeps quietly into their room.

Saidun is sitting in the chair in the corner, one low candle burning on the dresser as the electricity is off in the town for the evening as usual. Dina keeps her eyes on the floor and walks softly to her side of the bed. She keeps her back to Saidun and quickly undoes her headscarf. She is unbuttoning her cardigan when a tight fist closes around her upper arm and Saidun spins her around.

"Look at me!" he hisses at her furiously, and she trembles as she raises her eyes to his. The hatred she sees there makes panic rise in her throat. *What is he going to do to me?*

"Do not *ever* talk back to me again! Do you understand?!" Saidun keeps his grip on Dina's arm with one hand, and with the other he slaps her hard across the face. She cries out with pain and shock as her head whips to the side.

Saidun grabs a handful of her hair, twists it in his fist, and yanks her close. He bends his face right against hers and she can feel his hot breath. Her stomach twists at the stench of garlic and onion emanating from his mouth.

"You shamed me today and that will never happen again. You will pay for it tonight in a way that you will never forget." Saidun pushes Dina down onto the bed. *Don't struggle,* she tells herself, closing her eyes. *Pretend you're not here. Pretend you're somewhere else. The sooner you give in, the sooner this will be over.* She can feel Saidun's weight on top of her and she turns her head to the side as he pushes his mouth against her ear and whispers harshly, "I *will* break you, you feral filly."

CHAPTER 16
Sureti Valley, Georgia

July, 2018

By the time they're two hours into their horseback riding trip, Callie's inner thighs are burning and her lower back is complaining insistently. The scenery around her is stunning, but she has a hard time focusing on anything but her physical complaints. *Come on, suck it up— you were the one who wanted to come,* Callie reminds herself.

A few days before, Leila had mentioned an upcoming three-day horseback trip that a young couple wanted to do, "Locals have been riding through these mountains for generations, but very few foreigners have ever seen the incredible beauty that is accessible by horseback only a few days from here— beautiful woods, turquoise mountain lakes, thundering waterfalls, and fields of wildflowers. I'm wanting to expand to offering horseback tours as an option for our guests. This couple is coming from Russia on their honeymoon and has asked that we help organize a guided horse tour for them. I was thinking that maybe you could go as the photographer and get good material for your social media accounts."

"Oooh, I would love to!" Callie had responded excitedly, clapping her hands.

"Abdullah will go as your guide. Do you have any experience with horses?"

"Ugh, not nearly as much as I wish I had! I rode a few times as a kid. I even took riding lessons for a couple months— in fifth grade, maybe? But it's been a very long time," Callie had grimaced.

"It's not a problem— we will give you Bunny, our most docile horse. And it will be good for Abdullah to have guiding experience with a guest who is not good with horses."

Callie had nodded, so excited at the idea of a three-day horseback trip to explore the mountains that she had decided to let the slight insult roll off of her. She had been sure that she would be fine on a horse— she was in good shape, after all.

But now Callie is beginning to regret her earlier confidence. No matter which way she shifts, she can't get comfortable. Despite the horse moving at a slow, steady pace, Callie feels like she is constantly at risk of falling off. She doesn't remember horseback riding being so awkward when she was a kid. *Maybe this saddle isn't a good one? It certainly isn't ergonomic.* She holds onto the pommel with white-knuckles on both hands at all times, except for the brief moments when anyone glances her way and then she gives a hearty (fake) smile and lets go quickly for a thumbs up.

The Russian honeymooners speak very little English, so Callie isn't able to communicate much with them. Which doesn't seem to matter to them, because they're mostly focused on staring sappily into each other's eyes, whispering softly to each other, or attempting to hold hands while riding horseback. Callie can't decide whether to be annoyed or jealous, so she decides to be both. In their defense, both Oleg and Nastya seem very nice and do their best to use their limited English to make small talk with Callie when they stop for meals. They also seem much more comfortable on horseback than she is.

In spite of her initial unease on the horse, which does lessen the longer they ride, Callie's still able to take in the views around her. The scenery for the first few hours of the morning is beautiful— for the most part they follow a shallow meandering brook that looks to be about as wide as a two-lane road. The brook runs through a small ravine that is only a couple of feet deep. On either side of the brook lies a stretch of green grass, bordered by homes and gardens on the east and by trees and then low mountains to the west. The grass and leaves are both that lush, vibrant green that only appears in late spring and stays through early summer. A breeze blows, crisp and clean. Occasionally, Callie catches a scent of freshly mown grass. At one point she notices an acrid smell and a stream of black smoke billowing from someone's backyard. She points it out to Abdullah in concern. He laughs and assures her that it's no big deal— it's only locals burning leaves or trash.

The sounds of the first few hours contribute to the sense of peace and tranquility Callie feels— the gentle bubbling of the brook, the soft murmurs of Oleg and Nastya as they talk quietly beside each other, and the occasional trill of birdsong. Overall, it is truly idyllic. Callie hadn't even realized that she'd been feeling cooped up at Leila's until now, when she feels incredibly enlivened by the sense of freedom and wide open space. *If only I could figure out how to get comfortable on this dang horse,* she thinks with frustration, glaring at her stupid saddle. She glances over at Oleg and Nastya, who seemed so engrossed in each other that they don't even seem to notice they are *on* horses, to Abdullah, who moves with such grace that he looks like he is actually *part* of the horse. *Like some sort of Ramazi centaur,* Callie laughs to herself.

For most of the morning Abdullah rides up front, Nastya and Oleg ride in the middle, and Callie brings up the rear. Once they leave the village, they enter a forest of deciduous trees. They ride through the forest for over an hour, which Callie starts to find monotonous, but then the trail begins an uphill climb that eventually opens up onto a wide plateau. Callie's horse follows the others out onto the plateau and Callie sucks in her breath at the incredible beauty all around her. On every side, green hills rise to meet darker green mountains that stretch beyond them as far as the eye can see. Callie sits in appreciative silence, the wind whipping her hair about her face. She glances over at Oleg and Nastya, who are taking grinning selfies.

"What do you think?" Callie doesn't notice Abdullah ride quietly up beside her until her horse turns towards his.

"It's stunning— really. The mountains are beautiful. And I can't remember the last time I was in a place where there wasn't a single sign of human habitation."

Abdullah nods in agreement, "I love coming up here— it's probably my favorite place on earth. Not that I've been to many others to compare it to," he grins at Callie. "But I'm always glad when tourists book a horse trip because it means I get to get up into the mountains."

"Have you done many horse trips for tourists?"

"Only a couple, unfortunately." Abdullah shakes his head, looking out admiringly over the expanse of mountains.

"Well, hopefully that will change after this trip! I'm gonna make it so appealing on Instagram that you will have guests banging down your door to do a personally guided horse tour through the mountains!" Callie laughs, her left cheek dimpling.

"We'll see about that," Abdullah smiles, but Callie can hear doubt in his voice.

"You don't believe me, do you? Come on, we're up to over five hundred subscribers in only a couple of weeks!" Callie prods him.

Abdullah looks embarrassed, "No, no, it's not that. I'm sure you are right— I believe you can do anything you put your mind to. I am just not much of an internet and social media man myself. More of an out-in-nature man."

Callie nods, "That's probably a much healthier kind of person to be anyway."

***

At 1:00 p.m. they stop for a picnic lunch from Leila, and Callie is relieved to rest her back and legs. *Who knew that riding a horse could be so much work? Movies and TV always make it look so simple and convenient! I hope I get used to it quickly or I'm gonna be hobbling around like an idiot.*

Callie is impressed with the packed picnic— it's baked chicken breasts, the ever-present *khachapuri* cheesy bread, pickles, sliced tomatoes and cucumbers, and fresh plums. Overall, much healthier than the usual American picnic fare of sandwiches and chips! Callie thinks back to family picnics as a kid— every October, her family would head to the mountains a couple of times. Sometimes to camp, sometimes just for day trips. Callie's parents loved to see the trees in autumn. As a kid, Callie didn't appreciate nature very much. But she did like that it was the one time of the year when her parents would let them get slurpees at the 7-Eleven off Exit 100 in southern Virginia, and they would drink them as they rode along the Blue Ridge Parkway, turning their mouths blue and filling their stomachs so full that they rarely had room for the PB & Js that Callie's mom had packed them for lunch.

In some ways, the views from the spot where they'd stopped for lunch reminds Callie of the scenic overlooks they would stop at on the Blue Ridge Parkway— in both places, rolling hills lead to mountains that stretch as far as the eye can see. Only this time Callie doesn't have her parents or her siblings with her. Callie glances over to see Abdullah engaged in conversation in Russian with Oleg and Nastya. From what Callie can see, it seems like his Russian is as good as his English. *And his Ramazi and his Georgian!* Callie feels a rush of stupidity for only speaking one language.

As she watches Oleg and Nastya talk animatedly with Abdullah, their fingers intertwined, she feels a wave of loneliness and homesickness. *I miss my dad,* she realizes. *And the way he would make corny jokes to keep us distracted and help us not complain on hikes. And I miss Mom— how she was always the last one in hiking order because she would walk slowly so as not to miss an opportunity to notice some small detail, like a brightly colored salamander or a delicate leaf. I even miss Nathan and June. I really need to call them to catch up. Though the internet connection here is terrible. Maybe I should email them. June probably won't respond, but I bet Nate will. And Dad certainly would. I need to write him too.* Callie feels a soft pang of guilt for not being in better touch with her dad. It is so easy for her to get distracted with her own life, especially in San Francisco where she is always rushing from one activity to another.

I can't remember the last time I've had so much time to just be out in nature, away from noise and people and technology, Callie realizes, basking in the fresh air and the mountains all around her. She finishes her chicken and wraps up her trash so that they can pack it out with them. Callie is glad that Abdullah is insistent about not littering and doing their part to keep the trail clean.

"Tea?" Abdullah hands a thermos to Callie which she gratefully accepts. *Only Georgians would bring a thermos of hot tea with them on a horseback riding trip,* she thinks, cheek dimpling. The herbal tea, made with mint from Leila's garden, is still hot and is sweetened with honey. Callie wraps her hands around the thermos, appreciating its warmth.

"Are your hands cold?" Abdullah asks with concern.

"Not bad, though it is chillier than I expected."

"It will get really cold at night," Abdullah warns. "But our sleeping bags should be thick enough to keep you warm."

***

Though Callie's butt and thighs and back complain distractingly throughout the afternoon, her eyes still manage to soak in one incredible view after another. She also makes sure to take plenty of pictures of everything she sees so that she can update the website and Instagram. They make their way through the rolling hills and by late afternoon, they have ascended up to the top of a high ridge. Abdullah instructs them to tie their horses up in a stand of trees, and they walk together over to the edge of the ridge. Everyone stands in reverent silence at the view in front of them— in the distance, they can see a jut of snow-capped mountains thrusting up in fierce majesty. Closer, jagged peaks of tree-covered mountains rise in front of them. The wind whips Callie's hair so intensely that she has to hold it out of her eyes so that she can see. The roar of the wind is so loud that it reminds Callie of standing next to plane propellers. Abdullah points to the far east, yelling over the noise that the village they can just make out in the distance will be their destination on the evening of Day 3. It seems impossibly far away, but Callie reminds herself that horses can cover a lot of ground in two days. A gust jerks at Callie's turquoise North Face jacket and she takes a quick nervous step back from the edge of the cliff, which is a sheer drop off with hundreds of feet to the ground below.

Before sunset, they arrive in a small glen that is thankfully protected from the wind by the trees that surround it. Abdullah directs Callie and the Russian couple to look for firewood while he expertly sets up three tents— one for Callie, one for himself, and one for the newlyweds. Callie can't remember the last time she collected firewood; it's been multiple years for sure. She enjoys the slow process of rifling through last fall's blanket of crinkled brown leaves, hunting for tiny sticks. Once Abdullah gets a good fire going, they heat up dinner from Leila and then eat around the fire in tired silence. Callie also can't remember the last time she was so exhausted or sore. *Today was a better workout than any HIIT class I've done at home,* she thinks, *and I barely even did anything! The horse did most of the work! Though my thighs and back definitely don't agree,* she grimaces, reaching a hand behind her to try to massage her aching lower back. She glances over with a mixture of appreciation and dislike at Bunny, who is quietly munching grass next to the other horses. Abdullah hops up from the fire to rub each horse down and get them water.

By the time they finish dinner the sky is darkening and the first twilight stars are starting to appear. Oleg and Nastya wave quick goodbyes and head to their tent. Callie is tired, but she's enjoying the warmth of the dying fire and the glowing embers too much to move. Plus, her aching muscles have no desire to stand up. She scoots closer to the fire and holds her hands out, turning them frontwards and backwards to get them evenly heated over the coals.

"Can I join you?" Abdullah crouches across from her, and Callie nods, feeling slightly guilty as she remembers her conversation with Pat. She will need to be careful— firelight under the stars is just the kind of situation where she would be prone to get herself in trouble. Abdullah holds out his hands over the fire beside hers.

"How was the day for you?" he asks, seeming sincerely interested.

"It was good. The views were amazing! I think I got some nice pictures. Though I'm definitely going to be sore tomorrow!" Callie smiles wryly, "It's been quite some time since I was on a horse!"

Abdullah picks up a stick and pokes the fire, "You did a great job. Some people are really skittish around horses. I think Bunny could tell that you were confident and comfortable."

Confident and comfortable! Callie laughs internally. *I must have been putting on a better show than I realized because I definitely was not either of those things. More like unsure and uncomfortable!*

"And how has it been for you being here in Sureti this summer?" Abdullah's eyes are warm as he watches her from across the fire.

"It's been... different than I expected I think. I thought it would be more like a job. I didn't realize how much of a family atmosphere you guys would have here. After years of living away from family, it's been nice to be back in a family. You and your mom and your sister seem to be really close."

"We are close. We kind of had to get that way after my dad died." Abdullah shrugs.

"Oh, I'm really sorry," Callie reaches out a hand instinctively and lays it on top of Abdullah's. Abdullah freezes, looking distinctly uncomfortable. *Gosh I'm such an idiot! I forgot men and women don't touch here!* Callie realizes her mistake, and quickly removes her hand. "I had wondered what happened to your dad, but I didn't want to ask."

"I don't really know the details of his death," Abdullah shrugs his shoulders. "Mom said it was high blood pressure, maybe a stroke? She doesn't like to talk about it— I think it makes her too sad. And my dad's family was pretty unusual— in most Ramazi families, as you know, all the relatives live close together, in sort of a clan set-up. But my Dad didn't have any brothers, and his two sisters married and moved away, one all the way to Norway. So normally I would have aunts and uncles around to ask about stuff, but I don't."

"That must be really hard," Callie says sympathetically.

"It's ok— he died when I was really little. I don't even remember him. Fariza thinks she has a couple of vague memories of him, but she was only a toddler, and I was not even a year old. So it's hard to miss something you never had," Abdullah leans forward, and pokes the embers with a stick. "Plus, I always had my grandfather nearby."

"Still, I'm sorry you didn't know your dad. I'm sure he would've been really proud of the man you are."

Abdullah's eyes dart up from the fire and catch Callie's. She realizes that her offhand remark had struck a deeper chord with him than she intended.

"Really," she continues, locking eyes with him, "You're a very good man. You are hard-working and responsible. You care for your mom and sister very well— you clearly really value family, and you're incredibly hospitable to the people who come to the guesthouse."

Abdullah laughs, trying to make light of her comment, "Hard-working, devoted to family, and hospitable— you just described every single Ramazi in existence!"

Callie laughs, "Actually, I think you're right! Every single Ramazi I've met has those character qualities! But not every one is as great as you. Just take the compliment," Callie grins at him, and after a moment, his eyes sparkle golden in the firelight and he grins back. "Ok, compliment accepted. Thank you."

"Seriously," Callie adds, unable to stop herself, "You're an Excel wizard, brilliant at languages, an amazing woodworker, an expert fire builder, and a horse whisperer. *And* you're building me a bathroom! I basically will eternally owe you! And you can't say *that* about every single Ramazi out there!"

"Ok, fine," Abdullah grins, and switches from the squat he'd been sitting in to settle on the ground beside Callie (though she notices that he leaves a couple of feet of space between them). The embers are slowly cooling from bright orange to a dusty gray. Callie shivers and Abdullah hops up.

"I'll be right back," he says, and lopes off in the direction of the tents. A moment later, he returns carrying a blanket. Callie takes it gratefully, her heart warming at his sensitivity and awareness of her sensory issues. If only he could fix her throbbing back and the blisters on her thighs! She watches as Abdullah grabs two logs and places them, angled like a teepee, over the fire. His dark bangs fall over his eyes as he nestles some smaller twigs around them which quickly catch flame. Soon there is a fire crackling again and Callie soaks in the warmth. *This guy would put eagle scouts to shame,* she thinks appreciatively.

"You really didn't have to get me a blanket— I totally could've done it myself," she says, not wanting to seem needy or weak.

"You are very American," Abdullah smiles at her. "I know you *could* have gotten yourself a blanket. I know you are strong and capable and independent. But that doesn't mean you can't let someone else do something for you sometimes. Don't you ever get tired of always taking care of yourself?"

Callie turns her head back towards the black forest, feeling incredibly surprised to feel sudden tears forming. The fire crackles and pops loudly during the conversational pause.

Callie gets quick control of herself and turns towards Abdullah, "I do get tired," she admits quietly. "But I've pretty much been taking care of myself since I was a teenager, so I guess I'm used to it."

Abdullah raises his eyes questioningly, and Callie sighs, *I wasn't planning to get into this with him. Though I guess he would understand, with his background, with his dad.*

"When I was a sophomore in high school, my mom was diagnosed with breast cancer. My sister was a freshman in college in another state, and my little brother was in seventh grade. My dad worked full-time and my mom was sick, so a lot of the household duties fell to me."

Abdullah nods, his dark eyes full of empathy.

"She was sick throughout my last two years of high school, and our whole lives pretty much revolved around her various treatments. She tried not to let it— she made me go to prom for example, and I went even though I didn't want to because I knew it meant a lot to her. My little brother and I got really close during that time, since I basically parented him. I think I still resent my sister for leaving the work to me and for kind of getting a free pass from all the sadness since she was away at college. And I think she kind of resents (or regrets, maybe) that I got those final last years with Mom that she didn't get. We get along fine, but we aren't really close these days."

"Mom took a turn for the worst during spring semester of my senior year," Callie continues, eyes on the flickering flames of the fire. "She wanted so badly to hold out and see me graduate. But she died a couple of weeks before graduation," Callie pauses, quiet. Abdullah doesn't say anything, but he scoots closer to her. "I almost didn't go to graduation— my dad had to force me. I honestly don't really even remember it— it feels like a blur. My dad was a rockstar though— he did a great job at being there for all of us despite really grieving himself. He and Mom had been really close."

"And you? How did her death change you? Or maybe, how did you process?" Abdullah asks quietly.

"It probably changed me more than I realize, honestly. When I was a kid, I was pretty quiet and shy and insecure. I often avoided other kids and social situations because they were sensory overloads for me. But those few years Mom was sick, I had to grow up really fast— because I had to take care of her and Nate. I even handled a bunch of the insurance paperwork after she died because my dad was totally overwhelmed by it. It forced me to be capable, I guess."

"Skills you still use today, huh?" Abdullah smiles gently at her.

"Pretty much," Callie gives a half smile. She hesitates for a moment before admitting, "My belief in God pretty much died with Mom too. She and Dad were super religious. Somehow Dad's faith got stronger when Mom died— he clung to it. But I got really mad at

God for not answering our prayers and healing my Mom, and I think I'm still mad at Him today." Callie is shocked at herself for opening up like this with him— it had been years since she'd talked with anyone about her mom's death or her thoughts on God. *Maybe that conversation the other night with Pat and Rob has me thinking about things.*

"I think that's understandable," Abdullah says quietly. "And I'm really sorry about your mom. I can't imagine what it would have been like to lose my mom. She is our family rock. We cannot always understand why God allows certain things to happen the way they do in the world."

"You believe in God?" Callie frowns, "I thought you were a Muslim?"

"Muslims believe in God," Abdullah laughs. "We just normally refer to him by the name Allah, which is Arabic for God."

"Oh!" Callie blushes, feeling embarrassed at her lack of knowledge of Islam, "Are you religious?"

"I'm pretty sure almost all Ramazis are religious," Abdullah smiles. "But I believe in Allah. I have read the Koran and I try my best to be a good person and to follow the five pillars of Islam— including praying five times a day, which I think you have noticed…" Callie nods in affirmation, thinking of all the times he has ducked out to pray.

"And during Ramadan, I fast for the month," he adds.

"For a whole month??!" Callie has heard of Ramadan of course, but doesn't know any details.

"Not 24/7 all month," Abdullah's eyes crinkle in a laugh, "We fast from sunrise to sunset, and then we eat at night and in the early morning. It's a special time to seek Allah." Abdullah sits up straight, his eyes intense and proud.

"And have you found God, or Allah, when you've sought him?" Callie asks, truly curious.

Abdullah shifts his shoulders and looks uncomfortable, "Honestly? No. But you can't expect to find Allah, right? He is holy and perfect— of course He has to be separate from sinners like us. I just hope that my good deeds will outweigh my bad deeds so that when I die, I can go to heaven," his voice is intense with longing.

"I'm definitely not the expert, but I know Christians think that getting into heaven is not based on your good deeds. And they also believe you can experience God personally," Callie adds, thinking about their recent conversation with Rob and Pat.

"How though?" Abdullah asks, and Callie can hear raw desire in his voice.

"Well, based on what I remember from my long-ago days in Sunday school, the Bible says it's through a relationship with Jesus. But I'm really not the expert. It's been quite some time since God and I had anything to do with each other," Callie adds uncomfortably. She stares into the embers, which are once again turning a deep red now that the flames have died down.

"Have *you* ever experienced God?" Abdullah asks, staring intently at Callie, ignoring her discomfort.

Callie has a flashback to a worship night at a Christian summer camp when she was in ninth grade— that night, she had felt *something*, something that she had been sure at the time was the presence of God. But the intervening ten-plus years had left her with more doubt than faith.

"Do you people always have conversations like this?" Callie laughs in exasperation, avoiding Abdullah's question. "Americans really do not talk about religion much with others. We kind of view it as a private thing."

"Ha! Ramazis are as likely to bring up religion as they are to bring up the weather or who won the most recent MMA match," Abdullah laughs. "For us, Islam is communal, not private or individual."

"Is anything private or individual for Ramazis?" Callie asks with a cheeky grin.

"Basically, no!" Abdullah smiles, "Our whole lives are pretty communal."

"You even live in family communes! I can't imagine that!"

"It has its pluses and its minuses, but for the most part I like it," Abdullah's amber eyes are sincere.

"That's just because you haven't experienced the freedom of living on your own!" Callie winks.

"Not true!" Abdullah laughs. "I went to university in Tbilisi for four years! I tasted freedom there, and then happily returned home to my mom's cooking!"

"She is a pretty great cook," Callie acquiesces. "Do you think you will live in the family commune your whole life?"

"First of all, we call it a compound, not a commune," Abdullah adds with a twinkle in his eye. "But since I'm the only son, it's my duty to live with my mom and take care of her my whole life. And then when she dies someday, hopefully not for many many years, *inshallah*, I will inherit the property."

"What if your wife doesn't want to live there?" Callie asks, eyebrows raised.

"What wife wouldn't want to live there? We have one of the most beautiful properties in Sureti Valley, and one of the most successful businesses. Plus, my mother is much easier to get along with than many mothers-in-law. Any wife would be thrilled to marry into our family," Abdullah says with pride and self-assurance.

Any Ramazi, maybe, Callie thinks, but doesn't say anything.

"What about you and your family?" Abdullah asks. "I know Americans tend to move around a lot and not live communally, so how do you manage to look out for each other and take care of each other? How about your dad? Your boyfriend?" Abdullah asks, keeping his tone carefully neutral when he mentions Lucas.

"We do stay in touch— the internet definitely helps, since we can text and call and email. I know they all love me. But they're all very busy with their own lives and very far away. We're not intertwined in each other's daily lives the way people are with their families here, " Callie does a little hiccup laugh, suddenly feeling very alone in the midst of this giant Georgian forest, with no one for miles but Abdullah and the sleeping Russians.

"I'm sorry," Abdullah pauses, and then very intentionally reaches out and squeezes Callie's right hand. "If you need anything while you're here, I'm your guy, ok?" His golden eyes look intently into her blue ones, and Callie feels as if every nerve ending in her body is located in her hand, which is surrounded by the warmth of his strong, calloused hand. Somehow, with the 'no touching' rules and restrictions of Ramazi society, a simple hand hold feels far more intimate than many kisses Callie has had in the past.

"Thank you," she whispers, squeezing his hand back. She holds on for a moment, and then slips her fingers out of his. *You've got to be careful*, she tells herself. *Developing feelings will not do either of you any good. Remember what Pat said. And this setting certainly doesn't help*, she sighs, glancing up at the canopy of stars above them in the night sky. The forest is loud with the sounds of crickets and the occasional hoot of an owl.

"It's really beautiful here," Callie whispers, pulling the blanket tight around her shoulders and staring up at the stars.

Abdullah nods, "I love it. I wouldn't want to live anywhere else. My family has lived here for generations— this land is in our blood," he says proudly.

"What were your grandparents like?" Callie asks, curious. "I know your grandfather taught you woodworking?"

"My grandmother died when I was twelve. Until then, she definitely ran the place with an iron fist— she adored me, but I couldn't get away with anything! I think it was hard for my mom, having to serve my grandmother all the time. But she didn't complain to us about it. And once my grandmother died, my mom was finally able to get the idea for a guesthouse and to start working on it. My grandfather got dementia about five years ago, and passed away less than two years ago," Abdullah's eyes cloud. "I really loved him. He was quiet but strong, and everyone in the community looked up to him and respected him. He was from Ramazistan, in Russia, but he moved here for work when he was young. When he was alive, our property was a revolving door of neighbors and relatives constantly in and out — guests for every meal! When Mom got the idea for the guesthouse, he supported her, despite major backlash from the town."

"Why would people not have wanted your mom to start a business here?" Callie frowns. "It seems like anything that would bring money here would be a good thing," she spouts, before realizing that her words may sound judgmental. "Sorry," she flushes. Abdullah doesn't even seem to notice her discomfort and takes no offense at her words.

"You're right, you would think that. But people were worried about bringing foreigners and foreign influence to the village and the corrupting influence it could have on our culture."

"Like the terribly corrupting influence I'm having on you right now," Callie jokes, leaning forward and giving Abdullah an exaggerated, overtly teasing seductive wink.

"Pretty much exactly like that," Abdullah whispers, staring intently into her eyes. Callie's stomach twinges, realizing that while she thought she was being innocently flirty, he was dead serious.

She looks at the fire and scrambles for a change in conversation topic.

"How about your mom's family?" Callie asks, curious. Leila has never mentioned family.

In the silence, Callie can feel Abdullah still looking at her. But she feigns unawareness and eventually, he moves on.

"Well, in Ramazi culture, when women marry they join the family of the person they marry. So they don't really see their own family much anymore. And in a Ramazi marriage, the groom is not allowed to see his mother-in-law!"

"Wait... at the wedding?" Callie frowns.

"Nope— ever!" Abdullah laughs, "We joke that it is why we have such strong, lasting marriages— because the bride's mother cannot interfere!"

"Well, I think that's terrible," Callie frowns.

Abdullah shrugs, "People aren't quite as strict about it as they used to be, though I guess it does depend on the family. You have to value traditions for being part of your culture, even if you don't always agree with them."

"So if you get married, you would be ok never getting to know your mother-in-law??" Callie is shocked.

Abdullah looks nonplussed, "Honestly, I never really thought about it. I guess I would talk to my wife about it."

"Wait," Callie realizes, "But Sayid and Fariza come to your place and interact with your mother all the time."

Abdullah grins, "We all say Sayid isn't a real Ramazi— he breaks all the rules! For my sister's sake, I am glad. She is very close to Mom and it would be very hard for them if they were limited in their ability to see each other. It also makes a huge difference that Sayid is the oldest son."

"What does that have to do with anything?" Callie asks, confused.

"Well, it is the responsibility and privilege of the younger son to live in his family compound for his whole life and for him and his wife to take care of the grandparents into their old age."

"Oh! So that's why your mom is still living in the family compound and she was the one to care for your grandfather? Because your father was the youngest son?"

Abdullah shakes his head, "My dad was the *only* son. That's what made his death even more tragic for my grandparents. And also why they were so connected to me. Not only was I their only grandson, but I was their only heir, the only way that their family line will continue. When my grandfather died, I inherited their property— even though, let's be honest, we all know Mom really runs the ship for now," he grins and Callie nods in agreement. "Eventually when I get married and have children I will live there with my family and be responsible for caring for Mom when she gets old."

"Honestly, that's probably a better way of doing things than the American nursing home system," Callie admits.

"I do not mean to offend," Abdullah shudders, "but I do not understand the American system of putting old people in institutions. It's like putting them in an orphanage. If you wouldn't place your own child in an orphanage, why would you place your parent or grandparent in what essentially amounts to the same thing?!"

"An assisted living facility is not the same thing as an orphanage!" Callie quickly responds, feeling defensive. "A lot of them are really nice. And a lot of elderly people need medical help that their family isn't able to provide at home." *How have I never thought about this?* Callie wonders, *I guess Americans really don't pay much attention to old people or value them very much*, she acknowledges guiltily.

Abdullah shrugs, "All I know is that I would never put my grandfather or mother in a facility, no matter what the situation. We Ramazis revere our elderly— we value the wisdom they have gained through living a long life."

Callie nods. She has definitely noticed the respect that Ramazis accord to the elderly— everything from standing whenever an older person enters a room, to asking grandparents' opinions on all family matters. *I think I would rather grow old in a Ramazi village than in the US!* Callie realizes with surprise. *Though I definitely would not like to live in a Ramazi village as a young girl or a young woman. It's so strange that different cultures value different genders and ages differently.*

Callie shivers again in the night air— the fire is almost completely gone, and she can barely see Abdullah in the darkness. Everything in her wants to stay sitting close beside him under the starry sky. *Does he feel the same way?* Callie glances over at him. "I should probably head to bed," she says regretfully, "I'm guessing it's gonna be an early day tomorrow?"

"It's always an early day in the mountains," Callie can't see Abdullah's face, but she can hear the smile in his voice.

"Here," he holds out a hand, and pulls Callie to standing. When he lets go, she feels the absence of his hand like a missing limb.

CHAPTER 17
Khev, Georgia

May, 1992

The "night of the horse comment" is the first time Saidun beats Dina, but not the last. The business investment that Saidun and Anzor had made in a water purifying factory collapses when their business partner flees in the night with their investment capital. Anzor and Saidun are both furious, but Anzor has seen enough life roller coasters in his day to handle things a bit more stoically. Saidun, on the other hand, is used to things going his way. He storms around the compound, making life miserable for everyone. Even the barn cats, who he is normally surprisingly affectionate with, hide when they see him coming— they've learned the hard way that a boot may be heading their way.

Dina's life becomes even more miserable than before. Previously, Saidun was away at work most days. Now, he is moping around and often looking for trouble. Dina tries her best to steer clear of him and not say anything to upset him, but, despite her best efforts, some evenings he still finds something worth beating her or yelling at her for. The walls in the family home are thin, and their bedroom is right next to Hava and Marta's, and one room down from Anzor and Khadijat's. Dina is mortified to know that the entire family is certainly able to hear everything that goes on between her and Saidun. And she is hurt and angry, though not surprised, that none of them do anything to intervene. Dina has learned that according to Ramazi culture, it is acceptable to "train" your wife and your children by beating them.

One morning, after a particularly bad night, the women are silently serving breakfast to the men when Dina is startled to hear Anzor's fork clatter to the table.

"Ав у рофлы щтолфыр фывров цукцяз влыла?" he yells at Saidun, pointing to Dina's nearly swollen-shut blackeye. Dina glances at Saidun, who looks sheepish and shocked at his father's raised voice.

"Длу ав шыв ядасл вшэ лоу цуз яч фылв," Saidun replies defensively. All of the women freeze, glancing back and forth between father and son. Dina hates that she can't understand what they're saying.

"Enough!" Anzor switches to Georgian, clearly so that Dina can understand. "This ends here!" he reprimands his son. "Beating a weak woman is not something to be proud of. Have you ever seen me beat your mother? Well?"

Looking sullen, Saidun shakes his head.

"The Koran tells us that we are supposed to honor our wives. You are not honoring your wife by treating her in this way. Instead, you are bringing shame to our whole family. What would the neighbors say if they saw her like this??"

Saidun has the decency to look embarrassed. "I'm sorry for bringing shame to the family, Father," he says quietly, hunching his broad shoulders.

"I don't want your apology," Anzor sighs. "And anyway, it's her you should be apologizing to," Anzor points at Dina and everyone in the room looks shocked. Clearly the idea of a man apologizing to a woman is novel for all of them.

"No more of this, do you understand?" Anzor says in a stern tone, and Saidun quickly nods.

The women silently gather the breakfast dishes and Khadijat herds them out of the room.

***

True to his promise to his father, from that point on Saidun refrains from raising a hand towards Dina. She is overwhelmed with gratitude towards Anzor, but still feels that she always has to be on guard around Saidun; she doesn't trust that he won't snap again at some point. He of course does not apologize. Though his physical abuse stops, the verbal bullying continues unabated. Dina feels a bitter surge of frustratingly impotent hatred rise like bile in her throat whenever he approaches her. But to protect herself, she makes her face blank and tries to comply with his demands.

Thankfully, she doesn't have to see him that often these days— summer is in full swing and they are all very busy— the women with tending the summer garden and picking the vast variety and quantity of fruits and vegetables that grow there. To their deep disappointment, Hava and Marta tan a caramel brown from being out in the sun so much. Dina's pale skin, on the other hand, just burns and freckles. She's grateful for her long sleeves and long skirts— though they make her hot, at least they protect her from the sun.

As soon as the women pick anything, they have to then decide what to do with it— some of the produce they use right away, some they turn into canned jams and veggies. It's long, hot work; Dina has never been so exhausted in her entire life. She works harder than she has ever worked before, and still she cannot keep up with Khadijat, Marta, and Hava, which Khadijat doesn't hesitate to remind her about daily. The monotony is occasionally broken up by a couple of Khadijat's elderly aunts coming over to pitch in with the work. Unlike Khadijat, they are lighthearted and welcoming and quick to laugh. After meeting them, Dina knows who Marta got her spunk and sarcastic sense of humor from.

The men are busy making repairs around the property. They replace some rotten floor boards throughout the house, re-tile the back wall in the kitchen, patch the roof, and begin discussing plans to build a second house on the property for Saidun and Dina to live in once they start having babies, which everyone thinks they should be doing already, seeing as they've been married for a few months. Every time relatives or neighbor women come to visit, the first question they ask Khadijat is if Dina is pregnant or not. It pains Khadijat to tell them 'no'.

Dina's periods used to be regular as clockwork, but since the kidnapping, they've been sporadic. She thought at first that she might be pregnant, but then realized it was probably all the stress and physical labor that was throwing her body off. And so she didn't think anything of it that July when her period did not come as expected. When it hadn't come midway through hot dry August, Dina had started to worry— she didn't want a baby with Saidun. Inside, she still held onto a smidgen of hope that someday she could escape this place and go back home to Tbilisi. But if she had Saidun's baby, she knew that she would be tied to Khev forever— the family would never let her take their grandchild, and Dina knew that she would never leave her child. Plus, she was terrified that if she had a son, he would grow up to be domineering and aggressive like his father.

But by the end of August, there's no denying that Dina is pregnant. Though her stomach is still flat as a board, she's throwing up every morning and any slight smell makes her nauseated. For once, Dina is grateful for Saidun's fastidious hygiene— at least he doesn't stink.

Khadijat quickly catches on, and begins to treat Dina a bit less harshly. As each day of pregnancy drags on, Dina struggles to make her nauseated, exhausted body complete her long list of daily chores.

***

It's dark outside by the time Dina slips off her slippers outside her bedroom door, hangs her long dress up on a peg on the wall, and collapses into bed with a sigh of relief. She curls into a fetal position and takes deep breaths, trying to calm the roiling in her head and stomach. She has never been on a boat before, but she imagines pregnancy is what seasickness would feel like. Perpetual, never-ending seasickness. Dina allows herself a brief moment to moan with misery and self-pity, after having pretended all day to be totally fine.

A light rap sounds on the door, and a moment later Saidun's head peeps in.

"Can I come in?" he asks, sounding awkward. Dina raises her eyebrows— he's never asked her permission for anything before. She nods and gingerly sits up in bed as he lumbers in.

"My mother... told me..." Saidun turns uncharacteristically red and stumbles over his words. "She told me about the baby!" he finally manages to get out. "It's true?"

Dina nods, and Saidun smiles such a big grin that Dina can't help but smile back. He hurries over to the bed and carefully grasps her hand, "I can't believe it! Finally! You don't know what this means for my family! I'm the only son, and so it's essential that I have a son to carry on the family name and bloodline. I can't believe we're having a baby!" Dina has never seen him so genuinely excited, not even when he got back from his hunting trip.

"I have a gift for you. I'll be right back!" he hurries out the door, and when he comes back a moment later Dina is shocked by what he's holding in his hands— a tiny calico kitten. In Saidun's large hands, the kitten looks minuscule.

He carries it over to the bed, and gently hands it to Dina, who coos as she feels its tiny body cuddle up into her hand. She looks at Saidun, eyebrow raised questioningly.

He barks a laugh, "You cannot ever tell my mother that I gave you a kitten! She would have my head! I wanted to give you a gift as a thank you for carrying our first child, but I was not sure what you would like. Normal Ramazi women would want gold jewelry or a new canning pan or something, but none of those things seemed like something you would like," Saidun laughs and rolls his eyes. "But I thought maybe a kitten would be good company for you. When I was a boy, I had a cat named Smokey. He had a broken tail and was missing an eye from some street fight. Mother told me to put him out of his misery, but I nursed him back to health instead. After that, he followed me around like a shadow! Man, I loved that cat!" Saidun admits, looking sheepish. "And I know it hasn't been easy for you living here. And I know I sometimes lose my temper. But I am trying to be better. And especially with the baby coming, I want to be a father our baby can look up to. I can't ever fill the shoes of my own father, but I will try my hardest, I promise."

Dina nods, unexpectedly choked up at his uncharacteristically kind words. For a moment, she dares to let herself hope that maybe things will be different moving forward. She lowers her eyes and distracts herself by petting the tiny kitten, who is curled up, asleep in her lap.

***

"You are an idiot! My son was a fool to ever marry you!" Khadijat rages at Dina, who had thoughtlessly attempted to pick up one of the jars of pickles they were canning, forgetting that it would be burning hot. She had dropped it with surprise, and now glass, cucumbers, and steaming briny pickle water swim across the kitchen floor.

"Did you never help at home at all? You are worthless in the kitchen! In fact, you are worse than worthless— you're a liability!" Khadijat continues to rant as Dina wordlessly gets a broom and begins to sweep up the glass pieces.

"Oh for heaven's sake, now you've gone and ruined the broom— it will stink of pickles forever! Don't you know not to clean up pickle water with a broom??! I swear our cow has more sense than you!"

Hava and Marta busy themselves at the sink, washing and peeling vegetables and pretending not to hear yet another session of their mother yelling at Dina for her incompetence.

Suddenly, Dina throws down the broom and stands up straight, "That's enough!" she shouts, "I've had it! I have bent like a reed trying to serve your every whim, yet nothing I can do is good enough for you. You treat me like a slave! Why do you do this to me? I do not understand! You are a woman. I am a woman. Should we not band together and stand together and treat each other well? Instead you yell at me and demean me."

Hava and Marta freeze in shock and horror that Dina would dare to shout at their mother.

Khadijat stands up, somehow looking much taller than her stout 5'2". Her voice is furious, "I should beat you for such insolence! How *dare* you raise your voice at me! If you weren't carrying my grandson, you would be severely punished! It is your *job* to be my servant! That is how it is in our culture— you married my son, which means you are *his* wife and *my* servant. It is up to me to raise you up as a woman and train you in everything around the house! If you don't like how I do it, I don't care. But someday when you are capable of running this place, you will thank me. Mark my words." Khadijat thrusts a finger out towards Dina.

"But why can't you train me kindly?" Dina almost whispers.

Khadijat snorts, "Kindness is for soft people. Ramazis are strong! Our men are warriors on the battlefield, and our women are warriors at home! We have survived and can survive anything. My mother-in-law treated me harshly, as her servant, and her mother-in-law did the same before her, and her mother-in-law before her. It is how life works. And someday, *inshallah*, you will have your own daughter-in-law to serve you. You better hope that she is not as useless and incompetent and insolent as you are," Khadijat rolls her eyes and throws her hands in the air. "Whatever you do, make your son marry a Ramazi so that you don't have to put up with this kind of mess," Khadijat gestures at the briny floor and storms out of the kitchen.

***

"We can't believe you stood up to her! No one ever stands up to her!" Marta and Hava come running to Dina, each putting an arm on either side of her. Dina leans into their arms, and they ease her down into a chair.

"Sit here, we'll clean up the mess," Hava says gently. Dina nods gratefully.

"You really shouldn't have done that," Marta says authoritatively. "She already hated you— now she's really gonna have it out for you."

"I'm afraid Marta's right," Hava glances up from the floor with a look of concern.

"Whatever," Dina shrugs, "It's not like it could get any worse than it already is."

Dina catches a quick glance between Marta and Hava, and realizes that they don't agree with her prediction.

"Well, at least you're pregnant," Hava says hopefully, "that is really the most important duty for a daughter-in-law to perform. When you have a son, everyone here will have more grace for you."

"Unless she has a daughter," Marta tosses out sarcastically, and both girls shake their heads knowingly.

"Look," Hava lays a gentle hand on Dina's shoulder. "We know the way things work around here. We can teach you the ropes. Anytime you have a question about how things are done, ask *us* instead of confronting Mother."

"Yeah, unless you wanna get your head chopped off again!" Marta pulls a finger across her throat and rolls her eyes back in her head, and both Dina and Hava reluctantly laugh.

"Come on, let's get the rest of these pickles canned before mother comes in and finds none of us working! Then we would *all* be in hot water!" Hava pulls Dina to standing, and Dina surprises the younger girls by giving them each a quick hug, "Thank you girls so much! Of everyone here, you two have been kindest to me. I can't tell you how much it means to me. And Hava, you remind me a little bit of my sister Sofi, which is the biggest compliment I can give you."

Hava blushes, and Marta quips, "No offense to Sofi, but she must be a sissy if she reminds you of Hava!" Hava grabs a towel and tries to pop Marta with it, but Marta quickly catches the towel and saunters over to the sink.

***

Dina carries the mens' lunch dishes into the kitchen, thankful for the thousandth time that she lives in one of the few houses in Khev with a real stove and a water pump in the kitchen. As she places the dishes in the sink, she catches a whiff of lamb scent from the dirty plates and immediately begins to gag. *Curse this stupid morning sickness! Will it never go away?? This pregnancy is going to be the death of me,* Dina despairs, holding her nose and standing very still, taking in slow deep breaths through her mouth in a vain attempt to quell her stomach.

"Daydreaming again?" asks a voice dryly, from the doorway. Dina had not heard Khadijat come in.

Dina spins around, and Khadijat can see how pale Dina looks. Khadijat sighs and a momentary look of compassion passes across her face. She comes over, takes the rag from Dina's hand, and points Dina over to a chair. Dina sinks in gratefully, watching as her mother-in-law washes the lunch dishes with expert efficiency.

"Pregnancy can be hard," Khadijat surprises Dina by breaking the silence. "I was very sick with my children, especially with the girls for some reason. But there is nothing to be done but work through it. Coddling does no good. And anyway, the morning sickness will pass and soon you will start to feel better. And it will all be worth it when you have your son."

I can't believe she just spoke to me, and shared with me about her own life, Dina thinks with amazement. *Maybe our relationship will improve! Though of course a son is all that matters to her or to anyone here,* Dina thinks bitterly, and then fear creeps in— *what will they do if I have a girl?* For some reason, Dina is sure that the baby inside of her is a girl. Its flutters and kicks are dainty and delicate, and she feels connected to the child already. *I will love you no matter who you are, baby,* she silently reassures the little one inside of her.

CHAPTER 18
Caucasus Mountains, Georgia

July, 2018

"We think we'd actually like to stay here this afternoon, if that's possible," Oleg pulls an arm around Nastya's slender shoulders and she smiles up at him. Abdullah translates for Callie from Russian into English.

The morning's route had been even more beautiful than the day before, with the mountains around them getting progressively taller and more jagged. The horses had handled the terrain like champs, and are now placidly eating a well-earned lunch of grass while the humans sit on stumps and eat their own lunches. The plan had been to tie up the horses for the afternoon, and do a sunset hike to the top of a nearby peak. *Finally getting some legit exercise of our own,* Callie had thought with excited anticipation. Then they were going to camp that night in the glade where they are currently having lunch.

"Oleg can put up the tents and build a fire while you guys hike, and then everything will be ready for the night when you get back," Nastya suggests.

Abdullah looks unconvinced. "I really don't like to split up groups. There is safety in numbers, and plus you will miss a great view from the top. With all these clouds, sunset is likely to be spectacular. I am a little concerned that it might rain. Some of the clouds we saw in the distance this morning looked like storm clouds." Abdullah pauses, frowning. He thinks for a moment then decides, "How about this— if you guys don't want to do the hike, we can all stay here and hang out in the glade this afternoon. I'm sure Callie won't mind a break?" Abdullah raises his eyebrows at Callie, who looks non-committal. *I really want to do the hike,* she thinks, *but I don't want to be the one to force the group to split up.*

"Oh no!" Nastya exclaims, leaning even closer into Oleg's side, "We don't want you guys to miss the sunset hike! You guys do the hike. We will be waiting here for you when you get back!" Oleg kisses the top of Nastya's head, and nods in agreement to her plan.

They're newlyweds on their honeymoon! Of course they want to spend the afternoon alone together! It clicks with Callie, and she grins, "You know, Abdullah, it really would be good for the website and Instagram if we could get pics from the hike. Especially if there is a good sunset. I think Oleg and Nastya will be fine here."

It takes some convincing, but eventually Abdullah agrees to split up, against his better judgment. He leaves his cell phone with Oleg and Nastya and makes them promise to call the guesthouse if they have any issues. Oleg insists that everything will be fine, and reassures Abdullah that he and Nastya have done lots of wilderness camping in Russia, and that they're experienced and capable of looking after the horses. Abdullah nods— he has seen the confident way both of them handle the horses.

Around 2:00 p.m., Abdullah and Callie set off up the mountain. When they're a couple of hundred meters up, Callie glances behind them and sees Oleg pull Nastya in for a deep kiss. *Kinda jealous of their afternoon plans,* Callie thinks with a grin and momentarily wishes it was Lucas there with her instead of Abdullah— Lucas would definitely be up for making out in a scenic mountain meadow.

She glances at Abdullah, hiking a few feet ahead of her. He and Lucas couldn't be more different, physically or otherwise— Lucas is tall and broad-shouldered and blond and is the life of the party wherever he goes. He's loud and fun and a huge sports fan. Though he definitely also has a short-fused temper. Abdullah, on the other hand, is of medium height with a lean build, dark hair, and amber eyes that go warm when he looks at her. He's quieter— a deep thinker, intense, protective, and very committed to and proud of his people and his family. *They do have in common that they're both incredibly hard-working and very good-looking,* Callie acknowledges. *And they're both in better shape than me!* Though Callie worked out daily in San Francisco, the altitude of the mountains has her out of breath and the steep climb has her calves burning. *I definitely didn't train for this,* she thinks with chagrin, slightly embarrassed at how loudly she is breathing.

And it's not only the altitude that's bothering her— her inner thighs are still burning from the chaffing they got the day before from horseback riding. Callie does an awkward duck waddle, trying not to rub her thighs together. But even her pants hurt her when they rub up against the blisters. She grimaces, trying unsuccessfully to distract herself with the beautiful scenery around her.

Wordlessly, Abdullah hands Callie a bottle of water, which she gratefully accepts. They stop for a minute. Callie is very aware that Abdullah has no need to stop and is just doing it for her sake. *I hate being the weak link,* she thinks, frustrated. *It doesn't help that last night I barely slept between being cold and all those stupid rocks under my sleeping bag. This kind of roughing-it trip is definitely not for me.*

About an hour later, they reach a break in the trees that has formed a natural overlook. From the overlook, Callie can see back towards where they came, though the camp is hidden from view by trees. Abdullah points out the peak, where they're heading. It doesn't look impossibly far.

"I'm not happy about those clouds." Abdullah frowns at a patch of dark clouds on the western horizon, which, Callie admits, do look like storm clouds.

"It seems like they're really far away though?" Callie asks hopefully.

"It's impossible to tell," Abdullah explains. "Weather in the mountains can change really quickly and can be quite dangerous."

"If it looks like it's getting dangerous later this afternoon, we can turn around," Callie decides.

"It could be too late then," Abdullah warns, and then sighs. "I do think we're probably ok for now. Let's keep going. Maybe we can reach the summit before sundown and then get some sunset pics on the way back down."

Callie agrees, and they pick up their pace, which she had not even thought was possible. The stretch ahead of them is a steep hillside of barren dirt. Abdullah explains angrily that the mountains are being deforested for profit at a rapid rate, and companies are not required to replant trees in the places where they cut them down. Callie looks around, and she can see great swaths of naked land cutting like scars through almost each forest on the mountains around her.

Around five o'clock, they reach the summit. Callie collapses gratefully on the ground and Abdullah grins and squats beside her.

"Tired?"

"I think I've never been more tired in my life!" Callie admits with a laugh. "But man, was it worth it!" She sweeps her arms across the view in front of them. From the peak, they have a 360° view of the mountains around them. The darker clouds have moved closer than before, but still seem to be a ways off. Despite sunset not being until seven o'clock, some of the clouds closer to them are starting to lightly pinken. Rays of sunlight stream through the dark clouds, making distinct golden lines around their edges. After a few minutes of rest on the ground, Callie grabs her phone and begins to take photos. Though frustrated that the photos don't fully capture the majesty around her, she is pleased with some of the results. Abdullah stays seated on the ground, snacking on some nuts and dried fruit, watching Callie from behind. She turns to show him a photo, and catches him staring at her. He quickly averts his eyes. *Was he just checking me out? Is he actually interested in me?* Callie pretends not to notice and brings her phone over to show him the photos she has taken so far.

Callie wishes they could stay on the mountain top forever, but Abdullah reminds her that they need to head down as quickly as they can. He eyes the clouds with concern, which are rolling in with surprising speed. The wind has picked up and Callie is the uncomfortable mix of cold and wet with sweat at the same time.

"You cannot ever tell anyone we did this hike just the two of us," Abdullah abruptly says during the silence of their descent.

"What?" Callie is confused.

"In our culture, men and women are not allowed to be alone together unless they are married. And even once married, men and women don't spend much time alone together!" Abdullah explains.

"What about dating?" Callie frowns.

"Ramazis don't date— we normally do arranged marriages."

"And you don't spend any time alone together before the wedding?" Callie is shocked.

"Nope. That's how our society makes sure that everything stays pure and everyone stays moral and free from defilement."

"I'm pretty sure you can date and still maintain morality," Callie rolls her eyes.

Abdullah shrugs, "That's not how our society sees it. Anyway, we just have to be careful, ok? I especially wouldn't want to taint your reputation."

"What does my reputation matter?? I'm a foreigner!" Callie says indignantly, "You should probably be more concerned with your own reputation."

"Well..." Abdullah looks uncomfortable, "Unfortunately, there are different standards for men and women. Women are pure and innocent and if their reputation is tarnished, then it is likely they will never find a husband."

"Well that is just ridiculous and unfair," Callie huffs. "And what about men?"

Here, Abdullah has the decency to look even more uncomfortable, "Well, it is understood that men have... stronger urges...that are harder to control. So men are allowed to make more mistakes, and maybe have a woman on the side. So long as he is discreet about it, of course. He wouldn't want to hurt the reputation of his wife," Abdullah hurries to add.

"So women are required to be faithful and pure and stick to these ridiculous archaic laws, and men just can have a free-for-all and go sleep with whomever they want?" Callie's eyes blaze with anger at the unfairness of it and she glares at Abdullah. *What is this— the Middle Ages??*

Abdullah puts his hands up in self-defense, "Don't shoot the messenger! I did not make the rules, and I agree with you that they are not fair. But they are what they are, and it is impossible to change them. All I am doing is trying to protect you, ok?"

"Fine," Callie huffs, calming down a little bit. "But I'm glad I am not a Ramazi woman!" she spits out.

Abdullah smiles disarmingly, "You would be a disaster as a Ramazi woman." Callie laughs unintentionally, and the tension breaks.

"Agreed!" Callie admits, "And don't worry, I won't mention this hike. But for your reputation, not mine. I could care less what people think of me," Callie insists, crossing her arms across her chest. Though inside, she knows she isn't telling the full truth.

"You need to care what people think about you here," Abdullah says quietly. "You could get yourself or our family into lots of trouble if you aren't careful."

"Oh," Callie reddens. "Yeah, I figured that out when I tried to go running my first week. I just didn't think about it in regards to this hike," she admits.

"Mom told me about your attempt to run," Abdullah laughs. "Well, and I had at least four different neighbors tell me about it too! You definitely scandalized Baba Maia," he grins.

Callie covers her face in mock horror and laughs. When she lowers her hands, she looks around, surprised to notice how dark it is in the forest. She had been so honed in on their conversation that she hadn't noticed the growing darkness. Suddenly, she hears a loud pattering and she realizes that the skies have opened up and rain is pounding on the leaves above them.

Abdullah groans, "We really need to hurry and try to get back to camp. We don't want to get caught out in this. But you need to be careful— you also don't want to go so fast that you twist your ankle on a root or something."

Callie nods and focuses on the ground in front of her. Abdullah pulls two headlamps out of his backpack and hands one to her. Callie, yet again, internally thanks him for his preparedness. *When we make it through this, I'm leaving him a glowing review as a mountain guide,* she decides.

It takes a few minutes for the rain to reach through the canopy of trees overhead, but once it does, Callie is quickly soaked to the skin. She can't believe how much water is dumping from the sky— within minutes, the ground around her is running with rivers of water.

"We haven't had much rain this summer, so the ground is really dry," Abdullah explains, "The water can't soak into it very easily, so it just runs down." Callie nods, and stumbles over a rock in her path.

Abdullah reaches out a hand and catches her arm, steadying her. The second time Callie stumbles, Abdullah doesn't let go of her hand. "It will be safer if we just stick together," he explains. Callie holds his steady hand gratefully. They hike through the dark forest in silent concentration. Callie can feel the worry radiating off of Abdullah, though he doesn't say anything and tries not to rush her. The rain continues to pour in such heavy torrents that streams of water run down Callie's face and into her eyes and make it hard for her to see. She continually wipes her eyes, but even when she can see, all around her is pitch black except for the thin streams of light from their headlamps, which are hampered by all the rain. Branches catch at Callie's hair and one scrapes a gash above her eyebrow. She doesn't mention anything to Abdullah. *I would be terrified if he wasn't here with me,* she realizes. *But with him close I feel safe, even in the pitch black and pouring rain.*

After a few minutes, the forest opens up onto the bare deforested slope that they had walked up earlier. At first, Callie is relieved to not have to watch out for trees and branches and roots. Soon her relief turns to dismay as she alternates between slipping down the slick slope and getting her shoes stuck in patches of gooey mud. Abdullah is tense and silent beside her. He lets go of her hand and grasps her elbow instead with a firm, steady grip. She realizes that he has turned sideways and is kind of sliding his way down the hill. She copies him, and finds that it is better than what she'd been doing.

In the distance, Callie hears a strange humming sound. It quickly gets louder and turns into a rumbling sound.

Abdullah jerks her arm hard and shouts, "Mudslide! Run!"

For a moment, Callie stands still, frowning at him in confusion.

"What?" she shouts over the increasing roar.

"Mudslide! Run!" Abdullah pulls her in desperation and Callie looks behind her. In the darkness, she can't see anything. But she can hear the rumbling turn into a roaring. The ground under her feet begins to shake. In a panic, Callie runs down the hill, no longer caring about trying to watch where she's going.

A moment later, an arm grabs hers, "Not down!" Abdullah shouts. "You can't outrun it! We have to go across!" Abdullah pulls

Callie sideways, towards the forest. They both run as fast as they can. *We're not going to make it! We're going to die here!* Callie thinks in panic, as the ground shakes and rain pours. She can hear the incredible roar of the mudslide coming towards them at an impossible speed.

And then, suddenly, it's upon them. They're so close to the edge of its path. Abdullah gives Callie a giant shove and she lands in a heap on the ground. She crawls forwards, away from the river of mud and trees and debris rushing at an awesome speed only a couple feet behind her. She scrambles up the slope of the hill she's on, shaking and crying with terror and relief. When she reaches the top, she stops and turns around, "I can't believe we made it! That was definitely the scariest thing I have ever experienced!"

Abdullah is not behind her.

"Abdullah?!" Callie shouts in panic, turning her headlamp in all directions, scanning the forest.

"Abdullah!" She shouts again, heart racing. She hesitates, and then carefully makes her way back down the hill, towards the edge of the path of the mudslide. She groans— between the dark and the rain, she can see no more than a few feet in front of her. Even with what little visibility she has, she is in shock at the path of utter destruction the mudslide has left. The trail where she and Abdullah had walked earlier that day is totally gone— in its place is a pulsing river of mud and branches.

"Abdullah!" Callie screams again and again until her voice is hoarse.

There is no answer.

CHAPTER 19
Khev, Georgia

Summer, 1992

"I have the thermos of tea— don't forget the picnic blanket!" Hava calls over her shoulder towards the kitchen.

"I've got it! Do you think I would forget the picnic blanket? Mother would have my neck," Marta grumbles, hoisting the rolled up blanket in one arm and a bag of food in the other. Normally Dina enjoys the sisters' banter, but her morning sickness makes it almost impossible for her to enjoy anything these days.

You better be the most wonderful, beautiful, brilliant, peaceful child in the world, to make up for all the suffering you have brought me, she thinks down towards her belly as she grabs a stack of empty pails from the storage closet. By the time she gets out to the courtyard, it is filled with women— she recognizes the six great-aunts and their daughters, as well as a few neighbors from up the street. In all, probably about twenty-five women mingle in the hot August sun, happily chatting.

"Бя лвоцза!" Khadijat shouts, and all the women stream through the gate like water from a pitcher. Dina lags behind, partially because pregnancy has her feeling short of breath, and partially because she still doesn't feel like she fits in here. She's starting to be able to understand a lot of what people say when they speak in Ramazi, but she still has a hard time speaking it. Plus, these women seem so different from her friends back home, who cared about fashion and music and the latest makeup trends. She watches the gaggle of women in front of her, moving together in a quiet clump of long dark skirts and headscarves. *I will never have anything in common with them,* she thinks bitterly. *I will always be an outsider, always alone.* Her eyes rove over the group again, and she spots Marta's tall broad-shouldered frame walking next to diminutive Hava. A wave of gratitude and affection for the two sisters rolls over her. *That's not true,* she realizes. *Though our backgrounds are really different, we have many things in common just because we are human. And because we are Georgian. And because we are women. I'm going to try not to feel so sorry for myself, but to make the best of this crappy situation.* Dina takes a deep breath and picks up her step until she's walking next to Hava, who smiles kindly over at her.

"Dina, have you met Luli? She's our... hmmmm... second cousin? Or maybe third cousin?" Hava and Luli laugh and shrug, and Luli throws a plump arm around Hava's shoulder. "We're family, that's all that matters!"

Luli looks searchingly at Dina, clearly quite curious. "You're from Tbilisi?" The way she says it makes Tbilisi sound as exotic as Paris or New York. Dina nods.

"What's Tbilisi like? I've always wanted to go!" Luli exclaims.

"It's wonderful!" Dina enthuses, happy to wax eloquent about the things that she loves, and misses, about her home city as they walk. Talking about Tbilisi momentarily distracts her from her morning sickness.

Once the women get out of the village and into the countryside, Dina notices a distinct shift in the atmosphere of the group. Everyone seems more relaxed; the volume of the group drastically increases as women begin to talk and laugh freely. A couple of the young girls remove their headscarves under the heat of the baking August sun, and their mothers don't even reprimand them.

They walk for probably thirty minutes through fields and woods until they reach the side of a mountain. There is almost no tree cover — instead, the hillside is covered with low, scrubby bushes.

"They're perfectly ripe, Mama, just like I told you!" a young girl of about ten shouts, holding a fat blueberry up victoriously, before unceremoniously popping it into her mouth.

The women and girls spend the afternoon filling their buckets with juicy berries which they will then take home and either can, bake into pies, or sell at the market in Maidana. Dina has never picked wild blueberries before, and she can't help herself from sampling a few as she picks. Amazingly, they sit well in her rebellious stomach and it seems like the mountain air has helped quench some of her morning sickness. The actual picking of the berries is backbreaking labor though— by the end of the first hour, she feels as if she will be perpetually hunched over.

"Honey, it's easier if you sit," kindly suggests Khadijat's sister Louisa. Dina looks over in surprise— she didn't expect kindness from one of Khadijat's siblings, especially not after the glares she got from them at the wedding. The woman squats down among the bushes, scans for a spot that seems particularly bountiful, and sits down. "I just sit and pick all the ones I can reach in one spot, and then move to a new spot once I've picked this one clean," she smiles. "In your condition, you could probably use a rest."

"Her excuse for sitting down is because she's pregnant! What's your excuse?" Khadijat shouts over towards her sister sarcastically, but not meanly.

"Not all of us need an excuse to sit down!" Louisa rolls her eyes towards her sister. "She's a taskmaster, that one! Can you imagine what my life was like as her younger sister, with her always bossing me around?" she laughs. *More than you can possibly imagine*, Dina thinks.

"You think you had it tough? As the eldest child, I basically had to raise you! And the rest of the siblings! I had to do more work than the rest of you combined!" Khadijat huffs, jerking a berry so hard from the bush in front of her that it squishes in her fingers and squirts a stream of purple juice onto Khadijat's black dress. "Now look what you made me do!" she grumbles, but eventually relents into a purse-lipped smile when Louisa just laughs.

"She is tough on the outside," Louisa murmurs quietly to Dina while looking affectionately at her older sister. "Her life has not been easy. Our mother died when we were young, and Khadijat basically had to raise all of us. Our aunts helped where they could, of course, but they all had families of their own to care for. And then when she and Anzor first got married, they lived in Ramazistan for a few years with Anzor's family. She was basically their slave. Until his younger brother got married, and then *his* wife became the family servant. And then Anzor and Khadijat were free to move back here. She has a brusque way about her, but she has a good heart. And more than anything, she wants what is best for her family. Your unexpected arrival was very hard for her," Louisa explains, looking at Dina as if searching for understanding. Dina carefully maintains a passive expression— no amount of explanation can justify the harsh way Khadijat has treated her. Eventually, Louisa forces a cheery smile, "But everything will be fixed now with the arrival of your son. He is all everyone has been waiting for!" Dina's stomach twists, and she knows it isn't from morning sickness.

But that comment aside, she finds herself surprised to legitimately enjoy the day. The surrounding mountains are beautiful and the blueberries are delicious. The women take a break in the mid-afternoon and spread blankets under some trees near a brook in the meadow at the base of the mountainside. Once the blankets are spread, a plethora of food appears from hampers and baskets and the women flop on the blankets and chat and eat. The mood is light and happy— for women who spend most of their lives in backbreaking labor, any chance to get away with each other is treasured. It is clear to Dina that their relationships with each other are tight-knit and affectionate. They even make a point to include her, translating for her into Georgian when it is clear that she doesn't understand some story or another that they're telling.

At one point, the women start telling childhood stories about Saidun— many of them hilarious, lots of them involving animals. Apparently he was quite the high-energy mischief-maker, which doesn't surprise Dina in the least. All the women congratulate her on her pregnancy, and tell her they hope and pray that she gives birth to a son as energetic as his father.

When everyone has had their fill of lunch, Dina is surprised to see a couple of flasks surreptitiously pulled out of baskets and passed around among the women (though not to her of course, since she's pregnant). Khadijat's six elderly aunts, almost indistinguishable from one another with their plump bodies, cheery faces, cheek whiskers, and abundance of moles, pull harmonicas out of their bags and lurch to their feet. The other women start to clap as the aunts burst out a rowdy, noisy tune. Dina is impressed— they sound like a legitimate band! Clearly, they have years of experience playing with each other. Soon the other women are up on their feet, swinging each other round and round in a carefree, laugh-filled dance. Skirts swirl, boots tap, and cheeks get red from exertion. Hava pulls Dina to her feet and the whole group forms a merry, clapping circle around Marta, who spins and jumps in the middle with dizzyingly fast footwork. In a moment, Hava leaves Dina's side and glides into the middle with such delicate steps that it looks like she isn't even walking. She raises her arms above her head and twists them in elegant, gentle motions as she circles around her stomping sister. The crowd whoops and hollers and Dina finds herself laughing and clapping along with them. The great-aunts play even faster, and Marta grabs Dina's hand and pulls her into the circle with a dizzying spin. Dina lets her inhibitions go, picks her skirts up, and spins. Two of the cousins grasp her arms and suddenly the whole group is moving together in a tipsy giggling circle.

CHAPTER 20
Caucasus Mountains, Georgia

July, 2018

Callie's throat is raw from screaming Abdullah's name and her eyes are playing tricks on her in the darkness, vacillating between seeing monsters in the shadows or Abdullah's body. But every time, it's only a collection of sticks and debris. After an indeterminate amount of time of desperate, fruitless searching, Callie realizes that she needs to try to go for help. But where to go, she has no idea. Her best guess is to head down the mountain and try to find some sign of civilization. She walks through the night, stumbling from exhaustion, trying not to think about what may have happened to Abdullah or what could happen to her if she stays lost out in this vast wilderness. Close to sunrise, she simply can not go any farther. She collapses to the ground, allowing herself a small rationed portion of the snacks and water from her backpack, and curls up on the wet ground to sleep. If you had told her that she, who usually needs three different pillows and white noise and ear plugs and just the perfect temperature, would have been able to sleep on hard, muddy ground, she never would have believed it. But clearly, the trauma and sleep deprivation kicked in because thirty minutes later, the alarm she had set on her watch wakes her up. She's groggy and sore and running low on hope. But she knows that for Abdullah's sake, she has to keep going. She takes deep breaths, repeating a mantra over and over in her mind, *He's going to be ok. I'm going to find help. He's going to be ok.*

About noon she reaches an overhang and spots a rough lean-to shepherd's hut in the distance, across a valley from where she is. With determination, she cautiously edges her way down a steep embankment and makes her way towards the hut, hoping against hope that it is occupied. As she gets closer, she can make out hundreds of sheep around the hut, which she takes as a good sign. Sure enough, when she arrives at the hut, she finds three rough-looking bearded men sitting on low stools inside the hut, drinking tea around a small metal stove. They are probably all in their 50s or 60s and look and smell like it has been a good while since they've had a bath.

All three men jump up in surprise when she enters their hut. They quickly begin to question her in a language she recognizes as Ramazi. Callie lifts her shoulders and shakes her head. The youngest man, wearing a navy blue tracksuit and low cap, switches to another language. *Georgian, maybe?* Callie guesses. Again, Callie shrugs and shakes her head. The oldest man, with a grizzly gray beard and at least half of his teeth missing, switches to yet another language, which Callie thinks she recognizes as Russian. Again, Callie regretfully shakes her head.

"I'm lost!" she explains, "I was on a horse trek and a mudslide came down the mountain and my friend got lost and I need to get help!"

The three shepherds look back and forth between each other and shake their heads.

"I need... to get... help!" Callie explains louder and slower, feeling tears of frustration and worry rise.

Again, the men shake their heads and then group together and converse. Callie stands in the doorway, waiting. After a moment, the man in the navy tracksuit comes over to her and directs her to sit on a stool. Callie hesitates, feeling an intense need to get help for Abdullah as quickly as possible. After a moment, she realizes that these shepherds are probably going to be her best chance to get help. And so she drops, exhausted, onto the low stool and gratefully accepts a cup of hot herbal tea that the eldest man presses into her hands. All of them gather on the stools around her, concern clear in their eyes. Callie realizes that her best chance at communication will be trying to pantomime with her hands, since her phone is completely worthless—no service, a dead battery, and maybe destroyed thanks to the deluge it had gone through.

Callie stands up to begin her pantomime, and all three men immediately stand out of respect. She waves at them to sit back down, and reluctantly they do.

"I was hiking down the mountain," Callie says, as she moves her hand up and down in the shape of a mountain and then does exaggerated hiking around the room. The men nod— *they're tracking so far.*

"I was hiking, and a mudslide came," Callie pauses, trying to figure out how to act out the mudslide part. Eventually, she mimes to them to pretend that the stool she is sitting on is a mountain, and she walks two fingers down the side of it. The men watch closely. Then, she says, "Whoosh!" and uses her other hand to come sliding down the mountain like an avalanche or mudslide.

"Цу выдлодячос угя фывдло ячстло!" the youngest man exclaims.

"А! Зуя эждывчя воф шаощ!" The middle one replies, nodding his head vigorously.

"Йзы вдлодло цод?" one of them asks her.

"Argh," Callie groans, unsure what the man is trying to ask. As she sits and thinks, the youngest man shyly brings her a blanket, and motions for her to take off her backpack and soaking jacket and wrap up in the blanket instead. With a mix of gratitude for the men's kindness, as well as worry for Abdullah and frustration at the language barrier, Callie accepts the blanket and hands over her backpack and jacket. The men hang her jacket and backpack on a peg near the fire and go talk in a corner. Callie sips the thickly sugared herbal tea, grateful for the zip of energy that she can feel it bringing to her veins. She yawns, the smoke of the fire and the darkness of the warm little room making her drowsy.

The oldest man brings Callie a hunk of bread, torn from a loaf. Callie eats it gratefully and then watches with relief as he pulls a battered Nokia "dumb phone" from the pocket of his vest. Callie smiles with gratitude as he hands it to her— and then she realizes that she has no idea who to call. She doesn't have a single phone number memorized. Feeling suddenly hopeless and overwhelmed and exhausted, she starts to cry. All three men rush about her like worried hens. One of them hands her a handkerchief. Callie blows her nose into it with relief, not even caring that it looks and smells less than clean.

"I just wish one of you spoke English!" she sobs. "Or that I had memorized or at least written down Leila's phone number!"

"Leila?" the older man asks, looking excited. "Khev?"

A ray of hope! "Yes, Leila's guesthouse in Khev! You know it??!"

The men jabber excitedly between themselves, and then one of them makes a call. He talks in Ramazi for a few minutes, and his friend hands him a scrap of paper and pen and he writes down a phone number. A few seconds later, he calls the second number, speaks in Ramazi for just a moment, and then hands the phone to Callie.

"Callie?" It's Leila's voice, sounding both worried and relieved. Callie sighs with gratitude at having finally gotten through to help, and then her stomach drops. How will she tell Leila about Abdullah?

Somehow, she gets through the story. Leila is all business on the other end of the phone, trying through the poor connection to get every detail that she can. She reassures Callie that Oleg and Nastya are safe— the mudslide went down the opposite side of the mountain from where they'd been camping. When Abdullah and Callie had not returned by nightfall, the Russians had immediately called Leila using Abdullah's phone. They had heard the sound of the mudslide and were concerned that Abdullah and Callie had gotten caught up in it. And so at first light, a large search party had left Khev and was headed on a combination of four-wheelers and horses into the mountains to search for Callie and Abdullah, and to pick up Nastya and Oleg.

Callie tries her best to explain exactly where she was when she and Abdullah got separated, but she finds it nearly impossible— it had been so dark and so chaotic and scary that she had gotten totally turned around. She remembered them coming down through the cleared out slope, but that didn't give Leila much direction, since so many places in the mountains had been deforested.

"It's ok, Callie," Leila sighs. "I know you are doing your best. We will find Abdullah, *inshallah*. You just need to focus on getting yourself home safely, ok?"

"But I should go back to the mountain! Maybe in daylight I could retrace my steps, try to help find Abdullah!"

"Callie, after a mudslide, nothing will look like it did before. Believe me, they happen here every couple of years and they make a place unrecognizable. There is nothing you could do," Leila insists. "Besides, twenty men are already on their way there— men who know these mountains like the backs of their hands and have rescued people before. The shepherds told me you haven't slept all night. They have a cot in the back of their hut— get a couple of hours of sleep, and then they will bring you back here, ok?"

"Leila?" Callie's voice cracks, "I'm really sorry about Abdullah."

Callie hears a shuddering breath on Leila's end, but Leila doesn't say anything.

"Leila? Do Rob and Pat know what's going on?" Callie asks.

"Of course. I told them last night," Leila replies.

"I'm glad," Callie sniffles. "Can you ask them to pray for Abdullah?"

Callie can hear a wan smile in Leila's voice, "My dear, they haven't stopped praying for the two of you since I told them last night. They will be relieved to hear that their prayers for you have been answered."

Callie nods, grateful, "Thank them for me, ok? And tell them to keep praying for Abdullah. I'm praying for him too," Callie says quietly, realizing with surprise that what she was saying was true— she had been praying for him under her breath a lot of the time as she had stumbled through the woods the night before. *When was the last time I prayed?* Callie wonders. *Probably when Mom was sick. And look how that turned out. Maybe it would be better if I didn't pray for Abdullah,* she thinks bitterly.

***

"Callie?! Oh honey, we're so thankful you're alright!" Pat's warm arms envelop her and Callie sinks into her pillowy embrace. She and the two shepherds who brought her down the mountain are immediately surrounded by a crowd of people— Pat and Rob, Leila, Fariza and Daud, Rosana, and multiple neighbors whom she recognizes but doesn't know the names of. Thankfully the shepherds field many of the questions from the crowd and Callie nestles against Pat's round shoulder. As the crowd questions the shepherds, Leila approaches Callie.

"Callie... we are very glad that you are safe. How are you doing?" Leila's words and voice are calm, which Callie finds amazing considering the inner turmoil that Leila must be going through.

"I'm ok," Callie replies. "Tired and a bit scraped up, but nothing major. I'm just really worried for Abdullah," Callie tears up, and Leila looks away. She slowly twists a slender silver ring on her left hand.

"We're all worried for him, honey," Pat squeezes Callie's shoulder.

"The men will find him," Leila says resolutely. "You need some food and a shower and sleep. Rosana will help you with everything, ok?" Callie nods, grateful, as Rosana approaches shyly and holds out a hand to lead Callie to the dining room.

Callie is famished— she downs a large bowl of steaming vegetable stew with warm crusty bread, then gratefully takes a much-needed hot shower in the gleaming, newly completed bathrooms. *He made these for me, and now he's gone,* Callie runs a hand down the smooth cream-colored tile on the wall, overwhelmed with grief as the water courses down her. She had held herself together throughout the harrowing previous twenty-four hours, but now that she is alone and safe, she gives in to her emotions and sobs her way through the shower. When she is physically clean and emotionally spent, she heads up to her room and collapses into bed. Just before Callie falls asleep, Pat checks in on her and Callie makes Pat promise to wake her if there's any news of Abdullah.

A couple hours later, Callie awakens to the sound of her door creaking open. "Did they find him?" she asks anxiously.

"Not yet," Pat says as she carries in a tray of savory potato dumplings with sour cream and a tomato, cucumber, and walnut salad. She places it on Callie's bedside table.

"May I?" Pat gestures to Callie's bed, and Callie nods for Pat to sit down. Pat awkwardly pulls her ample frame up into the bed and settles in at the foot of the bed while Callie begins to eat what she assumes is a late dinner.

"I'm really worried that they're not going to find him," Callie whispers, and Pat nods with sympathy. "What if... what if he... didn't make it? The mudslide was so strong! How could anyone survive it?!" Callie starts to cry, and Pat scoots closer and places a comforting hand on Callie's foot.

"We can't give up hope yet, ok? We're gonna continue to hope and pray until we know for sure."

Callie nods, and then hesitates. "I... I really like him. We had a lot of time to talk on our trip... I think... I know what you said about how hard it would be with us coming from two different cultures, and you're right, I know, but I wish... I think I wish that something could work between us." Callie cries harder, and Pat pulls a small package of Kleenex from her pocket and hands it to Callie.

"It's just... I've been praying for him to be safe, but I'm not sure that I trust God to answer those prayers," Callie admits, blowing her nose noisily into a tissue.

"Because of your mom?" Pat probes gently, and Callie nods—she had told Pat about her mom the previous week on one of their walks into town.

"It's just... God didn't answer when we prayed for him to save Mom's life, so why would I trust him to answer now when we're praying for him to save Abdullah's life?" Callie tugs a blanket roughly up her chest, tears streaming down her cheeks.

CHAPTER 21
Khev, Georgia

Winter, 1992

Compared to the frenzied pace of work in the summer, winter in Khev seems tame. The women spend many of their days indoors, working on the darning and knitting that they don't have time to get to the rest of the year. A couple of times they gather together with neighbors and relatives for communal knitting and quilting, which Dina enjoys. She is pitiful at knitting, to Khadijat's very vocal judgment, but she's deft with a sewing needle— thanks to having had to alter all of her own clothes over the years growing up in Tbilisi, and often the clothes of her siblings, for that matter.

Snow drifts cover the yard by late October, not long after the final grapes have been harvested and crushed for wine and chacha, the Georgian equivalent of moonshine. Technically Muslims aren't supposed to drink, but Sureti's Georgian roots seem to trump Islamic tradition in this regard. The men in the family often drink when relatives and neighbors are over, particularly in the winter when cold nights come early and there is nothing else to do. And of course she has gotten to know Sahib, the neighborhood drunk. He is endlessly friendly, chatting with her on the rare occasion when she is allowed to leave the compound to go to the little store up the street. He seems kind, but she has never seen him sober, not even in the early morning. She knows from experience with neighborhood drunks in Tbilisi, as well as with her own father, that he probably doesn't have long to live.

By mid December, Dina is twenty weeks pregnant and finally her miserable morning sickness is abating. Her previously flat stomach is curving slightly— imperceivable under the flowing dresses she wears around the compound, but very noticeable to her. She loves running her hand along her belly, talking in her mind to the little one inside her.

Dina keeps an eye out for Christmas or New Year preparations, but as the end of December nears, it becomes clear to her that neither holiday will be celebrated. She finally asks the sisters, who confirm that Muslims celebrate neither New Year's Eve or Orthodox Christmas on January 7th.

New Year's Eve, the most important holiday of the year for Georgians, dawns bright and beautiful. A fresh snow has fallen overnight and the orchard is magical with streams of sunlight refracting through the icicles like crystals. Dina pulls on her boots and her wool coat and wraps a thick scarf about her before heading outside for a walk in the icy air. *Mom will be in the kitchen already and Sofi will be with her. They will be mixing the dough for khachapuri, so that it can rise in a warm oven all afternoon. Giorgi will be sleeping like the dead on his side of the pullout living room couch, probably snoring like a freight train. And Dato will be whining at Mom from the other side of the couch to keep it down in the kitchen so that he can sleep.* In her mind's eye, Dina can see the whole thing— the familiar, homey rooms. The curtains on the windows that she helped her mom sew in her first sewing project when she was only seven. Her brother's unruly curls. The big blue plastic tub with the broken handle where they always mix dough.

I wonder what it will be like for them, celebrating without me? Dina wonders, knowing deep down, that it will be really sad for all of them. Her grandfather and mother and sisters and brothers will all miss her on this, their first New Year and Christmas apart. *It will be sad for them, and they will miss me,* Dina acknowledges. *But at least they will be together,* she thinks, full of bitter self-pity and sadness as she lifts her icy hands up to her lips, cups them, and blows warm air into them.

"Dina, there you are!" Marta calls from the edge of the house in Ramazi, which Dina has finally started to get under her belt. "Mother is looking for you! We need to get started making breakfast and then after breakfast she wants us to change all the sheets!"

Dina takes a calming breath and steels herself to get started on another long day of chores.

The day passes as usual, with no mention of the holiday. The women do chores all day and then head to bed early. It's dark every day by 4:00 p.m. and there is no electricity, which means no light and no heat. So there really is no reason to stay up. Dina lies in bed under piles of thick blankets, listening to Saidun's deep breathing beside her as her breath frosts in the icy air. He splays his arms and legs out wide like usual, forcing Dina to tuck herself into an awkward ball. She gives in to self-pity again, and allows herself to imagine her family. Tears trickle from the corner of her eye as she pictures them sitting together at a table laden with all their favorite foods, toasting each other and exchanging small gifts. She knows that when midnight approaches, they will all bundle up in a noisy, excited crowd and head down to the riverbank with all the neighbors to watch the midnight fireworks light up the sky. Everyone will shout, "Happy New Year!" and couples will kiss and her siblings will swing one another round and round in circles. Will Mariam and Giorgi still be little enough to jump up and down and blow noisemakers? Will Mariam be able to stay awake and hang out with the rest of the family at the table until the wee hours of the morning, or will she fall asleep on the couch like she did last year? Dina hates not knowing. But more than that, she hates the overwhelming loneliness that encompasses her as she lays tucked between the limbs of her husband. Just as she's feeling extra sorry for herself, she feels a thump from within her, and then she feels the baby twist and turn.

"Hello, little one," she whispers, rubbing her belly gently. "Are you trying to remind me that I'm not alone? Thank you," Dina cries. "Next year, I promise, you and I will celebrate the New Year. We will be together, and neither of us will be alone."

CHAPTER 22
Sureti Valley, Georgia

~~~

July, 2018

It is late and dark when Callie is woken up by excited knocking on her door. Rob bursts in, throwing his long arms wide— "Callie, they've found him! He's alive! They're getting him to a hospital now!"

Callie jumps up out of bed and throws her arms around Rob, "Really?! Oh, that is the best news ever!"

"I know!" Rob laughs, and then Callie laughs with him, overjoyed and relieved. She quickly throws a sweater over her pajamas and follows Rob through the dark night and downstairs to the dining room, which has the festive feel of a party.

Fariza runs and grabs Callie's hands, "They've found him! He's going to be okay!"

"I'm so glad!" Callie exclaims, and the girls hug over Fariza's protruding stomach.

"What happened? Tell me all the details," Callie begs.

"We don't know much," Fariza admits. "Sayid called about an hour ago and said that they'd found Abdullah and that he was alive but pretty beaten up. For sure he has a broken leg, and probably some other injuries as well. But he is conscious and lucid, which is a very good sign. They're taking him now to the hospital in Maidana. If his broken leg is the worst of his injuries, then they should be able to treat him there. If it's anything more serious, then they'll do triage in Maidana and then send him to Tbilisi. Mom's on her way to Maidana now to meet him in the hospital."

"Why didn't you wake me earlier?" Callie exclaims. "I want to go to the hospital too!"

Fariza and Rosana exchange a quick glance which Callie is too worked up to try to interpret.

"It's almost midnight— the only thing you need is a good night's sleep!" Rob steps in, booming cheerfully. "In the morning, we can figure out who is going where. But for now, everyone here needs to head to bed so that we can be well-rested in order to give our boy all the help he will need tomorrow."

"You guys go to bed," Fariza insists. "Rosana and I are going to wait up and prepare food for the search party and for Oleg and Nastya. We're expecting them to return around midnight."

"I'll help," Pat offers, and after a moment, Fariza nods in acquiescence. She is standing awkwardly and holding her back and Callie can tell that she must be in a lot of pain— the day Fariza has had would be grueling for anyone, much less someone who is eight months pregnant. Callie moves to join the women in the kitchen when Rob puts a gentle hand on her shoulder.

"Go back to bed," he says softly but firmly, his gray eyes warm and caring. "You were up all night last night, and your body and spirit have been through massive trauma. You need rest in order to be able to recover. So go rest. We will help down here." At once reluctant and grateful, Callie lets herself be steered up the stairs. As she's about to get to the second floor, she hears a loud rapping on the gate. Callie looks over the railing and sees Rosana open the gate to nearly fifteen neighbor women, all carrying pots of food. One by one, they embrace Rosana and Fariza and then head to the kitchen, where Callie is sure they will be serving well into the night. *Progressive San Francisco could learn a thing or two about community from this little mountain village,* Callie thinks as she slips into bed minutes later. She utters a heartfelt spontaneous prayer of gratitude for Abdullah's safety before falling into a deep sleep.

***

Dear Dad and Lucas,

It's been a crazy past 48 hours here and I just wanted to fill you guys in. Remember I had mentioned to both of you that I was going to be doing a 72-hour horse trek through the mountains? Well, the horse trekking part was great, but the second night we had a ton of rain and a mudslide came down the mountain where we were hiking. It was scary, but I'm totally fine. So no need for you guys to worry about me. Abdullah, my guide, actually did get caught in the mudslide and thankfully made it out with a broken leg as his main injury. He is currently headed to Tbilisi for surgery and the doctors think he should make a full recovery after some bed rest.

So anyway, just wanted to let you guys know. I'm fine, just tired. Will talk soon.

Love, Callie

***

"Callie?? I got your email! Are you alright??" Lucas' worry is palpable through the phone line.

"Yeah, I'm fine, honestly. Like I wrote, I was really lucky– I came out with just a couple of scrapes and bruises. It was Abdullah who had the actual injuries." Callie is surprised to find herself not wanting to talk to Lucas, feeling too physically and emotionally drained to answer the same string of well-meaning questions that her concerned father had asked her over the phone a couple of hours before.

"I really think it's unwise of you to stay there. Can't you leave now and come home?" Callie sighs— her dad had said the same thing. She repeats the explanation she'd given to her father— how the mudslide was a fluke, a once-in-a-lifetime unlucky incident, but that in general she is very safe.

"The mudslide might have been a one-time thing," Lucas admits, "but still, couldn't you go ahead and come home early? I mean, it seems like you've already done a ton to help Leila with her business, right?"

"I'm not coming home now, Lucas. I said I'd stay through the end of the summer, and I'm sticking to my word. There are multiple projects we're working on that I still haven't finished— I'm still finalizing the listings for the guesthouse on Airbnb and booking.com. I'm trying to get an Instagram travel influencer to visit here. We are going to make a buying trip into Tbilisi next week to pick out a bunch of new bedding for the rooms. And lots of other things," Callie adds, feeling defensive.

"Ok, I hear you," Lucas appeases her. "It's just that I miss you, Callie. Three months is too long to go without seeing each other!"

"It is a long time," Callie agrees, feeling surprised to realize that she has barely thought about Lucas over the past few weeks. *It must be all the chaos and drama of the mudslide,* she tells herself, knowing that it's only a partial truth— in reality, all her brain space these past few weeks has been filled with distracting feelings for Abdullah and questions about God.

"Listen, I really should go," Callie makes an excuse.

"Ok, but I wish you didn't have to. Be careful, ok? I love you." Callie can hear the emotion in Lucas' voice and she feels distinctly guilty.

"You too. We'll talk more soon when I'm not so tired, ok?"

Callie hangs up, and sinks into her mattress with relief. She has no idea the massive drama that will be coming her way the next time she talks to Lucas.

***

After an exhausting morning spent weeding the vegetable garden and an afternoon and evening spent washing lunch and dinner dishes and helping with check-in for four Croatian backpackers, Callie heads to the back orchard around 10:00 p.m., once the guests have all retired to their rooms and the dinner dishes are washed and stacked in their appropriate cupboards. She is relieved to have a few moments to herself after the people-filled day she's had. With Abdullah and Leila still at the hospital in Tbilisi, Callie has taken over managing the guests. It is an exhausting job.

Callie grimaces as she feels a pull in her lower back— it seems like this is the first time she has had a break all week. On Monday, it hadn't taken the doctors at the small local hospital in Maidana long to realize that they weren't equipped to handle Abdullah's injuries. So he had been transported over the Zudi Pass to Tbilisi, and had spent the past few days in the hospital there. He'd had surgery on his shattered tibia the first day, and a couple of metal pins put in. He'd gotten fourteen stitches on a big gash on his head, and been told to rest his two broken ribs. The doctors had said that he was incredibly lucky to be alive and not be in worse shape. They were keeping him for observation in Tbilisi for a week, and then he would come home and recuperate for six to eight weeks with a cast and crutches.

Leila had been by Abdullah's side the entire time. Callie wished that she could go visit him, but she knew that it would not be culturally acceptable for her to go to Tbilisi to see him. And so she stayed in Khev, where there was more than enough work to do. They were slammed with guests, and there was an unending list of things to do— bed linens to change, laundry to wash, meals to cook, floors to mop, dishes to scour, chickens to feed and eggs to gather, vegetables to weed, etc. Not to mention all the bookings to deal with online and email correspondence with guests. In their absence, Callie quickly grew to appreciate the incredible amount of work that Abdullah and Leila did on a daily basis to keep the guesthouse running.

Despite being only weeks away from her due date, Fariza came almost every day and was a lifesaver with the cooking. Rosana also stayed extra hours and handled a lot of the cleaning. Despite being guests themselves, Rob and Pat graciously spent their final week at the guesthouse joining Callie in pitching in wherever they could. Most frustrating to Callie personally was having to deal with persnickety guests— they had a middle-aged couple from Paris who, with their snobbiness and endless demands, fit Callie's every worst stereotype of French people. It seemed that every time she turned around, one of them was complaining about something— the bed linen wasn't soft enough, or their tea was too cold, or the hot water in the bathroom took too long to heat up, etc. *I am never going into the hospitality business,* Callie promised herself.

Walking in the orchard at night relaxes her. Callie takes a deep breath in and rolls her shoulders, then stretches her arms up over her head. She glances over her shoulder to confirm that no one is around, and then bends down on the grass into "downward dog" and gradually moves into one of her favorite ten-minute yoga routines. *I haven't even thought about yoga or exercise all month!* She marvels that something that had been such a foundational daily habit in San Francisco had so quickly fallen to the wayside in Georgia. *Though I suppose I'm getting plenty of exercise with all the chores I'm doing!* Callie rolls her eyes and then stretches, luxuriating in the familiar feel of the yoga positions she is working her way through. Though it has been a couple of days since the mudslide, her body is still sore and, if she admits it, her mind is still in turmoil. Staying busy around the guesthouse has helped keep her from having time to think about what she recently went through.

When Callie finishes her yoga routine, she stands and looks up. The sky is black and so clear that she can see countless stars. Coming from starless San Francisco, Callie does not take Khev's night sky for granted. She walks past the chicken yard, silent and abandoned since all the chickens are safe in their enclosed pen for the night. An owl gives a lonely call from a tree only a few feet from Callie. A chill breeze raises goosebumps on her sunburnt arms as she approaches the clearing behind the orchard. She hugs herself, wishing she'd grabbed a sweater.

She strains her eyes, trying to make out the shapes of the mountains that she knows are so close. But the darkness is so thick that, despite the faint starlight overhead, she cannot see anything.

This is what Rob was talking about with God, Callie realizes with a jolt, thinking back to a conversation she'd had with Rob the previous day. *That just because you can't see Him, doesn't mean He isn't there.* She blows out a frustrated breath and kicks at a clod of dirt. *It's not fair— Rob and Pat at least seem to see and experience God sometimes. How am I supposed to believe in something that I can't see? Do you hear me, God?!* Callie looks up at the sky, shouting in her mind.

I'm here, ok? You have my attention! I'm so grateful to be alive and beyond grateful that Abdullah's okay! But maybe that was just a fluke. How am I supposed to know you're real?! I can't see you any more than I can see those mountains in the darkness! I need some sign that you even exist!

At the exact moment Callie whisper-shouts those final words, a shooting star arcs across the sky. Callie sucks in her breath, and instinctively glances around, wishing there were someone there to confirm what she just saw. In all her time in Georgia, she has never seen a shooting star. She looks back up at the sky, which is as still and placid as if nothing had happened. But inside Callie something has shifted.

I think that was for me, she thinks with awe. *Was the God of the universe really communicating with me?* Callie shivers, and chokes up inside. Slowly, she heads back to her room, where she digs the slim Bible Pat and Rob had given her out from under the pile of books on her bedside table.

Gingerly, Callie opens the Bible, unable to remember the last time she had actually read it of her own volition. Early high school, maybe? Unsure where to start, Callie flips open to a random page, whispering in her heart, *God, I think you just tried to communicate with me outside. Pat and Rob say that you speak through the Bible. If you're real, would you…* Callie feels almost foolish to ask, *…would you speak to me?*

She flips open the Bible, holding her breath. The page opens to Jeremiah 31, and Callie's eyes immediately fall on the third verse, "I have loved you with an everlasting love; therefore with lovingkindness I have drawn you."

This verse is for me, Callie is thunderstruck. Tears begin to trickle down her cheeks. *God is trying to show me that he loves me, that he wants to draw me to himself. Oh Lord, I'm so sorry that I doubted you for so long. I'm sorry for all the anger and resentment that I've held against you for all the years since Mom died. I'm sorry that I've run so far and been so distant. I want to come back, Lord. If you will have me, I want to know what it's like to have connection with you. I want what Rob and Pat have. What my Dad has. I want to know your love.*

Callie closes the Bible and places it gently at the top of the pile on her bedside table. She turns off the light and climbs under her blankets, still half unable to believe the combination of the shooting star and the verse that both seemed so perfectly aimed for her. She feels a combination of being known and loved that she hasn't felt for a very long time. For years to come, that night will be a cornerstone for Callie, a turning point in her story.

***

The next morning, Callie wakes up early. Her normal routine is to lie in bed and scroll Instagram for a few minutes after she wakes up. But this morning, she hesitates as she reaches for her phone. Instead, she picks the Bible up from the bedside table and opens to the middle, to Psalms. She remembers that Psalms were her mom's favorite part of the Bible. She reads one, does some stretching, and heads to the shower. It feels freeing to start her day without social media.

On the way to the shower, she glances out across the back pasture. To the left of the woodshed, she again notices that little shack that she'd seen out back before, but never explored. *I'm gonna go check it out this week while Abdullah and Leila are gone,* she thinks, looking forward to doing some sleuthing. *Maybe I'll find out some things about their secretive family.*

Later that afternoon, once the guests have had lunch and Callie has helped Rosana clear the table and wash the dishes, Callie has a few minutes of free time to herself. Rob and Pat have gone to their room for their daily afternoon nap. Callie throws her hair up into a high ponytail and, making sure that no one is watching, heads back into the orchard. She passes the chicken coop, the garden, the gazebo, and the swing. The sun is pleasantly warm on the back of her neck and the sky is blue. It's a perfect summer day.

At first, when she can't get the shed door open, Callie thinks her mission is a failure. But eventually she realizes that the base of the door is overgrown with weeds. She lifts the door and pulls, and it creaks open. Inside it is dark and dusty, like the woodshed. Callie assumes that both were built at the same time by the same person, since their construction seems identical. She does notice that the inner walls of this shed, unlike the woodshed, have been painted.

This must be their storage shed, Callie realizes, looking at the piles of boxes and belongings stacked precariously to her right. Everything is covered with layers of dust and looks ancient. *Pretty sure I would just get rid of everything in here,* Callie thinks with distaste as she eyes a broken lamp shade and a stool that is missing a leg. *Maybe I don't want to go through this after all...* she hesitates. *I will just leave that stack for later,* she decides, turning towards the narrow bed and table on the left side of the room. *Did someone once live out here?* she wonders. *And if so, who?*

She does a preliminary search around, but finds no clues. She glances over at the stack of boxes and junk, still not wanting to go through them. She's also slightly worried that Leila might realize that someone had been through them. *Though honestly, it seems like no one ever comes out here.*

Just as Callie is trying to decide what to do next, she hears footsteps outside. The hair on the back of her neck stands up and she ducks quickly. Did someone see her come out here and follow her? If Rosana finds her out here and tells Leila, Callie will have no good explanation. She holds her breath and waits. Eventually, the footsteps die down. She risks peeking her head up and looks through the grimy windows to see Rob loping across the lawn to the swing. She breathes a sigh of relief and turns back to the room.

On a hunch, Callie lifts the thin mattress. There is no dresser and no drawers in the hut, so she figures that if she wanted to hide something somewhere, she would hide it under her mattress. She sucks in her breath when her search reveals two yellowed letters sitting on the plywood under the mattress.

Gingerly, she picks them up. They both look quite old. With bated breath, Callie lays the mattress back down, sits on it carefully, and opens the first letter.

Shoot! she mutters. The letter is in beautiful, looping Georgian cursive, which of course Callie cannot read. She opens the second letter, expecting a second disappointment. Like the first letter, the second letter is in Georgian. But the second letter contains a photograph. It is sepia-toned and, from the clothing and hairstyles, looks like it's from the 1980s. Callie holds it up to the light from the window and sees an old man, a woman, and five children of various ages. They're all standing close together and smiling. In the center, a slender girl wearing curvy jeans is holding a birthday cake and grinning.

"Wait a minute...," Callie squints, and holds the picture closer. With her long auburn waves, the girl in the center looks familiar. Callie is certain that it's Leila, though it doesn't make any sense for her to be in non-Ramazi clothes, surrounded by people who clearly aren't Ramazis.

"Who were you in the past?" Callie whispers to the picture, "and how did you get to be where you are today?" The picture in her hand offers no answers, only more questions. After a moment of hesitation, Callie carefully slips the letters and the photo into the waistband of her floor-length skirt and heads to her room to find a better hiding place for them.

CHAPTER 23
Khev, Georgia

March, 1993

"Take the back burner completely off and scrub underneath," Khadijat directs, even more uptight than normal about cleaning.

"It's a really big deal that they're coming," Hava explains. "I was a kid when they last came— maybe seven years ago? And Grandfather's health isn't ideal, so it wouldn't surprise me if this is the last time they're able to come."

"Why do they live in Russia and you guys live in Georgia? Did they get separated when the Soviet Union fell?" Dina guesses.

Hava nods— it's an all too common situation, families divided by the collapse of the Soviet Union. What used to be one giant conglomerate country split almost overnight in 1991 into fifteen countries, and many people suddenly found themselves separated by country borders from friends, family, and homes.

"As you know, Father is from actual Ramazistan," Hava explains as she scrubs the small windows behind the kitchen sink. "His ancestors have lived there for generations," she says proudly. Dina nods, well aware of this fact. She's pretty sure each member of the family has mentioned it to her at least ten times in the past six months — their Ramazi roots are something they all take very seriously and hold with great pride and honor. To Dina, it seems like they view Ramazis who live in Ramazistan as kind of the royalty or upper class, whereas those who live in the Ramazi villages in Georgia are sort of seen as second class citizens— not of the true, purest blood. It seems dumb to Dina, but quite important to the family.

Hava continues, "Since my father is the oldest son, he was able to go to university, while his younger brother stayed home to take care of their parents. Father studied forestry at an agricultural college in Tbilisi, which is where he learned Georgian. When they were first married, he and Mother lived back in Ramazistan. But later he got a job in the woodworking factory here in Khev, so they moved here. Of course it collapsed like all the other factories around here when the Soviet Union fell," Hava sighs and Dina nods. She's seen the looted remnants of the once vibrant factory on the edge of town. For most Georgians, the collapse of the Soviet Union has made life much less stable. While Dina is theoretically all for the ideas of democracy, so much so that she willingly risked her life attending pro-democracy protests during her student days, on a practical level, the vacuum of power left by the collapse of the Soviet Union has led to nothing good — mostly poverty, instability, and crime.

Dina scrubs the burners, using her fingernail to scrape off the most stubborn crusts. "So your grandparents and cousins are coming here to visit?"

"I can't wait!" Hava exclaims. "My cousin Selima and I used to be best friends, back when we could easily travel back and forth between Georgia and Russia, when there was no border. We'd spend almost every summer there when I was little. But now we need visas even to get into Russia, and they're almost impossible to get. So our only chance to see our relatives is if they come visit us here."

"Have your parents thought about moving back there?" Dina asks, curious, and hoping that the answer is no— the thought of getting dragged with the family to another country sounds terrifying.

"They've talked about it these past few years, especially after the factory collapsed. But the visa situation is complicated, and plus Ramazistan is really unstable right now. There are even rumors of a war with Russia," Hava frowns, looking really concerned. "Plus, their whole lives are here. Mom and Dad have spent years building this house. I can't imagine them leaving it. For better or for worse, Khev is home for all of us now."

"Are you done with the stove?" Khadijat looks over Dina's shoulder, and takes the rag from her hand. With a huff, she expertly scours the side panel— an area Dina hadn't even thought to scrub.

"There!" she says with satisfaction. "Hava and Marta, keep cleaning the kitchen. Dina, come with me," Khadijat folds her thick arms and struts out of the room, leaving Dina to lumber after her as fast as her giant pregnant belly will allow her. She follows Khadijat, assuming she is heading toward some new chore. She is surprised and concerned when they enter the dining room to find Anzor and Saidun seated at the table, clearly waiting for her.

"Sit down," Anzor gestures to one of the chairs at the table. Dina raises her eyebrows, surprised— the men and women never sit together.

"Come on, just for today. You could probably stand to take the weight off your feet anyway," Khadijat presses a hand lightly to Dina's back and steers her to the table. Her unexpected kindness makes Dina even more suspicious.

Anzor clears his throat, looking uncomfortable. He takes a deep breath, then begins, "As you know, my relatives are coming from Ramazistan next week. This is an extremely big deal. They are very important people," there is pride in his eyes and in his voice and Dina nods hesitantly, unsure of where this conversation is going. *Maybe there are some sort of traditions that I am supposed to learn for how to interact with paternal extended relatives?*

"As I'm sure you are aware," he continues, "your initial arrival and marriage created quite the scandal and drama in the village here in Khev. Half of our neighbors would not talk to us for months. Thankfully, the rumor mill has died down."

"Or moved on to other topics! Like how Pasha Raxminov gambled away his family's car in one drunken poker game!" Saidun guffaws, only to be silenced by a stern glance from his father.

"Thanks to Allah, the village has accepted you. Especially now that you are understanding and speaking Ramazi well, and that you are...are..." Anzor gestures awkwardly to Dina's belly, unable to say the word 'pregnant'.

"Our relatives from Ramazistan, however, are much more fundamentalist than the villagers here. They hold to higher standards. Marrying a non-Muslim would be unthinkable there," Anzor explains.

"Basically, you're gonna have to fake it while they're here," Saidun tosses in.

"What?" Dina frowns, confused.

"Pretend you're Ramazi," Khadijat explains, as if it should have been obvious. "We have told them you are from a Ramazi family that has lived in Tbilisi for decades, so they will understand that your Ramazi language isn't perfect, and that you don't perfectly understand all of our customs. But it cannot *ever* get out to them that you are actually Georgian. Our friends and relatives in Khev have agreed to help us in keeping this secret."

Dina's eyebrows rise in shock. She can feel her cheeks getting hot with anger and frustration at the ridiculous, stupid charade she is about to take part in.

"You have to understand, reputation is everything," Anzor tries to explain. "If they find out, our reputation would be ruined. It would be a giant shame on our entire family. If others in Ramazistan find out, it could have massive repercussions. My family members there could lose jobs."

Dina sighs, "Fine, I will do what you need me to do while they are here."

Saidun, Anzor, and Khadijat exchange quick glances, and Dina's heart beat picks up.

"What else is there?" she asks with foreboding.

"Mother told them your name is Leila. That's what she wrote them last year, when we first got married. It's a Ramazi name," Saidun blurts. "Dina is such a classic Georgian name— it would've been a dead giveaway."

"Seriously?" Dina throws her arms up in the air. "This is ridiculous! You can't just *change my name!!* Sooner or later, somehow, they will find out! You know that, right?"

"Enough disrespect from you!" Khadijat slams a fist on the table and Dina quickly shuts her mouth and crosses her arms over her chest, on top of her bulging stomach. "You have been a problem from the beginning. In fact— I chose your name for a reason— Leila means 'darkness' in Arabic. And *you* have brought darkness and trouble to our family!" Khadijat glares at Dina, her round cheeks red and hot.

Yeah, well blame your precious son! Dina wants to shout, but keeps her mouth closed, unwilling to risk physical harm to herself or to the baby if she dares to disrespect Saidun again in public.

"I know it is a lot to process," Anzor says gently. "But you have handled the past year bravely and I trust you to do the same with this new adjustment. And anyway, it is good that we are making this change now, before the baby comes. Your child cannot ever know that he isn't one hundred percent Ramazi."

"What are you talking about?" Dina asks, quickly scrubbing at unwanted tears that had started with Anzor's kind words.

"If people outside of Khev find out that our kid isn't full-blooded Ramazi, no family will want their daughter to marry him. They will be afraid that he carries bad blood," Saidun explains, as if it should be obvious. "For the sake of his future, we have to keep your past hidden. And besides," he grins, "look on the bright side— you get to pretend that you are a real Ramazi!" He says this as if it is the greatest honor possible.

***

And so, for the next few weeks, Dina plays the role of dutiful Ramazi wife to the best of her ability. It's honestly not hard to fool the visiting Ramazi relatives, because her role as a bride is to be a wordless servant. She avoids the relatives as much as possible and sticks to her chores, of which there are plenty. Slowly, she and the family get used to her new name. *Darkness...* Dina thinks bitterly, deciding to embrace the name. *It appropriately sums up my new life.*

CHAPTER 24
Khev, Georgia

April, 1993

The April mountain weather is cold and gray and snowy. Leila sits propped against pillows in bed, holding her baby girl in her arms and marveling at the overwhelming love she feels. In fact, she feels as if her heart will burst. Surely there was never a more beautiful baby in all of Georgia, with her porcelain white skin and head of dark curls. The baby begins to grunt and root and Leila gingerly exposes her tender, swollen breast and guides the baby's small mouth to attach.

"I hate that you don't have a name yet, little one," she coos. Ramazi tradition is that the paternal grandfather names all grandchildren when they're eight days old— and parents get no say in the matter. Though Leila respects Anzor, she is afraid he will choose a name that she doesn't like.

Saidun stomps his feet at their bedroom door, knocking the snow off his boots and brushing it from his jacket before entering. Leila discreetly wraps a blanket around her nursing daughter.

"How's my little princess?" Saidun asks, glancing towards the blanket.

"Wonderful," Leila smiles, "and hungry!"

"Good, good! She should eat all she can to grow healthy and strong. Are you feeding her often enough?" Saidun looks concerned.

Leila laughs, "All I'm doing is feeding her! Around the clock!"

"Can I see her? When she's done?" Saidun asks gruffly.

Leila reaches under the blanket and gently unlatches the baby, whose eyes roll back in her head with a look of milk-drunk satisfaction as she slips into sleep. Leila glances at Saidun, who is staring at the baby with the same naked wonder and adoration that Leila herself feels. *Maybe my mother is right,* Leila thinks with surprise. *Maybe children can bring a man and woman together even in a hard marriage.*

"Do you want to hold your daughter?" Leila holds the baby towards Saidun, who glances furtively at the door, before hopping up and closing it.

"What are you doing?" Leila asks.

"I'm not allowed to hold her with the door open," Saidun replies, as if it is the most obvious thing in the world.

"What do you mean?" Leila frowns.

"Men aren't allowed to hold their children if anyone can see."

"What??!" Leila explodes. "You have got to be kidding me! So are you telling me for her whole life, you will never pick up our daughter if anyone is around??"

Saidun shrugs his shoulders and shakes his head.

Leila blows out a big breath of air and mumbles angrily under her breath, "I thought I already knew all the pig-headed backward idiot traditions of this stupid place, but clearly I was wrong."

"Hey! That's enough!" Saidun's shoulders tense and his mouth tightens in anger, and Leila realizes belatedly that the seeming closeness between them after the baby's birth had lulled her into letting her guard down. But Saidun is still Saidun and she still needs to guard her mouth and be careful.

"I'm sorry, I didn't mean that. Honestly. I just want you to be able to have a good relationship with our daughter." Leila realizes with surprise that she actually didn't mean it. While there are certainly Ramazi traditions that she thinks are ridiculous, there are plenty of other things that she's slowly come to really appreciate about the society.

"I want that too," Saidun looks sincere. "Here, hand her to me while we know no one is looking!"

Saidun cradles his daughter with the same tenderness that he uses for animals. He gently strokes her cheek with one of his thick hairy fingers and whispers to her that she is the most beautiful thing he has ever seen.

***

Two weeks after Fariza is born, Leila gets a terrible case of mastitis. She runs a raging fever, her breasts are red and burn like fire, and she's racked with chills. The great-aunts bring cabbage leaves and stuff Leila's bra with them, sharing their own nursing stories from decades past and promising the cabbage will leach out the excess milk and infection. Khadijat tries various teas and herbal remedies, but nothing seems to help. Finally, Anzor travels an hour to Maidana where he can get antibiotics from a pharmacy— a sacrifice of both time and money that the family can ill afford, as Khadijat makes Leila painfully aware. The antibiotics quickly nip the fever in the bud, but Leila still takes a long time to recover. The combination of the hard birth, mastitis, and not sleeping much at nights takes its toll on her.

On the one hand, Leila feels guilty that she is missing so much of the critical spring planting season, whereas on the other hand, she's grateful for the time she gets to spend lying in bed and marveling at her precious daughter. Every movement, every expression seems unique and exciting. Though Leila remembers clearly when her younger brothers were born, the level of love she feels for Fariza is totally different. She is completely smitten. She's grateful that Saidun seems smitten as well and saddened that neither Anzor nor Khadijat is interested in the baby. Instead of being grateful for a healthy granddaughter, they are both disappointed that it was not a boy. Leila got furious one day when she heard neighbors stopping by to give Khadijat their condolences on the birth of a granddaughter.

"If it had been a boy, we would have slaughtered and roasted a lamb in his honor," Leila had overheard one of the neighbors say with regret. "But hopefully, there will be another baby soon. *Inshallah*, it will be a boy next time!"

All week, Leila notices Marta and Hava passing worried glances her way. She knows something is up, but neither of them will say anything, which only serves to worry her more. She hears many heated conversations between Khadijat and Saidun, but they're all in Ramazi and so, infuriatingly, Leila can't fully understand them— her Ramazi has definitely improved, but it's hard for her to follow when people speak quickly. She builds up the courage to ask Saidun what is going on, but he refuses to explain.

Finally, after a week of waiting for the other shoe to drop, Leila is relieved to see Khadijat striding purposefully towards her across the orchard, where she'd been out getting a bundled-up Fariza some fresh air. Whatever Khadijat had to say was likely not going to be good news, but at least Leila would no longer be in the dark.

"We're getting another wife," Khadijat announces resolutely.

Leila frowns, confused, "Excuse me?"

"For Saidun. We're getting him another wife." Khadijat says the words slowly and clearly, with no intonation or inflection.

"Wait, he's divorcing me?? I just had his baby!" Leila's cheeks start to burn and her heart beats fast.

"Of course he's not divorcing you!" Khadijat throws her hands up in the air. "Calm down. He's just getting a second wife."

"A second wife?! What?! That's even worse! He can't do that!"

"Of course he can," Khadijat says calmly. "The Koran allows men to have up to four wives. And Saidun is the only son in our family. You just gave birth to a daughter. We need to ensure that our family line will have sons." Khadijat explains as if she is explaining simple addition to an elementary school child.

"This is ridiculous! I am not going to be a second wife!" Leila huffs, thrusting one arm down by her side, which jostles Fariza, who starts to cry.

"Here," Khadijat looks at Leila judgmentally, like she is a bad mother, and grabs Fariza out of her arms. She holds Fariza up on her shoulder and pats her back. To the frustration of Leila, Fariza quickly quiets and nuzzles into her grandmother's solid shoulder.

"Stop being so dramatic," Khadijat says sternly. "You *won't* be a second wife. You will always be the first wife, no matter how many women Saidun marries."

Leila blanches, collapsing against the tree behind her as Khadijat huffs away, softly patting sleeping Fariza.

***

"You know she doesn't like that," Leila blows out a frustrated breath as she watches Saidun try to tie a red-faced, wailing Fariza to the wooden board that Ramazi babies sleep on. The board is attached to rockers and looks like a cradle with no sides. To keep the baby from falling out, you wrap a swaddle blanket tightly around the baby and tie it to the board. Fariza wiggles and squirms, and Saidun eventually shouts, "I've had it! Enough! Here, you deal with her!" as he thrusts the furious baby towards Leila, knowing full-well that Leila will not tie her to the cradle board.

"She's going to have a crooked back because of you," he grumps at Leila, who cuddles Fariza close in her arms and whispers calming "shhhhs" under her breath. "Mother says babies need plenty of board time in order to keep their backs straight. Everyone in our family slept in these cradles, in fact— this was my father's cradle when he was a baby!" Saidun says proudly. "And it's not even good enough for you!" he frowns at Leila.

"It's not that," Leila sighs. "It's just that she doesn't like it." Leila smiles down at Fariza's dark curls and holds out a finger for Fariza to grasp in her little fist. "You know what you want, don't you, little one?" she coos at her daughter.

"I know who she gets that from!" Saidun rolls his eyes in exasperation and looks pointedly at Leila.

"Hey! I have gone over and above to try to fit in here, to try to adjust to your family's expectations."

Saidun at first looks like he is going to contradict her, but stops himself and eventually nods with reluctant agreement.

"Speaking of going over and above…" Leila hesitates, twisting the ring on her finger, wondering whether the moment is right to bring up this "second wife" plan that Khadijat mentioned. Her former self would have flown off the handle and gone storming to Saidun the second Khadijat mentioned it, but after spending almost a year in Khev, she has been forced to learn to swallow her emotions and bide her time. She glances at Saidun, who is sitting beside her on the bed and smiling down at Fariza's foot as he tickles it. The calico kitten he gifted to Leila when she was pregnant has now grown into a sleek, self-satisfied cat they named Whiskers. Whiskers hops up onto the bed and nudges her head between Saidun's hand and Fariza's foot, clearly suggesting that Saidun rub her instead of the baby. Saidun laughs good-naturedly and rubs them both. Leila realizes that with Saidun in this relaxed of a mood, now is probably as good a time as any to bring up what she has been burning to ask him.

"Speaking of going over and above," she says again, "your mother mentioned to me that you are planning to marry a second wife."

Saidun's eyes dart up, and he has the decency to look briefly ashamed. Then he squares his shoulders, "It is the best thing to do for the family. I am the only son, after all. It is essential that we have an heir to pass down the family name."

"Your daughter is only two months old!" Leila shrieks, unable to control herself any longer. "How can you talk about getting another wife?? How do you know that I won't have five sons in the next ten years??!"

Saidun's face hardens, growing defensive in response to Leila's anger, "Of course nothing is certain. *Inshallah* you will have sons. But we cannot risk our family name and honor on one woman. Plus, it will be good to have a Ramazi wife."

"That's what this is all about then?! You look down on me because I'm Georgian?? It's not fair! I never even wanted to come here to begin with!" Leila whisper-shouts, aware of Saidun's family in the adjoining rooms. Tears stream down her cheeks. "You forced me to come here when I didn't even want to come. I have tried so hard to fit in here since I came. And now you are just throwing me away like trash! What will become of me and Fariza?" Seemingly on cue, Fariza lets out a wail and, automatically, Leila begins to bounce her in an attempt to quiet her down.

"Hush, hush, don't get hysterical," Saidun crosses his arms and frowns at Leila. "Can't you see that you're upsetting the baby? No one is throwing you away, or Fariza. Fariza will always be the beloved first daughter. We will make sure she grows up and is provided for and marries a good husband. You're making way too big a deal out of this. Having a second wife is normal. You know Pavel, who runs the grocery story? He has three wives! I'm sure none of them complained when he remarried," Saidun frowns at Leila, communicating with his eyes that she is being overly dramatic. "It's for the good of the family."

"Everything you do is for the good of the family!" Leila accuses.

"Of course it is," Saidun says slowly, looking bewildered that Leila is speaking words that should obviously be a compliment in a tone of accusation. "How else would it be?"

"I'm going to bed," Leila huffs, rolling towards the wall and cuddling Fariza close in her arms. Talking with Saidun is pointless.

***

"It might not be so bad," Hava offers hesitantly, hands deep in a sink of dirty dishes and soapy water.

Marta snorts so hard that tea almost comes out of her nose, "Oh yeah, second wives are often an *awesome* addition! I'm sure we'll all be one big, happy family!" her voice drips with sarcasm. She tips her large teacup up towards the ceiling and downs it in one gulp before tossing it into the sink of dishes Hava is washing.

Leila runs a hand down her face, "It's going to be awful! I can't believe your mother is doing this to me."

"She's not doing it *to* you, she just feels pressure to have an heir. It's of critical importance in our culture," Hava gently explains.

"I know, I know. That's what everyone keeps telling me! But I don't have to like it! And it's not fair that it's all happening so soon." Leila gives the broom an extra hard shove, accidentally sending dirt flying across the kitchen floor.

"It might be nice to have an extra set of hands around here," Hava suggests. "There's more than enough work."

"That's for sure!" Marta grunts, heaving a huge bucket of dirty mop water towards the door. "Actually, why don't you see if you can convince Mother to bring THREE new wives!" she jokes. "We'll give them all the laundry and dishes!"

"And sweeping and mopping!" Hava smiles.

"And canning!" Leila adds, and all three girls laugh.

"Definitely the canning," Marta agrees.

Leila pauses, then asks, "Do you know who the bride will be? Or when she will come?"

Hava shakes her head reluctantly.

"You think Mother keeps us apprised of her scheming?" Marta snorts. "We're as in the dark as you are. The only thing we know for sure is this time, Saidun will not get away with kidnapping some poor Georgian girl. Mother about killed him last time— he's smart enough to let her choose this time." Marta darts a glance at Leila, "No offense. For our sakes, we're glad you're here. You just were not Mother's first choice."

"Oh, I'm well aware of that," Leila returns the broom to the corner and begins to dry the dishes that Hava has washed.

Hava looks sideways at her and says seriously, "We don't know who will come, or when she will come. But prepare yourself, because when it happens, it will happen fast."

***

Hava is right. A week later, Leila is nursing Fariza in her bed when she is surprised by a knock on the door. Leila tosses a blanket across her shoulder and shouts, "Come in!"

Khadijat enters the room, looking unperturbed at the sight of Leila nursing in bed, and closes the door behind her.

"I am here to tell you that the new bride will arrive in two days," she announces, her back straight and her eyes averted from Leila.

"Two days?!" Leila jolts, shocked at the speed at which things are changing. Fariza unlatches and begins to fuss. Distractedly, Leila reaches under the blanket to try to feel for her nipple and put it back in Fariza's mouth. Fariza fusses and squirms and refuses to latch.

"Oh for heaven's sakes, get rid of the blanket!" Khadijat huffs, "It's not like I haven't seen dozens of women nurse before."

Leila hesitates, and drops the blanket. Now that she can actually see what she's doing, it's much simpler to latch the baby. Fariza guzzles contentedly and Leila turns her attention back to her mother-in-law.

"You will need to pack up your room."

"What?" Leila asks, confused.

"Where do you think the new bride will sleep? This is the only room we have for her!"

"What about *us??*" Leila asks in shock. "Where will Fariza and I go??"

"We are getting the building ready behind the orchard," Khadijat explains awkwardly.

"Wait… the storage shed?? That building is falling down! We can't live there!" Leila replies in horror and desperation. She looks down at her beautiful baby girl, who has fallen asleep at her breast. "Please," Leila pleads, looking entreatingly at Khadijat, "you can't make us live there."

Khadijat sighs regretfully, "I know it's not ideal, but it's the only option. We can't send a new bride out there— her family would never allow it."

"And since my family is far away, you can just do whatever you want with me?! You already made me give up my family, my language, my religion, even my own *name*, for crying out loud. You can't make me give up my room, too!" Leila sputters, her anger beginning to get the best of her.

Khadijat, who normally clamps down on any outbursts of Leila's, decides to let this one slide. "Look, it's only temporary. We all have to make sacrifices for the good of the family. It's the beginning of summer. The weather is nice. You and Fariza will be fine out there. And soon we will build the new house, and then there will be room for everyone, ok? Just pack up your things. Have the girls help you. You need to free up this room by tomorrow. Understood?"

Leila grits her teeth and refuses to answer. She feels so vulnerable and helpless, pinned to the bed with a sleeping baby attached to her exposed breast. Khadijat stands by the door, arms crossed and eyes stern.

They stay in a stalemate of silence and glares for a few minutes, before Khadijat finally turns around and walks stiffly out of the room.

When the door closes, Leila deflates. "What are we going to do?" she moans, burying her face in Fariza's soft black curls.

CHAPTER 25

Sureti Valley, Georgia

July, 2018

"Honey, you need a break!" Pat pokes her head into the guys' dorm room, where Callie is changing the sheets on both sets of bunk beds. Three college buddies from Colorado had spent the past two days at the guesthouse. They had been rowdy and friendly, but left quite the mess after themselves. Poor Rosana had cleaned the bathrooms twice a day while they were there instead of her usual once a day. And the amount of food the guys had plowed through was unprecedented in Callie's guesthouse experience. But they'd already left glowing reviews online, and one of them had asked for Callie's number, which she had graciously declined, saying that she already had a boyfriend. Callie was glad Abdullah had not been around for that exchange.

"I'm almost done," Callie grimaces from the top bunk, where she's trying to get a fitted sheet to tuck in around the mattress edges. "Man, I'm terrible at this! If I wasn't working for free, Leila should fire me!" Callie laughs, tucking a loose strand of dark hair behind her ear.

"I'm sure she appreciates all your help, especially pitching in now with what a hard week it's been for everyone." Pat enters the room and hands a comforter and two pillows up to Callie.

"Speaking of pitching in, let me help you finish flipping this room."

"Oh Pat, you really don't need to! You're a guest here!"

"Come on now, you're gonna offend me! Rob and I sure hope we feel more like family than guests after all this time together," Pat smiles, shaking out the sheets for the bottom bunk.

"You really do, honestly," Callie says sincerely. She pauses, holding the pillow in her arms. "Getting to know you guys has been an unexpected bonus of my time here."

"For us too, honey," Pat smiles. "Speaking of, we want to get a meal with you before we leave tomorrow."

"Tomorrow! In all the chaos of this week, I forgot you guys leave tomorrow!" Callie almost wails.

"It's gone by fast, that's for sure. But we will stay in touch. We were thinking of going into Maidana for lunch. They have a great burger place there and Rob has been hankering for a burger."

"Oh, a burger sounds amazing! I mean, I love the food here, but I have definitely missed some foods from home!" Callie climbs down the bunk bed ladder awkwardly in her floor length skirt and begins to gather up trash from around the room— candy wrappers, scraps of paper, soda cans. On one bedside table she crinkles up her nose as she finds three wizened, half-eaten apple cores.

"Boys!" Pat shrugs and laughs. "I raised two of them. Three, if you count Rob! Honestly, this isn't so bad! So, are we on for lunch?"

"It's a date!" Callie agrees, "let me just finish this room and we can go. Do you mind if I run by a photo store when we're there? I've got an idea for a goodbye gift for Leila that I want to do before I leave."

"That sounds great! I'll go tell Rob to get ready."

As Callie is grabbing her sunglasses and purse twenty minutes later, she spontaneously reaches into the drawer of her bedside table and pulls out the two letters from the shed. *Maybe I can find some random Georgian in Maidana to translate them for me,* she realizes. She'd been at a loss for how to get them translated— she knew she couldn't ask anyone in Khev, because they all knew Leila and her family. But Maidana was a city of almost twenty thousand people. Surely she could find someone there who could translate for her. She would just have to find an excuse to slip away from Pat and Rob for a while.

***

Callie stretches out on a patio recliner, glancing up at the lush grapevines and wishing, not for the first time, that the grapes were already ripe. Leila had explained that the grapes wouldn't ripen until

September— Callie is disappointed to realize she would miss them. The summer seems to be hurtling towards its end— she can't believe it is almost August. Saying goodbye to Pat and Rob the night before had been super sad— she is really going to miss them.

Callie adjusts her body on the lawn chair and tries to savor the few minutes she has to relax, but she just can't. She glances down at her feet in their strappy golden sandals and forces them to stop fidgeting. Her toenails are painted coral— this morning was the first time she'd painted them all summer. Rays of sunlight beat down through the slats in the grape arbor and Callie feels a trickle of sweat run down her back. She shifts deeper into the shade, trying to avoid the heat from the sun— being hot makes her extremely uncomfortable and grumpy. But even her new spot isn't shady enough— a sliver of sunlight runs an aggravating line across her calf. She stands and drags the lawn chair to a section of the yard in complete and total shade, and then sits down, pleased with herself.

In her new shady oasis, Callie runs her fingers through her hair— she'd straightened it that morning for the first time in weeks and she is wearing a long fuchsia maxi dress with a floral print that she'd bought on a whim at a store in Maidana two days before when she'd gone for burgers with Pat and Rob. She knows she looks nice, but she feels taut as a string— Leila and Abdullah are on their way back from Tbilisi; they should arrive any time now. The hot summer air from the first real heatwave they've had all summer wraps around Callie, still and silent and oppressive. From the grapevines above her head, she can hear the drone of bees.

Abdullah had saved her life. All week, at night in bed after exhausting days of working her butt off around the guesthouse, Callie's mind had replayed the mudslide over and over— even when she tried her best to push the thoughts away, they still came clawing back. She repeatedly relived the terror in the dark moments before sleep, and then again in her nightmares. When she was awake, she remembered the giant push she'd felt from behind as Abdullah had thrust her out of the path of the river of mud, letting himself get swept away in her place. She churned with guilt and frustration at her own idiocy, remembering how she had run straight down the mountain instead of running across. If she had responded immediately to Abdullah's warning, they would have gotten out of the way of the mudslide in plenty of time. If she had listened to him earlier in the day, they wouldn't even have gone on that hike to begin with. She knew that nothing she could do or say would be enough to apologize to him or to thank him.

But that wasn't the only reason Callie was anxious about seeing him— they had connected in the mountains on a deep and meaningful level on which she rarely connected with her friends at home. In fact, she couldn't remember the last time one of them had asked her about the state of her soul. She couldn't wait to talk through her God experience in the orchard with Abdullah and see what he thought of it. He, who was clearly yearning so much more than even she herself had been for such an encounter.

Callie swats at a fly that buzzes near her face and admits to herself that there's a third reason she's in knots about seeing him— she can't stop thinking about the way he had looked into her eyes. *Will he still look at me like that, after what happened with the mudslide?* Callie wonders, twisting a strand of chocolate hair around her finger anxiously. Just the memory of the feel of his fingers enclosed around hers that night by the fire sends shivers down her spine whenever she thinks about it. Callie closes her eyes, allowing herself to savor the memory of his touch. Suddenly, she hears the sound of wheels crunching on the gravel outside. Her heart begins to thump and she stands up quickly, adjusting her dress and running a nervous hand through her hair.

"Is that a car I hear?" Fariza's cheery voice shouts out from the kitchen and she waddles heavily towards Callie. Both of them look expectantly as the gate creaks open.

"Surprise!" he throws open his arms, a huge grin across his face as he rushes through the gate and hurries across the patio towards a shocked Callie. Fariza looks on with a confused frown.

"Lucas??" Callie whispers. She stands stock-still, dazed and confused as Lucas reaches her and catches her up in an exuberant bear hug.

"Woah, I've missed you girl," he laughs.

At that moment, Callie hears the gate creak again. She pokes her head out of Lucas' embrace in time to see Abdullah limp into the courtyard on crutches, Leila supporting him on one side. Their eyes lock across the distance and Callie cannot read the expression on his face.

***

Callie's head and heart are churning with such a sea of emotions that she can't make head or tail of them. She belatedly gives Lucas a weak hug back and sets her face into the surprised smile that he will expect her to have. He pulls back from the hug and grins down at her.

"Well? Are you surprised?" His blue eyes twinkle merrily.

"Honestly, I don't even know what to say!" Callie laughs weakly and Lucas throws an arm around her shoulder. She had forgotten how tall he is— she barely comes halfway up his broad chest.

Lucas pulls back and whistles as he looks down at Callie, "Look at you all made up and fancy today! It's like you knew I was coming or something!"

Callie shrugs as guilt twinges her insides. She's saved from having to answer by Fariza running towards Abdullah and Lucas belatedly realizing the commotion going on behind him. Keeping his arm draped around her shoulder, he turns around and steers Callie towards the gate.

"Dude! You must be Abdullah! Man, I owe you a big one for keeping my girl safe! Sounds like you guys had quite the crazy experience." Lucas stretches out a friendly hand and Abdullah glances at Callie before awkwardly adjusting his crutches so that he can return Lucas' handshake.

"No problem," Abdullah answers, putting on the polite, smooth tone and smile that he uses with guests. "I'm just thankful everyone is safe."

"You can say that again!" Lucas replies heartily. Callie inwardly winces at how loud and larger than life he is— the things that make him so charismatic and winsome in America make him stick out like a sore thumb in this reserved Ramazi village.

"You guys really have a beautiful place!" Lucas looks around, legitimately impressed. "Callie told me about it and I've seen her

Instagram posts of course, but it's even better in real life! And you must be the famous Leila?" Lucas grins winsomely at Leila, who returns his smile with abnormal warmth.

"And you must be Lucas! What a happy surprise! I'm sure Callie must be thrilled to have you here!" Callie frowns in confusion at Leila — Leila is never this chipper and enthusiastic. *What is going on?* She glances at Abdullah, whose face is an unreadable mask.

"Callie, why don't you give Lucas a tour of the gardens and you two can catch up while we get Abdullah settled in," Leila suggests, and Callie reluctantly nods. Lucas, oblivious, grabs Callie's hand happily. "Lead the way, babe!"

CHAPTER 26
Khev, Georgia

Summer, 1993

The summer morning air is fresh and breezy and the sky is a bright blue. Birds flitter in the trees and the butterfly bushes Marta and Hava planted are thick with purple blossoms and buzzing with bees. Through the fresh green grass, still wet with morning dew, the girls make a somber procession— Leila carrying Fariza in one arm and a bag full of baby things in her other arm. Hava is carrying a stack of bedding and blankets that is so tall that, with her diminutive height, she can barely see over it. Marta leads the way, hefting a cardboard box filled with Leila's meager possessions.

Marta sets her box down outside the shed and cautiously opens the door. On her first pull, it refuses to yield, stuck in the dirt. Grass has grown up around the base of the door.

"Sorry," Marta frowns sheepishly. "We don't come out here very often. I think you kind of have to lift it to get it to open."

She lifts and pulls, and the door opens. Even the bright summer sun doesn't make the inside of the shed any more appealing than it was two days ago, when Leila came and examined it after receiving her ultimatum from Khadijat. An ancient, thin wooden bed and a rickety table are the only furniture in the room. The floor is dirt, and cobwebs abound. The shed isn't large to begin with, but most of the room is taken up with a towering stack of old belongings— a trunk, boxes of clothes, a teapot with a broken handle, a stool missing its third leg.

"I guess your mother's love for cleanliness doesn't extend to out here?" Leila says drily, kicking the toe of her shoe in the dirt.

Hava's eyes fill with tears and she looks at Leila with pity, "We're so sorry! We hate that you're having to move out here! We wish we could move out here instead!" Marta gives a hard nod of agreement. "But it's unacceptable for two wives to be under the same roof. Tradition dictates that a man can only bring on a second wife if he can provide a separate place to live for each woman."

"Yeah well, he's clearly done a great job at that," Leila spits out bitterly, and then immediately regrets her words when she sees the pain in the eyes of both sisters. She reaches a hand out towards them and sighs, "I'm sorry I said that. I know it's not your fault. This whole situation is just pretty awful. Thank you for your help."

"We'll do anything we can to help, we promise!" Hava says, as she carries her stack of bedding towards the bed. When she sees the mattress, she hesitates, and sets the bedding on the table instead. "You know what, we should probably beat this mattress out before we set it up. Marta?"

Marta grabs one end of the mattress, and together the sisters carry it outside. Leila can hear them beating it vigorously. She turns around, searching for somewhere to set Fariza down so that she can help get the room set up. But there is nowhere to put the baby— the floor is dirt, the table is full, and the mattress is gone. Fariza begins to fuss in her arms.

"It's probably time for you to eat anyway," Leila sighs, heading out into the sunlight with the baby. She walks a dozen meters behind the shed and sits on a fallen log in a small clearing. The sun feels wonderful on her head and she unbuttons the top of her simple floor-length dress and Fariza latches like a pro. Leila glances down, and realizes that her daughter's dark eyes are staring up at her.

"Well aren't you the best baby in the world," she coos, and Fariza never breaks eye contact. Leila's heart tightens and she whispers, "We're gonna be ok, you and I. We're going to make it." Fariza stares back up at her, totally trusting.

By the time Leila switches Fariza to the other breast, the baby is starting to doze off. As Fariza's eyelids close, Leila looks up at the mountains around her. They tower majestically, lush with the new green of summer grass at their bases but still snow-covered on the peaks. They are so strong and steady and unmoving. Leila stares at them and feels strength and resolve enter her soul for the road ahead.

CHAPTER 27
Sureti Valley, Georgia

July, 2018

Callie gives Lucas a tour of the property, and he is duly impressed. Meanwhile, her mind feels like it is being ripped in two— on the one side, she is trying to wrap her mind around Lucas being *here*, in Sureti. Around him flying across the ocean to see her. While the other half of her mind is stuck on Abdullah— aching to find him and talk to him. To try to make things right.

As they wander through the orchard, Callie takes in deep calming breaths of air and tells herself to forget about Abdullah— to give Lucas her full attention. He is so happy and charming that she finally begins to relax and engage with him.

When she shows Lucas the outhouse, he gets a big kick out of it, peeking inside and laughing heartily, "Seriously, girl, I cannot imagine you using this thing!"

"Yeah, well, be glad you came now that the bathrooms are already built!" Callie retorts, sticking out her tongue with her hand on her hips. Now that some of her shock has worn off, Callie is starting to slip into the easy back and forth banter that she and Lucas have always had.

"Woah, check out the size of this tomato! It's like a mini watermelon!" Lucas grins, holding up a luscious red tomato attached to its vine in the garden.

"I know, right? Leila is an amazing gardener. They grow everything organically and a ton of the food that she serves to the guests is straight from their own gardens. It's awesome."

"You should do an Instagram post with pictures from back here!" Lucas enthuses.

"Oooh, I like it! Maybe some shots of these?" Callie gingerly plucks plump purple berries from a thorny raspberry bush that climbs up the fence at the backside of the garden. She hands a few to Lucas, who pops them in his mouth and moans in appropriate appreciation. *I forgot how comfortable it is with him,* Callie thinks, glancing at him as he ambles around the garden.

"Hey," he smiles, mouth still half full of raspberries, "We can explore the garden more later! As great as these raspberries are, they are not what I flew halfway across the world for." He tugs at her hand, and Callie lets him lead her to the bench swing that Leila recently purchased for the orchard. Its cheery green cushions are plush and super comfortable. Lucas sits, patting the seat beside him. As soon as Callie joins him, she remembers that she hates swinging with him— he exuberantly pushes off the ground with his long legs and gets them going at a clipping pace back and forth. Callie's head begins to spin.

"Lucas, you've got to stop! You know I can't handle too much motion!"

"Oh, right— sorry!" Lucas stops swinging and Callie breathes a sigh of relief before turning to face him with an eye roll and grin, "You never could swing at a normal pace."

"Can't help it!" Lucas laughs, reaching up and gently stroking the dimple on Callie's cheek.

"I missed your dimple," he whispers. From the way he is looking at her, Callie can tell that her dimple is not all he has missed.

"Lucas— what are you doing here?" Callie asks quietly, turning serious. "Why did you come? I'm coming home in a couple of weeks anyway."

"I couldn't stand it, being so far away," Lucas admits. "And the terrible internet connection has not helped. All summer, I've felt like we've been missing each other. I felt really distant from you and I hated it. And then the mudslide happened, and oh man, Callie… it really threw me for a loop. I began to imagine what it would have been like if something had happened to you," Lucas' face gets abnormally sober and he squeezes Callie's hand. "And it made me realize that I've been an idiot this whole time for not realizing sooner what we had, and how special it is. It made me realize how heartbroken I would be to lose you. And it made me realize that there's nothing I love or value more than you. So Callie Leffler," Lucas pauses, and slips out of the swing, kneeling with one knee on the ground, "I love you with all of my heart. Will you marry me?"

Callie's first reaction is an instinctive head swivel to see if anyone is outside, if anyone saw. She's relieved to find the orchard empty except for her and Lucas. She turns back to him just as he pulls a dark blue velvet ring box out of his pocket. Her heart beats faster and she can feel her spine tensing.

"I wasn't planning to do this so fast upon arrival," Lucas laughs, "but now that I'm with you, I just couldn't wait!" Lucas opens the small box and Callie's eyes widen— the ring is stunning. The band is slender white gold with small inlaid diamonds around it and in the center is a large marquise-cut diamond that glitters up at Callie in the sunlight. Lucas places the ring box gently in her palm.

"It's absolutely perfect," she whispers, setting her shock aside for a moment as she glances at him with wonder— the ring is her dream ring.

"All Lucy," he winks. "I knew I'd need a professional's help for a purchase of this magnitude."

Callie gives an awkward half-laugh, "Well, you can tell Lucy that she did a fabulous job!"

"So?" Lucas looks up at Callie, expectant.

Callie twists a strand of her hair, shifting unconsciously on the swing. Lucas' eyes fill with a combination of surprise and hurt and uncertainty as Callie hesitates, unsure of what to say.

"Lucas, I..." she starts, and then stops. She takes quick breaths as she continues to twist a strand of hair.

"It's ok, really," Lucas puts on a falsely cheerful voice and hops up off the ground, trying unsuccessfully to rub the dirt out of the knee of his khaki pants. "I know this is a huge surprise and shock, and nothing that we've specifically talked about. And I know I hadn't even given you time to think since the shock of me arriving."

Callie latches onto his words like a lifeline, "That's it! This is all just so sudden, and such a surprise. I am so honored that you would ask me to marry you. And it's not out of thin air for me. I'm pretty sure I was doodling "Mrs. Callie Woods" in my daytimer before you and I ever even started dating."

The comment lowers the tension and Lucas gives a half smile. "Good thing I didn't see it then, cause I would totally have freaked out!" he admits.

"Ha, you definitely would have!" Callie smiles. Her smile fades as she slowly hands the ring box back to Lucas. "You keep this for now, ok? Give me some time to process and for us to reconnect."

Lucas slips the ring box back into his pocket, trying hard to be understanding and to mask his own hurt and disappointment. "Take the time you need— I don't want to pressure you. But if I'm not going to get a fiancée right now, can I at least get a kiss?" he raises his eyebrows.

"Actually…" Callie glances around the garden. When she looks towards the neighbor's fence, she notices a head duck quickly down. "Unfortunately there's not much privacy here. And PDA is a major no-go in this part of the world. So we're probably going to have to wait and be creative."

Lucas moans in mock distress, "Aggghh! But I've already waited two months! I can't wait another second more!"

"Well, you're going to have to. Come on, let's get you something to eat. I'm guessing you're starving?"

"Have you ever known me to be anything else?" Lucas grins and pats his flat stomach. For the millionth time, Callie cannot figure out where Lucas possibly stashes all the food he eats. *He probably burns it off with all the weightlifting and running he does,* she thinks, rolling her eyes.

"How'd your half-marathon with Pete go?" She asks, glancing over at him as he hops off the swing and follows her to the dining area. She's glad to steer the conversation away from their relationship.

"It was awesome! Pete is a beast— he beat me by seven minutes, but I still managed to run a PR! We're planning to do a triathlon in September in LA!"

"Triathlon?! You're gonna drown," Callie grins, swatting him playfully.

"Ha ha, laugh it up. Not all of us did swim team their whole childhood! I am gonna have to work on the swimming part though.

Oooh— wanna be my trainer? Wait— seriously," he pauses, eyebrows raised with excitement, "can you be my trainer?"

"Lucas, I have no clue how to train someone for a triathlon! I guess I could help you with the form on your strokes, but you really should train with someone who knows more about what they're doing."

Lucas shrugs and winks mischievously, "I'm just trying to figure out how to get time with you and me alone in a pool."

"You're hopeless!" Callie laughs, her laughter abruptly catching in her throat as they round the corner and see Leila and Fariza setting the table for dinner. She glances around, but there's no sign of Abdullah. *He's probably in his room in bed, resting his leg,* she realizes. *The doctors did say he's gonna need to do bed rest for a while.*

***

Lucas moans with pleasure as he downs a third piece of *khachapuri*. "Callie, you wrote me that you thought I would like the cheesy bread here. You didn't tell me that it would be maybe the most incredible thing I've ever eaten! This stuff is amazing. And the egg— who would've thought to put a raw egg on top of a piece of cheesy bread! But the way it soaks in and makes everything so moist— oh man, it's brilliant! And all the butter!"

"I'm glad you like it," Callie grins, handing him a napkin to wipe the melted butter dribbling down his chin.

"Please tell me you've learned to make this," Lucas begs, reaching for a fourth piece.

"Well... I have tried. But mine did not turn out nearly as good as Leila's. For some reason my dough was dense, whereas hers is always light and airy."

"You just need more practice," Leila says as she removes the dirty dishes from the table and sets down a steaming tray of apple cake slices.

"You can practice your *khachapuri* skills on me as much as you want!" Lucas promises. "And Leila, that apple cake looks and smells amazing! Callie didn't warn me there would be dessert!"

Leila smiles, "There's always dessert, and always tea with dessert. It's tradition."

"Tea and sweets is actually a tradition after every single meal," Callie informs Lucas. "It's basically become a habit for me. I think I'm up to five cups of tea per day!"

"She is pretty much half Georgian now," Leila smiles at Callie and Lucas as she gathers the final dirty dishes and heads back into the kitchen.

"So how long have you been here?" an Australian lady with bright red hair and freckles asks curiously from Callie's right side.

"Almost two months," Callie replies, "but it's flown by!"

"Wow, I'd love to spend two months here! You must feel so rested and relaxed!" the Australian lady's husband pipes up from across the table.

Callie laughs, "Actually, I think I've worked harder this past week than I ever worked at any other time in my life! Running this place is no joke. The amount of work Leila and her family do is incredible. I only grasped the extent of it this week when they were out of town. Just the vegetable garden alone is basically a full-time job!"

That gets the conversational ball rolling on the vegetable garden, and then the guests transition to raving about the amazing food. Callie zones out— she's heard some variation of the same conversation multiple nights per week from various groups of guests. As Lucas happily engages with the people around him (quickly winning them all over with his winsome smile and engaging personality), Callie glances down at her hand in her lap, at her empty ring finger. Briefly, she lets herself imagine what Lucas' stunning ring would've looked like on her hand. She still can't believe he's here, and that he proposed. *This is the dream*, she chides herself. *You have literally been dreaming about him proposing to you for two years. And now he did (and he flew halfway across the world to do it!), and you aren't happy. Why didn't you say 'yes' immediately?!* Callie cringes inside at the memory of the hurt look in Lucas' eyes when she had hesitated after his proposal.

It feels so natural and easy being back together with Lucas. He's so easy to be around and to joke with. It's so light and normal, and we understand each other's cultures without even having to explain anything. But I don't feel the depth and the intensity and the fire that I feel with Abdullah. If only I'd never met Abdullah, Callie groans. *Then this would've been a no-brainer.*

Would it have been?

Callie startles at the unexpected thought in her head. *Where did that thought come from?* she wonders, examining it. *Maybe from reexamining faith,* she realizes. *How does that tie into things? Does that affect things with Lucas? As far as I know, he's agnostic. We haven't really even talked about what we believe much. Though Abdullah is Muslim, so he and I obviously aren't on the same page either. But he at least believes in a God and wants to find spiritual truth. Ugh, why is this so hard? Maybe I should just become a nun and go join a convent and never have to deal with dumb boys,* Callie thinks sulkily.

"Earth to Callie..." Callie startles as she feels a light tap on her arm, and looks around to find the whole table staring at her expectantly. "Nancy here," Lucas points to the Australian, "was asking you what you'd recommend they do in the area over the next few days."

"Oh, sorry!" Callie blushes, "I guess my mind wandered! There's loads of stuff to do around here—"

Callie fills the guests in, and Lucas watches silently and proudly, clearly impressed with all she's learned over the summer.

When dinner is over, Lucas stands and immediately begins to gather dishes and carry them to the kitchen. Just as he's about to enter the kitchen, Rosana exits and they almost bump into each other. She startles, shocked at the sight of a guest, particularly a male guest, with an armful of dishes. She quickly starts jabbering in Ramazi, pulling the dishes from Lucas' hands. Callie comes to his side, grinning.

"Don't even try to enter their kitchen! It's sacred ground," she smiles. "And anyway, men here don't do dishes."

Lucas hesitates, "I'd like to help, really."

Callie puts a hand on his arm, "I know you would. And when we're back in SF, you can do the dishes anytime you want. But if you did them here, it really would just make them uncomfortable. They don't even like to let me wash dishes, and I'm a woman and have lived here for two months!"

"Ok, got it. No dishes." He gives a slight head bow to Rosana and hands her the rest of the dishes which she quickly accepts, relieved.

"Wanna go for a walk?" Callie asks, heading back towards the orchard.

"Hang on," Lucas stops her with a hand on her arm. "I've already seen the garden and the orchard. Could we walk around the town? Maybe towards the mountains, or the river that you've written about?"

Callie hesitates. She's sure that an unmarried man and woman walking together in the evening would be completely against Ramazi cultural norms. And generally, she's tried to accommodate and adjust to what she knows is accepted here. That being said, she knows that as a foreigner, she is held to looser standards than the strict ones that local women are held to.

"It's probably ok," she decides. "Let's just make sure we're back before it gets too late."

Lucas frowns, unsure of the reasoning behind her hesitancy. "I'll explain when we get outside," she assures him. "Let me just grab a headscarf and a jacket. It's chilly by the river— you might want to grab a jacket too."

***

Callie has done the walk down to the river so many times this summer that she hardly notices the sights along the way anymore. But with Lucas walking beside her, it's like she's seeing everything again for the first time, seeing it through his eyes. *I can't believe I've only been here for a couple of months and it already feels so much like home,* Callie marvels, glancing up at the majestic mountains bathed in the soft yellows and pinks of late summer evening. Like Callie, Lucas' eyes are focused on the mountains.

"It's really beautiful here, so peaceful. I can see why you like it so much," Lucas says quietly, glancing down at Callie.

She nods, "I almost forgot how much I love nature, living in downtown San Francisco. Being here has reminded me how good nature is for the soul. Hang on— watch your step!" Callie warns, pointing at a giant pothole in the road that Lucas spots just in time. Callie has gotten used to walking while looking at her feet so that she doesn't fall. Leila has tried unsuccessfully for years to get the local government to pave the roads.

Callie walks a few feet away from Lucas. At one point, he reaches for her hand, but she pulls it away. "Let's wait until we're sure we're where no one can see us. No PDA here, remember. I don't want Leila to have any trouble because of me."

"Because of hand-holding?" Lucas laughs in disbelief but then straightens his face when he realizes Callie is serious. "Sheesh, you didn't tell me how strict it is here!" Callie can tell that he is frustrated. "And what's with the headscarf? You didn't tell me you wear one here!"

Callie shrugs, "It's not a big deal. I don't wear it around the guesthouse. But outside the guesthouse, I stick out like a sore thumb if my head is uncovered, since all the other women keep their hair covered. I got tired of all the looks I was getting when I would go out, so I decided it would be easier just to cover it."

They get to the end of the road and Callie points out the river, a couple hundred yards away through a grassy field. A handful of cows graze in the grassy meadow. By the time they get down to the river, dusk is falling quickly. They stand under a canopy of thick trees, listening to the water bubbling merrily. A chilly breeze blows across the water and Callie shivers. Lucas looks around, confirms there is no one anywhere nearby, and takes Callie in his arms. He rubs his hands up and down her arms to warm her up. Callie allows herself to relax and lay her head against his chest. *Between the dimness of dusk and the copse of trees we're in, there's no way anyone could see us unless they walked right up to us.* Her head tucks under his chin, and Callie remembers why she likes their height difference. She takes in a deep breath and catches a whiff of the sandalwood cologne he wears that she really likes. His navy fleece sweater is soft against her face. His arms, so familiar to her after almost two years together, feel like home.

They stand there for a moment, holding each other close. And then Lucas reaches his hand under her chin and tips her face up towards him. Callie stands on her tiptoes and wraps her arms around his neck as his lips reach hers and he sighs contentedly.

His lips are warm and soft and familiar and Callie happily opens her mouth to him. As soon as she does, she cringes inside— a million neurons firing in her brain. *Uggggh, he tastes like onions! Disgusting! What did he eat for dinner?* She racks her brain and realizes it must have been the onions in the tomato and cucumber salad. She had eaten the salad, but only *after* picking out the onions. *Concentrate, Callie. Let it go. Just enjoy being kissed. He is clearly enjoying you. You know it will aggravate him if you say anything.* Callie wars with herself internally for a few moments, completely distracted and not enjoying the kiss at all. Lucas catches on and pulls back.

"What's wrong?" he frowns.

"It's just… ummmm…" Callie looks at the ground and digs the toe of her tennis shoe into the soft moss under her feet. "It's just that you taste like onions!" she spits out in a rush.

"Seriously??!" She can hear the disbelief and frustration in Lucas' voice. "This is our first kiss in two months and you're stopping it because I happened to eat the dinner that I was served like a good guest?" his voice starts to rise.

"I'm sorry!" Callie whines. "Really! It's just… onion breath tastes so gross. You know I can't concentrate around bad smells or tastes," she pleads.

"So that's it? Are we just not gonna kiss tonight? Unbelievable." Lucas thrusts his hands into the pocket of his fleece and takes a step away from Callie, who shrivels with regret.

"Hang on…" Callie reaches into the pocket of her jacket and digs around for a minute. She pulls out a folded Kleenex, a receipt, a hair rubber band, and finally, at the bottom, a stick of gum.

"Look!" she holds it up triumphantly and Lucas squints to see in the darkness.

"You are ridiculous, you know that right?" he asks, laughing, as he reaches for the gum, his flash of anger gone as quickly as it had come.

"I really can't help it," Callie insists, and Lucas rolls his eyes with a half-grin and pulls her close.

"It's a good thing I am so patient and flexible," he whispers with self-deprecating sarcasm.

"Oh yes, your patience and flexibility are at the top of your good qualities!" Callie laughs with an eye roll.

"Okay, patience maybe not, but come here and let me show you how flexible I can be. My tongue in particular is *very* flexible," Lucas whispers, tugging Callie up against him.

***

Callie lays in bed, aware with every nerve in her body that Lucas is sleeping in a bed only a few feet away from her, through the thin wall of the guys' room. She feigns sleep so she won't have to talk with the two female guests sharing her room for the night. Both girls seem quite nice, but Callie needs quiet so that she can process the unexpectedly crazy day.

He proposed, she thinks, still shocked. *And he's here. And he is such a good kisser.* She gives an internal moan of pleasure remembering their time in the woods only an hour before. Once they got past the onion breath fiasco, the actual kissing had been quite enjoyable. *What would marriage to him be like?* She wonders, allowing her mind to wander, trying to picture a potential future with him. She pictures a cute house with a yard and towheaded children. Unbidden, thoughts of Abdullah keep pushing in. For a moment, she imagines what it would be like to live here, at Leila's guesthouse, married to Abdullah.

I know what that life would be like, she realizes. *I just spent the week helping run this place. One week of it was almost more than I could handle. How on earth could I spend a lifetime doing it? And I like Leila, but I don't want to spend my life living with my mother-in-law.*

Then Callie remembers the night by the fire, camping out under the stars. She remembers how intently Abdullah had stared into her eyes and the depth of feeling that she had seen reflected there. Her insides turn as she realizes that no matter what choice she makes, someone is going to get hurt.

***

"Knock, knock— can I come in?" Callie stands awkwardly at the door of Abdullah's bedroom, holding a tray of soup and bread. In all her time in Khev, she's never seen his bedroom. She's not surprised to find it as simple and austere as the rest of Leila's house. It's a small room with a narrow bed, a dresser of drawers, and a desk. Everything is spotless. Callie looks around at the room, avoiding for a moment looking at her friend, lying on top of the bedspread, propped up on pillows. His laptop is open in his lap and an occasional breeze comes in through the window, though it doesn't do much to cool down the warm room.

"Sure," Abdullah's tone is neutral, and Callie steps over the threshold. "I brought you lunch," she explains unnecessarily, handing him the tray. As she gives him the tray, she looks down and sees his eyes watching her intently through the fringe of his dark bangs.

"Where's your boyfriend?" he asks, spooning a bite of steaming soup. "Or is he your fiancé now?" Callie raises her eyes in shock– she hadn't told anyone about Lucas' proposal.

"Just boyfriend," she frowns, defensive. "Why would you...?"

"Mr. Koshashvili from next door saw him propose," Abdullah shrugs. "Can't keep anything a secret in Khev."

"I suppose not," Callie laughs shakily. "He did propose, but I didn't say yes. And now he is napping. He's still really jet lagged," Callie explains, feeling guilty but justified in waiting till Lucas had lain down to come talk to Abdullah. She still hasn't gotten to talk to him since the accident.

"Gotcha. Ok, thanks for lunch," Abdullah says, dismissing Callie with a wave of the hunk of bread in his hand.

"I didn't ask him to come!" she blurts out, trying to justify Lucas' sudden arrival and proposal. "I had no idea he was coming!"

"It's fine, really," Abdullah sighs. His shoulders lower and some of the tension seems to go out of his back. "Of course he can come visit you. I was just surprised, that's all."

"Abdullah..." She hesitates, and slowly sits down at the desk chair. Abdullah watches her. "I... I haven't thanked you. I don't even know how to thank you. I owe you my life." Callie's eyes begin to tear up. "You pushed me out of the way," she says softly. "You saved me, You... you sacrificed yourself for me." She looks into his amber eyes which stare intensely back into hers.

"It was nothing," he replies softly. "I would do it again, a million times." Callie reads love in his eyes and his voice. A confusing mixture of exultation and guilt churns inside of her.

"It was my fault," she whispers, twisting her hair in anguish. "I was so stupid. I paused when you told me to move, and then I ran down the hill instead of across. All of this," Callie gestures to Abdullah's casted leg and the lacerations on his face, "these are all my fault. I'm so sorry," her voice breaks.

Abdullah sets his lunch tray on the floor beside his bed and moves towards Callie. He reaches a hand out towards her and Callie thinks for a moment that he is going to take her hand in his. But then he stops and, to Callie's disappointment, lays his hand on his lap instead. "It wasn't your fault. Really. There's no way you could have or should have known what to do in a mudslide. If anything, it was my fault for going on that hike against my better judgment, when I knew the weather was likely to turn."

"But that's my fault too!" Callie moans, "You never even would have gone on the hike if I hadn't twisted your arm!"

"I'm pretty sure you were just trying to help two lovebirds have a good honeymoon," Abdullah smiles.

"Well, that is true," Callie sniffles. "I didn't know you realized what was going on."

"Of course I knew! You would have to be blind not to see how smitten those two were," Abdullah gives a half-grin, and winces when his smile pulls at the stitches running across his cheek.

"Does it hurt a lot?" Callie asks, hesitantly reaching out and running a gentle finger down the skin near his stitches. His eyes hold hers as she touches his face and heat suffuses Callie's cheeks— *does he feel the same sparks I do when we touch?* She quickly jerks her hand away.

"I've gotten worse scrapes from messing around play fighting with my buddies," Abdullah brushes off her concern and changes the topic.

"Well, your friends must play-fight much harder than Americans!" Callie shakes her head. "Actually, I'm pretty sure most American guys don't ever fight with their friends. At least, not physically."

"There's a reason most of the world's best MMA fighters come from this region— wrestling is in our blood," Abdullah says proudly.

"How about your leg?" Callie hesitates, "I'm guessing you never got anything like that from messing around with your buddies?"

Abdullah grimaces, "Yeah, the leg was no fun. But the doctors say I should make a full recovery, so that's good."

"So… so you're not mad at me?"

Abdullah looks surprised, "How can you even think that? Of course I am not mad at you! I am so thankful you are ok! I was so worried about you in the woods at night by yourself!"

"You were worried about me?" Callie laughs incredulously through the remaining trickle of her tears. "I was panicked for *you*! I looked for you for so long, and you were just gone." Callie shudders as a flashback of that night runs through her mind, and she looks into Abdullah's amber eyes. "I thought you were dead, and that I'd never see you again." An unexpected sob catches in Callie's throat as all the emotions she had felt when she thought Abdullah was dead come rushing over her. Suddenly she's crying so hard she's shaking.

"Oh, please don't cry! Really, everything is fine!" Abdullah, looking uncomfortable and unsure of what to do, sits frozen like a deer in the headlights. Belatedly, he puts an arm around her shoulder. Without even thinking, Callie turns towards him, wraps her arms around his neck, and cries into his shoulder. Slowly, he puts his arms around her and holds her in silence. Somewhere underneath her grief, she registers how nice his lean arms feel wrapped around her, how safe and protected she feels with him.

Slowly, her sobs subside and she sniffles into the crook of his neck, "I'm sorry, I didn't mean to fall apart like this! I guess I'm more of a mess than I realized. It was really scary. And I was so scared for you." She glances up at him, unaware that she has black mascara rivulets running down her cheeks. "I'm just so thankful you're ok. I guess God answered my prayers this time."

"You prayed for me?" Abdullah looks surprised and touched.

"Of course! All the time! Well, maybe not as much as Pat and Rob, but they're pretty much professionals compared to me," Callie gives a light hiccuping laugh and pulls out of his arms, scooching back on the bed so that there's a couple of feet between them.

"I didn't think you prayed much these days?" Abdullah asks, curious.

"Well, you being in mortal peril pretty much pushed me into it!" Callie admits. "But since then, I've actually started to more often." Sheepishly, Callie tells Abdullah about her various spiritual conversations with Rob and Pat over the course of the week he was in the hospital, and then she tells him about her experience with the shooting star out behind the guesthouse. He listens with rapt attention, and is particularly fascinated by the verse that Callie read which seemed to confirm her experience.

"You don't think I'm crazy?" she asks hesitantly. "I actually haven't told anyone this but you."

"I know you aren't crazy!" Abdullah says. "In fact, I think you are very blessed. To find God, I think, is the core of humanity's deepest desire, and you have found what you were looking for."

"Even if I didn't really even know what I was looking for?"

He nods.

"And even if I'm not exactly sure what I have found?" Callie's forehead wrinkles.

Abdullah nods again. "I think that you are at the beginning of a journey of discovery and that God is opening up truth to you. And I think you should keep seeking."

"What about you?" Callie asks, deeply curious.

Abdullah runs a hand down his neat beard and laughs, "I will never stop looking! My mother says my curiosity got me into countless scrapes as a child, but I hope that in this case, it will have a better outcome! I think truth is worth striving to find, and then worth suffering to hold if necessary. So I will keep searching," he smiles carefully, aware of the thread of stitches down his face.

***

"There you are! I was looking for you!" Lucas greets Callie from across the courtyard.

"Oh, sorry! Leila asked me to take some lunch to Abdullah!" Callie holds up the empty tray, relieved that she remembered to grab it on her way out the door.

"Awesome. How's he holding up?" Lucas asks, without a hint of jealousy or suspicion. Callie feels a stomach-churning mixture of relief at his total trust in her, and guilt that perhaps she doesn't deserve it.

"He needs to take it slow, which I'm not sure he will do," she says, heading to the kitchen to return the tray. "But considering what he went through, it's really just a miracle he is alive."

Lucas stops Callie with a hand on her arm and a concerned look in his eyes, "Hey, you never really told me in detail what happened. I know it wasn't just Abdullah who went through a rough experience. I'm here if you want to talk about it."

Callie finds herself getting choked up again. *Good grief, pull yourself together! You don't need to fall apart twice in one hour!* she chides.

"I'm fine, really. I came out with barely a scratch," Callie replies, attempting a breezy tone of voice.

Apparently it doesn't work. Callie starts walking towards the kitchen again, but Lucas grabs her hand and gently pulls her back towards him. He puts a hand under her chin and tilts her face up to his. "Hey, were you about to cry?" he asks, concern in his voice.

Dang it, I hate that he can read me so well. Callie looks away, not saying anything. Lucas looks closer and frowns, "Hang on, you already were crying! I can tell because you have mascara streaks on your cheeks. When were you crying?" His voice is full of empathy, not accusation.

Callie licks a finger and quickly scrubs at the mascara on her cheeks, a thread of guilt stirring in her stomach. "Here, I don't want to talk in the courtyard— we would likely be interrupted any minute by some guest needing something," she tells Lucas, knowing that she owes him some explanation. "Let's go to that swing in the orchard and we can talk."

"So? Tell all!" Lucas insists the second they sit down. Callie sighs in aggravation— *why is he always barreling ahead? Doesn't he know that I need time to collect my thoughts?*

She ignores the impatient tapping of his foot and stares off at the mountains for a moment while she tries to figure out what she wants to say. To his credit, Lucas doesn't say anything. Finally Callie takes a deep breath and begins, "When I went to take Abdullah his lunch, I apologized to him because I've been feeling like everything that happened was my fault."

"Wait, what? Callie, you can't blame yourself for a mudslide!"

"I don't blame myself for the mudslide, but we never even would have been up on the mountain if I hadn't insisted on us going." Callie gives the short version of what happened, and is able to hold herself together as she does. Lucas doesn't say anything until she's done telling her story.

"Sounds like that was really hard and scary. I'm so glad you're ok," he holds both her hands in his and gives them a squeeze.

"Me too," Callie nods. "And I'm really glad Abdullah is ok." Unintentionally, Callie's eyes fill with tears. She quickly looks away, but not before she sees devastating suspicion dawn in Lucas' eyes.

"Callie..." Lucas hesitates, unsure whether to go down the conversational path he is about to start. Callie's stomach flips, knowing where he is going.

"You seem really connected to Abdullah, more than I realized." Callie almost jumps in to contradict him, but holds her tongue.

"I'm just wondering..." Lucas looks away from her and runs a hand down his face. "I just have to ask... does he have anything to do with why you said you needed time to think about my proposal?" Lucas tries to keep his voice neutral, but Callie knows him well enough to hear the worry and anger under it.

I don't know what to say! she panics. *Answer him, quick! But what do I say?? And how do I answer in a way that is honest but also not hurtful?*

"I... I'm not sure. I don't think so," Callie's eyes beg Lucas to understand. "I mean, he and I have become good friends this summer, which I definitely didn't expect at the beginning! Remember when I told you how standoffish he was on that first car ride when he picked me up in Tbilisi?"

"Yeah, well he seems to have gotten over that," Lucas spits out bitterly, and then looks regretful. "Sorry, didn't mean to lash out."

"It's ok, honestly. You have every right to. Nothing has happened between us, I promise. We are just good friends. I think it's more that being here has made me see the world differently than I saw it before. It's opened my eyes to different cultures— not just Ramazi culture, but all the cultures of the guests we've had from around the globe. And I've begun to reevaluate my life and my priorities and even my personal beliefs and I'm just not sure where I stand on anything anymore. Which I know doesn't help you at all," Callie says ruefully. "I just thought I knew what I wanted in life, and what I wanted my future to look like. And now I've had all these new experiences and seen all these different people and different ways of living, and it's made me want to take a deeper look at my own life and just make sure I'm really where I want to be, and really heading where I want to go. Does that make sense?" Callie asks.

"I guess? Kind of?" Lucas shrugs. "I am very glad, though, that you aren't in love with someone else. You had me worried there for a minute!" He tucks a strand of hair behind Callie's ear and she gives him her bravest smile, trying not to feel like a total liar.

"Take the time you need to figure things out, ok? I'm not going anywhere. I definitely want you to feel like you can talk with me. I know it's been partially due to bad internet and time difference, but it seems like you've been doing all this deep thinking and soul searching this summer and I've pretty much been in the dark about it. Which kind of sucks." he admits.

"I'm sorry! That's totally my fault! I just hadn't really been ready to share while everything was so jumbled and mushy in my head. Does that make sense?" Callie explains, feeling like she's trying to justify herself.

"I guess… but you can still talk to me about things, even when you don't have them 100% figured out. You know that, right? I mean, I certainly don't have everything in my own life 100% figured out. I'm pretty sure very few people our age do."

"You're right," Callie nods. "I'll try to be more open and better at communicating."

"It will be easier once you're back home," Lucas assures her.

"I'm sure you're right," Callie nods. But inside, she is unsure of whether she actually could talk to Lucas about all the soul-things she's experienced this summer. She's pretty sure he wouldn't understand her experiences. Would he even take them seriously? Though to be fair, she hasn't given him a chance to try.

CHAPTER 28
Khev, Georgia

Summer, 1993

Leila thought she would hate her, this unknown usurper who has caused her and Fariza to be tossed aside like yesterday's spoiled milk. This woman who is the reason she has lost her room— the one place, other than the orchard, where she can find a bit of peace and solace. The reason behind her banishment to the crumbling, miserable shed that she detests.

And yet, the first time Leila lays eyes on the new bride, she feels an unexpected, unwanted stirring of pity in her chest. Marina is *young* — her face fresh like a child's. Hava later tells Leila that the new bride is only 17. She is tall and sturdy, but her eyes have that same terrified look that Leila has seen in sheep as they're about to be shorn. Marina walks with her shoulders hunched as if she's trying to avoid being noticed. Which, considering the temperaments of Saidun and Khadijat, she probably is.

Leila realizes that she alone can truly empathize with this poor girl— being torn from her family, being forced against her wishes to be Saidun's wife, and having to live under the authority of a harsh and demanding mother-in-law. Leila went through all of these things herself over a year ago. She resolves to treat the new bride civilly, and not to hate her. She feels guilty when a stray thought crosses her mind — relief that Saidun will be so busy in Marina's bedroom that he won't have time nor the desire to visit her.

***

Leila lies in her narrow bed, the piece of plywood beneath her hard through the thin mattress. Fariza nuzzles at her side, and Leila wraps a blanket tighter around the baby as the wind gusts through the cracks in the wall. Whiskers curls contentedly on top of Leila's ankles, impervious to the cold. Though the shed is warm enough during the summer days, the mountain nights are brisk. Fariza has had a cough for the past week and Leila is sure that the night breeze is at fault.

"Leila?" Saidun's baritone voice startles her from the other side of the door. Leila gently kicks Whiskers off her feet, tucks Fariza tight amongst the blanket, and grabs the candle from the makeshift table in the corner and opens the door slightly. Outside, the night is pitch black.

"Fariza is already asleep. You'll have to come back tomorrow to see her," Leila says shortly. It was a long day of backbreaking weeding in the garden, and the combination of Fariza's coughing and Leila's uncomfortable bed and insufficient walls are combining to give her not much sleep at night. Her patience is running thin.

"I actually wasn't here to see Fariza. I'm here to see you," Saidun pushes open the door and makes his way into the room. The walls are only a few meters apart, and between the narrow bed and the rickety table, there's barely any room for Saidun and Leila to stand. His broad shoulders and barrel chest seem to fill the room.

"What do you want?" Leila sighs. "Tell me quickly and quietly so you don't wake up the baby."

Saidun looks uncharacteristically sheepish, and begins to hem and haw. Finally, it dawns on Leila. "Wait, are you coming here to sleep with me?!" her eyes open wide, incredulous. "You have a new wife! Go sleep with her!" Leila hisses as she thrusts up her right arm and points her finger to the door.

"I've tried!" Saidun whines. "She's so timid! And boring! It's like trying to be intimate with a fish!" Saidun mimics a fish flopping for a moment and then lying totally still, eyes closed.

"Oh for heaven's sake!" Leila throws her arms up in the air. "What do you expect??! The poor girl is only a child!"

"She's not a child!" Saidun growls, defensive.

"Yeah well, I hope you've changed your tune by the time our daughter is 17!" Leila tosses back, happy to see Saidun's face blanche temporarily.

"You know what, I don't want to sleep with you now anyway!" he says angrily.

"Great!" Leila hisses back, all of her pent up anger at being forced out to this miserable, dirt-floored, bug-infested hut coming out in a sleep-deprived rage.

"You know what, you deserve this hovel," Saidun glares at her. "Maybe when we build the new addition, we will move Fariza there with us and leave you out here!"

"You can't take Fariza!" Leila's eyes go wide in fury and horror.

Saidun gives a cruel laugh. "Have you not yet learned that I can do whatever I want?? You have no power or authority here." He looks at her with derision. "Fariza is my daughter. I control where she goes and what happens to her." With that, he storms out.

As Leila sinks onto the bed, the weight and truth of what he said overwhelms her. Earlier in the spring, a lady in the village had left her husband and returned to live with her parents. Marta had whispered to Leila that the husband was a notoriously abusive alcoholic. For two months, the woman had lived with her parents and was not allowed by her husband's family to have any contact with her children. Eventually, she had given up and returned to the abusive marriage so that she could be with her children.

That could be me, Leila thinks with despair, glancing over at her daughter. She knows that she will do whatever it takes to stay with Fariza, even if it means sacrificing herself in the process.

***

"Come on, we're almost home! Quiet down!" Leila begs Fariza, who screams, red-faced, against her shoulder. Leila gingerly opens the front gate, which is still damp with a fresh coat of green paint, and then crosses the orchard. When she turns the corner of her hut, she's horrified to see her bed and table standing in the yard outside the hut.

"What on earth—" she hurries inside, where a startled Anzor looks up at her, embarrassment on his face as he kneels on the dirt floor. He is in his work clothes, spattered with white paint. Leila glances around the room and realizes that he is almost done caulking all the gaps in the walls. Fariza continues to cry in her arms as Leila bounces her.

"I didn't think you'd be back so early," Anzor explains.

"I wasn't supposed to be. We were supposed to be at the market all day. But Fariza is teething and was impossibly grumpy, so they sent me home early. I'm going to see if I can get Fariza to nap."

"Oh," Anzor looks around regretfully, "It seems I have ruined that plan."

"No, no!" Leila quickly reassures him. "You keep working! Thank you! I'm sure I can put her down in the girls' room."

Anzor nods and turns back to his work without another word.

Throughout that fall, Anzor quietly makes other improvements to the shed. As fall turns to winter, he installs a small metal stove so that Leila and Fariza can keep warm. He fixes leaks in the roof. Leila doesn't even know how he knows what needs to be fixed, but she is extremely grateful to him. One day, he brings her out a narrow chest of drawers that he has clearly made himself— it is carved with the traditional Ramazi curlicue motif that Anzor's work is known for in Khev. When Leila examines it, she tears up at the beauty of it. She knows the hours and care that went into making it.

The winter is harsh and miserable. The Georgian economy continues to tank, and people across the country are suffering. Leila hears rumors that in Tbilisi things are even worse than in the mountains— at least in the mountains, they can grow their own food and chop down trees for firewood. Against all odds, Fariza grows strong and hearty.

One abnormally sunny winter day, Hava bursts into the kitchen with uncharacteristic noise. Leila looks up, startled, from the eggplant she's slicing.

"Leila, come quick!" Hava almost bounces with excitement. "Remember the Soviet library in Ruvi? The one that's been closed ever since the collapse?"

Leila nods vaguely, unsure where this is going. Ruvi is the next village over. Though hardly larger than Khev, it is the county seat and so boasts the only post office and, now-shuttered, library in the area.

"Well, the town council finally decided to sell the building! And they're giving away the books to anyone who wants them!"

"Okay..." Not being a huge reader, Leila still isn't sure where this is going.

"They have a whole section in English!" Hava exclaims.

"Really?!" Leila's eyes light up.

Hava nods, excited. "You've been saying this whole time how worried you are that you are going to lose your English!"

"That would be amazing," Leila agrees. "But I don't think I can go. Your mother told me to make eggplant rolls, and I have Fariza." Leila points down at her feet, where Fariza is happily banging away on a pot with spoons in both hands.

"Mother said Marta can watch Fariza, and Father will drive you!"

Leila raises her eyebrows, shocked.

"Even mother knows that in this economy, any chance to improve upon a marketable skill should be taken!" Hava laughs. "Plus, I think she will make you promise to teach all of her grandsons English."

"And granddaughters!" Leila insists.

"And granddaughters," Hava agrees.

CHAPTER 29
Sureti Valley, Georgia

August, 2018

Gratefully, Callie learns that Lucas only has four days to be at the guesthouse before he has to get back to San Francisco for work. Both of them try very hard to act normally, but Callie can read Lucas well enough to tell that he is still bothered by her lack of response to his proposal, as well as her connection to Abdullah.

Thankfully, the following three days go quickly and are much less drama-filled than Lucas's first day in Khev. Lucas and Callie take walks in the mornings, and in the afternoons and evenings Lucas often has to work remotely. For once, Callie is grateful for his workaholic tendencies. And so they spend many hours at a picnic table in the shade under the grape orchard, Callie working across from Lucas on her own laptop. They pause for meals and Callie helps with guests as needed. Abdullah is still recuperating in his room, so, to Callie's relief, the three of them see very little of each other.

"Oh, this is strange!" Callie blurts out one afternoon, pointing her phone towards Lucas. "See this message I just got on Instagram? This guy just messaged me from England— he said he used to know Leila, back when he lived in Georgia. He wants to come for a visit soon and reconnect! He's wondering if I can help him book a room at the guesthouse."

"Coming all the way from England to visit here? An old flame?" Lucas raises his eyebrows with interest.

"I don't know... maybe? Though from what I can see from scrolling his Instagram feed, it certainly doesn't seem like he's Ramazi. He seems really western. And look at this picture— that looks like a wife and daughter? Maybe they were just friends? Though women here don't usually have guy friends..." Callie trails off, thinking.

"Did he say when or how he knew her?" Lucas asks with the laser-focus Callie recognizes from when he is following a lead on a story.

"He says he was friends with her in college."

"College?" Lucas frowns, reading the message over Callie's shoulder. "Do girls from here go to college?"

"Actually... not normally," Callie realizes. "Leila definitely seems different than a lot of the other women here. And she is certainly educated. She's just always so frustratingly tight-lipped about everything. I have about fifty million different theories on her past! Did I tell you about the little hut out back?" Callie asked, relieved to focus their attention away from anything having to do with her and Lucas' own relationship. Talking about a story with Lucas feels so natural— it's the most relaxed they've both been all trip.

Lucas shakes his head, and Callie fills him in on the snooping she did while Leila and Abdullah were gone, and about the things she found.

"Should you really have been going through their private stuff?" Lucas frowns.

Callie rolls her eyes, "Come on! You, as a reporter, can't judge me for that!"

"Haha, I guess not. Gotta do what you gotta do to get the story! So you think she has some secret past life?" he asks.

"I think so. And more than that, I think her kids don't know about it. As far as I can tell, they think she's from here."

"I don't get why that's such a big deal," Lucas shrugs. "I mean, I think my mom is from Dayton, but it wouldn't change anything for me if I found out she was from Minneapolis or something."

"But it's not the same thing at all!" Callie insists. "You don't know what it's like here! Being Ramazi is the end all, be all of identity. It's a really insular society, for the good and the bad. If people found out Leila wasn't actually Ramazi, it would be a massive scandal— for her and her kids."

"I still don't get why it's such a big deal," Lucas' forehead wrinkles.

"Well, it's not for Americans. Our whole society is one giant melting pot of cultures and ethnicities. But it's not that way here. From what I understand, if people found out Abdullah wasn't a full-blooded Ramazi (or had questionable roots), they likely wouldn't want him to marry their daughters. His marriage prospects would be drastically reduced."

"Sheesh, that's harsh! Well, in case you had any concerns about *my* pedigree," Lucas changes the conversation direction with a cheeky grin, "I can assure you that I'm 100%, full red-blooded American! And by that I mean 15% Irish, 20% German, 30% Norwegian, 15% English, and who knows what else!"

"You need to do one of those DNA ancestry testing things so that I can know your actual genealogy," Callie teases, relieved to be joking with Lucas again.

"Nope, not interested. I'm content just being me, here and now." Lucas shrugs with a smug smile, his blue eyes twinkling.

Just then, Callie glances over Lucas' shoulder, across the lawn. She sees Abdullah, hanging frozen on his crutches on his way to the bathroom, watching the easy camaraderie of Callie and Lucas. When Abdullah catches Callie's eyes he quickly turns and hobbles into the bathroom. Callie twists a strand of hair, feeling distinctly guilty. *How long was he watching? Did he see us laughing and flirting? But why should you feel guilty for flirting with your boyfriend??* Callie tries to convince herself. *It's just that I don't want to hurt Abdullah's feelings. Ughhh!*

"You should write him back and get more information, just to make sure that he really knew Leila and isn't just chasing a rabbit trail," Lucas suggests, oblivious to Callie's inner turmoil.

"Huh?" Callie fumbles, trying and failing to pick up the conversational thread.

"The guy who wrote you on Instagram— Nika? You should write him back to get more information."

"Oh yeah, good idea," Callie ducks her head and quickly types a reply. A few minutes later, her phone pings.

"Woah, that was fast," Lucas grins. "This mystery might be solved before dinner!"

"Look!" Callie exclaims, bouncing in her seat, her own boy drama totally forgotten in the excitement of digging into Leila's mystery past, "He says that she used to go by the name Dina! That lines up with what I found in the hut— remember that letter I told you about addressed to Dina from her mom?? What if Leila and Dina are the same person, and she was bride kidnapped here!"

"Bride kidnapped?" Lucas asks, never having heard the term.

"I did some research after I found those letters out back, that the lady in that store in Maidana translated for me," Callie explains. "It's an old custom where men in this region would kidnap a woman and force her to become their wife."

"Wow, that's awful." Lucas' voice is somber.

"I know," Callie nods. "I think that's what happened to Leila," she says quietly. "Wow, that would explain so much of why she is like she is. It would explain how she's so educated, and how she knows English too."

"What are you going to tell this guy who wants to come visit?" Lucas asks.

"I'm not sure…" Callie pauses, thinking. "I'm not sure if Leila would want to see him or not…"

"Maybe you should ask her? Let her decide?" Lucas suggests, packing his laptop into the bag on the ground beside the picnic table and clearing his things off so that they can head inside to dinner.

"I could. That would probably be the wise thing to do. But see — he specifically asks me not to tell her. Says he wants to surprise her."

Lucas laughs, "Does Leila seem like the kind of woman who likes surprises?"

"Ha, touché. Probably not. But honestly, I'm really curious. And who knows, maybe this could be good for her. Maybe it would be nice for her to reconnect with an old friend?"

"Admit it, you just want to get to the bottom of the story, maybe grill this guy," Lucas pokes Callie in the side playfully and she sticks her tongue out at him.

"Ok fine, I admit I'm curious. I think I'm going to book a room for him. What's the worst that could happen? If Leila doesn't want to see him, she can tell him herself and he can check out early."

When Lucas leaves for the airport, Callie feels guiltily relieved to see him go. She enjoyed much of the time they had spent together, but always felt like she was on pins and needles, looking over her shoulder for Abdullah. She promises Lucas to try to sort things out in her head and heart during her final few weeks in Khev, and to come back to San Francisco with some clarity.

CHAPTER 30
Khev, Georgia

March, 1995

"Apple. A-a-a-a-pple," Leila holds the red fruit out towards her daughter, who takes it in her chubby toddler hands. It's wrinkled and slightly wizened from being in the cellar since the previous fall, but Fariza doesn't seem to care.

"Ap-puhl!" Fariza shouts lustily, then dramatically sinks her teeth in for a big bite. Though not quite two years old, she is precocious and incredibly advanced verbally. Leila glows with pride, certain that she has the only toddler in the entire Sureti Valley who speaks and understands Georgian and Ramazi, and has begun to learn a handful of words in English.

"Ba-ba-ba-ba!" Leila turns towards the voice piping up from the blanket on the brittle brown grass.

"You want in on the conversation too, do you?" Her cheek curves as she smiles over at her eight month old son, who is sitting in the middle of the blanket, bundled in a hat, scarf, and winter snowsuit, and reaching towards his older sister's apple.

"Ohhh, that's what you want! You're not really old enough for one of those, but I suppose it won't hurt you to gnaw on it with your two tiny teeth," Leila hands an apple towards her son, who immediately starts gumming it.

"What is he doing with that?! He could choke!" Leila turns to see Khadijat marching across the grass towards them. "And what on earth are you doing letting him sit on the ground in this cold weather?! He could get sick!"

"He's fine!" Leila says. "He's in his snowsuit, and it's a sunny day and there isn't even any snow." Leila gestures around at the ground, where finally, for the first time in five months, there is no snow.

"Humph, of course I cannot trust you to take care of our precious boy. Here, give him to me." Khadijat bends down towards the baby, and her face breaks out in a huge smile, which the baby quickly mirrors. She coos in Ramazi, "Look at you! Who's the most handsome boy! You are! You are! You're the best baby! Let's go get you some milk and tea and honey!" After two years in Khev, Leila finally speaks and understands Ramazi. She still, however, chooses to speak to her children in Georgian and English— the first because it is the language of her heart, and the second because it is the language that she hopes will provide them with a leg up in the world.

"Gran'ma! Gran'ma!" Fariza bounces excitedly up and down at Khadijat's feet. "App-uhl! App-uhl!" She proudly says her new word and holds out her partly eaten apple.

Khadijat ignores her granddaughter, cooing over Abdullah. As Fariza continues jumping around and shouting, Khadijat frowns at Leila, "What is she saying?"

"She said 'apple'. I'm teaching her English!" Leila smiles hesitantly, unsure of how Khadijat will take this news.

"Humph, what use is it filling her head with useless knowledge that she will never need. Better to fill it with useful things like how to milk a cow or make cheese or sew a dress. English. Humph!" Khadijat struts towards the main house, Abdullah on her hip. Fariza looks forlornly after them.

"Hey, who is mama's best girl?" Leila puts on a forced cheerful voice, and swings her daughter's hands back towards her. "Grandma has baby brother, that means you and I can spend time together! Want to come help mama feed the chickens?"

"Chick! Chick! Feed chick!" Fariza squeals excitedly, flapping her arms up and down.

Leila laughs genuinely, "You, my dear girl, are the very best! May you never lose your joy and your spunk. Let's go feed those chickens."

As they head towards the chicken coop, Leila looks down at her daughter's mess of dark black curls. *I was like her as a child, all laughter and fun and bubbly energy,* she marvels. *Life has pressed me down and sucked me dry. I don't even know who I am anymore. Please God, don't let my daughter lose her spirit.*

Leila grabs the buckets of kitchen scraps from the back gate and hefts it in one arm, while holding Fariza's hand with her other arm.

"Careful," she warns Fariza as she opens the gate to the chicken yard, and a rush of chickens swarm them, squawking demandingly. Unfazed, Fariza runs into the middle of the flock of chickens, flapping her arms and shouting, "Chick! Chick! Eat! Eat!" The chickens avoid Fariza, having learned from past experience that her small, chubby hands are capable of yanking out tail feathers, and peck at Leila's skirt.

"Ok, ok, I'm coming!" she laughs, and hurls the contents of the buckets as far as she can, in the opposite direction of her little daughter. The chickens scurry after the flying food, and Fariza runs after the chickens. Leila smiles, watching her daughter's awkward, toddler run— she's slow as molasses, swinging one arm intently, while the other stays close by her side.

Splat! Fariza trips, falling face first into the mud. She is stunned for a moment, then lets out a furious wail, "Dirty! Mama! Dirty! Yucky! F'iza fall down!"

"Ugh, you've got to be kidding me," Leila groans under her breath, hurrying towards the muddy toddler. She gingerly picks her up, holding her out away from her chest, and heads towards the main house.

After Abdullah, the long awaited heir, was born, Khadijat had moved Leila and her children back to the main house, and exiled poor childless Marina out to the shed behind the orchard. While Leila felt distinctly guilty for Marina's plight, she was extremely grateful not to have to worry about her children freezing in the winter.

She was, however, less than pleased about having to once again share sleeping quarters with Saidun. His mercurial moods continued to be difficult to navigate. Sometimes he was a warm, loving father, and unlike his mother, he didn't show the expected favoritism towards his son over his daughter, so Leila appreciated that in him. But his tolerance for any childhood "misbehavior", including crying, was extremely low. He was quick to fly into a temper with Fariza, who seemed to share his own iron will.

Leila felt like she was walking on constant eggshells, needing to keep her children quiet and well-behaved when Saidun was around so that he wouldn't fly off the handle. It was exhausting. She was unsure whether the emotional and mental stress were a fair trade for the warmth and comfort of being in the main house. But the winter had been harsh and snowy, and she had been thankful to have a roof that didn't leak for her children. If and when Marina had a son, Leila was unsure what would happen with their living situation.

But perhaps she wouldn't have to worry about that— the second building that the family had been working on slowly for years, bit by bit whenever they had the money, was finally coming together. The floor and walls had all been built, and neighbors had come over the previous summer and worked together to help frame a roof. Anzor was hopeful that if they had a good apple harvest, they would be able to earn the money needed to put on the finishing touches. Two of their cows were also pregnant, and Anzor was planning to sell one of the calves to help cover costs. Maybe Marina could move back into the main house with Saidun, and Leila and her children could move to the new house? Or maybe Saidun and Marina would move to the new house, and Leila and her children stay in the main house? Leila had no say in the matter, and was well aware that she wouldn't know what was going to happen until Khadijat informed her long after the decision had already been made. But at least either way, her season of suffering in the shed out back seemed to be over.

Once back at the main house, Leila strips the snow suit and boots off of screeching Fariza, leaving them in a crumpled heap by the front door. *I'll deal with those later,* she sighs.

She is in the kitchen scrubbing Fariza's face with a rag when a blood-curdling scream rends the air in the courtyard. Scooping up a startled Fariza, Leila rushes outside.

In the courtyard, Marta and Hava are struggling to hold up Khadijat, who seems to have fainted in their arms. Two neighbor men stand in front of them, faces grim and caps gripped in their hands.

"What is it? What's happened?" Leila rushes over, almost tripping over her long skirts in her hurry. Fariza bounces, whining, on her hip.

"It's Saidun," Marta says tonelessly, her eyes wide and face blanched.

CHAPTER 31
Khev, Georgia

Summer, 2001

"Mama!" Abdullah charges into the kitchen, his amber eyes alight.

"My love!" Khadijat scolds gently, "Look at you! You are a mess! Get out of the kitchen," she shoos him indulgently with the swat of a towel.

"How did you get to be such a mess?" Leila approaches her son, who is covered head to toe in wood shavings. "Did you get into grandfather's wood shop? You know you aren't allowed to be out there," Leila frowns.

"It's ok, Mom!" Abdullah hops up and down with excitement, his pudgy cheeks pink. "He said now that I turned seven, I am old enough!"

"It's true," Musa eagerly insists. "He let us both come out and taught us how to use the lathe!"

"Well, that sounds like fun," Leila smiles and ruffles her son's hair, trying to get out some of the shavings.

"Mooooommmmm!" he squirms away from her and the two boys take off towards the orchard.

"He has Anzor wrapped around his little finger," Leila shakes her head, not unhappily. She returns to the pile of onions she had been dicing.

Khadijat shrugs, "It is how it should be. Abdullah is Anzor's only heir now that…" her voice chokes up and she turns abruptly back to the sink of dishes. It has been six years since Saidun suddenly passed away while hauling logs by the river, but Khadijat is still mourning. The grief has softened her a bit, or maybe just made her so weary that she doesn't have the strength to be fierce. Often these days, Leila finds herself pitying Khadijat instead of hating her as she did in those early days in Khev.

Marta and Hava are both married now, Hava to Isa who she had been so smitten with for so long. Very rarely do love marriages happen in Khev— usually parents arrange marriages that they feel will be most beneficial for the extended family, so Leila is thrilled for Hava's sake that it worked out for her to marry the man she loved. Leila suspects that the soft spot Anzor holds in his heart for his gentle, peaceful daughter may have something to do with the marriage. Though perhaps he is regretting his indulgence now, since the couple did the unthinkable and moved to Norway for work a few years ago and have yet to come back to visit. They do regularly send much-needed money back to the family, and Hava often writes letters. Though she hasn't had children yet, she seems happy.

Marta and her husband, on the other hand, live only two villages over. She gave birth to three sons in her first four years of marriage, so her husband and his entire family are quite pleased with her! She has her hands quite full so only rarely can she come visit. When she comes, it is like a whirlwind with her rowdy boys, so different from Abdullah. But he always enjoys playing with his cousins. Leila misses both sisters far more than she misses Saidun; it's been lonely in Khev without them. She is slowly starting to get to know the neighbor women, though. They're a tight-knit group and slow to accept outsiders, but all were sympathetic and supportive after Saidun's death and she feels like they're beginning to warm up to her. She might even go so far as to say she has a couple of friends. Last spring, they'd invited her to both a quilting bee and an outdoor picnic. And of course, the great-aunts come over all the time, pockets full of sweets for Fariza and Abdullah.

But most of all, she's had Fariza and Abdullah to keep her busy. The two of them are her lifeblood, what keeps her going every day. And she can't believe how different their personalities are— Fariza is extroverted and chatty and hilarious and strong-willed, whereas Abdullah is more introverted. He's talkative around his handful of close friends and family, but he's shy in public. He's certainly more of a deep thinker than Fariza and is more interested in learning. She's been teaching them both English since they were little, and while Fariza's is passable, Abdullah's is excellent for a child of his age.

After Saidun's death, his poor second wife Marina returned to her parents. As a childless widow, nothing was tying her to Saidun's family. It's honestly been nice for Leila to have her gone, and she hopes Marina is happier back at home. Though the second building is finished, Leila and her kids still live in the main house with Anzor and Khadijat. They weren't about to let her move their grandkids even across the courtyard from them.

Though she can't live in the new house like she wishes, the second building has been an unexpected blessing— Leila has been able to use it to house the English tutoring business she started a few years ago. Saidun's death strapped the family financially, and so Anzor and Khadijat reluctantly agreed to let Leila start working. It's generally viewed as a dishonor to families when women work outside the home, but times are hard and people understand that. Plus, there is not a single other qualified English teacher in the village, so the locals have been willing to make an exception for Leila. With Georgia having separated from the USSR and trying falteringly to turn towards the West, English is growing increasingly popular. She has loved starting a business and having some space and money of her own. At night, she likes to lie in bed and daydream about other future businesses she could potentially open.

When Saidun first died, Leila's initial thought had been overwhelming relief that she would finally be able to leave Khev and return to her family in Tbilisi— something she had dreamed of for so long. She wrote a letter to her family a few weeks after Saidun's death and they quickly wrote back. It was a joy to be back in touch with them after all the years of not being able to risk communication while Saidun was alive. Her mother and sisters especially begged her to leave Khev and bring her children home to Tbilisi.

For a while, she had considered it— turning the idea over in her mind every which way. Being back with her family again would be so wonderful. But would it be wonderful for Abdullah and Fariza? Their whole lives were in Khev, their identity was Ramazi. They knew nothing about her family in Tbilisi. And how would she support them in Tbilisi? Her family there was poor. At least in Khev, they had stability and grandparents who adored them and a home and land they would inherit.

She also knew that Anzor and Khadijat would never let her take the children, especially not their precious heir Abdullah. She remembered her long ago conversation with Saidun's uncle, threatening her family in Tbilisi. She had no doubt that his threats were not idle. If she tried to take the children to Tbilisi, the Ramazi clan would never stop looking for them. And so she came to terms with staying in Khev — she would never do anything that put her children at risk. Her family didn't understand her decision, but they were grateful to at least be back in touch with her.

So she continued to write, hiding their letters from her children so that they didn't get suspicious and begin to question their identity. When Sofi wrote and mentioned in passing that Nika had moved to London and married a British woman, Leila was surprised at how heartbroken she felt. She realized that Nika had symbolized her last chance at a different life, at a life where she was loved by a good man. But, after grieving, Leila decided that she was grateful to know. Now she could fully throw herself into life in Khev without having to constantly second guess and wonder "what if". And by that point, she could speak Ramazi fluently and had come to appreciate the tight-knit community and to love the mountains. She didn't want to uproot her children, or herself. Especially not for old dreams that would never come to be. She needed to leave them in the past where they belonged.

Leila felt at home in the orchard in a way she never had in Tbilisi. She knew every flower in the garden, and thanks to a neighbor up the street who generously shared her seeds and bulbs and knowledge, she was planting new ones each spring. Beauty stubbornly clawing its way through the dirt every spring spoke to Leila's heart in a deeply personal way. From Hava, Leila had learned to identify all the different birdsongs. In Khev, Leila, who had spent her childhood surrounded by Tbilisi's concrete, grew to feel and appreciate the seasons, and how each season had its own unique beauty: the winters, with their giant mounds of snow that sometimes reached the second story of the house. Abdullah and his friends building snow forts and having endless snowball fights. The way the icicles crystalized like jewels on the apple and cherry trees after a good frost. The early darkness in the evenings that gave her an excuse to hibernate in bed with her children and read stories out loud to them.

The springs, which came achingly slowly, so slowly that one despaired of them ever coming at all. But then they would burst on the scene in a riot of color. First, the brave snowdrops, delicate and white, poking their green leaves and tiny bell-shaped heads up through the frosty snow, anxious to be the first to greet the sun. Leila felt such camaraderie with them— when she bent towards them, she felt that she was not the only one who had thrust her way through snow and ice and hardship to find her light. And after the snowdrops came the cherry and apple blossoms, boughs laden with pink and lacy clusters that smelled heavenly, the scent so strong that the whole property would smell like them while they bloomed. Leila spent as much time as she could outside while the apple blossoms were blooming, soaking in their scent, though her children religiously avoided the orchard when the trees were in bloom after having gotten one too many bee stings.

And the summers, when the mountains finally greened with a lushness that made Leila's heart swell. The grape vines, which stood all winter looking like hopeless, pitiful, brown, broken branches, suddenly burst to life seemingly overnight and grew long, green tendrils that stretched and reached across the arbor Anzor had built over the courtyard. Between the garden and canning, Leila was busiest of all in the summer with chores that stretched from morning to night. But her years of hard work in Khev had made her lean and strong and she no longer felt the same exhaustion that she had felt that first hard summer.

And finally, the falls. Fall in Khev was so different than in Tbilisi. Almost all of the trees in Tbilisi turned a golden yellow. Leila had been shocked her first fall in Khev at the variety of colors on the mountains — looking at them was like looking at some giant, vivid quilt— light banana yellows, deep golden yellows, fiery oranges, cheery apple reds, deep scarlets, chocolate browns. During the rest of the year, she rarely found the time to hike in the forest down past the river at the edge of the village, but Leila made a point every fall to take the children hiking a couple of times to look for brightly colored leaves. Sometimes Anzor went with them, searching along the way for wood that would be good to carve. As they walked, he pointed out various types of wood to an eager Abdullah and explained their uses.

Once or twice, Leila saw Abdullah grab his grandfather's hand and hold it on their hike. The old man had hesitated, looking taken aback, and then wrapped Abdullah's hand tightly in his own and smiled down at his grandson. The two of them were peas in a pod, Leila thought with a smile as she watched the gray-haired old man and the dark-haired little boy walking in front of her through a pool of fallen leaves.

CHAPTER 32
Sureti Valley, Georgia

August, 2018

Leila exits the pantry with two jars of jam and heads to the kitchen to start preparing dinner. Thanks to Callie and the miracle of social media, they have been booked solid the past two weeks, and are booked for the coming two weeks as well. Leila still almost doesn't believe it. *Let's see if it actually keeps up this way once the summer rush is over*, she thinks.

She sees a guest standing near the gate, suitcase in hand. She doesn't recognize him from behind, so he must have just arrived. He is wearing a western business suit and is tall and thin with short salt and pepper hair. Callie had mentioned something about a businessman from London coming to stay. He is their first London booking, so Leila veers away from the kitchen and heads over to welcome him.

At first, when he turns around, she doesn't recognize him. The roundness of youth is gone from his cheeks, leaving his face long and angular, with fine wrinkles around his eyes. His face is clean shaven— no scrawny mustache, and his once long curly black hair is now cut to a crisp graying crew cut.

"Welcome to Sureti," she smiles politely. "How was your trip?"

"Dina?" he whispers, his eyes misting. *She hasn't changed at all*, he thinks with wonder. Aside from the headscarf and the long skirts, she looks just as he remembered.

Leila startles— she hasn't heard anyone say the name Dina in years.

She frowns, and leans closer. "Do I know you?" she begins to ask. And then she sucks in a breath, "Nika?"

He nods, so overcome with emotion that he can't speak.

"I can't believe it's you! I didn't even recognize you! What are you doing here?" Leila feels blindsided and confused.

"You look just the same— you're as beautiful as you were twenty-five years ago!" Nika exclaims, his voice rich with feeling.

Leila blushes, unsure of what to do or how to respond. She stands in the courtyard, awkwardly balancing the two large jars of jam in her arms. He has taken her completely and totally off guard. She glances around, searching for his British wife, but it seems like he has come alone.

"It's so good to see you! Here— let me take those jars for you. Where do you want them?" Nika asks. In a daze, Leila directs him to the kitchen. He walks in without hesitation and Rosana looks up in shock to see a strange man in the kitchen. "I'll explain later," Leila mouths to her in Ramazi. She guides Nika back to the patio, still unsure of what to do with him. At that moment, Callie peeps her head over the second story railing, where she has clearly been spying. *Callie,* Leila thinks. *And her blasted social media. That has to be how Nika found me. Now what am I supposed to do?*

"I have been wondering what happened to you for years," Nika explains, confirming Leila's suspicions. "Despite all my googling, I couldn't find a trace of you until one day I happened upon an Instagram page for 'Leila's Guesthouse' in Sureti. When I scrolled through the pictures, I saw one of someone making *khachapuri* and I knew immediately that it was you, and that I had to come. Dina— is there somewhere we could talk in private?"

He can still read me, Leila thinks with shock. *He can tell that I'm uncomfortable out here, where neighbors or guests could potentially see us.*

Leila nods, "I've got to go get dinner ready now— we have twelve guests eating here this evening— but after dinner is cleaned up, we can talk in my office. For now, let me show you to your room. And Callie," Leila raises her voice so that it carries to the second story, "you can come out now. If you're going to spy, at least make yourself useful and give Mr. Shashashvili a tour of the guesthouse and property."

Callie looks slightly sheepish as she hurries down the stairs, two steps at a time. She introduces herself to Nika and soon the two are talking like best friends. Callie shows Nika to his room so that he can store his suitcase, and then offers to give him a tour of the grounds.

Leila heads for the kitchen, but instead of entering it like she knows she should, she slips into the pantry and closes herself in, sinking to the floor and forcing herself to take slow deep breaths in and out as she counts to ten.

I can't believe he found me. I can't believe he has been searching for me for years— that he remembered me. He looks so different! He was such an awkward, gangly kid, and now he's matured into a handsome man. But what is he doing here? What about his wife? London? What does he want? I can't have him here. My life is finally somewhat settled and stable. My kids are stable. I don't want to mess up the delicate balance I have finally achieved here. Having him here is a risk. I will have to be really careful. Maybe he will just stay for a few days and we will reconnect as old friends and then he will go back to his life and I can go back to mine.

But is that what I really want? Remember that day on the piano, when he played your soul with his music? Surely he remembers it too. But he's married. Leila's mind is a rushing jumble, jumping from one thought to another. Things that she hasn't thought about in years come barreling into her mind. Finally, she decides that she has let herself have enough space for panic and that it's time to pull herself together and get dinner ready. At this point, they will be hard-pressed to be done with everything in time for the daily 7:00 p.m. dinner time. Leila takes a long, slow inhale and then exhales.

When she enters the kitchen, Leila is so calm that Rosana can't even tell that anything is amiss.

"Hand me the carrots please, and I will start peeling them," Leila instructs.

***

To Nika, it seems like dinner will never end. The eleven other guests around him, hailing from four different countries, relax around the table, enjoying the multiple-course dinner— sumptuous pumpkin stew, meat dumplings, vegetable salad with walnut sauce, mashed potatoes, and bread. Callie regales the table with tales of her various adventures over the course of her time in Sureti, glowing with excitement and a clear love for the region, and fields questions and offers suggestions like a pro. Normally Nika would be impressed, but he is so distracted that he has a hard time following the conversation— he can't help himself but stare at Dina every time she comes in and out of the kitchen, bringing some new dish to the table. After dinner, she and her assistant cook come out bearing a teapot and a steaming apple cobbler that smells divine. Until this very moment, never in his life has Nika been disappointed to see an apple cobbler. *Did Dina remember that it is his favorite dessert? Did she make it on purpose?*

The guests linger around the table, enjoying tea and apple cobbler and talking about their plans for exploring the region. Two sisters from Ohio sit beside Nika and try to engage with him— they tell him about the cooking class Leila organized for them the previous day, and the horseback ride they're planning to do the next day. He manages to carry on a semblance of a conversation with them; they're surprised to find out he grew up in Georgia, since he speaks English like a Brit. He explains to them that he's lived in England for over twenty years, and is just here to visit family and friends in Georgia.

After what seems like hours to Nika, the guests begin to drift back to their rooms or out to the gazebo and swing in the orchard. It is a crystal clear night and Nika can see more stars than he's seen in years. He waits for Dina but she doesn't leave the kitchen. Finally, he decides to explore the property and let her come find him when she's ready. He's waited for twenty-five years— surely he can wait another thirty minutes.

Nika explores the grounds, impressed by the landscaping and the well-tended flower beds. He wonders if Dina has gained a green thumb and love of gardening in her adult life. He almost laughs at the thought of her gardening in college— she definitely would not have had patience for it back then.

Finally, Nika hears footsteps on the stone path behind him. He turns, relieved to find Dina standing in front of him. She, however, does not look relieved. She glances furtively around and whispers, "Our business office is the first room on the right in the small white building across from the guesthouse. I will go inside now. Wait ten minutes, and you may follow. But please, *please,* make sure no one sees you. Do you understand?" Her voice carries such concern and urgency that Nika wants to give her a hug to calm her down. But he realizes that that would probably just make her more stressed in this situation. And so he nods, and she hurries off.

As agreed upon, ten minutes later Nika knocks lightly on the office door. Leila opens it and glances furtively outside and then motions him quickly inside. The office is plain and functional— a desk with an old desktop computer, two straight-back chairs, a filing cabinet, a book shelf, and a lamp. The only sign of personality is a beautiful large potted fern and a framed black and white photo of a horse on top of a mountain. This is not the kind of office his Dina from the past would have had— hers would have been messy, full of comfy couches and vibrant colors. It is a good reminder to Nika that he needs to take time to get to know this Dina, and not to expect everything to be like it used to be.

"What are you doing here?" Leila whispers. "How did you find me? What have you been doing the past twenty-five years?"

"I've been looking for you, Dina," he stares at her with intensity. "I never stopped looking. Well, ok, that's not entirely true. I knew you were in this general region, but your mom would never tell me exactly where. She made me promise not to contact you."

"I know— she wrote me," Leila once again feels her old hurt and anger stir up at her mother, even though she knows Nika contacting her back when Saidun was still alive would have been a disaster. She backs away from Nika and sits in the chair behind the desk.

Nika blows out air, frustrated. He holds his hands up, in a gesture of peace. "How about I just start at the beginning? I will tell my side and then you can tell yours?" He folds his lanky frame into one of the straight back chairs across the big desk from Leila.

"You tell yours, and then we will see," Leila replies softly, glancing at the window to double check that the curtains are fully drawn. Nika sees that it is as good as he is going to get, and so he begins.

He tells her about the day of her kidnapping, and the days afterwards. Even though it was so long ago, his retelling is so fresh that it's as if it happened yesterday. Leila can feel his anguish. He tells her about their frantic attempts to find her, and the police's unwillingness to help, and then about the relief her mother felt when she received Leila's letter and was just so very thankful that her daughter was still alive and safe. *"Safe,"* Leila thinks with a frown.

"But I didn't share her relief," Nika admits. "Everything within me wanted to go rescue you. Your mom had your *address*, for crying out loud, though she never would give it to me. She insisted that me trying to find you would likely end in my death and in your getting beaten."

"She was probably right about that," Leila admits softly. "My husband and his relatives would not have taken kindly to interference."

"I didn't care about risking my own life, but I didn't want to put you in danger. I spent my days vacillating between worrying about you, and fantasizing about scenarios where I could swoop in and rescue you." Nika smiles sadly, "And then your mom got your letter that you were expecting a baby. And I knew that any chance I had to get you back was over. Your mom made me swear to never try to contact you, a promise that I kept until after she passed away."

Leila nods, understanding. Sofi had written a couple of years ago that Natela had died, and Leila had managed to go to Tbilisi for the funeral, telling her children that she was going on a shopping run for the guesthouse. It was one of her biggest life regrets, that she had been unable to spend more time with her mother and siblings during adulthood. And that Natela had never gotten to know her grandchildren.

"Why now? And what have you been doing these past few decades?" *What about your wife? Where is she?* Leila wonders.

"Well, the year after we lost you, I was offered a chance to intern with the London Symphony Orchestra. Looking back, I'm sure my dad pulled some strings in a desperate attempt to get me out of Tbilisi, where I was despondent. And his plan worked. London was an entirely different world from post-Soviet Georgia. There was food on the shelves in the stores! I gained fifteen pounds in my first month living there!" Nika grins, and pats his stomach, which Leila can see does have a tiny bit of pudge.

"London was full of life and people and gave me a chance to practice my English with native speakers. Plus the London Symphony

Orchestra was phenomenal. I had been something of a prodigy in Tbilisi, but in London, I was a nobody. I had to practice day and night in order to keep up. Eventually I made some friends— can you believe it? You weren't my only friend in life," Nika smiles self-deprecatingly. "After five years of being there, I became really close with the principal flutist for the orchestra. We got married in 1998, and had our daughter Ali in 2001."

"Ali, named after your grandmother?" Leila asks and Nika nods, touched that she remembers. Leila glances at his hand, looking for a wedding ring. Nika notices and holds up his bare hand.

"Steph and I separated in 2013 and officially divorced in 2015. She got remarried last year, to an electrician, and they seem really happy together. I guess she learned the hard way that it wasn't wise to be married to another musician! We were both introverted and tended towards being loners, and plus we worked long hours. We just grew apart over the years, I guess. We always had a decent relationship, and we still get along. We do stuff together with our daughter. Want to see a picture?"

Leila nods, trying to take it all in. Nika pulls out the newest iPhone and opens iMessage. He shows Leila a picture of a smiling woman with a short blond bob who has her arm around a teenage girl — the girl has Nika's chocolate eyes and her mother's blond hair, which is up in peppy pigtails. She's wearing a sports uniform and holding some kind of stick that Leila can't identify. Her face is smeared with dirt and she looks absolutely radiant.

"Steph sent me this pic last night," Nika grins. "Ali is hardcore into lacrosse." *Ah, the stick,* Leila thinks. "Her team won their qualifying match for regionals and she is over the moon, as you can tell! I think she learned from her mother and I not to become a musician, haha! The kid doesn't have a musical bone in her body, and can't carry a tune to save her life. But other than that, she's fabulous."

"She looks wonderful," Leila smiles sincerely. "Children are the biggest blessing. But I'm sorry your marriage didn't work out."

"Me too. We tried, though maybe not hard enough. I think part of the problem…" Nika trails off, and then glances up at Leila. She is sitting far back in her chair, looking stiff and defensive and uncomfortable. Her face, which was always so expressive, is utterly unreadable. Despite all of that, she is so beautiful that it almost takes Nika's breath away. He inhales and decides to forge boldly ahead— something he has regretted for years not having been brave enough to do with her when he had the chance.

"I think part of the problem was that I never got over you. Never in my life have I felt about anyone the way I feel about you, Dina. And so I decided to try to find you. My biggest regret in life is that I didn't try to find you twenty-five years ago."

Leila stands up, and backs against the back wall of the office, shaking her head. "You can't say that," she says in a low voice. "There is no future for us. You don't know me now. The girl you knew and loved so long ago is dead and gone. Even her name is gone! I am Dina no more. I am just her dark shadow, her empty shell," Leila fights tears of frustration, "or maybe I am just the hard, crusty part that fought to survive for the sake of my children."

Nika stands, and slowly walks around the desk towards Leila. He gently reaches out and grasps her hand, "Please let me know you. I want to know who you are today. I didn't have a chance to be with you and love you twenty-five years ago. Can we at least take the chance to get to know each other again– the people we are today? I want to know you, Dina," Nika searches her eyes in a way that no one has looked at her for many, many years. Dina has a flashback to that moment in his living room, with his piano. "I want to know who you are today. I want to hear your story, whatever part of it you're willing to share with me. I am willing to go slow, to do this however you want. I finally, miraculously, found you. Don't make me lose you again," Nika's voice is impassioned and his eyes so sincere that everything in Leila wants to forget her current life and give him hope that they could have some sort of future. But she can't.

"Nika, you don't understand," she sighs. "Maybe things would have gone somewhere between us all those years ago had I not been abducted, but maybe they wouldn't have. Now I am here, and I have built a life here. A life that I fought tooth and nail to build– for myself, but mostly for my son and daughter, and now for my grandson."

"I knew you had at least one child, but I had no idea you have a grandson! I would love to meet him!" Nika exclaims.

"No!" Nika is taken aback by the intensity of Leila's vehemence. "Under no circumstances can you get to know my grandson. You don't get it. This is a Ramazi town. There are strict rules. If anyone found out I was in a room alone with a man in the evening, there would be severe consequences. My children are Ramazi, my grandson is Ramazi. For their sake, I have to fit in with society and abide by the rules and customs. And after twenty-five years here, honestly their rules and customs feel like my own in many ways."

"So you are unwilling to give us a chance because of societal rules and customs?" Nika feels a stirring of anger and frustration.

"I'm unwilling to give us a chance because a chance is impossible — there is no future for us. My children know nothing about my past and I have worked hard to keep it that way. I don't intend to change that now."

"Wait— your children don't know your past? They don't know you were bride kidnapped?"

"They don't know, and I intend to keep it that way. There's no reason to bring up old hurts and old skeletons now." Leila crosses her arms across her chest.

"But Dina—"

"I'm not Dina!" Leila explodes. "You have to stop calling me that!"

Nika sighs, "Ok, ok, I'm sorry. Really. Though I don't understand how or why you have kept your life story from your children—"

Leila looks at him threateningly, and Nika changes tracks, glad to see that Dina hasn't lost all of her fire and spark.

"Ok. I see that I don't understand. But help me to understand. Please," he begs. "I have missed you for twenty-five years. I never stopped loving you," he whispers, his brown eyes holding Leila's green ones. "Can I please just… give you a hug?"

"A hug??" Leila half laughs, looking up at the ceiling to try to keep tears from forming in the edges of her eyes. She can't remember the last time someone other than her children and grandson gave her a hug. It's been decades since a man touched her at all. She cannot believe that Nika has loved her and missed her this whole time. *Oh, how I wish you could have come for me twenty-five years ago,* she thinks with regret as she glances at Nika out of the corner of her eye. Finally, against her better judgment, she nods.

Nika closes the gap between them and pulls her gently into his arms. He is so tall that Leila doesn't even reach his shoulders. He wraps his arms around her and for a moment, she lays her head against his chest, the brushed silk of his navy dress shirt soft against her cheek. He smells good— like fresh linen and coffee. Leila smiles, breathing him in, overwhelmed by how wonderful it feels to be held. Gently, Nika rubs one hand in slow, tender circles on her lower back.

He rests his chin on top of her head and whispers, "I always knew you would fit perfectly in my arms." Leila stiffens and reluctantly pulls away, immediately regretting losing the warmth and comfort of Nika's arms.

"I can't," she whispers sadly. "This will only make things harder. I wish things could be different, but they can't." Leila straightens, and points firmly towards the door, "You have to go."

Nika stands still, glancing from Leila to the door. He pauses, clearly considering his options. "Ok," he finally says. "I understand. I just had to try. But I won't force anything you don't want, ok?" He looks at Leila with such sincerity that she nods, grateful. *A man not forcing what he wants— I forgot that was even possible,* she thinks sadly, wishing for the thousandth time that her life could have gone another direction.

"I did book a four-day stay," Nika adds, hesitatingly. "If you wouldn't mind, I would love to keep my reservation and just stay as a guest. And get a little taste of your life and this beautiful place you have built. And maybe reminisce as friends a time or two? If we get the chance?"

Leila bites her lip and stares towards the window. Honestly, she would love to get more time with Nika— to talk to someone who knows her past and her family and who knows who she used to be. And she is proud of her guesthouse and of the life she has built for herself and her family— she would love for Nika to see it. But every day having him around is a risk, one that she's not sure she's willing to take. She glances over at him— his back is to her and he's examining the photograph on the wall— one of her favorites that a Georgian photographer took a couple of years ago when he did a horseback riding tour through the mountains with Abdullah. *Back when Abdullah did those*, Leila shudders, thanking the Almighty for protecting her son.

"Alright," Leila eventually agrees. "You can stay as a guest 'til the end of your reservation. I would enjoy spending more time with you as friends if we're able to find an opportunity when we can do it discreetly. BUT— you have to pretend to be just a guest, not to know me. And you *can't* call me Dina. You have to call me Leila, ok?"

Nika nods, willing to agree to any parameters Leila sets. Then he frowns, "But wait— your assistant? Callie? She knows that I know you from the past."

"Shoot," Leila mutters. "Alright, let me worry about Callie. The key is that my children do not find out, ok?"

Nika nods agreeably, "Got it," he smiles. "Undercover friends it is!"

Leila gives him a purse-lipped smile and furtively shoos him out the door once she checks to make sure that the coast is clear.

***

Leila knocks on Callie's door later that evening. Callie opens it, surprised to find Leila. She's even more surprised when Leila slips into her room and closes the door behind her.

"What's up?" Callie asks, eyebrows raised in curiosity.

"You know the man you saw earlier?" Leila asks, going straight to the point.

Callie nods, "Nika, I know. He and I have been writing on Instagram for a couple of weeks."

"I'm aware," Leila says. "Listen, Nika is a friend from my youth, from a part of my life that I would rather leave in the past. I would appreciate it if you would not mention anything about him to anyone here, particularly my children."

Callie nods, unsurprised that Leila wants to keep things under wraps.

"So…" Callie asks hesitantly, "You're not going to introduce him to Abdullah and Fariza?"

"Absolutely not," Leila says sternly. "Some things are better left in the past, ok?"

Callie raises her eyebrows questioningly and Leila sighs. "Listen, I know you and Abdullah are close." Callie blushes. "But I would really appreciate it if you wouldn't say anything to him. Mr. Shashashvili will be here for a few days and then leave, and we will never see him again. Let's just treat him with the same courtesy that we would extend to any guest, ok?"

Callie nods, and Leila looks relieved.

"Well, that's it then. Goodnight." Leila awkwardly slips out of the room, leaving Callie, her journalist instincts ramping up to full steam, more curious than ever to get to the bottom of the mystery of Leila's past. *But how to do it without upsetting Leila or breaking the promise I just made?* she wonders. *Maybe I can talk to Nika? I didn't make any promises about not talking to him! I'll do it the first chance I get!* she decides.

***

True to his word, Nika plays the role of a guest perfectly the next two days. He explores the property, enjoys the delicious meals, and takes one of the new cooking classes that Leila is trial running with a couple other guests. He is a perfect gentleman and even Abdullah, who is normally situationally aware, does not pick up on anything.

Nika hopes for another chance to get alone time with Leila, but the guesthouse is packed and Leila is busy from morning to night. So Nika contents himself with watching her covertly, and getting a small taste of the world she has forged for herself. He is in awe of how gracefully and expertly she handles the herculean task of running the guesthouse. She always seems calm, cool, and collected— nothing like the spunky, dramatic girl he remembers, who was so quick to roller coaster between gleeful highs and sudden outbursts of anger. He simultaneously misses the girl from his memories, and wants to get to know this new matured side of her.

Nika is also impressed with what he sees of Abdullah, who manages to be quite helpful and hands on with the guests despite hopping around on crutches. Nika wishes that he could actually get to know Abdullah, but he honors Leila's wishes and keeps a polite distance. From what he can tell, it seems that Leila has raised a hard-working and respectful son. He knows Leila has a daughter and grandson, but he does not see them.

When Nika wakes up on his third morning, he finds a note slipped under his door. His heart beats faster at the sight of the handwriting, so familiar even after all these years.

Nika—

Abdullah and Callie will leave around 11:00 a.m. to take a group of guests to grill kebabs for lunch at the river today. I have given my assistant the morning and early afternoon off, thinking that perhaps you and I could have more of an opportunity to catch up. Meet me in the dining room at noon and we can have lunch together.

Leila

Nika holds the letter to his chest and breathes in a sigh of relief that he will get time with Dina after all. He keeps trying to think of her as Leila, but it is nearly impossible for him after thinking of her as Dina for all these years. He goes over to his small suitcase, and pulls out his limited variety of clothing options. After some deliberation, he settles on a pair of dark narrow jeans and a short-sleeve hunter green polo. Green used to be Dina's favorite color, but he has no idea if that has changed. Just like he has no idea what else about her has changed. She definitely comes across as far more serious and disciplined than she was when he knew her before. *But she didn't really reveal any of her story when we talked,* Nika frowns in frustration. *Was it because it is too painful? Or because she doesn't trust me? Or just wants to keep her distance and her walls up? Or maybe we just didn't have enough time?*

The morning crawls by for Nika, who is both excited and nervous. He showers in the newly completed bathroom and then enjoys a filling breakfast with the other guests of omelettes, crêpes with homemade cherry jam, fruit, veggies, and cheese. At eleven o'clock he is relieved to see a white Sprinter van pull up to collect the party for the river outing. Abdullah immediately greets the driver, and together with Leila they load a bunch of food and water and coal and skewers into the back of the van. The sisters from Ohio congregate at the van, talking with noisy animation that immediately pegs them as Americans. Soon, a quiet German gentleman joins the group and the friendly girls turn to include him in their conversation.

"Sure you don't want to join us?" Callie appears at Nika's side, holding a basket of plates, forks, and cups.

Nika smiles down at her cheery face, "Thanks for the invitation! I've got some computer work I need to catch up on. Gonna try to tackle that while you guys are gone," he lies smoothly.

"Suit yourself," Callie gives him a smile, and he notices the dimple in her left cheek. "You'll be missing out though! *Shashlik* is delicious! And the whole process of cooking the kebabs is super interesting. And then we get to eat them! Though we do come home smelling like fire," Callie crinkles her nose with disgust and Nika smiles — *Leila has done a good job finding someone so peppy and enthusiastic,* he thinks.

"Thanks for the invitation. Unfortunately, I really do have to pass for today— there's too much I need to get done. And besides, I've grilled *shashlik* a time or two in my day," Nika smiles gently at Callie.

"Shoot!" Callie replies, lightly slapping her forehead. "I keep forgetting you're actually Georgian! You look and sound so British! And I mean that as the highest compliment because obvs British accents are the best," Callie gives Nika a wink and he laughs.

Nika bends at the waist, giving a deep bow and putting on the most exaggerated British accent he can, "Of course madam, why else do you think I moved to England?"

Callie laughs and picks up the heavy backpack at her feet and swings it onto her back. "Ok, have a great day!" She gives Nika a quick wave and skips her way over to the van, wondering as she goes if his "computer work" is just a ruse to get alone time with Leila. The romantic in her hopes so!

I can barely even remember what it was like to be that young and have that much energy and enthusiasm, Nika thinks nostalgically, watching her skip away. *Though to be honest, I probably never had as much energy as Callie.* He glances over at Leila, who is busy helping the guests settle into the van. *She was definitely the one who had the energy for the both of us. Though it looks like now all the energy she has just goes towards hard work.* Nika shakes his head and turns to head upstairs to his room. He writes his daughter and tries through his distraction to handle some email. Eventually he gives up and decides to go looking for Dina early.

He finds her in the kitchen. Her back is to him as she stirs something on the stove and she's humming under her breath in Georgian— he smiles when he recognizes it as a song from their youth. He is amazed yet again that from behind, she looks just as slender and lithe and young as she did twenty-five years ago, though her body, which she once loved to show off with tight shirts and curvy jeans, is now modestly cloaked in a high necked, floor length dress. Nika finds that he likes her in the floor-length dress— it somehow suits her naturally regal bearing.

"Anything I can do to help?" Nika slips beside Leila at the stove and she jumps, startled.

"Nika!" she scolds him, "Men aren't allowed in the kitchen! Get out— I'm cooking!"

"And it smells amazing!" Nika bends over the pan and sniffs appreciatively at the wafting aroma of garlic and onions caramelizing in butter. "I can cook, you know," Nika grins, reaching a long arm to grab an apron hanging on a peg on the wall, and tying it expertly around his waist. "Steph doesn't really like to cook, so I was pretty much the family chef for the past twenty years. I've tried to get Ali to join me, but unfortunately she seems to take after her mother in regards to not liking to cook. She does like to bake though— we have a father-daughter tradition of baking a different kind of cookie every Friday night and then eating them with milk while we watch an episode of Gilmore Girls." Nika smiles at the fond memories.

Leila stares at him, not knowing what to think. *Nika cooks? Georgian men don't cook! Wow, England must have changed him. What would it be like to be with a man who helps in the kitchen? A man who engages with his own children? His daughter is so lucky.* Leila feels at once glad for Ali's sake, and sad for her own children, who never had the opportunity to connect with their father. *Though honestly, I'm glad they didn't really get to know Saidun,* she thinks, not for the first time. *Their grandfather is a much better father figure than Saidun ever would have been.* Leila glances out of the corner of her eye at Nika, who has taken over chopping the cutting board full of red summer tomatoes sitting on the counter, and stops herself from trying to imagine what it would have been like for her children to get to grow up with a father like him. *Stop,* she chides herself, *there's no point in dwelling on it and regretting something that can never be.*

"If you're going to help, at least dice them smaller, so that no one will realize that it wasn't me who cut them," Leila comes over to Nika and quickly demonstrates how she wants the tomato cut. He nods, and duplicates her example.

"So, men aren't usually allowed in your kitchen?" Nika smiles at Leila, and she laughs. "Ramazi men wouldn't come within ten feet of a kitchen if they were starving to death! Though neither would most Georgian men, for that matter!"

"I'm not 'most Georgian men'" Nika smiles.

"You never were," Leila smiles back, reaching for the tomatoes that Nika has cut and adding them to her pan of garlic and onions. Nika watches her as she slowly folds all the ingredients together with a wooden spatula.

"If you're going to help, you might as well de-bone the chicken," Leila points with her spoon to a whole baked chicken that is sitting on a plate on the counter.

"Oooh, finally a chef-worthy task!" Nika grins and the two of them cook in companionable silence, both of them marveling at how natural it feels to be back together.

"Tell me about your kids," Nika lobs a conversational softball— what mom doesn't like talking about her kids?

"They're mostly great," Leila smiles, tossing the deboned chicken pieces into the now simmering tomato sauce. "You've met my son Abdullah— he's my right-hand man around here," Leila smiles affectionately. "He's very Ramazi in some ways— strong, and proud, and protective and hard-working. But he is also a thinker— he doesn't just immediately follow the rules without knowing why they exist. He questions things and is insatiably curious. He is very religious— he seems to have an intense desire to find truth that I think the rest of us are too tired to even try for," Leila gives a regretful half-grin. "I'm worried about him now though— he and Callie have gotten really close, and his accident in the mountains only seems to have intensified their bond. I'm worried Callie will leave and go back to her bright American life, and he will be left behind with a broken heart."

"I can attest to what that is like," Nika smiles sadly, looking deep into Leila's green eyes. She swallows, twisting a dishcloth in her hands, and changes the subject.

"As for Fariza, she is married to a good man named Sayid and they have a two year-old son named Daud and she is eight months pregnant with a baby girl. Daud is already a handful, so she will have an interesting life once the new baby comes along!"

"What's she like?" Nika heads to the sink to wash his knife and cutting board, but Leila rushes over and takes them from his hands. "It's ridiculous enough for me to let you help cook— there is no way I'm letting you wash dishes!" She reaches for the cutting board and their fingers connect for a moment. Leila feels a rush down to her toes. She ignores it, and grabs the cutting board quickly and washes it. She hurries back to their previous topic of conversation as if nothing had happened.

"Fariza? She looks more like Saidun, with his dark hair and stature. She has my green eyes, though," Leila smiles.

"Then she's very lucky," Nika winks.

Leila sighs wistfully, "She reminds me so much of myself when I was young! Her whole life she has been full of energy and mischief and laughter. Not even this place could steal it from her," Leila adds quietly. "Her husband is a good man, a very devout Muslim. He teaches history in the local *madrasa*. He really loves my daughter. Since she got married, Fariza has still maintained her bubbly personality, which I'm so grateful for."

Nika moves towards Leila and pulls a chair out from the wall. She reluctantly sits, and he pulls a second chair up for himself near her.

"Dina, what—"

"I'm not Dina," Leila whispers, looking up out the window and avoiding eye contact with Nika.

"What happened to Dina?" Nika asks, holding out a hand towards Leila. Slowly, she puts her hands in his and he wraps his warm fingers around hers.

"She died. A long, slow, painful death," Leila gives a humorless laugh. "Really, it's not worth talking about." Leila tucks a loose strand of long auburn hair under her headscarf and moves to stand up.

"Wait! Please," Nika continues to hold her hand. "I want to hear your story. I want to know how you changed from the fiery, emotional, spunky girl I used to know into this organized, professional businesswoman."

"Basically I was a square peg, hammered and hammered and hammered until all my edges wore off and I would fit into the round hole I had to fit into. Does that tell you what you need to know?" Leila laughs but there is hurt in her eyes. She sighs. Nika sits still and quiet, like one would if trying not to scare away a skittish fawn. His brown eyes are warm and accepting.

Leila's face grows serious and she stops joking. "I've never told my story to anyone," she glances over at him, tears in the edges of her eyes. "And anyway, my story is no different from any of a thousand others. In many ways, others' are much worse. I at least survived," Leila shrugs and lets go of Nika's hand, then heads back to the stove. She stirs the contents slowly and Nika worries that she will stay there and their conversation will be over. But finally she turns the burner off and puts a lid on the pot before returning and reluctantly sitting next to Nika.

"Please tell me your story," he whispers, eyes holding hers.

She is quiet for a long time, and Nika can see her internal debate. Finally she takes a deep breath, looks up at the ceiling, and begins. "I was walking to university, the day you had your competition…"

Over the course of the next two hours, as lunch grows cold on the stovetop, she tells him everything— the initial kidnapping, the failed attempt at running away, how she felt like a deaf person with the language barrier, the harsh treatment she received from her mother-in-law, the saving grace of the kindness her sisters-in-law showed her. She cries as she gives broad strokes over the beatings and the season in the hut out back and Saidun's second marriage and subsequent death. Nika cries along with her and holds her hands the whole time she talks, squeezing gently at all the right places. She tells him how the mountains and the garden and motherhood saved her. She tells him how she and her father-in-law grew to love each other. She tells him how proud she is of her children and of the guesthouse they have built together.

Finally, exhausted and spent, she looks up into his adoring brown eyes.

"Thank you for letting me tell you my story," she whispers. "I never told it to anyone before. That was hard, but cathartic I think."

"Dina... Leila. I am in awe of you— you are an incredible woman. I hate that you went through everything you went through. And I hate that I didn't come and rescue you. I should have." Nika says, fierce with frustration.

"I wish you could have," Leila says sadly. "But it really would have just made things worse. And anyway, the bad days are behind me. I'm content with life as it currently is. I have my children and Daud and the other baby on the way. And I have a growing business that I enjoy. And I live in a place whose beauty I don't think I could bear to be separated from," Leila smiles gently.

Nika shakes his head in admiration, "I always knew you were strong, but now you are even so much stronger than you were back then."

"Ramazi women have to be strong," Leila smiles sadly. "We have to fight for life."

Nika nods, understanding. He reaches a tentative hand out and runs it gently down Leila's cheek. "Leila, I want you back in my life so very much. Is there nothing we can do to give us a second chance? You are free. I am free. I think we could be really happy together."

"I wish we could," Leila says with true regret. "I think... I think I could really love you. I thought about you so many times over the past few decades," she dares to admit in a whisper. "You have always been a very good man. And now that you got rid of that terrible mustache you used to have, you are a good-looking man!" Leila grins, and Nika can see a glimmer of her old teasing nature.

"The mustache was terrible!" he laughs. "I thought it made me look so grown up!"

"Ha, it just made you look scraggly!" Leila grins, and stands up and pushes away her chair. She glances at the clock on the wall and blanches. "Everyone will be back soon! You have to get out of here right away!"

Nika stands up, reluctantly pushing his chair against the wall. He is about to try to talk her into the two of them at least eating lunch together since his stomach is starting to growl, but when he sees her panic he quickly acquiesces and exits the kitchen.

"Bring your laptop or a book down to the dining table and you can eat and I will serve you," Leila instructs.

"Dina, no! You don't have to serve me! Please, I can get my own food. You need to eat too!"

"Do not call me Dina!" Leila hisses, frowning. "You could ruin everything!"

"I'm sorry— Leila! Honest mistake, seriously."

"I know," Leila sighs, taking a calming breath. "Just be careful, ok?"

***

Later that night, Nika is lying in bed trying unsuccessfully to read the novel he brought along for the trip. His mind keeps returning to Dina/Leila, and to all the terrible things that she had been through. He feels heartsick thinking about them, and he knows instinctively that she didn't tell him the half of what she had actually endured.

In the late afternoon, after the *shashlik* crew had returned, Nika had taken a walk into the orchard and then into the back pasture. He had glanced around to make sure that no one was looking, and then had surreptitiously snuck behind the back hut and looked in the dim windows. He could see one narrow bed, covered with a natty wool blanket. From what he could tell, the floor looked to be made from dirt. There were piles of junk— old lamps, boxes, abandoned rugs and more piled up in the corners of the room. He had stared through that dirty window, into the even dirtier hovel inside and ached for the hurting girl who had suffered there so many years before. Even now, lying in bed, he felt like he was on the verge of tears. He was emotionally spent, and it hadn't even been his story.

Suddenly, Nika is startled by a creaking sound as his door opens quickly and then closes. He hears soft footsteps tiptoeing across his floor towards his bed and he holds his breath, hoping against hope for it to be the one person whom he wants more than anyone in the world — the one person he has loved for more than half of his life.

The footsteps stop by his bed and Nika barely breaths. Then the steps begin to retreat towards the door.

"Wait!" Nika whispers desperately. "Leila?"

The footsteps head back towards the bed.

"I thought you were asleep. I really shouldn't be here." Leila's voice is so soft that Nika has to strain to hear it. Suddenly, he is shocked to feel her sit down on the bed beside him.

"I'm glad you're here," Nika whispers, trying to reassure her and to not startle her away.

"It's just that…." Leila takes a long pause and Nika holds his breath.

"It's just that… I know we can't actually have a relationship or a life together. But I thought maybe… maybe we could have a night together?" Leila's voice sounds at once scared and hopeful. "No one has ever held me," she whispers sadly. "I don't know what a kiss feels like from someone who loves me. And I don't want to go to my grave never experiencing that. And this will likely be my one chance." Leila's voice cracks.

In the darkness, Nika clambers up to his knees. "Let me show you what it feels like," he stretches out his arms to Leila in the darkness and she moves into them. She startles away for a second when she touches the bare skin of his chest— he had been heading to bed in just a pair of flannel pj pants. But he pulls her back, and she snuggles close. This time, since they're both on their knees, she is about the same height as him and she can tuck her head into his neck. Nika begins to stroke the long strands of hair coming out from under her headscarf. Wordlessly, Leila lifts her hands and unties the headscarf. Nika runs his fingers through the length of her hair and she sighs contentedly.

"Can I kiss you now?" Nika whispers, gently running a finger down her cheeks and then across her lips.

Leila nods in the darkness, opening her lips slightly to his finger, shivering with a desire she has never felt before.

Gently, Nika removes his finger and replaces it with his lips. His kisses are soft and slow and so tender that Leila starts to cry. *I didn't know it could be like this*, she thinks. *This is better than I ever imagined.* She puts both hands on either side of his head and caresses the back of his neck as Nika gently begins to probe Leila's lips with his tongue. She opens her mouth to him and sighs with pleasure and wonder— *how is it possible that at forty-six I am having my first real kiss?* Leila presses her body against Nika and she hears him moan gently as he wraps his arms around her and pulls her close. She allows herself to do something she has never done— experience the pleasure of being kissed by a man who loves her.

Nika's kisses get deeper and stronger and he slides down onto the bed. Leila slides down beside him, shocked at her own brazenness. His hands begin to move across her body, gently exploring over the top of her dress as he continues to kiss her. Leila is lost in the moment when Nika shifts his body and Leila suddenly has overwhelming, rushing flashbacks of Saidun and his rough handling. Bedroom memories that she has long suppressed come flooding back and she can barely breathe. She tears at the sheets and pushes Nika away from her in a panic to get out of the bed as quickly as possible.

"Leila, what's wrong?" Nika sits up, concern in his voice.

"This was a mistake! I'm sorry— I can't do this. I should never have come!" Leila cries, grabbing her headscarf and slipping out of Nika's room as quickly and quietly as she had come.

***

The next morning, Leila keeps her head down as she serves breakfast silently to Nika and the table full of happy oblivious chattering guests. Nika, who had tossed and turned all night, tries unsuccessfully to catch her eye. He drinks a second cup of black coffee and picks distractedly at the heaping pile of pancakes on his plate. The toddler next to him spills a cup of deep-red cherry juice on the white tablecloth and Leila cleans it up with a gracious smile.

At the end of breakfast, when the other guests are leaving the table in a noisy cacophony of scraping chairs, a hysterical toddler, and the gathering of sundry jackets and sunglasses, Nika hears a slight cough at his elbow.

"Mr. Shashashvili, I have a question about the receipt you said you need for your room. If you could come to my office to clarify, I would appreciate it." Leila is polite and formal and Nika nods, relieved. He follows her across the veranda and into the building that houses both her office and her home.

"My son is out for the morning," Leila explains, closing the door behind them. Nika sits in one of the two office chairs and waits as Leila sits across from him.

"I'm really sorry," she whispers, green eyes full of guilt and regret. "It was wrong of me to come last night– selfish. I never should have come."

"But I'm glad you came!" Nika insists. "I just wish you hadn't left!" He pauses for a moment, then asks quietly, "What happened? Why did you leave?"

Leila sighs and looks up at the ceiling, willing tears not to come. "It had nothing to do with you, I promise. It's just… my bedroom memories from my husband are not happy ones." Leila gives a sad shrug, "I thought that all that pain was far in the past, but I think being in a similar situation stirred it all up. All my old fear came rushing back and I panicked," Leila admits, at once ashamed for her behavior and incredibly grateful to be sitting across from a man with whom she can be honest.

"I understand," Nika smiles tenderly at her. "There's nothing to be ashamed of. I'm so sorry for everything you went through. Physical intimacy should be a beautiful thing, not a painful one."

"That's what I've heard," Leila makes a weak attempt at humor. "Thank you for your patience. And thank you for coming to find me. Thank you for still loving me, after all these years. Despite last night not ending the way we would have liked, I will always treasure the memory of our kiss."

Leila stands and Nika reluctantly stands as well. "You leave tomorrow?" she asks formally, even though she knows the answer quite well. Nika nods.

"We have someone checking into your room in the afternoon, so we will need to get Rosana in to clean around noon. But you're welcome to stay around the property 'til whatever time you would like in the afternoon or evening, and of course we can arrange a car for you back to Tbilisi."

"Is this it, Leila? Is there really nothing we can do?" Nika's eyes are pleading.

"I wish there was," Leila stands on tiptoe and barely reaches Nika's cheek, where she brushes her lips for a soft, quick kiss before slipping out the door. Nika sinks back into the office chair, unable to believe that he finally found the love of his life, only to lose her for a second time. His head is groggy from lack of sleep and he thumps his fist on the desk in frustration. After a few minutes, he heads to his room and starts packing his suitcase. If there's no chance for him and Leila, there's no reason for him to stay.

CHAPTER 33
Sureti Valley, Georgia

August, 2018

"You're leaving early?! I just overheard Abdullah call a cab!" Callie rushes out to the garden, where Nika is taking a last walk before leaving.

He turns to her with sad eyes, "Unfortunately my stay here did not go as I had hoped, and now I need to return home to London."

"I'm sorry," Callie replies sincerely, standing beside him and looking out across the mountains. Realizing that with Nika's departure, her last chance at answers to her questions will likely disappear, she throws caution to the wind and decides to get what answers from him she can.

"So…" she starts hesitantly, being as delicate and gentle as she can. She's had plenty of experience in her journalistic work getting wary subjects to drop their guard and open up to her. She probes tentatively, "You and Leila were friends growing up? Like you said in your initial messages on Instagram?"

Nika glances sideways at her, then nods. He stands under the gnarled branches of an apple tree, its green fruit small and new and unripe. Callie reaches up and gently pulls off a leaf, tearing it into small pieces in her hand, letting the pieces flutter one by one to the ground.

"Maybe you and Leila were more than friends?" she asks quietly.

Nika laughs ruefully, "Ha, I wished! But no, we were just friends. Maybe if we had had more time…" Nika glances at his watch and Callie realizes that his taxi is about to arrive. He is about to turn back towards the house when she grasps his elbow and asks quickly, "Leila was kidnapped, wasn't she? Brought here? She's not really Ramazi?"

Before Nika has a chance to answer, they hear a strangled voice behind them.

"What?!"

Callie spins around to see Abdullah leaning on his crutches, his face pale.

He stares hard at Callie, "What did you just say?"

She panics, "Ummm, nothing, really. Just my curiosity. No big deal. I think Mr. Shashashvili has to go now?"

Abdullah shakes his head, eyebrows drawn together and amber eyes blazing, "What are you saying about my mother? And why are you asking this man? Who are you?" He half shouts, his lean body taut with pent-up tension as he glares at Nika with suspicion. Callie is shocked— she's never seen Abdullah react so intensely and rashly.

Nika holds up his hands placatingly, "I'm an old school friend of your mother's, that's all. I am from Tbilisi, but I live in London now. I'm just here for a visit."

Abdullah's eyes narrow and he says harshly, his voice raised, "My mother is not from Tbilisi. You must be confused."

Callie and Nika cast desperate glances at each other, neither one sure what to do.

"What is going on out here? All the guests can hear you, and likely the whole neighborhood!" Leila hurries towards them across the stone path, her arms covered up to her elbows in flour from the bread dough she had been in the middle of kneading when she had heard the commotion through the open kitchen window.

"These two," Abdullah flings an arm accusingly towards Callie and Nika, "are saying that you're not Ramazi and that you're not even from here! Tell them the truth!"

Leila darts a withering glare at Callie and Nika, who both shrivel, before turning resignedly back to her son.

"They're right," she says quietly.

"What??!" Abdullah explodes, hitting a flat palm against his forehead in a ricocheting motion of shock. In his hurried movement, a crutch slips from under his arm and clatters noisily on the stone path.

"Hush! Keep quiet! Don't you know the potential scandal and repercussions if this gets out to the wrong people?" Leila glares at her son. "I know this is a shock, but get yourself under control."

Abdullah takes a steadying breath of air and leans on his remaining crutch. Just then, his cell phone blares, startling everyone.

Abdullah answers it. "It's your driver," he says to Nika. "He's here. I think it's time for you to go." Abdullah's clipped tone and tightly crossed arms leave no question of the meaning of his words.

Nika's eyes dart towards Leila. "I didn't want this to end like this," he whispers anxiously, reaching one arm out towards her hand. Leila takes a quick step back and holds up her arms, still covered in flour and dough. A piece of her long auburn hair has escaped her headscarf and is covering her right eye. Impatiently, she blows a puff of air out of the side of her mouth to get the strand out of the way.

"I know," she sighs. "But it's how things have happened, and now I will deal with them. Go home, back to your daughter."

Resigned, Nika turns and walks towards the guesthouse, then around the corner to the gate and his waiting taxi. Leila, Abdullah, and Callie stand in fraught silence, watching his lanky form and shoulders, hunched with dejection, until he is out of sight. Callie risks a glance at Abdullah, who is bouncing on the heel of his good leg.

"What do you mean—" Abdullah starts to whisper-shout at his mother the moment Nika is gone.

"Enough!" Leila raises a hand and her stern tone stops her fuming son. "You will get the explanation you want. I promise. And who knows, maybe I should have told you years ago. But not here. Come inside, where we can talk in private. Ok?" Her eyes plead for understanding and eventually, he gives a curt nod.

For a moment, Callie hopes that they have forgotten about her and that she will be able to back away, unnoticed. But before her wish can come true, Leila turns abruptly towards her, her eyes flashing.

"And you. You may return to your room for the day. You have done more than enough today already." Her tone is scalding and Callie nods rapidly, tears forming in her eyes as she darts around them. She almost trips on Abdullah's crutch, still lying across the pathway. He bends awkwardly to try to pick it up, and she reaches down and grabs it for him. There is apology in her eyes when she hands him the crutch, but he takes it from her without looking at her. She hurries to her room as quickly as she can, tears streaming, berating herself for being so nosy, so unwilling to let the past stay in the past.

***

In her bottom bunk, Callie turns to face the wall and cries quietly into her pillow, hoping the Austrian women sharing her room won't notice. But trying to cry silently when you really want to wail is pretty miserable, and Callie finds herself growing increasingly angry at the cheerful, oblivious banter of the mother and her two teenage daughters. *I've got to get out of here, find somewhere I can think in peace.* Callie wipes her eyes, grabs her phone, and hurries out of the room.

Where can I go? The orchard and garden are too public... Callie glances around the backyard and her eyes land on the woodshed. She heads towards it, looking forward to guaranteed solitude. As she enters the shed, she stumbles to a halt at the sight of Abdullah's lean frame coiled on a chair in the corner. He's furiously hacking away at a piece of wood. To Callie, it looks more like he's destroying it than trying to actually carve something. Slowly, she backs through the door as quietly as possible, hot tears streaming down her cheeks. Just as she is about to leave, Abdullah glances up and sees her. His eyes burn with a combination of such hurt and fury that Callie turns and runs. She runs all the way to the twin shed across the field, the one where she found Leila's letters. Glancing furtively around to make sure that no one is looking, Callie lets herself into the dusty, crowded little room. She collapses onto the narrow bed and all the pent up emotions of the past few weeks come pouring out of her.

When she's finally calmed down after a cleansing cry, Callie picks up her phone— she knows she needs to talk through what's going on with someone. She's about to call Lucy when she hesitates. Lucy would listen (*if she wasn't busy at work or at some party,* Callie thinks), but she wouldn't actually *understand.* Resolutely, Callie dials Pat, who picks up immediately. Callie jumps right in, starting with the most recent fiasco, explaining about Leila's past accidentally coming to light. It is so nice to not have to explain anything, since Pat knows all the people involved, as well as the Ramazi culture.

"I shouldn't have been snooping around!" Callie admits with a groan. "Now Leila and Abdullah are furious at me. I'm supposed to leave in five days and I really don't want to leave on a sour note!"

"Oh honey, I'm sure that must have been quite the shock for everyone," Pat placates. "Obviously not a big deal for Americans where people are from, but it is so important to Ramazis."

"I know," Callie sniffs. "I didn't think it would be such a big deal to Abdullah— he seems so modern. But I've never seen him mad like this; he's usually so good at keeping his cool," Callie whispers, twisting a strand of dark hair around her finger as she scoots around on the hard bed, trying unsuccessfully to get comfortable.

"How are you and Abdullah doing? How has it been since he got back from the hospital? And how's his leg?" Pat asks.

"His leg seems to be healing on schedule. He's gonna be on crutches for a while longer, though it is pretty impressive how quickly he gets around on them! He and I... ugh, I didn't tell you about that drama!" Callie gives a long pause and she can hear Pat listening.

"Lucas flew here without me knowing it and showed up at the guest house to surprise me!" she almost shouts.

"What?!" Callie feels vindicated hearing the shock in Pat's voice.

"I know! I couldn't believe it! And— get this— he arrived at the SAME TIME as Abdullah got home from the hospital!"

Pat begins to chuckle and Callie sputters, "Hey! It wasn't funny!"

"Oh my goodness, I'm sorry I'm laughing! But I can just imagine what a disaster that must have been! Poor you! And poor both of them!"

"I know," Callie groans. "It was pretty terrible. I felt so bad for Abdullah. Though honestly, I'm pretty sure Lucas didn't even realize anything was off, at least at first. He just thought he was happily surprising me."

"So? Did it end up being a happy surprise?" Pat asks.

"Pat, I didn't even tell you the craziest part— Lucas *proposed*, only hours after arriving! And he did it *in* the orchard— you know, on that swing I like? And to make matters worse, one of the neighbors was watching over the fence when he did it! So of course the entire village knew almost immediately!" Callie moans, and Pat murmurs sympathetically.

"What did you say?" Pat asks.

"I didn't know what to say! I was so shocked. On the one hand, I really truly love him. He is a great guy— he's confident and funny and outgoing, all the things I'm not," Callie laughs. "For years, I dreamed about marrying him. If I hadn't met Abdullah, I would've said yes right away. But Abdullah and I... we share a deeper soul-connection. I feel like he *sees* me, on a level Lucas doesn't. I think Lucas likes the *idea* of me... or maybe he likes me when I'm easy to get along with? Maybe it's that I feel like Lucas is willing to *put up* with my flaws, like my sensory issues, which he definitely sees as flaws. Whereas I feel like Abdullah actually *likes* all of who I am. Ugh, sorry I'm droning on! I just haven't had anyone to process with! I've been going in circles inside my own head, and I just needed to get everything out."

"Oh my dear girl, what a drama-filled summer you have had!"

"I don't even *like* drama!" Callie wails. "I like everything to be calm and peaceful! I generally try not to rock the boat!"

"Well," Pat laughs, "I'm afraid that plan failed this summer! Intentionally or unintentionally, you have rocked quite a lot of boats!"

"I know," Callie says miserably. "I'm afraid I've even sunk some... like my relationship with Abdullah. And Leila's opinion of me."

"I'm so sorry, honey. There is always hope for restoration though. What are you going to do?"

"I don't know... Lucas left, and I told him that I would give him my answer when I get back to the US."

"And what are you going to tell him?" Pat asks quietly.

"I'm not sure," Callie sighs. "I literally have no idea what I should do. But my first priority is to try to mend fences with Leila and Abdullah here before I leave. So I'm going to try to apologize to them. I'm just not sure if they will accept it."

"I think they will. It might take them time, but they both really value you," Pat's voice is reassuring.

"I just don't have much time," Callie's voice cracks. "Will you and Rob pray that I can smooth things out here before I leave? And that I will know what to do with Lucas? And I guess with Abdullah as well?"

"Of course, honey. Always." Pat's voice is as warm as a hug and Callie feels a glimmer of hope and comfort as she hangs up the phone and heads back to her room.

***

The next morning, Callie is grateful to be able to head to breakfast with the Austrian mother and her two teenage daughters who are bunking in her room. The mother's light, whiffling snores had contributed to Callie's tossing and turning through the night, but Callie is willing to forgive all for an excuse to blend in with the crowd and hopefully avoid a confrontation with Leila or Abdullah. She wonders whether they've had their talk. And if so, what Leila told Abdullah. Despite herself, she's incredibly curious.

Breakfast, though delicious as usual, is an abnormally quiet affair. The two teenage girls don't look up from their phones the entire time, except to reposition their plates to get better photos of their food. The mother ignores them, clearly having given up long ago on trying to get them off their phones. Callie glances at Leila out of the corner of her eye, when Leila is busy with the other guests. Leila looks subdued and, frankly, exhausted. It is the first time Callie has seen dark circles under her eyes. Callie swallows a lump in her throat and forces herself to finish the omelette in front of her.

There is no sign of Abdullah all morning.

After breakfast, Callie does a workout video in her room, takes a shower, and then grabs her sunglasses and laptop and heads to the picnic table in the orchard to get some work done. She checks all the websites and social media platforms that she has set up for the guesthouse, and everything seems to be running smoothly. They have over two thousand followers on Instagram, and between Airbnb and booking.com, they are booked for most of the fall. The new pictures Callie has posted on all the sites look, if not professional, at least very appealing. Callie can't believe the progress they've made this summer. And more than that, she can't believe she has only four more days here. *And I'm worried that I've ruined them. I can't leave things on this sour note,* she worries, twisting a strand of damp dark hair.

"Callie? May I sit?" Callie is startled to hear Leila's curt voice behind her.

"Of course!" Callie nervously clears off the table space across from her and Leila folds gracefully onto the bench. For a moment, Leila just stares at the mountains, not saying anything. Finally, she gives a tired sigh and turns back to Callie, who is sitting, taut.

"I'm sorry for how everything fell apart yesterday, and that you were caught in the middle of our private family business," she says formally.

"It's all my fault," Callie cries. "I never should have been snooping! I'm so sorry!"

"You're right, you should not have been," Leila agrees sternly, and then softens. "But honestly, it's probably good that the truth came out. I have been hiding myself and my past from my children this whole time. Fariza tells me that isn't healthy, and maybe she is right," Leila sighs.

"So… you talked to both of them?" Callie asks hesitantly.

Leila snorts, "I tried. Fariza was understanding and willing to listen. Abdullah… well, he was mostly just very angry," Leila's eyes look very sad.

"Angry… at whom?" Callie asks quietly.

"At the world, and pretty much everyone in it," Leila says. "Mad at me, for not telling him the truth. Angry that he isn't 100% Ramazi. Mad at his father, for his sins of the past. Angry at his grandmother, for the way she treated me. Angry at you, for digging everything up. Angry at Fariza, for not being angry. And scared, I think. Scared that this changes things. Scared that this changes who he is, or his understanding of who he is." Leila doesn't make eye contact with Callie, but just looks off at the mountains.

"Where is he now?"

"He left on a horse early this morning. I'm guessing he will ride out his angst in the mountains all day and come back calmer. The mountains and forest are good for that, for calming you down," Leila smiles sadly.

"I hope it works," Callie replies sincerely.

"It will. He will come around. It may take a while— he's a hothead sometimes, but his heart is good. And he loves me," Leila smiles gently.

"I... I have something that belongs to you," Callie admits spontaneously. She had been uncertain how or if to return the letters to Leila, but now there seems to be open communication between them, so she reaches into her purse and pulls out the two letters.

Leila gasps and takes the letters, looking up at Callie in confusion, "Where did you find these? I lost them years ago."

"I found them in the shed out back... under the mattress," Callie admits, cheeks reddening with shame.

Leila purses her lips, about to say something when the family photo falls out of one of the letters. She sucks in a breath of air, and pulls it close to her eyes. "I thought I'd never see this again!" she murmurs, running a finger longingly across the photograph.

"That's your family?" Callie asks gently.

Leila nods, absorbed in looking at the photo. "This was our last family photo, the last time we were together," she says quietly, a quiver in her voice. "Thank you for finding this— it is more precious than you can imagine to me."

Callie nods and quietly begins to gather her things, planning to leave Leila in peace with her letters and photo. But before she can leave, Leila looks up and stops her, "Callie."

"Yes?" Callie asks, awkwardly hunched partway to standing between the bench and the table.

"Since it seems we are baring all," Leila says drily, "I have a final thing to ask you. You leave in four days. Are you still together with your American boyfriend?"

Callie nods, not liking the turn this conversation has taken.

"Good," Leila nods firmly. "Does my son know that?"

"I... I think so. I mean, I'm sure he does," Callie reddens.

"Before you leave, please do me the favor of making it very clear to my son that you are together with Lucas. I would not want him to get any wrong ideas." Even though Leila is the one sitting and Callie is standing, the look in Leila's eyes makes Callie feel about two inches tall.

Callie feels herself growing defensive, "There's nothing going on between Abdullah and me," she insists more hotly than she should.

"Excellent. Keep it that way," Leila nods sternly, then softens. "He has had enough troubles this summer without needing to add to them. Your life is in America, and his is here. I know that you two have enjoyed working together this summer, and you have done excellent work. We will always be grateful for the ways in which you have helped our guesthouse develop and modernize. You have been a wonderful asset to our business. I am just worried that perhaps... perhaps some people got too attached over the summer. My son seems very strong and mature, but underneath he is young and tenderhearted and feels things intensely. I don't want him to get hurt."

"And I don't want to hurt him, I promise!" Callie insists, flustered at their sudden honesty after the arm's length Leila had kept her at all summer.

"Good, then we are in agreement. Enjoy your last few days here, and then you can return home to your friends and family." Callie nods and hurries back to her room, her head and heart spinning.

***

"You don't have to drive me," Callie whispers quietly as Abdullah loads her bags into the trunk of his beat up sedan. *I can't believe it was only three months ago that I came to Khev in this clunker,* Callie thinks in amazement, running a hand across the car's dented bumper. *It feels like a lifetime ago.* She glances up at Abdullah, who has avoided her the past few days.

"Of course I will drive you," Abdullah replies formally, as standoffish as he was that very first day he picked Callie up in Tbilisi. *I suppose we've gone full circle, just not in a good way.* Callie feels a catch in her throat as she climbs into the back seat, the cushions sticky in the summer heat. Her goodbyes a few minutes before with Leila, Rosana, and Fariza had been warm and heartfelt. They had gotten over the initial shock of her accidental revelation, and clearly wanted to end things with her on a good note. Callie glances at the tall green gate, where the three women are waving vigorously at her. She puts a brave smile on her face and waves back, laughing in spite of herself when Daud comes darting out into the road and tries to climb into the car. Fariza comes chasing after him.

"One last kiss for Auntie Callie!" Fariza calls, throwing open the door of the backseat. "He wants to come with you!"

Callie laughs and gives the squirming toddler a kiss on his sweaty curly head, then attempts to help Fariza finagle him, kicking and screaming, out of the car.

Callie turns and looks through the back windshield of the car as they pull away. She can hear Daud's furious screams all the way till the end of the street, when they turn onto the main road. She turns around, soaking in one last look at Khev. She tears up when she passes the homes of some of the neighbors who hosted her for meals over the course of the summer. When they pass the local fruit stand, Abbas waves happily to her and blows her kisses. Amira waves from the doorway of the store.

"You made quite the impression in your short time here," Abdullah says softly when they finally pull out of town. *He's talking to me!* Callie rejoices.

"I'm really gonna miss this place," she admits, teary-eyed. "It has gotten inside my heart in ways I didn't expect. I thought I was just coming for a job," Callie gives a hiccuping laugh.

"It seems perhaps you have gotten in the hearts of people in Khev as well," Abdullah says, eyes ahead on the road. *Is he talking about himself? I cannot handle the not knowing! We can't end on this note!* Callie thinks desperately, unsure of how to proceed. Finally, she decides to just barrel ahead like an American.

"Please Abdullah, we can't end like this! I don't want to leave on a sour note with you," Callie begs, cautiously reaching up to the front seat and putting a hand on Abdullah's shoulder. He sits very still, not responding. Callie feels like she can barely breathe. Are they going to spend their two-hour ride to the airport in awkward silence, and leave without having reconciled?? The air in the car feels hot and constricting. Callie shifts uncomfortably— she really hates being hot. She slips off her sandals and surreptitiously lifts her floor-length skirt up to her knees.

Suddenly, Abdullah pulls off the road. They're driving through the winding mountain pass that Callie remembers so well from their first drive together, when everything was the fresh vibrant green of early summer. Now the grass is dry, brittle and brown from the August heat and the lack of rain. Some of the leaves on the trees are even starting to prematurely turn autumn brown, but from a lack of water instead of cold weather. Abdullah's car rattles and shakes as he drives it down a bumpy path that is clearly not meant for cars. Finally he parks behind some trees, out of sight of the road. Callie holds her breath in the backseat, confused.

After a minute, Abdullah opens his door. Callie watches as he walks around the car and opens all four doors, letting in a surprisingly cool mountain breeze. Callie sighs in relief, soaking in the fresh air. Her heart thumps, unsure of what is happening.

Once all four car doors are open, Abdullah surprises her by sliding into the backseat beside her. She sees him notice her bare legs, and she quickly lowers her skirt, blushing. *I wouldn't think a thing of someone seeing my legs in the US, but here it feels inappropriate,* she realizes, marveling at how much this place has affected her.

Abdullah looks at the floorboard in silence while Callie watches him and waits. Finally, he raises his eyes to hers and they are burning with emotion.

"I'm so sorry," he whispers. "I was an idiot. I responded so rashly and so rudely. I'm not normally like that," his eyes plead.

"I know you aren't!" Callie hurries to reassure him. "It was my fault! I shouldn't have snooped around!"

Abdullah shakes his head, "It's good you did. Now so much of my life makes sense. It's like my life was this puzzle with missing pieces that didn't connect, and you found the missing pieces and connected them. But just not in the way I expected," his mouth moves in a half smile, half grimace. "You pretty much turned my world upside down, Callie Leffler."

"I feel really awful about it," Callie twists her hands.

"Don't," he sighs. "Now I just have to re-figure out who I am and who my mom is, without all the things I thought I knew. Though honestly, now that I know the truth about my mom, it explains so much."

"Abdullah, this doesn't change who you are!" Callie leans towards him, insistent.

"I think there are about 3 million Ramazis who would disagree with you," Abdullah gives her another grimace-smile and runs a hand through his dark bangs.

"Well, screw them!" Callie says vehemently.

Abdullah raises his eyebrows with a grin.

"Sorry," Callie smiles sheepishly, twisting a strand of her dark hair. "I just don't want you to doubt who you are. Because you are amazing just the way you are," she whispers, staring into his eyes.

"Don't leave!" Abdullah exclaims, grasping Callie's hand and pulling it to his chest. Her eyes widen. She can feel his heart beating through the thin cotton of his shirt.

"I... I've wanted to say something for so long," the words flood out of him, like a broken dam. "I've liked you since you first arrived. And then that photoshoot in the woodshed. Remember that?"

Callie nods.

"That was the first time we flirted," Abdullah grins and Callie blushes. "It was the first time I dared to hope that maybe you might feel something for me in return. And then the whole summer, we worked so well together. Callie, I've never met anyone who is so easy for me to be around and to be open with. And then that night by the campfire, on the horseback-riding trip..."

Callie nods, remembering that night— the warmth of the fire, how they had opened their hearts to each other, the look in his eyes, the electricity when he had held her hand.

"I was planning to tell you how I felt on the last day of that trip, but then..." Abdullah shrugs. "All the shit hit the fan. Is this the American expression you use?"

Callie laughs, "That's a fairly appropriate expression. Probably too mild even to sum up the mudslide."

Abdullah lowers their hands to his lap and begins to move his thumb in a slow circle on the bit of skin between Callie's thumb and finger. She shivers.

"And then Lucas showed up," she whispers.

"And he asked you to marry him," Abdullah's eyes are dark and probing.

Callie looks away. "And he asked me to marry him," she whispers.

"Callie," Abdullah puts a finger under her chin and pulls her head up till she is looking into his eyes. "Don't marry him! I know that on paper, you should choose him— you're from the same country, he is tall and handsome and everyone likes him. He probably has a lot more money than I will ever make. But Callie, I love you. I have never felt like this about anyone before. And I think maybe… maybe… you feel the same?" Doubt and insecurity and hope all commingle in Abdullah's warm eyes. *'Love', he said 'love',* Callie's heart thrums.

"I never imagined that I could fall in love with someone who wasn't a Ramazi. But then you came. Callie, you are kind and generous — you quit your job to spend a summer helping total strangers for free — who does that?? And when my mom and I were in the hospital, you helped run the guesthouse that whole week. Fariza and Rosana told me how amazing you were, that they couldn't have managed without you. And I love your gentleness— you put on a capable, driven face for the world, but underneath, you are soft and gentle. When I'm with you, I feel a peace that I don't feel other places. And have I mentioned that you are so very beautiful? Callie, I want to be with you. And not just for a short time, but for the rest of our lives. I want to marry you." Callie feels warmth spreading across her cheeks and neck at the love in his eyes as he stares at her.

This can't end well. Tell him you have no feelings for him, that he misread everything. You're dating Lucas. What are you doing? Callie thinks desperately. But her emotions outweigh her thoughts and before she knows it she has twined her arms around Abdullah's neck and pressed her mouth against his. It takes him a moment to respond— she can tell he is surprised and taken aback. But he quickly recovers and she feels his lean arms pull her up against his muscular chest. He reaches up and runs a hand through her hair as he kisses her— softly and gently at first and then more deeply.

For a few minutes, Callie allows herself to get lost in his kiss, which is so much sweeter than she had even imagined.

Finally her brain catches up to her body and she pulls away, hands pushing his chest away from her, "I'm a terrible person," she gasps. "I am so sorry. I didn't mean for that to happen."

"Don't apologize! Please!" Abdullah begs, gently tugging her back towards himself.

But Callie shakes her head and blows out a breath of hot air, "I can't do this. I am so sorry. I should never have kissed you." By now she is crying for real.

"You're going back to him?" Abdullah asks, stone still.

"I don't know!" Callie wails, burying her face in her hands. "How am I supposed to choose?! I love both of you, and in such different ways! And no matter what I choose, people will get hurt. I don't want to hurt you," Callie runs a finger gently down the jagged scar on his cheek.

"I know you don't," Abdullah raises her hand to his lips and kisses the inside of her palm. He takes a deep, shuddering breath and then squares his shoulders. "Whatever you choose, Lucas and I will survive. I think we are strong guys," Abdullah gives a half-smile. "I trust you to make the decision that is right for you. Though selfishly, I hope that that decision is me." Abdullah puts his hand to Callie's cheek and she leans into it and closes her eyes. He smells like wood shavings and Leila's lavender soap. She sighs, soaking in the scent of him that has become so dear to her over the past few months.

She opens her eyes, glancing up at him, "I'm sorry I kissed you," she whispers. "I shouldn't have. It won't make anything any easier."

"It probably won't," Abdullah admits. "But I'm glad you did. I probably wouldn't have kissed you."

"Wait— what?!" Callie asks, a bit offended.

"Not that I haven't wanted to! I have wanted to so much!" Abdullah quickly defends himself. "We just normally don't kiss until our weddings," he explains.

"Oh my gosh, are you serious??! I am so sorry!" Now Callie feels even worse— mortified, really. "Wait— was that your first kiss??" She asks, slightly horrified– and confused, because his kiss had certainly felt like he knew what he was doing.

"Actually, no," Abdullah admits sheepishly. "I dated a Georgian girl for a couple of months at university in Tbilisi— but you cannot ever tell my mother! I was eighteen and stupid and just exploring the world."

"And now you're a mature twenty-four-year-old?" Callie grins.

"So old and wise," Abdullah smiles back, then goes pale when he glances at the clock.

"Ummm, Callie, we're going to be cutting it close for you to make your flight."

"I completely lost track of the time!" Callie pushes him out of the door. "Drive!"

"Come sit up here beside me!" Abdullah shouts as he rushes to the front seat. Callie quickly jumps out of the back, slams the door, and scoots into the front seat. *Lord, please let this car make it on time and in one piece!* she prays as the old sedan rattles across the bumpy dirt path and back onto the main road. Even on the main road, it can't go much over 60 mph. Callie twists a strand of her hair nervously, kicking herself for getting so distracted in the woods. She glances over at Abdullah, who seems to be fully focused on getting her to the airport as quickly as possible.

"Abdullah," she hesitates, unsure of what to say. He glances over at her and grabs her hand, giving it a squeeze.

"I don't know what will happen down the road," she admits. "But I'm really glad we aren't leaving on a bad note. I was so worried that we wouldn't make up before I left."

"I think we officially made up," he winks at her and Callie blushes. His hand feels warm and solid in hers. He rolls down his window and she rolls down hers and the summer breeze blows her hair as they wind their way down the mountain road to the airport on the edge of Tbilisi.

Far too soon, the ride is over. Callie is so late for her flight that there is no time for lingering goodbyes or more conversation. Abdullah pulls up to the curb right by the terminal and they both hop out of the car and run for the trunk. Abdullah sets Callie's suitcase on the ground and helps her put her orange backpack on her back. And then he wraps his arms around her and she buries her face in his neck.

"I love you," he whispers. "Whatever you choose, I will never forget you and our summer. And if you decide to come back, I will be here waiting." Callie nods into his neck, and then pulls back. She runs her hand through his swoopy bangs that she loves so much, plants a quick peck on his cheek, and sprints to catch her plane.

EPILOGUE
Sureti Valley, Georgia

April, 2019

The grape vines are bare and shriveled, looking empty and forlorn after a long winter. Patches of snow lie in stubborn clumps in the shaded areas of the courtyard, refusing to melt. The April sun shines weakly from the sky— this high in the mountains, the spring sun is no competition for the cold. It will be at least a month before it gains enough warmth to bring buds to the trees.

Rosana sets the table carefully for lunch, excitedly awaiting the upcoming arrival. She lays out the white ceramic plates with soup bowls on top. In the middle of the table, a large glass vase holds sprigs of holly with a few red berries still clinging stubbornly to the branches. As she deftly folds a pile of cream-colored cloth napkins and places them to the right of each plate, she hears a knock at the gate and hurries to open it.

"We're here! Are they here yet?" Fariza rushes through the gate, thrusting a thickly bundled baby girl towards Rosana as she drags a tantruming Daud by one arm.

"I don't want to wear this hat!" he wails, yanking at the strings of the bright red hat tied under his chin.

"Look at the ground! See the snow??! You have to keep your hat on! You may take it off once you're inside," Fariza huffs with exasperation. "This boy is impossible! How did my mother manage with us on her own?"

"From what I've heard, you had as much of a mind of your own as Daud does," Rosana smiles at Fariza as she bounces the baby girl on her hip. "Maybe this one will give you some peace?"

"So far, she definitely seems more docile than her brother. But she's only seven months old, so it's really too early to tell. But you're a sweet one, aren't you, my girl?" Fariza coos at her daughter, whose round face grins back from under a giant snowsuit, hat, and scarf.

"So they aren't here yet?" Fariza asks, heading towards the dining room.

"Not yet, but we're expecting them soon. Lunch is almost ready."

"Perfect timing," Fariza smiles.

Just then, they hear the sound of crunching gravel on the road outside. "Oooh, I bet it's them!" Both women hurry towards the gate and throw open the door.

"Hello!" Rob shouts, hopping out of the car. "We're back!"

"Us and our eighty million bags and books," Pat adds from the back seat where she is surrounded by suitcases. Eventually she extricates herself from all the luggage and hurries over to the ladies, arms outstretched.

She gives them each warm hugs and then oohs and ahhhs over Fariza's baby girl. Just as Rosana is handing the baby over to Pat, Rob hustles over, "Any sign of the lovebirds?" he grins, red-cheeked from the cold and the exertion of hauling suitcases from the trunk of the taxi.

"Not yet, but they should be here soon," Fariza smiles. "We can't wait to hear about their honeymoon! Come on in— Rosana has lunch ready. You guys can get settled in your room and by the time you're done hopefully they'll be here."

"Sounds perfect!" says Rob, hoisting a giant suitcase. Pat returns the baby to Fariza and pulls a rolling suitcase towards the guesthouse.

Everyone is sitting down for lunch when they hear another car drive up outside. Soup spoons clatter as they rush to the gate just in time to see a taxi come to a stop. When the door opens, Leila steps out. The door on the other side of the taxi opens and Nika's lanky form exits the taxi.

"Mom! Welcome home!" Fariza throws her arms around Leila, who happily hugs her back.

"Grandma! Grandma!" Daud hurtles between them, insisting that Leila let go of Fariza and pick him up. "The cat in the barn had kittens while you were gone! Six of them!" he shouts excitedly. "You have to come see them now!"

"You've missed a lot of important things while you were gone, Mom," Abdullah grins, coming in for a side hug. Leila puts a hand to his cheek and blows an air kiss in his direction.

There's a brief moment of awkward silence when Nika makes his way around the car towards Abdullah, but the men quickly move past it and shake hands cordially.

"So, how was London?" Pat asks, leaning towards Leila for a hug.

"It was wonderful," she smiles, glancing up at Nika, who has moved to her side and put an arm around her shoulder. "I got to meet Nika's friends and family there, including his daughter. We had a simple wedding ceremony and reception with some of his close friends. It was much tamer than our upcoming wedding this weekend in Khev will be, I'm sure! And Nika showed me around London, like a professional tour guide."

"In true London fashion, the weather was cold and wet and gray," Nika shrugs, "but even that didn't dampen our time. Your mother was a hit everywhere we went," he smiles adoringly at Leila.

"That's definitely an exaggeration," Leila shakes her head with a smile. "We had a great trip, but I am so very very glad to be home. *We* are so very glad to be home," she corrects herself, glancing up at Nika.

"We're glad you're both home too," Fariza smiles at them. "Now come inside for lunch! We started without you guys and it's going to be cold if we don't hurry!"

"Can't let Rosana's amazing soup get cold!" Rob grins, leading the way.

"So how long are you here for?" Leila asks Rob and Pat over lunch. For once, she is sitting at the table with guests. Or, more accurately, Rob and Pat have been allowed to join a family meal.

"We're only here for a week this time. This should be our final week on Rob's language project, so we won't have work reasons to return here in the future. But we're planning to come back just to visit," Pat winks, serving herself a generous helping of cucumber and tomato salad with walnut sauce.

"You are always welcome here," Leila replies with a cordial nod.

"How did you guys end up getting back together? We were so surprised when we heard the news!" Pat asks curiously, breaking a piece of steaming *khachapuri* in half and handing half to Rob. "The last time I talked to Callie when she was here, she told me that Nika had left and gone back to London."

"Leila sent me packing!" Nika laughed. "But it wasn't long before she realized her mistake!"

"Actually, it was Fariza's doing," Leila nods gratefully at her daughter. "Though I tried to hide it, she saw how sad I was after Nika left. And she convinced me that if she and Abdullah could accept him, then the rest of the village would too. And she reminded me that love is worth fighting for. It didn't take long for Abdullah to get on board. And then all I had to do was swallow my pride and call Nika in London and tell him I had changed my mind."

"Best phone call of my life," Nika smiles at Leila and squeezes her hand across the table.

"So what's your plan now that you're back from London?" Rob asks.

Leila glances at Nika, who answers for them, "Well, first things first, as you know, we're going to have a huge wedding ceremony! We're so glad you guys could come! We've invited the entire village and we will roast four different kinds of meat in hopes that it wins them over towards accepting me," Nika laughs. "As for longer-term plans, we've decided that the guesthouse will be our home base for now. Leila has worked so hard to build this business, plus her family is here. So I will see what I can do to come alongside and contribute. Who knows — maybe I can help bring in more British clientele!"

"Or start a music school in Khev," Leila nudges him.

"Oh, that would be wonderful!" Pat exclaims. "I'm guessing there's nothing like that here now?"

"Khev isn't exactly the cultural capital of the world," Abdullah jokes. "We just got indoor bathrooms last year— you can't expect us to have a music school!"

"I'm not sure about a music school," Nika shrugs self-deprecatingly and runs a hand across his close-cropped salt and pepper hair, "but we will see how things go. I will travel back to London regularly to visit my daughter of course, and we are hoping that maybe this summer she can come spend a few weeks here at the guesthouse."

"Does she want to babysit one angel and one Tasmanian devil?" Fariza grimaces, "Because if she does, I have a job for her!"

"You can barely handle the two of them— how do you expect a teenager to manage?" Abdullah ribs her and she swats him in return.

"Have either of you heard from Callie?" Fariza asks Rob and Pat innocently, purposefully avoiding looking at her brother. Abdullah suddenly seems very interested in his bowl of soup.

"I've stayed in regular touch with her," Pat replies. "Seems like she's doing well. She's back in San Francisco, but she quit her job at the newspaper and has started working for a nonprofit, which she's really enjoying."

"Actually," Leila clears her throat, glancing quickly at her son. "I've been in touch with Callie as well. She's working on a development grant for Sureti Valley through her new job. I've invited her for the wedding, and she agreed to come. She was wanting to surprise everyone, but well, I think we've had enough secrets in this family."

Abdullah's golden eyes light up, "You really invited her? And she's really coming?"

Leila nods and glances at Nika, who squeezes her hand encouragingly. "She arrives the day after tomorrow," Nika smiles. "Think you can pick her up from the airport?" He asks Abdullah innocently.

"Thursday?" Abdullah's brows crease, fooling no one at the table. "Um… yes, sure, I should be able to fit that into my schedule." Nika nods, falsely serious.

"Well, hooray for a happy reunion!" Rob shouts, raising his water glass high in a toast.

After dinner, Fariza and Rosana wash the dishes while Abdullah chases Daud around the courtyard. Pat and Rob sit on the porch, with

Rob bouncing Fariza's daughter on his knee and speaking to her in the most over-the-top baby voice.

Nika comes up from behind Leila and gives her long skirt a tiny tug, "Let's take a walk out into the orchard."

"Hang on just a second," Leila continues her task, stacking up dishes on the dining room table.

"Leave the dishes— they can wait," he tugs her hand insistently and she acquiesces, following him out of the dining room, through the courtyard, behind the guesthouse, and into the apple orchard. The apple trees are bare, their gnarled limbs looking so naked without leaves and fruit. Leila shivers in the evening cold and Nika steps behind her and wraps his arms around her. For a moment she freezes, glancing around to make sure no one is looking, and then tucks her head under his chin and relaxes into him. They stand like that for a long time, content in each other's arms, watching the golden sun slip behind Leila's beloved mountains.

Dear reader,

Thank you so much for taking the time to read this book! I hope you enjoyed it! My family has lived in the Caucasus mountains for the past 10 years, so the culture here is near and dear to me. I hope that *The Valley Between Us* has given you a holistic glimpse into a unique world, with all its beauty as well as its hardship.

Over our decade of living in the Caucasus, I have gotten to know many women who were bride kidnapped. This book is a combination of bits and pieces of their stories, along with a fair dose of my own imagination. **Unfortunately, bride kidnapping still happens around the world today.** It is my hope that this book can educate people about this unjust practice. You can help by sharing this story with others!

If you enjoyed this book, I would so appreciate it if you would leave me a review on Amazon and/or Goodreads! I read and value every single review. As a self-published author, I don't have access to all the marketing money and networks that large publishing houses have. **Getting this story out into the world can only happen through help from readers like you.**

I also love to connect with readers. If you have any questions or comments, feel free to **reach out to me through my website www.cristislate.com or sign up there to receive my newsletters about future books!**

Thank you again,
Cristi

Leave an Amazon Review: **Leave a Goodreads Review:**

READING GROUP QUESTIONS

I would be *thrilled* if your book club or reading group would like to read this book! Below are a bunch of sample discussion questions and topics— feel free to pick and choose (or make up your own!). A free downloadable PDF of these questions is available at www.cristislate.com. And contact me at cristi@cristislate.com if you would like to discuss me making a virtual appearance at your group!

1) What was your favorite part of the book? Your least favorite? Were there any scenes that really stuck with you? Any parts of the book that were slow for you?

2) How did the book make you feel? What emotions did it evoke for you?

3) "Home" and "belonging" are big themes throughout the book. What are some ways that Callie and Dina each found a sense of home and belonging in Sureti? What are some things that they missed from their former lives? Think back to big moves that you have made — what are some things that you've missed from your former home, and what are some things that helped you feel a sense of belonging in your new home?

4) Callie and Dina both wrestle with adjusting to a new culture that is so different from the one they came from. What are some of the things that were hard for each of them to adjust to? What are some of the things they eventually came to appreciate? How did Marta, Hava, and Abdullah serve as bridges/guides for Dina and Callie respectively into their new cultures?

5) How is Ramazi culture different from the culture in your home country? Have you ever come in close contact with a culture that was different from your own? And if so, how have you adjusted? Think too about refugees and immigrants moving to your home culture — what do you think is hard for them to adjust to?

6) At first, Ramazi culture really rubs Callie the wrong way. Abdullah tells her that it's "just different, not wrong." But she's not sure if she agrees, especially in the area of women's rights. Do you agree with Abdullah or not? Where is the line between respecting another culture and standing up for human rights?

7) Georgia in the 1990s was a completely different world than it is today. Did you know much about the former Soviet Union before reading this book? What stood out to you as unique or interesting or new?

8) Callie struggles with sensory processing issues. Were there any parts of her struggle that were relatable to you or someone you love?

9) Throughout the book (and particularly once she starts interacting with Abdullah, Rob, and Pat), Callie wrestles with questions of faith and what she believes. Callie is agnostic for most of the book, Rob and Pat are Christians, and Abdullah is Muslim. What stood out to you (good or bad) about each of their faiths?

10) How does nature play a role in Dina's sanity? Do you connect with nature? Has there been a time or place or season in your life where it was particularly healing for you?

11) Dina/Leila's character changes a lot from the spunky, vivacious 20-year-old girl that we meet in the beginning of the book to the aloof, private, capable woman at the end of the book. How has she still maintained the core of who she is? Nika in particular notices the changes in her, as well as reminds her of who she used to be. How do you think you have changed since the time you were 20? What are some major ways you've changed, and what are some ways that you've stayed the same?

12) What did you think of Lucas? Abdullah? Was there a particular one of them that you were rooting for Callie to end up with? If so, why? The end of the book doesn't tie Callie's story up in a neat bow— it kind of leaves you hanging, unsure which guy she will choose (if either!). Were you ok with that ending or did you wish there was more clarity? How did you feel about Dina/Leila's ending?

ACKNOWLEDGEMENTS

The process of getting this book into the world took far longer than I expected! The actual writing only took 5 months, but then I spent a year and a half on editing and publishing. Phew — that's longer than it took to form any of my 4 human children :).

There are *so* many people who came alongside me in this process and I owe a huge debt of gratitude to all of them.

First of all, thanks to all of you brave Caucasus women who shared your stories with me. I hope that I have done them justice here. Any mistakes are mine and mine alone.

Thank you to Eli and Hollie— without Artist's Way and our Genesis Cohort, I never would have finished my first draft. And thanks to everyone who went through those groups with me— Mark, Kailey, Rachel, Jenn, Chris N, Chris T, Frankie, and Ira. My Beta-readers gave me invaluable feedback: Hollie, Jules, Trin, Mom, Dad, Trev, Savannah, Alycia, Jenn, Kailey, Anna, Jules, Trin, Julia, and Sarah. Savannah also was hugely helpful in all the design aspects of the book, and Frankie Emrick was copy editor extraordinaire— I think he found over 1000 errors in the original manuscript!

Special thanks to Alycia who, of everyone, has been the biggest cheerleader for this book. I sent her almost daily word count updates for the 5 months I was writing, and her enthusiasm was such a buoy.

A couple other authors have been so helpful to me in this writing process, and have patiently answered dozens of emails with all the questions from this first-time author— Robert Whitlow, Rachel Linden, Karen Springs, Athena Stevens, Max Moyer, and Bronwen Newcott— thank you! Thanks as well to Glenn Price, who gave me the gift of 24 hours away in a lovely hotel, where I was able to actually have the time and space to hear myself think and to write the first 30 pages of this book.

Thanks to Trin and Jules, for being the best friends a girl could ask for. Triumvirate for life!

And to my parents and siblings— growing up with the 12 of you was the craziest ride and greatest honor! And was never ever boring. I should have enough story fodder for dozens more books :). Mom and Dad, special thanks to you both. I look up to you both so much— your lives have been exemplary ones of love for the Lord and love for others.

And finally, to my kiddos: Elyse, Hannah, J, and Isaac— you four are the spunkiest, strongest-willed, most hilarious, brilliant, and fabulous bunch of kids I have ever known. I adore you. It is my greatest joy and privilege to be your mama.

And last, but certainly not least, to Andrew. You are more than I could have dreamed of or desired in a husband. You have been incredibly supportive during this time-consuming roller coaster of a process. Just being with you is my favorite thing. You have my heart, forever and always.

Made in the USA
Middletown, DE
02 August 2024